Lara spun. The noise was coming from the corner near Rue Vivienne where the streetlight was out.

She felt a chill run up her neck. "Come on…come on." She looked around for something to change. Silently, she began the chant.

From a distance, she heard a church bell begin to clang. It was eleven. As if her vision were bending, she saw the pillars in front of her warp. At first it was small, like a ripple when you throw a small stone in the water. Within seconds, the smooth waves became more pronounced, like something was trying to tear through the scene. The streetlights dimmed, making a charged noise as the scene in front of her—the massive building with pillars—gave way. In its place emerged a giant round arena with an opulent gold entrance complete with a Devil's open mouth.

Lara gasped. *The Devil's mouth.*

Praise for
THE LADIES OF THE SECRET CIRCUS

"Ambitious and teeming with magic, Sayers creates a fascinating mix of art, the belle époque, and more than a little murder."

—Erika Swyler, author of *The Book of Speculation*

"Encompassing as many genres as a circus carousel has animals to ride, this is ultimately a story about love.... Highly recommended for lovers of timeslip fiction, readers who enjoy their genres very bent indeed, and those who have dreamed of running away to the circus."

—*Library Journal* (starred review)

"At times decadent and macabre, *The Ladies of the Secret Circus* is a mesmerizing tale of love, treachery, and depraved magic percolating through four generations of Cabot women."

—Luanne G. Smith, author of *The Vine Witch*

"*The Ladies of the Secret Circus* is a dazzling tale laced with sinister magic, blood and beauty, love and loss. This is a book that will haunt you long after the last page is turned."

—Alyssa Palombo, author of *The Spellbook of Katrina Van Tassel*

"Romance, mystery, and a family curse—*The Ladies of the Secret Circus*...has it all."

—*PopSugar*

"Spellbinding. *The Ladies of the Secret Circus* is a dazzling, high-wire feat of storytelling."

—Catherine Taylor, author of *Beyond the Moon*

"Fans of Erin Morgenstern's *The Night Circus* will love this page-turning story of dark magic, star-crossed love, and familial sacrifice."

—*Publishers Weekly* (starred review)

By Constance Sayers

A Witch in Time
The Ladies of the Secret Circus

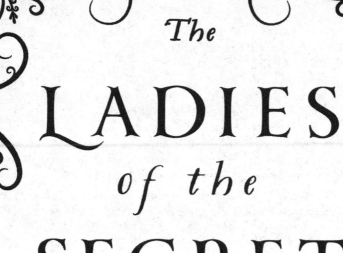

The
LADIES
of the
SECRET
CIRCUS

CONSTANCE
SAYERS

REDHOOK

Copyright © 2021 by Constance Sayers
Reading group guide © 2021 by Hachette Book Group, Inc.
Excerpt from *The Great Witch of Brittany* copyright © 2021 by Louise Marley

Cover design by Lisa Marie Pompilio
Cover art by Arcangel and Shutterstock
Cover copyright © 2021 by Hachette Book Group, Inc.
Author photograph by Rebecca Danzenbaker

Redhook Books/Orbit
Hachette Book Group
1290 Avenue of the Americas
New York, NY 10104
hachettebookgroup.com

First Paperback Edition: November 2021
Originally published in hardcover and ebook by Redhook in March 2021

Redhook is an imprint of Orbit, a division of Hachette Book Group.
The Redhook name and logo are trademarks of Hachette Book Group, Inc.

The publisher is not responsible for websites (or their content) that are not owned by the publisher.

The Hachette Speakers Bureau provides a wide range of authors for speaking events. To find out more, go to www.hachettespeakersbureau.com or call (866) 376-6591.

The Library of Congress has cataloged the hardcover edition as follows:
Names: Sayers, Constance, author.
Title: The ladies of the secret circus / Constance Sayers.
Description: First Edition. | New York, NY : Redhook, 2021.
Identifiers: LCCN 2020032854 | ISBN 9780316493673 (hardcover) |
   ISBN 9780316493666 (e-book)
Subjects: GSAFD: Fantasy fiction.
Classification: LCC PS3619.A9974 L33 2021 | DDC 813/.6—dc23
LC record available at https://lccn.loc.gov/2020032854

ISBNs: 9780316493680 (trade paperback), 9780316493642 (ebook)

Printed in the United States of America

LSC-C

Printing 2, 2021

To my ladies:
Barbara Guthrie Sayers
Goldie Sayers
Nessa Guthrie
and
Laura Beatty Fuller

The circus is a jealous wench. Indeed, that is an understatement. She is a ravening hag who sucks your vitality as a vampire drinks blood...She is all of these things, and yet, I love her as I love nothing else on earth.

—*Henry Ringling North*

PROLOGUE

Kerrigan Falls, Virginia
October 9, 1974

The Buick was both half on and half off the road, its shiny body blending seamlessly with the pitch-black night. He slammed on his brakes, nearly hitting the car's back quarter panel. Jesus. Who the hell would have left a car here of all places?

The vehicle was familiar. He racked his brain trying to remember where he'd seen it before.

Worried that someone might have been hurt, he stepped out onto the road, careful to leave his own car's right turn signal blinking to catch the attention of anyone else traveling on this desolate stretch. Despite the full moon, the dense forest made the road appear to be nestled under a tent even in fall as the leaves began to thin; the clusters of birch trees with their straight white trunks resembled sticks of chalk. The moon shining through them reassured him for a moment.

He peered inside the car's open window, revealing the empty front seat. An RC Cola can was turned over, dumping its contents on the leather upholstery as though the driver had been holding it when he'd come to a stop. The radio blared. Poor bastard was probably just relieving himself in the woods.

"Hello?" His voiced carried more than he thought it would, making him realize just how lonely this road was.

The stillness puzzled him. On an evening like this, the woods should be buzzing with nocturnal activity, yet the night was eerily calm. He turned to go back to his car. He'd call old Chief Archer as soon as he got home and tell him about the abandoned car.

"Hello? Anyone out here?"

He spied something moving at the edge of the tree line.

His pulse quickened and he hurried back to the safety of his own car, relieved when he placed his right foot on the floorboard with the intent of getting in and driving away. Instead he focused on something moving slowly, cat-like, weaving in and out of the trees. He knew there were cats in these parts, small, but nuisance enough to vex the farmers. His eye followed the movement of what appeared to be a shadow—until it stopped.

Where the thing had halted, there was now a heap of something by the roadside. Gingerly, he took a step around the trunk, the car still protecting him from what was over there. What was it? A pile of leaves? Dear Lord, not a body?

Inching, inching closer.

The air left him as he realized too late what was in front of him. The thing was swift and for a moment—his last moment—it had been oddly familiar.

When it was over, the forest seemed to reassemble itself and there was nothing, except the sound of the two car radios playing "The Air That I Breathe" in unison.

PART 1

THE WEDDING THAT WASN'T

Kerrigan Falls, Virginia
October 8, 2004

It was the wrong dress; Lara realized that now.

It was the color of old bones. The intricate platinum beading dripped down the dress's fitted bodice in a scrolled pattern. Mid-thigh, the long chiffon skirt emerged, sweeping the floor with a dramatic five-foot train. Tugging at the garment, she looked in the mirror and frowned. Yes, she was definitely disappointed with *this* dress.

It was the first time she'd actually been alone with the gown. No mother standing behind her pulling at the fabric with a hopeful tone in her voice. No "bridal consultants" or seamstresses fussing at her with their encouraging platitudes of just *how wonderful* she would look.

She did not look wonderful in this dress.

Cocking her head from side to side, hoping for an angle she'd like, Lara recalled the small stack of photographs she'd clipped from bridal magazines as a little girl. She and her friends would grab last year's dog-eared copies of *Modern Bride* from the waiting areas of the hair salons while their mothers got their perms and double processes. When no one was looking, they'd slide the old magazines into book bags, poring over them later in their bedrooms, each girl tearing out the pages of silk, taffeta, and tulle creations that they liked best. Lara had actually kept a few of the pages over the years and pruned them down to this *one* dress style, now reflecting back at her in the mirror. She sighed. No dress could possibly shoulder such expectation. But this one was too mature and vintage, more like a costume than a wedding gown.

Turning around, Lara strained to hear if her mother was on her way back upstairs. The hall was silent. She smiled. Studying her reflection, Lara began wishing the dress was fuller in the train, less form-fitting through the thighs. Tugging on it, she concentrated hard, and the fabric gave way and blossomed, like a time-lapse video of flowers blooming, folds of fabric bursting then tumbling down and arranging themselves before her.

"There," she said, and the fabric obeyed. "A little less." The fabric swirled as though it were alive, rustling and shifting to please her. "Perfect." She turned, watching it retract until she said, "Stop."

Lara spun in front of the mirror, admiring the way the fabric moved. Next she focused on the color. "A little lighter, more ivory, less platinum." Like a TV screen adjusting its brightness, the silver tones of the dress warmed to a pure-ivory hue. "Much better." She considered the sleeveless bodice for October. "Maybe sleeves?" She could feel the dress hesitate, like it was bubbling, unsure of her direction. "Lace sleeves," she clarified. Instantly the dress obeyed like a courteous bellman, creating ornate lace patterns along her arm as though the seams were being stitched together by the singing birds in Disney cartoons.

"Lara Barnes, what *are* you doing?" Her mother stood behind her with one hand on her hip and the other holding an elaborate twenty-strand pearl choker. In the center of the choker was a large Victorian diamond brooch.

"I didn't like it." Her voice was defensive. She smoothed the new skirt like it was an obedient pet, letting the dress know that she was done with alterations.

"Then you go to a store and buy another one. You can't simply *enchant* a dress, Lara."

"Apparently I can." Lara spun to face her mother, her eyebrow cocked. "We really didn't need to alter it. I do a better job."

"The sleeves are all wrong." Audrey Barnes frowned and ran her hand through her butter-colored bob. "Turn around," she said, gesturing with her hand. "You'll get nervous at the ceremony and the enchantment will wane. You mark my words. This is dangerous business."

"If the spell wears off, you can keep the dress together for me."

"As if I don't have enough to worry about."

Her mother was the superior spell caster, even if she hated using her magic. She handed the choker to Lara and turned her attention to the enchanted wedding gown. Audrey ran her hands over the lace sleeves, and they softened to a flowing chiffon under her touch. Unlike Lara, her mother didn't have to tell the dress what to do; it read her mind. Audrey returned the platinum beading to its original color but then seemed to change her mind, and it shifted to a softer embroidery pattern. "There," she said. "You need texture to contrast with the sleeves." The finished effect was an ivory dress with platinum detailing at the bodice, ivory sleeves, and a matching full skirt. "It's much more romantic."

Lara studied the changes in the mirror, pleased. "You should enchant dresses more often, Mother."

Audrey scowled. Taking the necklace from Lara, she fastened it around her daughter's neck.

Lara touched the choker, admiring it. "Where have you been keeping this bauble?"

"It was Cecile's," said Audrey, referring to Lara's great-grandmother.

Lara thought it looked familiar. "Have you worn this before?"

"No," said her mother, admiring her alterations to the dress, tugging here and there and shifting the hue and fit under her hands. "You've seen it, though. She's wearing it in the painting."

She'd passed the painting of her great-grandmother Cecile Cabot that hung in the hallway hundreds of times but never really stopped to study it. Lara tried to recall the choker.

"It belonged to her mother."

"I didn't know that." Lara touched the delicate strands, wondering how she'd never found this in her childhood raids on her mother's jewelry box.

"They say she was quite famous." Audrey smiled, spinning Lara around. "You look beautiful in it. And I do like the changes to the dress, but you can't risk getting caught."

"I'm in my room. Who is going to catch me but you?"

"You can't take risks with magic, Lara. People don't understand. What would happen if that dress began to unwind in the middle of your vows?"

"What you mean is that *Todd* won't understand." She folded her arms.

"Listen to me," said Audrey. "There are some secrets that you must keep—even from Todd. *This* is one of them."

Lara knew that her mother had always wanted them to be "normal." Instead they were the Cabots—the famous and strange circus family—former owners of Le Cirque Margot. Circus families were rarely normal. As a kid, Audrey had worked the horses in the summers, becoming an expert trick rider, but she'd hated performing for crowds and made it clear that she wanted no part of her family legacy. Instead the young girl had taken the Lippitt Morgan horses from the act and had begun breeding them, turning Cabot Farms into one of the most successful horse breeders in the South. Unable to compete with television, Le Cirque Margot came upon hard times and low attendance, closing in the early 1970s.

Then there were the strange powers—the simple "corrections" that both mother and daughter could perform. So incensed was Audrey when her precocious daughter cast a spell in school in front of other kids that she enchanted the doors and windows as punishment, leaving Lara grounded in the house for a weekend.

Lara turned her back to Audrey. "Can you unzip me? I have to go see Todd."

"Now?" Audrey put her hands on her hips. "It's ten. Don't stay too long. It's bad luck."

Lara rolled her eyes and gathered the dress, now changed back to its original version, and placed it on a hanger. She and Todd had given in to another one of Audrey's old wives' tales when they'd agreed to spend the night before the wedding apart. Lara would come back to Cabot Farms tonight with her mother while Todd spent the night at their apartment.

Audrey Barnes possessed all the coolness of a Hitchcock blonde, yet she subscribed to all the myths and romance of a Victorian heroine. She'd named Lara for the character in *Doctor Zhivago*—a film they watched together faithfully each year, a box of tissues between them. Tomorrow Lara's first dance with her father was going to be the Al Martino version of "Somewhere My Love," and she knew her mother would be weeping near the wedding cake.

As she drove her Jeep down the winding road from Cabot Farms to the highway, she recalled the disappointed look on her mother's face when she and Todd announced they were engaged. Audrey didn't care for him. She'd tried to talk them out of getting married, encouraging them to wait until spring. Lara knew her mother had hoped that given enough time, something would change, but Todd had been Lara's first love, her first everything. They'd known each other since they were fifteen years old.

Audrey had encouraged them to attend separate colleges, paid for Lara's semester in Europe, and even tolerated her year on the road with her father's band, anything to allow the relationship to cool. Todd had also left for college, finishing his sophomore year, then returning home and building a vintage car restoration business.

When they were apart on a break, other boys were only ever interesting to Lara for their likenesses to Todd. From the bevy of Lara look-alikes that Todd dated during their splits, she knew he felt the same way. Whether chemistry or magic, there was some inexplicable pull always guiding them back together.

Had Audrey been younger, Lara was sure that Todd would have been exactly the bad-boy romantic figure that her mother would have swooned over. In fact, her mother had chosen her own version of Todd back in 1974 when she'd married Lara's father, Jason Barnes.

Lara pulled into the driveway. The house was abuzz with activity and anticipation; lanterns lit the sidewalk to the front door that was now ajar. Relatives from places like Odessa and Toledo perched themselves on sofa arms and decorative side chairs. Plates clanged, and people caught up with one another over decafs and dirty dishes. She wondered why her house wasn't stuffed full of relatives, like this one.

Through the foyer, she spotted Todd going out the back door, bags of ice in his arms. As he went past, he spied Lara and smiled. His wavy, chin-length dark hair had begun to curl as the evening went on.

"Lara, why didn't you make him get a haircut?" asked his aunt Tilda, a hairdresser from somewhere in Ohio. Lara rolled her eyes conspiratorially. As if anyone could make Todd do something he didn't want to do.

Back from delivering ice, Todd kissed his aunt on the cheek. "Ah, you don't like my hair?" As Todd fixed his gaze on her, Lara could see the old woman straightening herself.

The aunt pulled at a lock, inspecting it. His hair was shiny and brown. Lara noticed a few gray hairs shimmering under the light like tinsel. Had Todd been a vain man, he'd have dyed it before the ceremony. There was an audible exhale from the woman as she smoothed an errant strand, seemingly agreeing that Todd's hair suited him. "Well…"

Todd wasn't just handsome, he was beautiful. There was a tragic sexiness to him, like a burgeoning James Dean, that was so intoxicating to women—all women. From the looks of it, even the ones who were related to him.

"I have to go soon." Lara sank onto the sofa next to him. These days he wore long-sleeved T-shirts because, even though he was nearly twenty-nine, he still cared that his mother hated the sight of the rococo-scrolled tattoos that now decorated both of his forearms.

After an hour, Lara began to rise from the sofa. "I'll walk you out," said Todd.

"Let her go, Todd," another pair of aunts teased. "It's almost midnight. Bad luck to see the bride on the wedding day." The overhead fans in the screen porch were rhythmically cycling above them, sending out waves of cool air that made Lara shiver.

"I'll make sure to send her out by eleven fifty-nine then." He pushed through the door. "How many times has your mother called you?"

"Twice in the last ten minutes." Lara slow-walked across the yard toward her Jeep. She looked up at the sky and thought that she should remember to look up more often—the stars seemed low, like they were glowing brighter for her.

"Before you go, I have something to show you."

Lara spun to see that Todd had begun to walk backward, leading her toward his stepfather's garage. That he never looked down as he walked and never doubted the sureness of his steps fascinated her. She'd have stumbled over an uneven paver or tree root, spraining an ankle, but not Todd. He was one of the most confident men she'd ever known, comfortable in his own skin to a fault, and it made him generous to others. He had nothing to prove.

"I thought I'd have this finished before the wedding, but I didn't get it done fast enough." He opened the door and turned on the light that hummed from a faulty bulb. In front of her was a pickup truck up on a lift, angled like it was taking off in flight. The truck was painted with a smooth dull-gray primer, as though it had been sculpted out of clay. She gasped.

Lara had a thing for vintage pickup trucks—the kind they made into Christmas ornaments, embroidered onto winter pillows, or put in front of businesses to make them *old-timey*. When she was a kid, they'd had an old truck just like this among the battered old circus equipment. One day it had been hauled away for scrap in one of Audrey's reorganizations, the dead-grass outline of it remaining for several years like a scar. "It's a 1948 Chevy."

"A 1948 Chevy 3100 five-window," he said. "Straight-six manual. I know how you like that." He walked around the truck and pointed past the body. About ten feet from the truck she spied a dusty pile of brown metal that looked like mechanical guts that he'd tossed out. "Wait till you see what's in store for her. Come with me." Todd led her around the truck to a wooden work space, rolling up his sleeves and pushing his hair back, completely focused on the plans and notes he'd drawn that were sprawled across the space. He placed his hands down on the bench and scanned the photos and sketches.

After he'd left college, failing out of the engineering program at Virginia Tech, Todd had returned to Kerrigan Falls and, on a whim, started a classic car restoration business with a man named

Paul Sherman who'd owned an old garage. Over the past two years, Sherman & Sutton Classic Cars had become one of the most sought-after vintage car restoration specialists along the entire East Coast, mostly due to Todd's reputation as a muscle car restoration expert— Corvettes, Camaros, GTOs, Chevelles, and Mustangs. Lara would never have thought that an obsession with ripping apart car engines in his teens would turn into a livelihood he loved, let alone one that was so lucrative.

"You see here"—Todd pointed to a photo of the very same Chevy with missing headlights and mismatched paint that resembled patches—"the fenders had rust all over." Lara saw from the photo that the entire truck had been a dull weathered brown when he'd found it. So engrossed was he in shaping this metal puzzle into a work of art and seemingly unhappy about some detail, he appeared to be lost in his own world, his arms folded and the line of his square jaw pulsing.

While Lara should have been looking at the posted pictures of the truck in various stages of ruin, she studied his face instead. Todd's long nose could have been a hair too feminine if not for the elegant bump at the top. When he walked into a room, people stopped their conversations and looked up, wondering if he was someone famous, perhaps a film star returning to his hometown for a holiday. That he didn't care, that he stood here agonizing over a sketch of a 1948 Chevy truck as a gift for her, was what truly made Todd Sutton beautiful to Lara. He never noticed the effect he had on people—or if he did, it never mattered to him.

"Where did you find this?"

"Oh, that's the special thing." He smiled devilishly, his hazel eyes shining, and pulled from a file folder a photo of the truck with faded livery painted on the side. "Recognize it?"

Lara took the photo from his hand and inhaled sharply. It was an old black-and-white image, the familiar logo painted on it almost overexposed in the sunlight—she felt a jolt of melancholy. It was her old truck. LE CIRQUE MARGOT.

Decorated in its circus livery, the old truck had once hauled a two-person crew to eighteen towns with the purpose of sticking posters up on every telephone pole, barn, and local business that would post them—the markets and pharmacies being the most likely prospects. This Chevy had sat among the rusted and abandoned circus props and trailers at Lara's house for years, grass and vines growing up through the floorboards as though the ground were reclaiming it.

"So, I was driving by an old amusement park supply in Culpeper, and I saw it from the road. It was hidden behind some old roller-coaster cars. I didn't know it was the old truck that sat out in your field until I was scrubbing it and saw the faded sign. Something about the lettering looked familiar, so I went to the historical society to see if there were any old photos of it in Le Cirque Margot memorabilia. And sure enough, I found plenty."

A blonde was posed leaning against the front bumper. She wore shorts and had legs that would have made Betty Grable envious. Turning back to look at the truck, Lara smoothed its rounded fender. This truck had belonged to *the Margot*.

"I had hoped to give it to you as a wedding present, but it's frankly been a bitch to find parts for, so it won't be ready in time, I'm afraid." He laughed a little too loudly, and she tilted her head and glanced up at him. Was he jittery? Todd was never nervous. He was searching her face, trying to read her, hoping this offering had meant something to her.

She pulled him toward her and kissed him, hard, then whispered in his ear, "This is the most thoughtful thing that anyone has ever done for me. I love it."

He looked down and his forehead touched hers. "Lara, we both know that I haven't always been so thoughtful."

It was true. Throughout their history, there had been many transgressions, many girls, then—as they got older—women. While she chalked it up to youth, Lara had slammed doors on him, thrown beautiful bunches of roses at him, ripped up apology notes and his poor attempts at poetry. She'd had revenge dates and surprisingly fallen in love with one of them for a short time but always returned to this man.

"You aren't getting cold feet, are you?" Lara tilted her head, only slightly joking.

He didn't touch her, and for some reason it felt sobering and honest that he didn't. He wasn't trying to charm her. "I'm sorry that I had to grow up—that you didn't meet me now instead of then."

Lara laughed this comment off, but he didn't. She realized as she looked around the room—the photos, the thoughtful gift suspended above her—that the change that had come over him in the last few years had been so gradual, it had escaped her notice. He leaned his tall frame against the workbench and faced her, folding his arms. "I was someone who had to grow into love. Not that I had to grow to love *you*. I always loved you, but I didn't know *how* to love you, so what you got was the equivalent of an attempt at a work of art from someone who didn't know how to draw. I said the words, but we both know often they were hollow. At times it was the very absence of you that shaped me. But that's what it is, isn't it? Both the presence and the absence of a person. The sum of it all. As a result, I feel it more deeply now. Love. My love for you."

The silence between them was thick. She could tell he didn't expect a response from her. There was so much shared history—both good and bad. Yet it was the things that were unsaid that charged the room. Lara met his eyes. She saw this wedding gift for what it was—an offering—more a piece of himself than even marrying her could ever be. Every inch of that truck had been shaped and sanded by his hands—it was created by him *for* her.

He took her hand. Her lips met his. Todd was a great kisser—slow, deliberate. She knew exactly where to press against him to fill the spaces between them. He put his hands on her face and the kisses became deeper, harder. As they pulled apart, he caught a strand of her hair, twirling it around his finger and studying it.

"It's nearly midnight." She didn't want to go.

"Ah, shit, not midnight," he teased. He turned back to the perfectly sanded truck in front of them. "Here is the color she'll be when she's all done." Taking her hand, he led her around and showed her a sample—the original Le Cirque Margot deep-red color that resembled a ripe Red Delicious apple.

She could easily imagine a lifetime of this. Smiling, she wished they could just go back to their apartment and their bed tonight. When they got back from their honeymoon in Greece, there was even a house, a stately Victorian with a turret and a wraparound porch, that they were looking at buying. "I really do have to go."

Lara looked back at the truck before he turned out the light. "Will I see you tomorrow?" It was a joke, and she said it lightly as she opened the door and walked out onto the sidewalk.

"Nothing could keep me away."

T he church bells began to clang as the forecasted thunderstorm let out its initial boom, sending a torrent of rain over the valley. For weeks, the weather had called for clear and sunny skies today, but in the last hour, an inflamed purple sky had fixed itself unnaturally over the town of Kerrigan Falls.

Was this bad luck? An omen, perhaps? That was crazy. Lara wiped the thought from her mind. From her vantage point in an upstairs classroom, she watched a classic white convertible Mercedes idling just beyond the steps. Rain was soaking the lavender tissue-paper streamers taped to the car's trunk, sending a stream of cheap ink down over the bumper and into the mud puddle below. She bit at a stray hangnail on an otherwise perfect manicure and watched as guests teetered across the gravel, then hopscotched over newly formed puddles and up the stairs in their good Sunday shoes, scrambling to get out of the downpour.

The dress—the enchanted version—complete with pearl choker, looked perfect. Her long, wild blond hair was now secured in an elaborate low twist. She'd taken off her new shoes, cursing herself for not breaking them in; then she decided to enchant them as well, the leather giving way under command.

It was nearly four thirty. Her wedding was about to start, yet no one had come to get her. Odd. She looked around the room. Where had everyone gone? She strained her neck to see. Her mother? Her bridesmaids, Caren and Betsy?

At the Chamberlain Winery five miles away in the heart of the Piedmont wine country, there was another group of workers preparing the reception. Long tables adorned with damask linens, mercury-glass votives, and elaborate hydrangea centerpieces awaited the 150 guests now seated in the pews and flipping through hymnals below her. Within hours, those guests would dance to a full Irish band overlooking the vineyard while dining on stations of cheeses from around the world—Manchegos, smoked Goudas, and bleus—then moving to short ribs, shrimp with garlic sauce, and finally a plated combination of a filet mignon with an herb-crusted salmon and patatas bravas. Around eight, they'd cut the wedding cake—a whimsical aqua-and-gold confection consisting of three layers of white almond cake topped with a cream cheese and buttercream frosting evoking just a hint of almond extract. Their friends and family would drink the wines that thrived during the humid Virginia summers—the peppery Cabernet Francs, tannic Nebbiolos, and creamy Viogniers all poured into heavy crystal Sasaki goblets with orbed stems.

Lara had designed every detail. In her mind, she was already worrying about the reception details, needing to get started, get moving. Minutes ago, the activity that had swarmed around her had all but disappeared and an eerie quiet had set in, the rattling boom from the storm providing a welcome reprieve from the stillness. She'd been dressed and ready for an hour now, the photographer capturing every moment of preparation from her hair, to the makeup, and finally the dress.

She lifted the bulk of her skirt and, like an extra from *Gone with the Wind,* rustled toward the hall. When she didn't see anyone, she went back to the window, but then heard faint whispering and turned back to the hallway to see that Fred Sutton, the town's undertaker and Todd's stepfather, was talking with her mother in hushed tones.

Finally. It was starting.

Their voices rose and fell. Lara turned her attention back to the window, sure whatever details the two of them were tackling didn't concern her.

Fred was heading back down the stairs when, out of the corner of her eye, Lara saw him stop, then march down the hall toward her, the floor pulsing with every heavy footstep. He placed his thick hands on her forearms with such force that he nearly lifted her up off the floorboards. His sudden movement shocked her so much that she stepped back, almost toppling over a half-moon kindergarten table behind her. Fred leaned in and whispered in her ear, his lips touching her borrowed diamond earring. "Don't worry. We'll find him."

Had she misheard? Lara spoke her next words carefully. "He's not here?"

Fred looked down at his black, mirror-shiny rental shoes. "Not exactly."

What did *not exactly* mean? She looked over at her mother for clarification. Audrey seemed to be taking in this information as she would news of a car wreck.

Fred's voice sounded more like a plea. "He went to clean his car and he wasn't back when we left for the church. We didn't think anything was wrong."

It was the word *wrong* that struck her. Something here *was* terribly wrong, wasn't it? She could feel it. "When did you see him last?"

"Around noon." Fred consulted his watch as though it somehow held the answer.

Things like this didn't happen. Lara searched her mind trying to remember the last *bad* thing that had happened in Kerrigan Falls. Old people died, although usually quite peacefully in their beds. There hadn't been a car accident or a house fire in her lifetime. And certainly, people weren't just plucked from the streets. They showed up for their weddings.

"Where is his tuxedo?" Lara's face flared hot, and her throat began to tighten. She could imagine the rented tuxedo still draped across Todd's childhood twin bed.

"It was still on the bed when we left." Fred met her eyes. "We brought it . . . just in case—"

"Just in case . . . ?" Lara cut in. This was all the answer she needed. A sudden hot pressure of tears welled up inside her. Looking down at the bouquet of tightly packed calla lilies in her hand, she felt as though she were holding a ridiculous prop. She lowered her arm and quietly dropped the bouquet onto the floor. If he'd left the tuxedo on his bed, Todd Sutton wasn't planning on coming to their wedding, that much she was sure of. *But why?* When she'd seen him last night, he'd been so different. She'd never been surer of him. Grabbing her stomach, she felt sick. Had she been a fool? He'd let her down before, but never, never like this.

"Have you checked the bars?" Audrey snorted.

This was unfair, but Lara knew Audrey was protecting her. At some point, if Todd really failed to show, her mother would need to begin a detailed accounting of his faults.

But he will show up. Todd would not leave me here like this.

Fred lowered his head. "Yes," he croaked. "We've checked everywhere. We also asked Ben Archer to inquire about any accidents, but there haven't been any. He even called the hospitals in Madison and Orange Counties. Nothing."

Ben Archer? If Fred felt desperate enough to involve the chief of police, then Lara understood that things were more serious than he was letting on. Fred looked smaller, shaken, remorseful.

"He's probably just late." Lara smiled, hopeful. That was it, Todd was just late. But late from where? Todd had many faults, but tardiness was never one of them. In fact, she thought back to their years together. She couldn't recall ever having waited on him.

Until now.

"That's probably it." Fred's smile was wooden, and the flap of hair doing its best to hide his bald patch was drooping down over his forehead now glistening with sweat. He held up his finger. "Let me check downstairs *one* more time." He walked to the top of the steps and turned like a dutiful waiter. "I just thought you should know."

Oh no. Lara had seen this look before. Fred was taking on the rehearsed demeanor he displayed when managing funerals and organizing grief—other people's grief. It was his business—reducing the messiness of loss into a tidy, well-executed ritual. Now it was her turn. With his carefully chosen words, he'd begun preparing her for the worst.

"What time is it?" asked Audrey.

"Four forty," said Fred without gazing at a timepiece.

"If he isn't here yet, I need you to tell everyone the wedding has been postponed," Audrey commanded. "*Postponed*," she emphasized. "Until we can figure this out."

Lara's father, Jason Barnes, had been standing in the doorway waiting for his cue to walk Lara down the aisle. Now he was taking in the conversation and tugging free of his bow tie, finally ripping it off. A musician, Jason didn't wear ties or tuxedos. "Let's just wait a little longer for him. He'll show." He met Lara's eyes and smiled.

That was Jason, the eternal optimist, Candide with a Fender.

As was the norm, Audrey ignored her ex-husband with an eye roll, turning her attention back to Todd's stepfather. "You have ten minutes, Fred. That's all. I will not have my daughter waiting up here for him any longer than that."

Lara walked over to her mother. Audrey had intuitions about things; her abilities weren't limited to enchanting gowns and turning on lights. Her mother could sense the hearts of people—what was in them—*really in them*, not just the pretend exterior sheen. If anyone would know whether Todd Sutton was on his way to the church or in the next state by now, it was Audrey. "Do you see anything?"

Her mother simply shook her head. "Nothing."

Yet Lara knew that her mother was lying. *Why?* "What aren't you telling me?"

"Nothing," said her mother, nearly snapping at her. "Lara, I see nothing."

"Nothing?" Lara dramatically looked down at her dress. "Really, Mother?"

"I don't see *him*, Lara." Audrey looked stricken. "I'm sorry."

That was impossible. Her mother could see everything. Each transgression Todd had ever made, Audrey smelled on him, like a dog.

"What does that mean?"

"I don't know." Her mother's voice was low now.

In hearing those words—*I don't know*—something in Lara shifted. The whole place began to sour. She tried to breathe, but the corset in the damned dress stopped her lungs from expanding. She grabbed at the bodice, but it wouldn't move. Lara concentrated and began to enchant the zipper, feeling her ribs relax as the fabric released. Looking up, she spied Caren Jackson, her maid of honor, standing in the doorway in her lavender taffeta dress, her mouth agape as she watched her friend's wedding gown appear to unzip itself with invisible hands.

Lara's knees buckled and she stumbled into the Baby Jesus doll in his cradle shoved against the wall. Caren pulled her back up, placing her in the regular-size teacher's chair. Lara began to pluck the baby's breath sprigs from Caren's updo, first just the strand that was too close to Caren's dark-brown eyes, but then another cluster near her ear.

"Fuck the baby's breath," said Caren, who began tugging at the other sprigs, pulling them out.

Somehow, this absurd gesture made Lara laugh. This situation was ridiculous, really it was. She needed to get herself together. She put her head down almost between her knees to avoid fainting. "What should I do?"

Caren had been her best friend since their morning kindergarten class. They'd sat together in the tiny chairs in this room as children. Caren crouched down and met her eyes. "I honestly don't know, but we'll figure this out."

"How could he—?"

Caren simply shook her head.

A few minutes later, Fred crept upstairs and whispered to her mother, just loud enough for her to hear. "I don't think he's coming."

"We need to get her out of here." Audrey grabbed her hand. "Now."

Lara and her mother managed the stairs down to the foyer one step at a time, her father two steps behind them. For the first time in her life, Lara used the handrail. The church door opened. Her heart leapt, hoping it was Todd. Instead, Chet Ludlow, Todd's best man, muscled through the doors, his face red. The first thing Lara thought was that he'd gotten a terrible haircut for this ceremony and that the pictures would look terrible. And then she remembered, and her stomach lurched. *The wedding pictures.* There would be many more moments like this in her future, cruel reminders of what didn't happen today. Her world was about to change to "before" and "after."

He seemed surprised to find a clump of people standing in the foyer. He turned to Lara. "I've been out looking for him for the last half hour. I swear I have."

"And?" It was Caren, her voice firm.

Chet furiously shook his head. "I can't find him anywhere."

Satisfied he was telling the truth, Lara nodded and pushed through the Gothic wooden double doors with a strength she didn't know she had. As she stepped outside, through a cruel twist, the sun was now peeking around a soft cloud.

Hearing steps on the pavement below, Lara looked down to see Ben Archer, Kerrigan Falls' chief of police. He was out of breath, his uniform rising and falling as if he'd been out for a hard run.

In this humiliating and intimate moment, she'd hoped to avoid seeing anyone, let alone a perfect stranger, but their eyes met and she could see that he, too, had nothing to report.

There would be no wedding today.

3

Kerrigan Falls, Virginia
October 10, 2004

With his phone on vibrate, it took Ben Archer a minute to comprehend the sound he was hearing until it traveled off the nightstand and onto the wood floor, clacking like a child's windup toy. *That* woke him up.

Sweeping his hand under the bed, he retrieved it just as it went to voicemail. *Damn.* It was Doyle Huggins, his deputy. He hated these new mobile phones. The idea that he was now tethered round-the-clock to Doyle was nearly unbearable. He hit the redial. "It's six A.M., Doyle." His voice was low even though he was alone.

"I know. I thought you'd want to know right away. They'd found a car about an hour ago—Todd Sutton's car."

He felt a lump in his throat. "Are you sure?"

"Oh yeah," said Doyle. "It's his car all right."

"What about Sutton?" Yesterday Ben had been out looking for the runaway groom for hours.

"No sign of him yet, but I'm looking."

"Where are you?"

"That's the fucked-up part." Doyle seemed hesitant to speak. "I'm standing in the middle of Wickelow Bend."

Ben inhaled sharply. "I'll be right there."

He slid out of the warm bed and got dressed quickly. Grabbing coffee at the 7-Eleven, Ben drove across the Shumholdt Bridge with its dramatic view of Kerrigan Falls' hundred-foot drop.

Seventy minutes southwest of Washington, DC, Kerrigan Falls was named for the wild and winding Kerrigan River that flowed south another sixty miles. Famous for its large rocks and fallen trees that crossed the small gorge like Pixy Stix, the Kerrigan River ran parallel to the Blue Ridge Mountains that loomed above the town's tiny skyline.

At the entrance of both wine and horse country, Kerrigan Falls was surrounded by the lush and humid rolling hills of the Virginia countryside with their old horse farms and new vineyards. In the past ten years, tourists had begun to flock to the area for its quaint downtown, buying up old farms, opening antiques shops and vintage bookstores. In its heyday after the war, the town had been the home of the Zoltan's Spicy Brown Mustard plant and before that, of the famous (or infamous, depending upon the story) circus, Le Cirque Margot. In the past year, a noticeable shift had happened here. A famous DC chef had opened up a restaurant that had earned a Michelin star. People who once worked shifts at the old mustard plant were now running bed-and-breakfasts in sprawling Victorians, complete with picket fences and porch swings.

The downtown itself was laid out like a movie set from the 1940s— awnings, sandblasted brick buildings, a state theater, big stone churches at the corners, and Victorian homes all restored with a meticulous devotion. The Orpheum Theatre still showed *It's a Wonderful Life* the Saturday before Christmas to a packed house. There was a strange, unnatural perfection to Kerrigan Falls.

Ben had his own Victorian that he still owned, although he didn't live in it. According to their divorce agreement, Marla was supposed to buy his half out, yet she'd shown little interest in selling. So he'd taken to stopping at houses with FOR SALE signs in front of them and determining whether the photos of the selling agents looked hungry enough. Any agent they hired would need to navigate between his eagerness and Marla's reluctance to sell. He glanced down at the passenger's seat where he'd listed a bunch of real estate agent numbers along with a little cartoon drawing of his own house, shading in the ornate trellis and crepe myrtle tree that adorned the front.

Honestly, the town was too perfect. Nothing—not a shooting or a robbery or even a petty theft—had happened here. Ben Archer was almost the laughingstock of every police gathering or convention in the Commonwealth of Virginia. The *Washington Post* had written an article about the "Kerrigan Falls Phenomenon" last year in the Style Section. (*The Style Section?*) If you searched back in the archives—as Ben had many times—the last murder within city limits had been in 1935. The surrounding counties had their share of murders, murder-suicides, and pileups on the highway, but those accidents never crossed the county line, almost so as not to offend Kerrigan County. But there had been that *one* case.

That one case was very much on Ben Archer's mind this morning,

Just past the bridge, his car approached the sharp turn in the road that was Wickelow Bend. Beyond the bend began the tree line leading to a strange patch of land aptly named Wickelow Forest. At night, especially in the summer, Ben knew it was hard to see the moon, so thick was the canopy of tall trees. Even now the bright-yellow and red leaves were still lush.

He pulled in behind Doyle's patrol car. As he stepped out of the car, his foot sank deep into a chocolate-colored mud puddle. "Shit!"

Doyle Huggins pointed at the ground. "I should have told you not to park there." His deputy was leaning against his cruiser. Six-foot-two and rangy with bulging eyes, Doyle Huggins was a man no one would have ever called handsome. He motioned to the car. "The gas company crew found it this morning."

And there it sat. Todd Sutton's white Mustang with the navy-blue center stripes rested cocked half on and half off the road. He'd been looking for this car until two this morning, when he'd finally given up and fallen into bed. God, he dreaded having to call Lara Barnes to tell her this news. There had been whispers that Todd had fled his wedding in this car yesterday; to find it here, abandoned, seemed to change things.

"Damned gas company nearly smashed into it. Sutton's registration is the glove compartment." Doyle was writing something like he was actually attempting to take notes.

"And Sutton?" Ben angled to get a look at what Doyle was scribbling, convinced it had to be a grocery list.

Doyle shook his head. "No sign of him."

"Call the hospitals," said Ben. "See if he's shown up there. I'll call his parents."

"Someone needs to tell Lara Barnes."

"I'll do that," Ben snapped.

"I figured." Doyle spit on the ground. "It's a nice car." Doyle was wheezing slightly. His shoes squeaked as he walked over and stood beside him. "The gas company driver says it's a 1977. He knows stuff like that."

"It's a '76, Doyle," said Ben. "Ford Mustang Cobra Two. Same car driven by Jill Munroe on *Charlie's Angels*."

"A fucking chick car?" Doyle inspected the body of the vehicle with a scowl.

"It's a classic, Doyle." It was as though his deputy was trying to get under his skin this morning. He looked out at the white forest of Wickelow Bend. It was quiet, eerie even, like the forest was holding its breath, waiting for him to leave so it could find peace again. "Have you searched those woods for a body?"

"A little," said Doyle. "We need to do a more thorough search, though. We'll probably need some volunteers."

"Okay. I'll call the state police and see if we can get some sent over, but try to assemble a team to start looking now." Ben looked up at the span of the Shumholdt Bridge unfolding behind them.

Wickelow Bend was one of those magic places on the earth. Even standing there in the eighth-of-a-mile bend in the road, Ben could feel its tug. For this very reason, lots of people wouldn't drive it, choosing the interstate that took them six miles out of their way to avoid this one little patch of road. During the end of World War II, Wickelow Bend had been the entrance to Le Cirque Margot's office, but when the circus closed in the early 1970s the old road had grown over, the woods erasing all traces. From his father he knew that lots of God-fearing folks in the area had hated the circus at the time, preaching against it to their congregations.

Now, in the fall, the forest played host to drunken dares. Kids taunted each other to see if they could spend just one night in Wickelow Forest. There were wild tales, like the man who supposedly tied two of his wayward dogs to a tree until he could retrieve his truck, only to find nothing but bones in the morning. Ben thought it probably had been hypothermia, then hungry animals that finished the dogs off, but wondered what ass would tie his dogs to a tree in the woods in the first place. With each passing year, the stories and the stupid dares around the place only grew.

Ben walked around to the car. "Why don't you try to pull some fingerprints from the car and see if there is any blood or hair? You do have your kit with you, don't you? If not, I've got some stuff in the back of the car."

"Won't the Staties be pissed? I mean, I've never pulled a fingerprint before. We don't pull fingerprints, Ben. We never need to." He reached into his back pocket and retrieved a tin of Copenhagen. Ben thought it took him forever to unscrew the lid.

"Just follow the directions on the kit." Ben didn't need him screwing it up. "Never mind. Just go get it and I'll get the damned prints myself. We need to mark off a circle from about here to that tree and over to that tree and search inch by inch. Look for anything out of the ordinary."

Ben took out a pair of latex gloves from the back of his car and began searching for the car keys inside the Cobra. They were missing from the ignition. He looked under the floor mats. Nothing.

"Did you find any keys, Doyle?"

His deputy appeared in the passenger's window. "No."

"Did you even look?" Ben muttered under his breath and inhaled as he walked around to the Cobra's trunk to see if there was a manual release button but came up empty.

Ben got in the backseat and was relieved when he didn't smell anything decaying. He wasn't in the right state of mind to find a dead body. Pulling on the backseat, he got a good look inside the trunk. Shining his flashlight into the space, he found it empty.

"I already looked in there," said Doyle. "There's *nothing* here, boss."

"You could have told me that, Doyle."

"You didn't ask," said the man with a shrug.

On the passenger's side of the front seat, GNR and AC/DC tapes littered the floor, and a Burger King wrapper was wadded on the seat. Ben checked the date on the receipt: *October 9, 2004 11:41* A.M. The morning of the wedding.

Ben shut the door and circled the spot, searching for something he was missing about the location. "Why *here* of all places?"

"This ain't no simple stretch of road and you know it, boss."

Doyle was right. The other famous case—Peter Beaumont—was a musician who went missing in 1974. Even if people didn't recall his name or weren't alive when it happened, Peter Beaumont had been the genesis of the lore connected to Wickelow Bend. He'd gone missing from this very spot, his Nova found running with a quarter tank of gas, 99.7 K-ROCK blaring on the radio, and the driver's door open for him.

But there was something even more disconcerting that Doyle didn't know because it had been left out of the papers. Ben Archer recalled the day Peter's tan Chevy had appeared here. For the fall, it had been an unusually warm morning. Ben had tagged along with his father, the chief of police, and he could still visualize the car. Todd Sutton's Cobra II wasn't just parked in the same general *spot*, it had been parked at this exact same angle as though it were staged.

Until he got back to the office and pulled Beaumont's file, Doyle also wouldn't connect another common detail between the two. The other car—Peter Beaumont's car—had been found abandoned here on October 10, 1974.

Exactly thirty years ago to the day.

Kerrigan Falls, Virginia
June 20, 1981

T hey were peering down at her.

"I think I've got grass stains?" The man lifted his knee. "Imagine that?"

"You've never had them before?" The woman studied the fabric.

"Where would I have ever gotten grass stains?" The man's voice was terse, like he was speaking to an idiot.

"Well, how would I know?" The woman held a parasol over her head. Then she crouched down, touching Lara's face. She could see her own reflection in the woman's mirrored sunglasses. "Do you think she's fainted?"

"*Elle n'est pas morte*," said the man.

He didn't know that Lara spoke perfect French. "I can understand you, you know. I'm definitely *not* dead."

"Well, a smart one too." He flashed a smile.

Before the pair's arrival, Lara had been standing out in the field, feeding a carrot to her favorite horse, which her mother had allowed her to name Gomez Addams. She changed the horses' names quite frequently. Whatever his moniker that day, the horse chomped loudly, exposing his teeth, causing Lara to laugh. It was then she spied them—an odd duo, walking toward her in the middle of the field.

They were completely out of place in the country. At first, Lara thought they were old performers from Le Cirque Margot. In the summer, performers often got nostalgic for the old days and visited her great-grandmother. She scrutinized the two in front of her. Usually, the old circus folk didn't arrive in their costumes, but you never knew; they were a strange lot. As the couple got closer to inspect her, Lara could see that they were too young to have performed in Le Cirque Margot.

He was a tall, slight man, handsome, wearing a white flowing shirt and light-brown pants. Beside him, a blond woman carried a parasol. Lara could hear a slight Southern drawl, and the woman wore a pink sequined costume. She had long legs, like a Las Vegas showgirl. Lara had just seen a *Starsky & Hutch* rerun on TV where they were in Las Vegas, and this woman definitely looked like those women. Her costume was the most beautiful thing Lara had ever seen. They appeared to be squabbling, because Lara could hear the woman's voice rise.

The next logical thought Lara had was that they must be some musician friends of her father's. Drummers were always coming and going. The man's hair fell in waves to the top of his shoulders like the men on the album covers in her father's record collection, but he walked toward *her* with purpose. And why not use the road? When they got closer, Lara couldn't see their eyes behind their matching round mirrored sunglasses. The man stopped walking and leaned toward the grade in the hill. He seemed winded.

"Are you looking for my father?" Lara shaded her eyes so she could get a better look at them.

"No, silly," he said. "I'm looking for you, Miss Lara Barnes."

"Lara *Margot* Barnes," she said, correcting him and folding her arms in front of her like she meant business.

"Oh, how delightful!" The lady turned to the man. "Did you hear that?"

"Of course I heard it, Margot. I'm standing here, aren't I?"

The woman snorted loud enough for Gomez Addams to raise his head.

His accent was French, like her great-grandmother Cecile's. The lady's was definitely Southern, like her mother's. It was an odd combination. *They* were an odd pair.

As she took in the two of them, something in the horizon *bent*, like the shimmer of air in extreme heat. Lara blinked furiously, making sure that she wasn't seeing things. The world began to twirl and she found that her legs were bendy as she slid down, like she did when she played dead after being shot from a cap gun.

When she opened her eyes, she found herself lying on the grass, looking up at the curious pair.

"Does she know?" The woman looked up at the man.

He seemed irritated. "Of course not."

"Know what?" Lara lifted herself up on her elbows. She'd heard of kidnappers, but these two didn't look much like kidnappers. Lara figured she could outrun the woman, who was wearing high heels in a field. At least her vision wasn't bendy and she wasn't dizzy anymore.

"That you're special." He smiled. "But of course, you know that already, don't you?" His voiced teased at something. "Someone's magic has just come in."

What was he talking about? *What magic?*

"I remember when my magic came in," said the woman, closing her eyes to savor a memory. "I could turn the radio on without touching it. Drove *Maman* crazy." She cocked her head, as if Lara were an exhibit in the zoo. "She's a pretty child, too. Don't you think she looks like me?"

The man closed his eyes in disgust. "Why do I bring you along?"

"Because I'm your favorite and you know it." She touched Lara's cheek again, maternally. "She's *definitely* the one."

"Oh, she's the one all right." The man finally leaned over her. "I've made sure of it this time. Remember this, my dear girl. We have bigger plans for you, Lara Barnes. That boy in your future, he is not your destiny."

"Oh, she'll never remember." The woman sniffed slightly with disgust. Her upturned nose and full lips made her look like a movie star. "She'll think she *loves* him. We always do."

"Sadly, yes, I'm afraid," said the man, pulling his sunglasses down so Lara could see his eyes. They were an amber color, and something struck her as oddly familiar about them. It took Lara a moment for it to register. His pupils were horizontal like those of the goat they'd kept on the farm last summer. She could never tell if the goat was actually looking at her and she had that same familiar feeling now, the desire to look behind her to see what he was staring at.

"Love. It is the bane of my existence." He shook his head pitifully. "And unfortunately, it's in the genes for this one, too." He shot the woman a look.

"Not my fault." The woman sat back on her high heels. Lara could see that the heels were still pristine, not a speck of dirt on them.

Lara looked around, wondering if anyone else—other than the horses—could see them, but the grass swayed quietly. From a distance she heard the screen door slam.

"One day," he said. "I'll find you again, Lara Barnes."

He touched her on the tip of her nose, causing her to faint again. When she woke up a few moments later, they were gone.

5

Kerrigan Falls, Virginia
October 10, 2004

Sometime in the night, Lara woke to find the curtain blowing softly over her bed. She'd downed a sleeping pill when they'd returned home from the church, so mercifully she'd slept until now. She looked at the clock: five fifty-two A.M. She'd been unconscious for nearly twelve hours. Nothing about her wedding day had happened as she'd planned. She slid out of the sheets and crept downstairs.

Before drifting off, she remembered hearing phones ringing and doors slamming. She'd half expected to find Todd standing by her bed when she woke with some wild story about getting drunk in the woods or falling down a well. She looked around her room. No note.

But nothing? Has he really not come here?

She padded into the dining room and searched for a sign that he'd called while she slept—even a terse note from her mother telling her "the boy" had left a message. Nothing. The house was silent. It was unthinkable, really. Surely there had been some mistake, some logical explanation. She wouldn't be forgiving him, not this time, but at least he owed her some kind of answer for standing her up at their wedding. There was a finality to this silence, like she'd been forgotten, abandoned.

Wedding gifts in silver wrapping sat on the dining room table in a haphazard jumble. She wondered if her mother hadn't knocked them from their neat pile on purpose. Audrey, still in her blue bathrobe, was asleep on the wingback chair in the living room with the light on. She'd been reading and hadn't bothered to take off the heavy layer of wedding makeup.

Lara padded softly through the foyer, passing all the black-and-white family photos as well as photos of their prized horses and the painting of her great-grandmother standing on a horse. As she passed it, a detail caught her eye: the choker necklace. She reached up to touch her own neck. It was bare. Still feeling the imprint of the necklace on her collarbone, Lara couldn't remember taking it off, but then so many things about the hour after she left the church were hazy. At some point, she must have cooperated with her mother because she was also out of her wedding dress and now in a long sleeveless cotton nightgown that looked like it belonged in another century.

The minute she stepped outside, the breeze hit her. Goose bumps dotted her arms, and she rubbed her hands over them. She walked out into the field where, as a teenager, she'd sat with Todd so many times. Easing herself onto a soft patch of grass, she thought there was something comforting about being here again. It recalled a simpler time.

Usually her mother was up by five, so the animals were stirring and restless, waiting for Audrey to feed them. They turned their hopeful attention to Lara.

She thought she heard rustling in the tall grasses behind her. Lara twisted to get a better look. "Todd?" Instead of his tall figure standing there, she found only the softly swaying grass. Thinking she heard movement again, she turned, hoping that Todd would emerge from the trees. There had been mysterious things—mysterious people— appearing here before, only now she welcomed them. She'd even dreamed about them again last night.

It was late harvest in the valley, and she knew the nearby winery's seasonal staff would be out this morning, racing against the clock for any late grapes that were ripening. Expecting to hear the firing up of tractor engines and the shouts and laughter from the early-morning pickers, she pulled her legs closer, meeting the eyes of the tall chestnut horse that had begun staring at her from his gate. It was as though time had stopped. Even the scene in the house looked like one of those episodes of *The Twilight Zone* where everyone had fallen into a deep sleep with Lara being the only person conscious and left wandering the earth.

She didn't know how long she'd been sitting when she heard the gravel shifting then saw the glare of headlights coming up over the drive. Her breath caught. *Todd! Oh, thank God.*

This had all been a terrible nightmare.

But the car that emerged from the trees wasn't Todd's familiar white Mustang. Instead it was a dark Jeep Cherokee. She'd seen this car before. The door opened and the outline of a man appeared. From the way he placed his hand heavily on the roof before he came around the car, she knew that whoever he was, he was delivering bad news.

Lara jumped up and ran down the hill, forgetting that she was only dressed in a thin cotton nightgown. The sight of her emerging from the field, her hair a wild tangle of blond and her makeup still in streaks, must have been a fright. "Did you find him?"

The face was familiar, and it took Lara a minute to place it. Ben Archer, the chief of police.

Immediately he removed his jacket and placed it around her shoulders. "How long have you been out here? It's freezing."

Lara looked out in the field blankly. It was definitely lighter now than when she'd come outside. She could make out the outlines of the mountains in the distance. "I don't know. Half an hour. I thought I heard something."

"Jesus, Lara," said a voice. Lara turned to see her mother at the door, pulling her bathrobe tight.

"I found her out here."

When they reached the house, Lara's mother grabbed her arm and ushered her up on the front porch and through the door.

Once they were inside, the police chief didn't move much past the stairs. "We found Todd's car."

Lara felt the room spin and could feel herself swaying. In a flash, thoughts came. What questions should she ask? Should she be sitting or standing? Would she need tissues? An eternity seemed to pass before she realized he'd said *Todd's car*. Not *Todd*. Ben had not said he was found dead.

"What about Todd?" Audrey had taken her by the shoulders.

"Is he hurt?" Lara added, her voice rising hopefully, because the alternative was worse.

Ben shook his head. "No sign of him."

"What do you mean no sign of him?" said Audrey. Her mother's voice had an edge to it, causing Lara to turn and look at her. Despite the woman's earlier denial, *her mother knew something*.

"We called the state police." Ben Archer rubbed the back of his neck. "They're going to take the car and analyze it." There was a haze of stubble on his face and a look of exhaustion. He clasped his hands in front of him like an undertaker at an unexpected funeral.

It occurred to Lara that, living in Kerrigan Falls, he probably hadn't had to give bad news to anyone before, so he had no practice at it. Nothing happened here. Until now.

"That's why I wanted to get down here to talk to you," he continued. "His car is going to be towed through town on a flatbed. People will notice it. They'll talk." He stammered. "I just wanted to prepare you. Now I've got to tell Fred and Betty."

"They don't know yet?" Lara's hand went to her mouth from shock. She imagined Betty Sutton hearing this news.

Ben shook his head. "I came here first."

"Where did you find it?" Audrey's voice was thin and tense, expectant even. "The car?"

Lara studied her mother's features, looking for something.

Ben hesitated before answering. "Wickelow Bend."

Audrey's eyes widened, but not with surprise. Lara made a mental note of that. There was something unsaid between her mother and Ben Archer. At the mention of Wickelow Bend, the air seemed to go out of her mother. "I see."

"Wait! The haunted stretch of road that kids are told not to drive on?" Lara looked at Ben. "*That* Wickelow Bend? Why on earth would Todd have been there?" Lara eyed her mother suspiciously. Audrey had turned completely pale and seemed to be trembling. "What aren't you telling me?"

"It was thirty years ago today." Audrey directed the comment to Ben. "You remember that, don't you?"

"I was there, Audrey," said Ben. He put his hands in his pockets and seemed fascinated with his shoes. "It was my dad's birthday. He always let me ride along with him in the police cruiser."

"Oh, I keep forgetting about your father." Audrey looked weary. "But you were *just* a boy."

"What are you both talking about?" Lara was watching their faces. "You didn't find Todd. That's good, right?"

Ben hesitated as though he were parsing out unfortunate news to a child. "Back in 1974—October tenth to be specific—we found an abandoned car along the road. It belonged to a man by the name of Peter Beaumont. To be perfectly honest with you, Todd's car was found in the exact same spot today."

"We've all heard the story," said Lara. "You're telling me that it's really true?"

"Yes." Audrey's voice was soft. "Peter Beaumont was your father's best friend."

"But Todd had no connection to Wickelow Bend or that missing man."

"Peter Beaumont wasn't just some missing man," said her mother, a surprising tone of annoyance in her voice as she clutched at the collar of her robe, pulling it around her neck. "He and your father grew up together here. They started their first band together in Jason's garage."

Lara was confused. While she knew never to drive on Wickelow Bend at night—no one did that—she'd never heard the name Peter Beaumont until now. Kids told wild tales of Wickelow Bend, but there were no names attached. It was an anonymous bogeyman... a missing man. The idea that someone real had actually disappeared hadn't occurred to her or her friends, ever. It was just an old legend. And Peter Beaumont? She'd toured with her father's band for a year. No one knew her father's musical career like she did. "And yet none of you have ever mentioned his name?" It was a sharp comment and she could see that it stung, but she couldn't exactly figure out why this revelation was bothering her so much.

"I have to go tell the Suttons," said Ben, excusing himself.

"Of course," said Audrey, taking his jacket from Lara's shoulders and offering it back.

He touched the doorknob and then turned back. "I'm sorry, Lara. I wish I'd had better news for you."

"You're still looking for him?"

"Of course we are," said Ben. "Doyle has a team searching the woods. But..."

"But what?"

"They never found Peter Beaumont." Her mother finished Ben's sentence for him.

"That's correct. Technically, the Beaumont case is still open," he said. Ben tapped the front door with his finger, nervously.

The weight of what they were hinting at hit her in waves. This wasn't some simple misunderstanding over their wedding. They were saying that she might never see Todd again. Pressure built up behind her eyes, and she fixed on something on the wall so as not to cry.

"I'll be in touch." Ben nodded at Audrey. Lara noticed the thick mud on the pants of his uniform and the dark circles under his eyes. It would be a long day. For that, she was grateful to him. He looked as miserable as she felt.

When she turned, she saw that her father had been standing in the doorway, listening to the entire exchange. It would make sense that he wanted to be here for Lara after what happened at the wedding, but she hadn't known he was in the house.

"I guess you heard." Audrey ran her hands through her hair, like she was trying to compose herself.

Anger rose up in her, but Lara wasn't sure why. "Why didn't either of you ever mention Peter Beaumont to me?" A name she had never heard until today had suddenly become significant. Now Peter and Todd seemed to be entwined by the same fate.

"I couldn't talk about him." Jason focused on Audrey.

Something occurred to Lara. She had been so stupid. She turned to her mother. "You knew." The common blood that flowed between them told her this much. "You'd tried to talk me out of getting married yesterday. It was the date, wasn't it? You knew something would happen on that day."

"They thought Peter actually disappeared on the ninth and that his car wasn't found until the next day. I've hated that day." Her mother inhaled deeply. "I'd hoped I would be wrong."

Lara shot her mother a disbelieving stare and laughed. "You're *never* wrong."

"No," admitted Audrey. "I'm not, but for your sake, I wish that I had been."

6

Kerrigan Falls, Virginia
June 20, 2005 (Nine Months After the Wedding)

After Todd—didn't show, split, went missing, jilted her, bailed, was abducted by aliens, insert wild theory—Lara had contemplated moving away from Kerrigan Falls.

Nothing had prepared her for the aftermath. First there were people who speculated on the connection between the Todd Sutton and Peter Beaumont cases.

Reporters camped out on Wickelow Bend as though they were expecting something to emerge from the trees. They stalked her, trying to get interviews about the last time she saw Todd and if he believed in the supernatural. A television show, *Ghostly Happenings*, sent a team of "hunters" for an episode titled "The Devil's Bend" that was the most watched show of the season, leading to odd phone calls at all hours from true believers in the occult. Lara had been so rattled by the intense attention that she didn't put up a fuss when Audrey insisted she stay out at Cabot Farms. When cars began driving up to the house in the middle of the night, Audrey installed a gate at the bottom of the hill, then changed their number. Lara wasted the days away reading her horoscope, watching *General Hospital*, drinking Chardonnay, and doing tarot readings for Caren and Betsy, who'd visited her like she was a high schooler home sick with mono. The apartment she'd shared with Todd sat empty. She couldn't bear to see it without him in it. The radio station gave her a month off.

Then there were the people who thought that Todd had just bailed on her. In some ways, they were the worst. Wild stories of him being seen at Dulles Airport the day of the wedding abounded, indicating that Todd might have sought a new life elsewhere on a 747. If this group saw her buying mac and cheese in a box at the supermarket, they turned their carts mid-aisle to avoid talking to her as though her misfortune were contagious. To avoid the look of pity, she started shopping at the all-night supermarket on the highway twelve miles away, peacefully steering her cart at three in the morning with the drunks and stoned college kids, bags of potato chips tucked under their arms. Then the daily copy of the *Kerrigan Falls Express* newspaper started going missing from the mailbox. Furious, Lara called the customer service line, only to learn that Caren, at Audrey's request, had driven by each morning, snatching up the morning edition so Lara wouldn't have to see that reporter Kim Landau had written yet another article on Todd's disappearance. MISSING posters from well-meaning people went up around Kerrigan Falls like Todd was some cat who'd been let out in the night and never returned. A fundraiser was held. What the funds were for, Lara was never quite sure.

And what did she think? No one ever had the courage to ask her.

If they had, depending on the day or even the hour, Lara switched camps between the two prevailing theories, causing her to exist in a kind of limbo. Certainly the idea that Todd might be dead was a real possibility, yet a part of her couldn't be sure. To give up on him felt like a betrayal. It was so tempting to get caught in the Todd Sutton and Peter Beaumont mystery, with its elaborate magical plot involving Wickelow Bend. In that theory, Todd was a victim, not a cad who'd abandoned her. She'd seen stories where loved ones left behind spearheaded these fantastical ideas only to look desperate and foolish when they were proven to be untrue. She couldn't bear to let herself be embarrassed again. The wedding had been enough.

Lara was more of a believer in Occam's razor. Publicly, this was the stance she'd taken, and it put her at odds with Todd's family, who still held vigils at Wickelow Bend. He'd left her. Pure and simple. But even then, the question became: Where was he? His empty car being found the following morning threw a monkey wrench in this theory. Todd might have left her, but everyone who knew him agreed, he never would have abandoned his car.

After the wedding, she'd taken on more of the regular overnight shifts at the radio station where, for years, she'd only been doing them on weekends. Providing the soundtrack to her fellow people of the night—emergency room crews, bartenders, security guards— had great appeal to her. A month after the wedding, a notice to 99.7 K-ROCK employees was tucked in her paycheck: The owners had put the radio station up for sale. Something in her stirred as she read the announcement on blue copy paper. It informed 99.7 K-ROCK employees that "While no immediate changes are expected, another owner will have the right to change the station's format." That meant that 99.7 K-ROCK could become a country station and they'd all lose their jobs. It felt like a sign.

Her grandfather Simon Webster, founder of the *Kerrigan Falls Express*, had left her half of his fortune—which wasn't so much of a fortune as he'd pretended it was, but it was enough to buy the radio station assets at the $200,000 asking price. Seeing an opportunity, she went to her father to see if he'd be interested in running it with her.

A week later, she saw that the FOR SALE sign was still up on the 1902 four-bedroom painted-brick Victorian that she and Todd had looked at before the wedding. They'd dreamed of fixing it up together. With its large porch, opulent woodwork, marble fireplace, and French doors, the house was $40,000. It also had ruined floors, drafty windows, and a non-functioning kitchen. She settled on the house for $5,000 less than the asking price the day before she bought the radio station assets.

She knew that both had been impulsive decisions, but she needed to put distance between herself and that wedding. All these things, these moving parts, night shifts, and broken-down houses, had kept her busy and exhausted and stopped her from thinking. She'd closed on the house in January. And after five months of sanding walls, painting, pulling out nails, replacing drafty windows with historically accurate ones, and replacing the old heating system, the mere mention of Todd didn't cause her heart to pound like an infected wound anymore.

Surveying the disaster that was now her dining room floor, Lara thought seriously about hiring a professional. She'd thrown herself into sanding the Georgia pine floors. Of course the house had no air-conditioning, and with summer approaching she was thinking of buying a few window units. Last week's heat wave had her sleeping in a puddle of sweat.

Her mother had been hovering over her lately, stopping by the station or her house daily under the guise of helpful remodeling advice, lugging paint chips and rug samples with her.

The door opened and Lara regretted giving her mother a key when the large Oorang Airedales, Oddjob and Moneypenny, came bounding into the living room, circling the sander and barking as though it were a menacing beast. The dogs were oddly old, yet they seemed like puppies. Lara could swear they'd been alive when she was a child, but Audrey insisted they were just different dogs with the same names. She guessed people did that kind of thing. Quickly, Lara turned off the machine and removed her goggles and respirator to find her mother standing in the hallway holding a painting under one arm and garment bag under the other.

"What's that?" Lara folded her arms. As she moved, her jeans, T-shirt, and Chuck Taylors let loose a fine sprinkle of sawdust.

Audrey held both out. "Your dress for the gala and Cecile's painting." She looked around the room and couldn't hide her horror. "You should really hire someone to do this."

Lara wasn't going to admit she'd had the same thought. Shooing her mother away with a glove, Lara turned to pet the dogs. "I'm learning a lot from doing it myself."

"Learning? At least get Caren to help you *learn.*" Her voice trailed down the hall and back again.

"She's got her own sawdust pile at the coffeehouse."

"Oh yes, I heard she's jumped into small-business ownership, too." Audrey had been against Lara purchasing both this house and the radio station, instead wanting her to move home permanently. Audrey turned the frame around to reveal the painting of Cecile Cabot, standing atop a white steed that circled the Parisian circus. "I thought it would look perfect in your dining room."

"But *you* love that painting." Lara's eye went immediately to the choker around Cecile's neck. While it was a very generous gift from her mother, she actually didn't care for the painting, fearing it would always remind her of *that* day.

"I do love it," said Audrey, holding it up to the light.

Lara stepped carefully to avoid the sawdust and leaned on the doorway to the dining room, ushering the dogs away from the dust.

Audrey handed Lara the garment bag and began walking around the room with the painting, placing it on each wall, looking for the desired effect.

Lara sighed. "You're bestowing a pity painting on me."

"Don't be ridiculous." Audrey was a slight woman, shorter and finer-boned than Lara with a blond bob that never varied in length, as though it was tended at night while she slept. Audrey had obviously come from the stable because she was walking around the room in a pair of beige riding pants and tall field boots that curved at the knee. "I'm doing some redecorating at the farm. You've gotten me in the mood to change things up a bit, so I thought it made sense for you to have it." She put her hands on her hips. "I'm empty-nesting."

Lara raised her eyebrow in doubt.

Her mother sighed, defeated. She pointed to the frame. "This painting—this woman—this is your legacy. Who *we* are. Anyway, I'm passing it down to you. There are some heirlooms that are yours. They're more sentimental than anything, but they need to be passed to the next generation."

"Oh please, Mother," said Lara. "This isn't about heirlooms. You're decorating. You've been itching to decorate this house since I bought it."

"A bit." Audrey gave her a sheepish smile.

"The frame is too much, though," said Lara, protesting.

"It does have a Versailles-meets-Vegas feel to it, doesn't it? Take it to Gaston Boucher and change it. Make sure he keeps it for you, though, it's probably worth more than the painting." Audrey leaned it against the wall.

Gaston Boucher, owner of the most successful art gallery and framing shop in Kerrigan Falls, was a name that was peppered in all of Audrey's recent conversations. Lara suspected they'd begun dating.

"She was brave. And you are, too." She turned Lara's chin with her hand and gazed into her eyes. "We owe this woman a great deal," said Audrey. "She needs to be with you now. She's been in my hallway long enough."

Crouching down to get a better look at the painting, Lara lifted the frame from the floor. The colors looked different in this room than they had in the dimly lit hall at Cabot Farms. "If I'm brave, Mother, I learned it from you. Thank you." Running her hands over the frame, Lara thought how her mother had held her together all these months. While she often rolled her eyes at Audrey's fussing, her mother had created a safe world for her when everything had fallen to pieces. "I couldn't have done any of this without you."

Audrey blushed and tugged at her shirt, taking deep breaths like she was about to cry. "Oh, come on now." Changing the subject, Audrey began unzipping the bag that held what Lara assumed to be a gown.

"You said this is for the gala, right?" As her mother held the hanger, Lara slid the garment bag down, allowing a wash of midnight-blue chiffon to reveal itself. With a strapless bodice, the dress was like something out of vintage Barbie. Cascading down from the fitted waist was a full skirt with multiple tulle layers arranged like ombré waterfalls in different lengths and saturations of peacock. "You must have spent a fortune on this."

"I did," said Audrey. "Don't get dust on it. I suppose you'll want to *alter* it?"

Lara smiled. "No. It's perfect. Thank you."

Audrey ignored her and turned, the mother-daughter moment broken. "And *that* painting will look great with the rug I just bought you. Eggplant and gold tones, ornate. Perfect for this room. You also need wooden shutters." Audrey scanned the room. "And a silver tea set."

Oddjob came and sat at Lara's feet. She could feel the dog lean slowly into her.

"You can also take him anytime you want. He misses you."

As if to answer, Oddjob let out a sigh and stretched out on the floor in front of Lara like the Sphinx. Oddjob was hers, while Miss

Moneypenny was her mother's dog. Hugo, the ringleader, a tiny Welsh terrier, was nowhere to be found today.

Audrey retrieved the sunglasses that hung on the neck of her T-shirt and headed toward the door. Oddjob and Moneypenny scrambled up, their paws and claws scraping against the floor in a mad rush not to be left behind by the woman who fed them.

"I'll come here around six tomorrow to pick you up for the circus."

Lara frowned. "I don't think I'm going this year."

"Nonsense," said Audrey. "The Rivolis will be hurt if you don't go."

Her mother pushed through the door and down the steps, walking around to the driver's-side door. When she opened the back door, the dogs leapt into the backseat, Oddjob putting his paws up on the front-seat cup holder so he could get a good view of the windshield. After shutting the door, Audrey slid into the driver's seat and lowered the passenger's window. "Six tomorrow for the circus. No excuses."

Lara saluted her.

Audrey slid her glasses down her nose. "And Lara."

Lara leaned down to see her mother's face.

"Him not coming back was always a possibility; you knew that. I'm glad to see you're getting on with your life."

Lara looked down at her dusty sneakers. She couldn't help shake the feeling that she wasn't getting the full truth from Audrey. They'd never lied to each other, but Audrey was definitely holding something back.

"And get a floor man in, will you?" Without another word, the door shut and the black Sierra Grande with the CABOT FARMS logo pulled out.

When she got back into the house, Lara stood and looked down at the painting before picking it up. The frame was small but heavy in her hands. She estimated it had to be fifteen pounds of gold or wood. The painting depicted a petite blond woman wearing a muted-aqua leotard with brown gemstones, standing on the back of a white horse. Her arms were held high in perfect balance. The horse was adorned with a matching costume of aqua feathers and looked to be in full stride. While a young Cecile's features were clear, it was as though the artist had placed the painting out in the rain; there was a noticeable dripping effect on the oil. At first glance, it was the dual subjects of horse and rider that caught the eye, yet great care had also been taken by the painter to capture the audience's faces in the front row. Dressed in their finest clothing, several patrons in the back rows were holding champagne flutes, their faces illuminated by the stage lighting. Midpoint in the audience, one man in particular had clearly drawn features, a shock of red hair and beard, as he pointed to the spectacle that was unfolding in front of him. The woman next to him held her head in her hands, presumably to avoid observing any fall.

While not a realistic style of painting, it wasn't exactly modernist, either. Lara had noticed how textured it was, with the heavy brushstrokes still visible. The painting lacked the smooth, baked finishes of the artwork Lara had seen at museums in New York, Washington, and even Paris and Rome during her visits there while in college.

Lara knew the story well. Cecile Cabot had left France in September 1926 with her infant daughter, Margot. Not much was known about Margot's father; Cecile indicated that he'd died of influenza and was a man of no real consequence. She sailed across the ocean, departing the port of Le Havre on the SS *de Grasse*, arriving in New York Harbor five days later. With little money, Cecile heard about work at the glass factory outside of Kerrigan Falls, landing a job on the assembly line making Zoltan's mustard jars. She'd been working on the assembly line for six months when she applied for a job as a seamstress for Daphne Lund, wife of the factory owner, Bertrand Lund. Cecile drew some sketches of dresses for Mrs. Lund and proved an inventive seamstress, bringing Parisian flair to Daphne's spring wardrobe. The Great Depression didn't seem to hit the Lund family as hard as other entrepreneurs, so Cecile was kept on, designing mostly evening dresses for Mrs. Lund, traveling with her to New York searching for silks and taffetas and sewing beading into bodices. Within the year, she'd proven herself invaluable.

On a rare outing at the house with the children, Cecile had saved the Lunds' youngest son from a runaway horse, chasing down the creature on her own horse and grabbing the boy by the belt just as the animal fled into a low patch of trees that would have surely decapitated the child. The couple had already lost two children, so Mrs. Lund was so grateful that Bertrand Lund rewarded Cecile for the heroic deed by giving her a job running his rather elaborate stables. Bertrand Lund hadn't known his seamstress was such a keen horsewoman. Later, she purchased fifty acres from Lund and built a modest farmhouse, raising her daughter, Margot, alongside the Lund children.

In 1938, using the money she'd saved, Cecile left the employ of the Lund family and began a traveling equestrian show with her Chevrolet pickup truck and a trailer full of old horses. The horses had been a final gift from her employer and were either aging or misfits that Mr. Lund was planning on retiring or shooting. She let the word get out that she was looking to employ clowns and, later, trapeze artists, naming her enterprise Le Cirque Margot, after her daughter.

In those days, weeks before a circus arrived in towns like Charlottesville, Roanoke, Gainesville, Pensacola, Mobile, and Gaffney, posters went up using young Margot as the draw. The circus did two shows in a town—the afternoon matinee and the evening performance—before they broke down the tents and seats. Trailers doubling as ticket booths pulled up at the entrance of the "big top." A ticket cost 75 cents; reserved seats were $1.25.

Thirteen when the circus was founded, Margot Cabot was becoming an expert horsewoman herself. Early posters in 1940 showed a teenage Margot Cabot hanging upside down on a white stallion, her right leg appearing to be the only thing connecting her to the animal's back. The second wave of posters for the 1941 season featured Margot wearing a red leotard with a head of plumes, standing astride a white horse with the red lettering that would become the company's logo: LE CIRQUE MARGOT.

The real Margot, however, made the circus look tame by comparison. A wild teenager who smoked and drank gin, Margot Cabot was also a great beauty. But the circus's namesake never seemed to take to her birthright. At the age of seventeen, Margot left the circus—a turn of events that would have been funny since few people run away *from* the circus. She'd fallen in love with a driver on the demolition derby circuit, and nothing Cecile could say would stop her.

In the fall of 1944, after about a year on the road, things with the man she'd run off with seemed to go south. Abruptly, Margot returned to Kerrigan Falls and within the year had married Simon Webster, the founder of the *Kerrigan Falls Express* newspaper.

While she settled down, Margot still wasn't "right," often not leaving her room for days—including not eating or bathing. The logistics of these episodes were difficult for a man trying to run a daily newspaper. Simon hired nurses to coax her to eat and twice a week to throw her into the bathtub. Then, as quickly as they began, the episodes would cease and Margot would be demurely seated at the breakfast table in her silk robe, buttering her toast and sipping coffee—having returned from wherever it was her mind had gone.

She'd also come and go at the circus in those days, Cecile dreading her arrival because she was unreliable, demanding her show be included but not practicing it enough for it to be safe. On a horse, Margot was an artist. While Cecile could ride, she couldn't hold a candle to Margot. It was as though the horse weren't even there—as though she were interacting with a chair, not a living, pulsing creature with a mind of its own.

After five years of marriage, Margot gave birth to a daughter, Audrey, in the fall of 1950. Margot's eccentric and impulsive nature began to get wilder and she began to exhibit odd signs, claiming to see the devil in the field. One day, Simon found her standing in the apple groves, watching the first winter snowfall in her thin nightgown and bare feet, Audrey dangling loosely in her arms, chanting a spell and saying that *he* had asked to see the baby. Her husband had had it by then. It was one thing to endanger herself but another to harm their young daughter. Simon called an institution to take Margot, but within a day, she'd developed a fever, dying three days later.

Cecile, who had been on the road touring, moved back and took over much of the care of Audrey, letting her manager run the circus in her absence. Le Cirque Margot continued to thrive through the 1960s when Audrey picked up trick riding like Cecile and her mother, working the shows each summer. In 1972, when Audrey made it clear that she didn't want a life on the road, Cecile, then seventy-two years old, decided it was time to retire the show. For years, ticket sales had been lagging, since families had other forms of entertainment. The age of the circus—and Le Cirque Margot—was at an end.

Now Le Cirque Margot lived on only in memorabilia. Posters and signs with Margot's face could be found all over Kerrigan Falls. The historical society had an entire collection of circus memorabilia as well as original Zoltan's mustard jars.

A jolt of nostalgia for Cecile gripped her, and she grabbed the frame. Her mother was right. This painting should be with her. She'd get Gaston Boucher working on it as soon as possible.

Walking the block down from her house to Main Street, she

stopped off at the Feed & Supply Coffee House, needing caffeine before a three-hour evening shift. Shortly after Lara had purchased the radio station, Caren opened Kerrigan Falls' only coffeehouse in the old hardware store next door to 99.7 K-ROCK. Feed & Supply was one of the new businesses that thrived due to the Washington, DC, transplants who'd moved out to the country and expected things like lattes, red velvet cake, and artisanal breads.

As the bell jingled overhead, Lara noticed that things were slow for a Wednesday evening. Caren was constantly suffering local college students who ordered only a tall drip coffee and sat for four hours on a sofa just for the new Wi-Fi. From the looks of it, she had four students and a book club tonight. The book club seemed to have an assortment of cakes and drinks with whipped cream, so that was a good sign.

The old hardware store was long and narrow with wide oak planks on the floor and a tin ceiling. Caren and Lara had removed the counter from the old pharmacy that had once stood in the space now occupied by the 99.7 K-ROCK studio and lugged it on two borrowed dollies over to the coffeehouse. It was a perfect fit along the wall, and Caren displayed scones and muffins there in covered glass domes. Then they scoured thrift shops and estate sales up and down Route 29, finding old velvet sofas and vintage leather chairs. The look was like a smoking room with deep jewel tones, brown wood, and aged leather—Lara had been pleased that such a mismatch of furniture styles could blend this well.

As she paid for her drink, Lara spied a Ouija board on the coffee table—not a Parker Brothers board, but an antique one that she didn't recognize.

"Where'd you get that?" She pointed to it.

"Isn't it great? I'm thinking we have a séance some night after close." Caren placed the lid on Lara's white mocha. "A customer donated it to the shop. It doubles as a tray."

Lara did notice the sides of the board scooped upward. "Who was it?"

"Dunno," said Caren with a shrug. "Some blond woman. She looked familiar, though I'm not sure from where." Caren raised her eyebrow. "Please tell me you're not still freaked out by Ouija boards?"

"No," said Lara, not convincing anyone.

"You're such a baby. They're just board games, like Clue."

"They are nothing like Clue!" Lara eyed the Ouija board. Lara's magic had "come in" during a sleepover at Caren's when Lara was six. As a prank, Caren's older sister and her friends tried to scare the younger girls with a séance. Instead Lara had moved the board with her mind, scaring six teenage girls, sending them squealing through the house. It had been the first time Lara had made a "correction."

As if reading her thoughts, Caren said, "My dad said it was static electricity that moved the board. It happens all the time."

"It does not *happen* all the time, Caren." After Caren watched her unzip her own wedding dress with magic, Lara knew that her friend was growing suspicious; she was probably connecting all the weird things she'd witnessed over the years.

"What was the name that appeared on the board? The one that had you so freaked." Caren looked up. "Alta..."

"Althacazur." Lara snatched the cup from the counter. It was a name that she had never forgotten. Lara had asked the board who was there and "Althacazur" had been the response.

"Betsy was going to name her cat Althacazur, but you were so freaked out that you cried. Those were fun times." Caren looked at the painting leaning next to the sofa. "How did you get that thing?"

"My mother," said Lara. "She's cleaning and thinks it would look perfect in my dining room."

"Or here," said Caren. "Would look great next to the leather

Chesterfield over there." Caren pointed toward the book clubbers, who had thick copies of *Jonathan Strange & Mr. Norrell* on their laps.

"It's an heirloom," Lara said with a sigh. "I'll put it up for a little while then gift it to you. Gaston Boucher is going to make the frame a little less...well, just a little less..."

"Yeah, a little less would be nice." Caren nodded gravely.

Lara headed past the Ouija board a little too quickly on her way to the door. She could hear Caren giggle behind her.

"You're so mean," said Lara as the door shut behind her.

She crossed the street and opened the door to Gaston Boucher's frame shop. Another bell rang overhead. Why did everyone in Kerrigan Falls need to announce their door was opening? It wasn't like crime ever happened here. Despite the old-fashioned touch of a bronze bell, the inside of the gallery was sleek. White framed prints in all sizes were arranged in neat stacks that leaned against the wall, with sleek laminate counters and up-lighting. Two chrome Wassily Chairs with brown leather were gathered around a small glass table with hulking art books in the center.

Dressed casually in jeans and a white shirt with the sleeves pushed up above his elbows, Gaston Boucher was leaning over his work desk studying a piece of paper rather intently. A slight man, he had blond wavy hair that fell below his chin while he worked and round tortoise-shell glasses perched on his nose. His face was stern, like he was a philosophy professor grading a poor paper.

"I heard you were bringing me something." Gaston didn't look up, his French accent slight. He held up a small painting to the light and studied it intently.

"Well, that depends. Are you going to try to talk me out of reframing it?" Lara struggled to hold up the heavy painting, which was only about two feet wide by two feet long. She could hear a promotional jingle for 99.7 K-ROCK playing and was touched that he was piping the radio station into the gallery. She'd taken Gaston for a techno or Velvet Underground fan.

"I've always thought that frame overpowers what is an unusually intriguing painting." Gaston peered over his glasses, abandoning the photo he'd been working on. "So, *non*." He motioned for her to hand it to him.

Lara had suspected something was going on between Audrey and this man. That Gaston had opinions about this painting meant he'd *seen* this painting at her mother's house.

"The thing has to be made of solid gold." He reached over and easily lifted the painting from her hands, then turned the frame over and studied each corner.

While he worked, Lara walked the perimeter of the gallery.

From Audrey, Lara learned that he'd graduated from the Sorbonne, then knocked around New York City for years trying to make his mark as a punk rock guitarist. When his music career hadn't taken off, he began working as a painter, then a photographer living in Chelsea back in the late 1970s. The photos of Gaston with famous people—Patti Smith, Lou Reed, Gary Numan, Debbie Harry, and Chris Stein—seemed to support this claim. In them Gaston's hair was spiky and he wore a suit with a thin black tie like a member of Devo.

He had a section of equine paintings. Also from Audrey, Lara knew that this was how he'd met her mother. Years ago, when he was still living in New York, he'd purchased a horse from Audrey. While driving the horse out of Kerrigan Falls, he noticed that there was an old art gallery for sale. He bought the place, tossing out most of the hotel-lobby-inspired fruit bowl paintings and bad landscapes and replacing them with more modern works that he brought in regularly from New York. He also had a robust wedding and graduation framing business that Lara imagined paid the bills nicely.

After making a full circle around the shop, she leaned over the desk, a tall, long worktable. "What do you think?"

"It's older than I thought." He turned on a light and slid the frame under it. "Audrey said this was her grandmother's painting."

"Yes. It's her grandmother, *my great-grandmother*, Cecile Cabot. That's her riding the horse in Paris."

Taking a loupe, Gaston studied the corner. "I hadn't noticed this before. Odd."

"What?" Again, the *before* implying he'd studied this painting at length.

"The painting is signed EG." He pulled away and handed her the loupe. "See."

"And?" Lara looked at the signature. It was, indeed, signed EG.

"Well." Gaston took his glasses off and wiped them on his shirt. "It's unlikely, but this signature does resemble Émile Giroux's. This painting is from the 1920s, *non*?"

"Yes, that's about right."

"This would be the correct time frame as well as the correct location for Giroux. It's just that..." He stopped and turned his head, looking at the painting at an angle. "Again, I highly doubt it. This painting was probably some street artist, but there *were* rumored circus paintings by Giroux. Lost paintings—three of them—Les Dames du Cirque Secret. It's an odd coincidence."

"You're saying this painting might be famous?"

"Perhaps," he said. "I'm going to contact Edward Binghampton Barrow to see if the paintings are all accounted for. The lost thing is always a bit of an exaggeration. Usually they're just in some private collection. This is probably just a cheap copy."

"Edward Binghampton?" Lara laughed out loud struggling to recall the third name.

"Barrow," said Gaston, clarifying. "Binghampton Barrow."

"That's a ridiculous name."

"*Troisième*," he said, smiling. "Or is it *quatrième*—as you say it, 'the fourth'? I can never remember. Anyway, there's a whole mess of Edward Binghampton Barrows, but *this* particular one has done most of his work on French Jazz Age painters. A few years ago, he wrote the only biography that exists of the painter Émile Giroux. So if anyone will know if this painting is one of his, it would be Teddy."

"How do you know him?"

"We studied at the Sorbonne together. His mother was a famous Nigerian model who used to hang with Warhol. In our youth, his mother's cachet could get Teddy and me into some terrific parties in Paris. His father, the rather stodgy Earl of Campshire, would often have to get us out of any trouble, but it was a marvelous existence." Gaston grinned, turning the painting over and bending over it, again studying the frame carefully. It was gold-carved with inlaid flowers that looked to have once been red but were now faded brown. "While I'm not a fan of this frame for this picture, I think it might be quite valuable—an original even."

"Let me know what you find," said Lara. "I think I'd like it more if it was framed in something like this." She pointed to a simple gold frame.

He nodded. "I'll call you when I hear something from Teddy or have something to show you."

Hearing the bell's off-key clang, Lara turned to see a petite chestnut-haired woman making a beeline toward Gaston. Recognizing her as Marla Archer—the recent ex-wife of police chief Ben Archer—Lara stepped out of the way as the woman approached Gaston and gave him a kiss on each cheek. Marla Archer quickly shifted her gaze to Lara as though she were a potted plant that was in the way.

"Hello," she said brightly. "So sorry, I didn't see you there."

"This is Lara Barnes," said Gaston.

"*Oh*," said Marla in *that* tone. Her eyes softened. It was the look of pity that Lara was used to by now.

"Well," said Lara, giving a final nod to Gaston. "Call me when you find out something, Gaston."

"That's quite a painting," said Marla, pushing her shoulder-length hair out of the way to get a closer look at it.

"It needs a new frame," said Gaston. "But we're taking care of that."

As Lara turned the knob, she heard Marla exclaim, "That's gorgeous." Lara turned to see that Gaston was holding up a frame with one of her recent photographs, the painting now forgotten. Marla was one of only two photographers in Kerrigan Falls. That Marla had taken her high school graduation portrait and still didn't recall her until Gaston's prompting didn't exactly make Lara feel memorable. Over the years, she'd been introduced to Marla several times, but it seemed the woman didn't recall her until the connection with Todd was made. It was tough when the only thing you were known for was not getting married. But her mother was right. Lara came from a long line of strong women. She would weather this. Thinking about the painting, Lara realized she really *would* like to see it hanging in her dining room.

As she shut the door behind her, she wondered what she would do if she found out the painting was valuable.

O nly in the quiet of the night, when Lara worked alone at the radio station, did she feel she'd learned the rhythms and creaks of the place, the music of old boards and rusted nails giving way. It was only then that she felt it was truly hers. After the sale, and at the urging of her father, she'd stopped doing the overnight shift to focus on the business side of things—which had sorely needed her attention—but she liked to do the occasional night and overnight shifts. Now her day was a constant stream of spreadsheets and advertising numbers, so she liked to get behind the booth and remember why she loved this station. Tonight she was filling in for the seven-to-ten shift.

As she came through the door, she was surprised to find her father still in the studio. He was sitting on the floor, a fan of albums spread around him.

"Looking for something?"

"I'm doing the Laurel Canyon sound tomorrow night." There seemed to be an order to the scattered albums, and he kept swapping them out. He looked like a teenager on his bedroom floor.

"Not enough David Crosby?"

"Too much Crosby," said Jason, his face stern. "Not enough Joni Mitchell."

Lara made a face behind his back. She wasn't as big a Joni Mitchell fan as her father. "How about Buffalo Springfield? Maybe 'Expecting to Fly'? Haven't heard that one in a while."

From the corner of her eye, she could see him smile. He was always proud when she knew her music.

Jason stood up, knees cracking, and plunked himself heavily in his desk chair, which faced hers.

Housed in the old Main Street pharmacy, 99.7 K-ROCK's focal point in the office was a giant stained-glass mortar and pestle that had once been centered over the bar. At some point, the glass at the top of the pestle had fallen out and been replaced by a wad of kelly-green tape.

Their desks sat in what used to be the candy aisle. As a kid, Lara and her friends raced to this very spot to grab a small paper bag and fill it to the top with Swedish Fish, salty pumpkin seeds, SweeTarts, and her favorite, the now unpopular fake Winston candy cigarettes.

Growing up, it had been nice having a somewhat famous father. His band, Dangerous Tendencies, had cut two studio albums in the late 1970s. He still had a lot of fans who wrote him, so they'd created a weekly syndicated radio show on music of the '70s across twenty-seven radio stations in the US, Europe, and Japan. It was a lucrative contract and gave her father a new fan base. Advertising was up and between the two of them, the radio station venture was beginning to work. The station still hadn't turned anywhere near a profit yet, so she was making payroll with the money she had left from her grandfather's inheritance. She calculated how long she had to turn around the business—about fifteen months.

While some radio stations had cushy budgets and their on-air talent didn't have to load reel-to-reel tapes or handle the production of their own shows, 99.7 K-ROCK was assembled on a shoestring. From the tattered purple velvet sofa in the waiting room to the records housed in the old display donated from the long-closed G. C. Murphy store where she used to go and buy Donna Summer albums with her allowance money, everything looked like it had been patched together. It made you feel that one wobbly old switch could feasibly shut off the station, sending the place into some sort of silent history. Yet there was a faded elegance to the building that Lara admired. Everything had earned its place here. Even her. It was this station that had saved her in her darkest hours.

The day she'd closed on the business, she and Jason had come here together, sitting amid the dust, the faint smell of old antiseptic and drug compounds still clinging to the space. He took out a photo and slid it across the floor to her. It was an old photo of a band—three members. It was a funny pose, like they were preening for an album cover. Even before he'd pointed Peter Beaumont out to her, she'd known who he was. The trio was assembled down near the Kerrigan River against the rocks—but the man crouching in the middle was pulling the photographer's eye to him. Jason and the third man were neatly assembled around the subject—orbiting him even—but it was clear they were supporting characters. Lara realized just how powerful a photo could be to sum up things that people couldn't articulate. Her father could have spoken for hours about Peter Beaumont and wouldn't have been able to explain *this*. Peter had been the focal point of the band. From the photo, she knew he was talented, too. His shoulder jutted out, just a bit, displaying a type of youthful cockiness that comes with knowing you have talent. He wasn't as tall as Jason, who hunched a little in the picture, but they looked like they could have been brothers.

"You were lost without him," she said.

"It just didn't matter without him," he said, correcting her. "It had been his dream, not mine. Hell, I'd have probably been a mechanic had I not met him."

"And now?"

"Some days I feel like an imposter living in his dream. Survivor's guilt they call it, I think."

Lara knew that feeling well. "It's strange, isn't it? The spaces they leave for you to fill."

He laughed. "My life has been a poor attempt at trying to live the life he didn't get to."

"So you think Peter Beaumont is dead?" They had never discussed it. She knew this was the first time he was able to broach the subject of his former bandmate.

"I do," he said. She heard a snap and saw that he'd opened a green bottle of Tanqueray. He pulled out two glasses and a tiny bottle of Schweppes tonic. "Everything I did was designed to fill the vacuum," said Jason, as if he could read her mind.

"And Todd?" It was the natural next question. Peter and Todd were now lumped together forever on Wickelow Bend. She'd watched his mouth tighten, but he did not answer her. Instead they both drank to the future.

Five years from now with a bit more reflection, she wondered what life would be like for her. How would she shift herself to feel less incomplete? Looking around the radio station, she thought she was off to a good start with that question. The old Lara Barnes, the one who would have married Todd, wouldn't have needed to buy a radio station. This one did.

Lately, she'd also begun to think of the man in the field. *That boy is not your destiny.*

As a child, she'd had a wild imagination. She'd been born with only one kidney and had been sickly, so some part of her had never been convinced that the man had been real; perhaps he was just an imaginary friend created by an overactive mind. Still, what he had said, real or not, had been on her mind lately. Had they known her fate? They'd certainly seemed to allude to it. These were the things you thought of in the middle of the night when you were alone at a radio station. It wasn't a healthy shift, that was for sure.

She waved to Bob Breen, the drive-time announcer sitting in the sound booth, the glow from his cigarette lighting the darkened space. She was sure she'd told him that he couldn't smoke in here anymore, but she'd likely have to add a sign near the clock—all the on-air talent watched the clock. She checked her own watch: fifteen minutes until she was on air. Her father began to gather up his stuff, finally satisfied with his albums.

At seven, Bob pushed back from the table and was quickly off. Lara heard the door shut behind him as she climbed into the chair and wheeled up to the control desk. She thought that she was probably one of the few DJs who didn't like the sound of her own voice. Her vocal cords sounded as though they'd been run over with sandpaper. "Smoky," they called it. Pulling her blond hair into a ponytail, she swallowed hard as she pressed the MIKE button and turned up the volume, then pushed the STATION ID button at the top of the hour.

99.7 K-ROCK played the deep or obscure tracks on an album, not just popular "top 40" songs, except for three hours each Sunday night when she'd play punk and new wave—Bauhaus, Television, the Cure, the Slits, Concrete Blonde, and House of Love. The college kids would call her and beg her for the Ramones and the Violent Femmes—always the Femmes. Lara laid out her first hour of songs, something she liked to do, although a lot of on-air talent chose songs on the fly.

First up was a Led Zeppelin two-set. She placed "Achilles Last Stand" on turntable one, turned the knob to the CUE setting, and set the needle on the track. Then she pressed the START button. The turntable belt wound the record slowly until she heard the beginning chords of the song. When she detected the first few notes, she hit the STOP button, rotating the record backward with her fingers until the vinyl made a growling noise at the opening chords. She repeated the ritual with "How Many More Times" on turntable two.

Lara activated turntable number one. The song melted perfectly into the fading chords of the station jingle. She flipped the window blind and stared out into the road. Enough cars were still going down the hill at this hour to cause a small traffic jam, but they would thin in the hours to come. Perhaps it was the loneliness of the job, but Todd was never far from her thoughts when she was locked in the radio studio.

She kept looking at the phone, hoping to see it blinking, almost willing it to do so. She supposed she could enchant it to ring, but there would be no one on the other end. If Todd was going to contact her anywhere—if he could contact her—it would be here. When she'd worked the midnight-to-six shift, he often called to check up on her, worried about her locked alone spinning records. But her father had been right: Just as with Peter, there had been no sightings of Todd. Christmas had come and gone, Valentine's Day, his mother's birthday—all points when everyone had thought he'd call. Despite his abandoned car being found, his credit cards had never been used. Like Peter Beaumont, he'd simply vanished.

Always, she scrutinized the final moments she'd seen him. They'd taken on mythic status, like a collection of valuable missing jewels. She'd combed through every minute, every word, gesture, and movement, looking for something that would provide the key. What had she missed?

Thinking back now, she couldn't recall the last image of him. When she thought about the moments in her life—the defining ones that had *truly* mattered—how much did they really add up to? For her, maybe ten hours in a total lifetime? Was that a lot or a little? She didn't know. But *that* moment. That was the *one*.

It had seemed so ordinary, almost pedestrian at the time. If only she could have stopped herself from sliding into the driver's seat and glancing at him so briefly, before backing her car out onto the road. She was so focused on the road ahead of her, the life in front of her, that she didn't stop and absorb that final image of him standing in his driveway. It had been her biggest regret.

Seeing her father tonight made her nostalgic for a Dangerous Tendencies album. Normally, she didn't play Jason's records—his music was saved for his own show—but "The One I Left Behind" was her favorite of their songs. Sliding *Tending*, the band's debut album, out of its battered paper sleeve, Lara placed it on the turntable, flipped the knob to the CUE setting, and then carefully set the needle on the vinyl groove for song number three. As she wound the disk backward, something odd happened. She picked up tones. *Is it a song?* It was definitely a song. Usually, the backward cue sound was pure garble that resembled a warped tape, but tonight she heard the beginnings of a perfect guitar intro.

That was impossible.

"I am *definitely* hearing things." She inhaled loudly and restarted the record until she heard the song start and positioned her hands on the record, stopping her fingers. Finding the start spot, she swallowed hard then wound her hand backward. Again, instead of dissonance, soft guitar chords echoed through the cue in the sound booth. She kept the rotation going steady, standing up so she could get a good angle above the turntable. Finally, after thirty seconds of winding, she heard a man's voice begin to sing.

You said I didn't know what I wanted,
That I didn't know about love.

"What the fuck?" Her hand froze. She stepped back from the turntable.

Moving quickly, she flipped the switch on the reel-to-reel tapes. The station could run on the four tape machines passing off songs to each other as if on autopilot, so she wouldn't have to worry about the sound board for now.

She pushed through the booth and out into the office, searching through drawers for a tape recorder. She found the one she was looking for, but when she hit the PLAY button it was dead. Finally, she grabbed Jason's guitar and ran back into the booth. Cuing up the record again, she repeated the process. The song was still there. She located the notes on the guitar and played the melody, repeating the record rotation until she had it. The song wasn't familiar. She tabbed the notes quickly on a piece of scrap paper so she wouldn't lose them.

As she heard the door open for the overnight person to relieve her, she tried the record once again. This time the familiar warble had replaced the guitar opening.

The song was gone.

After gathering her purse, Lara walked at a clipped pace down Main Street toward the restaurant two blocks away. The dress shop on the corner had closed a month before, leaving a vacant glass space with the bodies of naked plastic mannequins, legs and arms akimbo and piled in a corner like a crime scene. She was rattled.

What had just happened in there? It was clearly backmasking—recorded messages in an album that could only be heard when the song was played backward. Musicians did it occasionally, for effect. Famously, the Beatles did it in the song "Revolution 9"; listeners could hear "Turn me on, dead man," which led to the whole "Paul Is Dead" conspiracy. As a kid, Lara was sent to church camp with Caren. On the first morning, after singing rousing versions of "I'm in the Lord's

Army," the kids were served cookies and Hawaiian Punch and told how rock musicians were coding secret messages to the devil in their albums. Dutifully, the boys in the group pledged to offer their AC/DC and Led Zeppelin records for burning. When Jason heard that Lara needed to take some records to be destroyed at a camp activity, he never allowed her to go back.

But the song she'd just heard on that album *did* contain a recorded message that could only be heard when the album was played in reverse. Yet Lara had played that song hundreds of times and knew the sound had never been there before. And even if *Tending* had used it, backmasking was pressed into the vinyl and couldn't just disappear as that song had.

No, the song had been a message for her.

8

One of the two restaurants serving dinner until eleven, Delilah's was busy. Lara perched herself on a pleather barstool near the door. Soon she was swirling a glass of Chardonnay the color of concentrated piss. It was some tart, shitty vintage, "fruit forward" they called it, probably from a box in Delilah's giant fridge that would give her a headache in a few hours. Rubbing her neck, she thought a good night's sleep was soon in order.

"Poor girl. Didn't anyone warn you. The wine here is *awful.*"

Lara smiled at the sound of his voice, a hint of his deep Virginian Southern drawl coming through in the word *wine.* She turned to face Ben Archer. "What are you having, then?"

"Well, certainly not the *wine.*" Rolling up the sleeves on his crisp white dress shirt, he scanned the menu.

"How on earth do you fold those?" She reached over and tugged at one. "They're like plaster slabs. Can I hang them in my house?"

"Oh, shut up," he said, smirking. Unbuttoning the other cuff, he struggled as the fabric crunched. "It's heavy starch, I'll have you know, the Southern gentleman's wardrobe staple." He laughed, satisfied with the length of the sleeve.

"Where's the uniform?"

"I've got court this week." Next he began to tug at his necktie, twisting in an attempt to free himself.

Lara recognized the striped blue silk tie as one of his recent birthday gifts. Two weeks ago he'd turned forty—a cause for much celebration by everyone but him. There had been a party, an awkward affair with people from the courthouse and others who knew him casually. At his party, Ben had been gracious, but he seemed like he was dying to leave before the cake was wheeled out. His secretary (yes, they still called her that) had been the one to spot Ben's driver's license and notice the milestone date, which had led to a phone tree (they still had those, too). Since he was also newly divorced, his party had been filled with widows and divorcées who'd brought presents with them—house plants, beer mugs, golf balls (even though Ben wore a police uniform most days and never golfed), as well as neckties in every hue of blue.

She pushed her wine away and turned her stool toward him. "You don't have to wear them *all*, you know." She kept her hands on her glass, but the desire to touch the tie to feel the quality of silk under her fingers was strong.

"The *hell* I don't." He leaned in, and she felt his breath on her neck. "They watch."

Lara snorted and wine came out her nose. He wasn't wrong. As if on cue, Del—Delilah's owner, who was serving as bartender—put her hand on her hip. "Nice tie, Ben. Who got you that one?"

"Pepper Maguire, I do believe."

They'd have been better off tucked away in a quiet booth, but they always sat at the bar. She had never been self-conscious about their friendship, until recently. Lately Lara had noticed people glancing up over their salads or craning their necks to get a glimpse of them together. She wondered if they'd been doing that for months and she just never paid attention.

At a nearby booth, Lara could see Kim Landau, the *Kerrigan Falls*

Express reporter, watching them. She and Ben avoided each other in that charged way that people who'd accidentally slept together then regretted it later did. "I saw Marla earlier today."

"And how is my former half doing?" Ben glanced up as Del slid his usual drink, a Jameson straight, in front of him.

"She was picking up a photo at Gaston Boucher's."

"Well, he does do all of her framing." Ben took a sip of his drink. "And not at a discount, either, might I add." He shook his head. "She has a framing habit."

"She *is* a photographer."

"Well, wedding photography isn't that lucrative."

"I hired the other photographer in town," said Lara, considering what he'd said. "It was an early night for him."

From the corner of her eye, she saw Ben glance over at her, not sure what to make of her comment. She laughed, so that he'd know she was joking at her own expense. "The bastard charged me for the full booking anyway."

"You'd have thought he'd have given you fifty percent off." He flashed her a smile, and it was as if everything came into focus. His tousled brown hair had gray flecks that had become more pronounced in the time she'd known him.

She took a too-big sip of her wine and watched Ben talk. He was boyish with soft blue eyes—you could almost picture his sixth-grade photo. In fact, there were youthful versions of Ben in photos all around Delilah's. The walls were decorated with local photos from the town's past, grainy 1970s snaps, sharp black-and-whites where people dressed too formally and posed in awkward clumps. Near the wooden hostess station, there was a photo of a young Ben Archer from the 1982 Kerrigan Falls High baseball team lineup, kneeling and holding his glove in his lap.

Since Todd's disappearance, Ben Archer had been her lifeline to any details on Wickelow Bend or the case. In the weeks after the non-wedding, the mere sight of Ben Archer in her driveway had made her pulse quicken—hoping some thread of evidence of Todd's whereabouts would come to light. They worked together to formulate new and wild theories about the disappearance, often talking well into the night.

His apartment was only five houses from Lara's Victorian. Often they both worked late and then hit Delilah's for a few drinks. After missing each other or arriving just as the other was leaving, a few months ago, they began making plans to show up at the same time. Now their dinners had become a habit.

Del interrupted again and launched into a description of the special: Southern mac and cheese casserole with ham and shrimp.

After they'd ordered, Lara leaned in conspiratorially. "You never told me about the funeral."

Over the weekend, Ben had gone to his college roommate's funeral in Charlottesville. The roommate, Walker, had only learned he'd had stage four pancreatic cancer two weeks ago.

"Well, it was a keen reminder of my mortality." He hesitated. "His wife propositioned me at the luncheon."

Lara's eyes went wide. "No!"

"She did." He nodded shyly. It was rare that he was divulging something like this to Lara.

"How?"

"*How?*" He looked perplexed and his eyebrow raised.

"I mean, did she let her hand wander while trying to secure a cucumber sandwich?"

He shook his head and took a sip of his Jameson, wincing as it went down. "No. She put her hand on my ass."

Lara doubled over laughing. "Ewww, her husband was just buried."

"I know," he said gravely.

"So?" Lara pressed. "What did you do?"

"Oh, nothing." He shrugged a little too vaguely for Lara's liking.

As the conversation went on, he continued to gloss over the details of what had actually happened after the wake. That he'd slept with the widow was a real possibility. As their mac and cheese arrived, Lara had begun to *care* about this detail—it needled at her—and the vexation surprised her.

Over the hour that followed, Lara found herself noticing things about Ben Archer that she'd never paid attention to in the nine months that she'd known him well. There was a growing energy she felt, like the first flicker in a tinder nest. For the first time, she hadn't asked him for news on Todd. To her surprise, she was living in *this* moment. It was so unexpected that it only made the attraction she was feeling more interesting.

Well, that and the wine.

They traded favorite Hitchcock films (hers *North by Northwest*, his *Vertigo*), favorite James Bond films (his *Dr. No* and hers a tie between *Diamonds Are Forever* and *On Her Majesty's Secret Service*—to which he claimed there could be no tie for a favorite James Bond film, so she hesitantly chose *Diamonds*). He challenged her to recite the fifty states in alphabetical order (a rare skill she possessed from the song "Fifty Nifty United States") and wrote out each of them on a napkin, insisting she'd missed one. (She hadn't.)

As the evening wore on, Lara found that she *cared* about his answers to these mundane questions. With all these details, she was connecting the dots that formed Ben Archer. Stories he'd told her in passing— usually when she was crying and blubbering on about Todd—came flooding back to her as patchy memories. In her head she tried to reassemble them, because they mattered now. What had he told her about his first girlfriend? Where had he proposed to Marla? As she watched him talk, she strained to recall every detail from seeing Marla earlier today and wondering how she measured up to his rather stunning ex-wife. She racked her brain to remember their every conversation. In the early days, she cared less about his stories and more about how they related to Todd. But tonight, over dinner, their relationship began to shift. And she'd allowed herself this change.

She scanned the room, suddenly self-conscious about what people thought of them.

Hours later, after finishing the macaroni and cheese special, brussels sprouts, and another glass of wine that was definitely giving her a headache, Lara began to gather her purse.

Del presented one bill, and Ben Archer reached for it.

"You don't have to do that." Lara reached for the pleather holder with a faded Amex logo to pull it away from him.

"I know. I should make you pay for both of us." He lifted one eyebrow, something that Lara marveled he could do. "It occurs to me that among my recent loot, there was *no* birthday present from you. I'm a little hurt. I could have used a lighter."

"You don't smoke."

"For barbecuing and lighting candles," he said as he scanned the bill.

"I've never seen you barbecue anything and I'm pretty sure you don't own a single decorative candle, Mr. Archer."

"Quit being so smug that you know me so well. An oven mitt, then."

"You don't cook. You come *here* every night."

"A blood pressure cuff, then."

"Eh." Lara considered the cuff before waving goodbye to Del. It was a two-block walk to her house.

A light rain began to fall as they walked toward their respective homes. They stopped at the street where he went left and she went right and continued to make small talk about the state of the sidewalk repair. Lara remembered she didn't have to be at the station early the next day, so that was good.

"I must be doing a really poor job of this." Ben's face was getting flushed.

"Of what?"

"Hitting on you." He put his hands in his pockets.

"Oh." Lara laughed, pressing her hand to her face.

"And I'm getting wet, so if you're going to reject me, do it quickly so I can get inside. This carnival gala thing on Saturday. Do you need a chaperone?"

"I *could* use a chaperone, Mr. Archer. As the chief of police, you'd probably be an acceptable one." Lara wasn't sure if it was too soon to start something new. She didn't know if there was a time line for women like her, but she knew that with Ben Archer she didn't feel like a tragedy. She weighed them both in her mind: Todd and Ben; Ben and Todd. But it wasn't as though she had a choice. One was gone and one was standing in front of her. Maybe it was time she started living again.

"What color is your dress?"

"Why?" She laughed. "Are we matching?"

"No," he said, smiling. "You'll just be wearing a mask. I want to know who I'm looking for."

"Blue," she said. "My dress is blue. And I'll find *you*."

9

As a kid, Lara had loved to run across the field that connected the old Lund Farm, now owned by her grandfather Simon Webster, to the one that belonged to her great-grandmother Cecile. Like bookends, two generations of her family were connected by one sloping field. It took four minutes of a full-on run to make it from porch to porch, a timetable she often tested to make it to dinner on time at one house or the other.

In those days, Audrey and Jason were still living with Simon. Her grandfather's house was nearly a museum to the memory of Margot. Simon didn't like it when things were touched, and Lara seemed to explore the world with her fingertips—candied fingertips. As Cecile was much more forgiving with the furniture, Lara spent most of her childhood at her great-grandmother's. Simon disliked noise as well, so Jason converted Cecile's garage into a makeshift music studio where his bandmates came to jam at all hours, the sound floating through the open window screens.

Summers were blissful with the lush fields and the wavelike chorus of the locusts. Like their own personal amusement park. Lara and her friends wandered around the old circus equipment—trailers and rides—rotting in the field, eventually finding one of the old circus tents in one of the trailers, its canvas ripped but salvageable. Jason helped them stretch it out over the field and found the old poles to get it set up.

Shortly after the tent had been raised, Lara was twirling her baton, imagining she had an audience for her arm rolls and fishtails. It had been a year since she'd seen the mysterious man and woman.

She was working on her timed thumb tosses, counting the number of times she could flip her baton over her thumb and catch it with a quick wrist motion, Cecile's egg timer set for one minute. Lara counted aloud. As the timer went off, she'd done fifty-two tosses. There was a clapping and she looked up to see the man standing there at the entrance to the tent. This time, he was solo.

"It's really you?" He was dressed in a gold costume, kind of like Elvis. To her surprise, she realized how much she'd been looking for him in the last year.

"Did you fear that I was a figment of your imagination?" He leaned against a post, and she had a notion to tell him not to do that. All the posts in the tent were wobbly.

The little girl nodded. "I was beginning to."

Through mirrored sunglasses, he looked up at the sagging canvas. "I see you put up the old circus tent. Tell me, do you like it?"

"I love it." From the opening in the tent, she kept her eye on the horses beyond her—they were good judges of character. But they simply stood there watching the man, their tails swatting flies.

"That's good." The man stepped into the tent. It was a shabby beige-and-blue thing with uneven poles and a sag in the back that Jason had tried to fix by wedging an old tree branch under it. "The circus is in your blood, you know."

"I do know that," she chirped. Lara was confident as only a sheltered seven-year-old could be. "My family owned this circus."

"Yes," he said. "Remember the woman who was with me before? That was Margot, your grandmother. This circus was named for her."

Remembering the beautiful young woman, Lara made a face, thinking of Simon Webster, who was an old, grumpy man. They said he had been married to Margot, the woman from the posters, but that seemed impossible. "She's not *that* old."

"Well, she'd dead, *ma cherie*. She doesn't age anymore." The man smiled and put his hands on the back of his brown pants. "That was a fine circus, but that wasn't the only circus that belonged to your family, you know. There was another once." He had a rise to his voice like he was about to tell her a story. "It's a magic circus, and it belongs to you."

"Me?" This was news to Lara. She stood up straight. Now he had her attention.

"It's true." The man did something with his hands, and the circus tent seemed to perk up a little like extra poles had been added or an invisible hand had pulled it up. Color washed over it, brightening the blue and beige silks. A chandelier shone over them. The rusted and dingy artifacts that she'd dragged under the tent were soon replaced by clowns, and most of the space under the tent was now occupied by a spinning carousel. The man walked around to stand next to Lara. The girl looked up in wonder. Had this been what the circus was like? For some reason, she'd never imagined it so colorful. In her mind, it had been an old, shabby spectacle with aging clowns and rusted equipment. She thought all circuses were like that.

"How'd you do that?" Lara looked up in wonder.

"You can do it, too," said the man. "Try it. Make the carousel spin."

On cue, it stopped as though it were waiting for her.

She looked at him like he was crazy and giggled. "That's silly. I can't do that."

"But that's not true." He smiled, leaning down to face her. "You do move things, don't you? Ouija boards perhaps?"

Her eyes widened. It was one thing for this man to know her name, but to know about the Ouija board at Caren's was entirely another. "How did you—?"

"No matter," he said, brushing her off. "But you mustn't fear your power."

Yet she *did* fear the things she could do. Right here, with him performing for her, it was fun, like a magic trick at birthday parties. She was a spectator of sorts. Left to her own devices, though, this power frightened her.

"Go ahead." He twirled his finger. He picked up a tiny flower—a white clover—and began to spin the stem between his thumb and forefinger. "Here"—he handed her the flower—"instead of thinking of the carousel, keep your eyes on this flower. When magic is new, it's about drawing on the emotion of what you want most, my dear, not focus. Focus comes later. The magic knows what you want. Just want it harder."

"You said not to think about it." Lara watched the flower clumsily turning under her fingers.

"Thinking and wanting are not the same thing, my clever poppet. Wanting comes from your heart, not your head."

Always a dutiful student, Lara mimicked him with her tiny fingers, and, to her surprise, she could hear the creaking of the carousel as it began to move.

"Bravo," he said, clapping.

She shook her head. "*You* did that, not me."

"No. I swear that I did not, my pet." He leaned down. "You are the one. The circus—the *real* circus—it is your destiny. One day, it will need you to do your magic—I will call on you. Do you understand?"

While she nodded, she did not understand the things he said—she had no one, neither Cecile nor her mother, to filter, translate, or put them in context for her. Lara watched in awe as the carousel spun, so engrossed she'd forgotten he was standing there. As it wound down, like the batteries operating it had been drained, she turned to say something to him, but he was already gone.

Turning back, she saw that the carousel was fading and the tent was once again dirty, empty, dull, and limp. The sparkling chandelier was now gone as well, the top of the tent sagging like it couldn't support the weight of a glass Christmas ornament.

"Come back," she said. There was something about the man. Even if she didn't know exactly what he meant, she knew he was telling her the truth. Her mother could also do things—magical things. Lara observed Audrey unlocking doors, making the phone ring, and even stopping the thunder outside when she didn't know that Lara was watching. Once Lara heard Cecile and her mother discussing a spell. Audrey had been chanting something with Cecile's guidance. Lara had flattened herself in the wide space between the floor and the old door to get a look at them. She'd tried to memorize what they were saying, but they chanted too fast. The ritual and the language had been secret and exotic, with the candles flickering and the lights dimming then brightening in the house, like Audrey was drawing energy from everything around her. Lara could feel the tug of the chant, the pull of her mother's words.

When magic is new, it's about drawing on the emotion of what you want most, my dear, not focus.

After the man had shown her how to change the tent, Lara began to attempt simpler tricks. She began with the lock on Simon's office door. It was an easy door, requiring just a small movement of the notch on the doorknob. Closing her eyes, Lara thought not of the lock, but of rotating a penny between her fingers. Then she recalled Simon's candy jar. He'd filled it with peppermint patties that morning. Most of all, she *wanted* a peppermint patty. Focusing on her deepest desire for the crisp, sugary candy, Lara heard the lock click.

But now all her corrections were focused on fixing the tent. After a week, she came back to the tent. Starting with color, she focused on the faded blue of the canvas, thinking of the blue of the ocean. Coaxing the worn fabric, she saw it brighten. Next, using her hand to pretend, she lifted the top of it, like she was pulling up the dome of a candy jar. On command the tent lifted and the beige color began to brighten. "Carousel, come back."

Nothing.

"Carousel, *come* back." She barked the command loud enough to make Gomez Addams—now named Squiggy—look up in alarm.

She could see something flicker and could hear the faint echo of an organ as though it were somewhere else, just beyond reach, the volume low. Growing impatient, she said, "Carousel, come back." Again, she could see it shimmer, but then it faded. With that, the tent sank, returning to its dull state. Lara was exhausted. This was harder than turning locks.

Lara knew what her father and grandfather would say—she was a child with a "vivid imagination." An only child, she needed one to keep herself occupied. But when she'd gone to the place where the man had stood, she saw the dried, long-dead clover lying on the ground. The man had plucked it, not her. She gathered it up as proof that what she'd seen was real and took the flower fragments and pressed them in her *Rumpelstiltskin* book. Months later, she would pull out the book and see the dried flower in waxed paper.

He had plucked that flower. He had been real. She wasn't mad.

She came back to the field every day. If she had to practice the guitar, then she could practice this. For weeks, she brightened and tugged at the old tent. Once, she brought the carousel through but held it only for a few seconds until it disappeared. A week later, a storm blew the tent over, shredding the old fabric.

As the summer went on, several elderly men and women visited

Cecile to reminisce about the old circus. As if they felt the pull of the tide, performers drove their old, battered trucks up the long drive to sit on the porch with Cecile and drink iced tea or Tanqueray and tonic and reminisce about life in the old days.

Lara loved these visits. When she'd see an old truck sitting in Cecile's driveway, she'd run through the field at a clip to see who had come. Sitting on the porch, they talked while Lara played with her Barbies or Legos, pretending not to listen, but she never missed a tale. Circus people were great storytellers. One tall, gangly man of the gin-and-tonic set cried to Cecile about the loss of his beloved show horse from colic. Lara knew from her short experience with horses that they were mysterious, fragile creatures. The man was so distraught Lara presented him with her plastic butter-colored Johnny West horse, Thunderbolt.

"You can have my horse." Lara remembered loving the toy dearly and holding it by its legs, making sure she'd secured the little brown vinyl saddle tightly as though it would be a selling point.

The man refused the toy with a smile of gratitude and took a hankie from his back pocket and wiped his face.

After the man left, Cecile knelt down and sat next to Lara on the floor, and Lara could smell the L'Air du Temps perfume in the air. Cecile—still tan like a raisin with her cropped silver hair and heart-shaped face—was the only woman she knew who wore bright-red lipstick, but it was now faded from an afternoon of entertaining.

"That was a lovely thing to do, Lara. It was very touching." Cecile still had a strong French accent, and Lara found herself counting *un, deux, trois* or saying *n'est-ce pas.*

Lara shrugged, making Thunderbolt gallop. "It was nothing. I just needed to take care of him."

"What a curious thing to say." With her accent, there was a musicality to Cecile's voice.

"He said the circus is my destiny."

"Who said?"

Lara looked up. She hadn't meant to talk about *him*.

"Lara?" Cecile pressed; there was alarm in her voice.

"The man in the field." Lara looked down at the floor.

"*What* man in the field?" Cecile's voice rose.

She shrugged. "Just the man. Sometimes the woman is with him. Margot."

Cecile's face looked stricken. "Where did you see him?"

Lara pointed over to the field. "The last time was when we had the tent up."

"Tell me exactly what he said." She spun Lara toward her and drew close to her face. Something on Cecile's breath smelled like Christmas trees.

Lara told Cecile every detail, and her great-grandmother's face fell as she explained about the spinning carousel. The alarm in her voice was evident. She peppered Lara with questions as if she'd done something wrong. "You must not say anything about this. Never speak of it to anyone, do you hear me? Forget him."

Lara nodded, fearing Cecile was angry at her. "Did I do something wrong?"

Cecile was slow to smile, but when she did, she beamed at the little girl. "No, my dear. You are absolutely perfect."

While she had listened to Cecile that day and never told anyone about the strange man in the field, he had unlocked something in her. With the twirl or snap of her finger, she could move things.

Little corrections, she began to call them then.

"Who is he?" Lara asked Cecile once, shortly before the older woman died. Lara didn't need to clarify the *he*. Cecile understood her perfectly.

"His name is Althacazur," said Cecile. "And no good can come from him."

From THE NEW DEMONPEDIA.com

Althacazur (/altha-ca-zhr/) The spellings *Althacazar* (/altha-caz-ahr/) and *Althacazure* (/al-tha-caz-yoor/) have also been used. One of the princes of Hell, he is considered one of the most powerful demons, often called "Hell's king," primarily due to representing carnal pleasures, vanity, and lust, which affords him the greatest number of legions. He is said to command the eighth layer of Hell, where his subjects are sent upon their deaths. According to several texts, the River Styx flows primarily through the eighth layer of Hell, making him very powerful in that other demons must pay a toll to cross the main river of the underworld.

In lore, he is often depicted as handsome and vain, with flowing hair and amber eyes that he often covers with sunglasses when walking among mortals due to the permanent state of his horizontal pupils—an underworld trait that cannot be masked. An 1821 painting, *Althacazar*, by Bishop Worth, hangs in the British Museum and features the demon in his signature purple robe. In the painting, Althacazur has the head of a ram and dragon wings sprouting from his back. Some biographers of Worth (notably Constance van Hugh in her book *Worth: A Life*) have claimed the demon sat for the portrait, while many scholars of Worth have dismissed the idea as rubbish and hearsay. Van Hugh's claim largely came from the source notes of Worth's daughter who said that she met the demon on several occasions in the parlor while her father worked on the painting and that "when his wings were contained, he [Althacazur] was perfectly able to enjoy high tea."

Althacazur factors prominently in the book *Damsel and the Demon*, the 1884 novel by Andrew Wainwright Collier, where, in love with a mortal woman, Aerin, Althacazur plots and kills all of the maiden's intended husbands, causing the ultimate ruination of her as a marriageable lady. As a result, Aerin drinks poison and kills herself. In the underworld, she is given in marriage to Althacazur as a gift from Lucifer. Althacazur is then tormented by Aerin, who now resents him and can never love him. That the maiden retains her human memories is meant to be a punishment from the other demons who resent Althacazur for his growing power. Lucifer banishes the maiden to the angels, for she is too pure of heart for Hell, in an effort to rescue his favorite. In the novel, Althacazur is a tragic figure, torn apart by his own lust and the envy of the other demons of Hell.

It is interesting to note that Andrew Wainwright Collier's second wife was the actress Juno Wagner, who portrayed the maiden Aerin in the London stage adaptation in 1902. On October 9, 1904, Wagner died during childbirth. Collier went to his death destroying every copy of *Damsel and the Demon* that existed, claiming the demon, Althacazur, was responsible for her death. Collier never spoke of what had happened to the baby Wagner was carrying, but it is assumed the child died as well. After Wagner's death, Collier himself was not well, and many assume his assertions were not of Althacazur being responsible, but actually of the play being responsible for his wife's death—because the pregnant actress, against the advice of doctors, had traveled to Paris to see a performance of the play and had fallen ill. Collier died on December 23, 1905.

Collier's friend Pearce Buckley said that "Collier was not in his right mind at the end of this life and anything regarding Juno was, unfortunately, the ravings of a madman."

In the foreword to *The Selected Works of Andrew Wainwright Collier*, Jacques Mourier, the journalist at *Le Figaro* who had been an assistant to Collier, claimed that Collier went to his death claiming that Wagner had been seduced by a devil. "He came to see her one night after a performance—a dashing man in a black waistcoat and flowing brown hair. Collier suspected that his wife had begun an affair with the man and likened the cur to a vampire, who drained the life out of her." Many scholars of demonology suspect the "flowing hair" trait is a reference to Althacazur and that Collier's assertions were correct that his wife had been seduced by one of the most powerful demons of the underworld.

In **The Demonic Encyclopedia of 1888**, the entry on him reads: *While often written as a handsome and witty character, Althacazure often falls prey to his own lust and its consequences. His temper, which is considered the most volatile of the princes of Hell, is another one of his follies. Given his charm, he is often mistaken as a lighter demon, which is a grave mistake, for he is the most vain and unforgiving of all Hell's generals. He is considered Lucifer's favorite and a frequent foil of the angel Raphael.*

In Modern Lore

The Dinner Guests

Althacazur was a demon who factored heavily in stage magician Philippe Angier's occult show. Angier's show always had whispers of demonic leanings, especially after the occultist's hair was rumored to have transformed from black to flame red overnight. Angier was famously killed in a duel in 1898 in the Bois de Boulogne. While at a private dinner in Paris, Angier is said to have predicted the fates of all of his dinner companions—all well-known Parisian literati. The rumored fates were grim—imprisonment, poison, and suicide. In the following years, the predictions were rumored to have come true, resulting in the last living dinner guest, journalist Gerard Caron, charging Angier in the paper *Le Parisian* as a Satanist and challenging him to a duel. In one of the flats of the Bois de Boulogne, Angier's pistol failed to fire and he was mortally wounded, yet lingered for days until dying. Caron, overcome with guilt, took his own life, shooting himself with Angier's pistol—which "fired brilliantly," according to witnesses. After his death, multiple reports claimed that Angier had impregnated several of his stage assistants and sacrificed his own newborn children to appease the demon Althacazur. This story was the inspiration for the musical *The Dinner Guests*.

Association with Robert Johnson

While Lucifer is often cited as meeting guitar blues legend Robert Johnson at the "crossroads" in Clarksdale, Mississippi, some have suggested that it was actually the demon Althacazur who sealed the fateful deal in the legend. The guitar legend died on August 16, 1938, in Greenwood, Mississippi.

Demon Days

Althacazur factored prominently in the sitcom *Demon Days* as the foil to angels Gabriel and Raphael, who are roommates living in modern-day San Francisco. He was portrayed by actor Jacob Broody for Seasons 1–2 and then Elijah Hunt for Seasons 3–5.

10

Kerrigan Falls, Virginia
June 21, 2005

W hy hadn't she ever thought to look him up on the internet before? Hell, she'd researched enough dead musicians; the deaths of Mama Cass and Keith Moon at the age of thirty-two in the same London apartment was a favorite search. Yet it had taken Caren to remind her of his name. *Althacazur.*

She stared at the entry in disbelief, then hit PRINT. Was the man who'd visited her in the field a major daemon—or "Hell's king," as he was also known? Lara tried to recall if he'd ever introduced himself to her. It had been Cecile who had first pronounced a name that sounded like a children's cartoon villain, akin to Gargamel.

Surely Cecile had been mistaken. It had just sounded like this name. She'd been a kid. Maybe she'd misheard the woman. But then there was the spelling on the Ouija board. It matched this. The magic her family used—locks, dresses—that was innocent magic. This Althacazur was a different type of creature altogether.

As she gathered her purse and searched for her lipstick, she kept picking up the printout to read over and over, looking for any similarity between the description and the man she'd known. Vain? Absolutely. Flowing hair? Check. But it was the line…*amber eyes that he often covers with sunglasses when walking among mortals due to the permanent state of his horizontal pupils—an underworld trait that cannot be masked* that left her cold.

Of everything she'd read, this line felt like a concrete detail describing him. This begged the question: If a major daemon was visiting her, what did he want? At some point, he'd said, he would call on her. She took a seat and found her legs were trembling. Was *this* the source of her magic? Was he the reason Audrey insisted they hide their abilities?

After opening locks and emptying her grandfather's candy jars, Lara had graduated to copying her mother's signature and enchanting the phone to sound like anyone she wanted. As she got older, those skills were helpful when she wanted to get permission to go on a field trip. As she got better at it, she could match her friends' mothers' voices easily and so stay out later while Audrey thought she was safely tucked at home with Caren.

It was Caren's mom who inadvertently busted her. Caren and Lara were both allergy sufferers requiring weekly shots. At the doctor's office one spring, Mrs. Jackson, in passing, thanked Audrey for allowing Caren to stay over so much. In actuality, the two girls had sneaked out and gone to all-night bowling. Lara had always been careful to never let Caren hear her make the phone calls, not wanting her friend to have culpability. As Mrs. Jackson presented a thorough accounting of Audrey's generosity in lodging her daughter, Lara closed her eyes with dread.

It was the firm tug on the checkbook from Audrey's hand that served as the tell as Dr. Mulligan's check for $3 was ripped free.

"You have no idea what it is like to grow up without a mother because she went crazy from magic." Audrey had been silent until they'd turned into their winding drive. "I've spared you that knowledge. Sure, it's fun to have old equipment in your backyard, but you've never been taunted by your friends that you're a freak because you work at the circus. I have. You think it's cute and it's fun, but drawing attention to yourself is dangerous."

When Lara returned home, the punishment had been swift yet quiet. Since the phone had been the source of the problem, Audrey enchanted it so Lara couldn't call anyone for a week. Interestingly, her mother never mentioned to Jason what Lara had done, nor the punishment she'd doled out. Only then did Lara understand that Audrey had kept both of their abilities from her father. Magic was a shameful secret.

Shutting down her computer, she looked at her watch. It was almost time for Audrey to pick her up for the circus. Folding up the paper with Althacazur's entry, she placed it deep in her handbag.

For two weeks each June, the Rivoli Circus from Montreal settled in one of the open fields near the highway, the backdrop of the Blue Ridge Mountains peering over the big top at sunset. The stop at Kerrigan Falls was an act of respect for Le Cirque Margot, many of the performers having sought jobs with the Canadian troupe when the circus closed. Loyalties ran deep with these families, and even the children of many members who had died still recalled the stories. The Montreal troupe had picked up most of Le Cirque Margot's old stops, so the two companies' histories were richly entwined.

After kicking off the season, the Rivoli Circus would perform in twelve towns in Tennessee, Georgia, Alabama, and Mississippi before heading to the Southwest for the winter and then retooling the show back in Canada for the following year's performances.

Tickets were hard to come by, but Audrey always managed to get premium seats from the Rivoli family. The legacy between the families was something that her mother endured more than celebrated, but the horses were some of the most stunning animals in the ring. For that reason, Audrey always made sure they were front and center.

The trademark moss-green-and-blue-striped tents were strung together into a connected bazaar. As Lara and Audrey walked through the grand entrance, food stands and other carnival attractions like fortune-tellers, T-shirt sellers, and arcade games lined the avenue to the entrance to the big top.

Inside the main tent, the night air was cool. Above them an elaborate green-and-blue chandelier, resembling a Chihuly creation, dangled heavily from the center. From the props to the sound and concessions, Lara admired their attention to detail. The performance was always elegant and sophisticated, unlike some two-bit carnival that made its way through each fall, giving kids rides on rusted Ferris wheels and serving watered-down Coca-Colas.

On cue, the tent went dark and the light show flashed blue and green, like something out of Las Vegas. This was one of the rare circuses that still traveled with a full orchestra. There was a dark, dramatic pause. Somewhere in the audience a man coughed, then a child wailed. A small spotlight appeared at the top of the tent—where the form of a blond girl dressed in a chartreuse sequined leotard descended, lowering herself smoothly on a fabric rope, coiling then uncoiling herself down its length. As she moved, the fabrics twisted with and then against her body, giving her the illusion of winding and then letting go of the line before catching herself in a dramatically staged free fall. From the orchestra below, a lone singer crooned a melody in French, a set of electric strings accompanying her.

That a performer would fall was not out of consideration at the circus. Ropes ripped, hands slipped, but precision and practice as well as luck and talent stacked the odds in favor of tonight's seasoned performer, now twirling from a rope gripped in her teeth. While there was slim chance of disaster, with every spin and twist of the aerialist's back and each pump of her biceps, the audience was rapt and on the edge of their seats. This act was the perfect combination of spectacle and tension; beauty entwined with danger.

And then there were two of her. A twin second performer in a royal-blue leotard joined. They twisted and spun in unison, some silent count driving the precision with which they intertwined and switched their ropes in an elaborate aerial scheme. After they established their rhythm, a third acrobat appeared.

Lara craned her neck and noticed there was no net under them, only a soft padded floor resembling a gymnasium wrestling mat that wouldn't stop a leg from breaking or a body from being crushed if the timing was off. And that chance created such a marvelous spectacle that Lara found her heart racing. She was someone who cried at Broadway shows, caught up in the art and emotion of a live performance, yet even as a child, she couldn't recall ever watching an act with such wonder as she did now. The motions were fluid, like she was seeing dance in the air—what birds might do if they sprouted limbs. The three acrobats slid down into a dramatic finale, and the crowd went wild.

Another act followed, this one a more traditional trapeze act with the swinging poles that Lara was used to seeing. The four performers looked weightless, twisting then tossing their bodies, lightly handing off to one another as though connecting weren't really necessary. As they juggled themselves high above the crowd, grabbing the bar and twisting onto the platform where they were caught by sure hands until the next performer replaced them, Lara could feel the counts between them, hands reaching, bodies corkscrewing then landing softly, only to turn and repeat the performance with the ease of shuffling a deck. It was as though they were objects being juggled across the stage, not people, so when Lara felt a missed count, she inhaled sharply. Noticing a slight twitch, she could see the performer lose her grip on the catcher's hand.

Instinctively, Lara recalled the child's game she'd played where forced perspective made the person tiny, allowing you to "squish" them with your fingers. Using the same technique, Lara said "no" aloud as she slid her hand under the falling aerialist, holding her up with her palm, as if she were a tiny marionette. "Up, up," whispered Lara, lifting the performer. To anyone watching, she would have looked like she was holding an imaginary teacup. At that same moment, the acrobat would have felt she was now standing firmly on an invisible glass platform. Instinct kicked in, and the girl wiggled toward the catcher's awaiting grip.

"What are you doing?" Audrey whispered under her breath, her eyes wide. "Stop it."

The words interrupted Lara's concentration, and she could feel the spell break for a moment. The aerialist stumbled again. "Up," said Lara, ignoring her mother and refocusing on the performer. "Up, up." Lara began to sweat, recalling what *he* had said to her in the tent: *Keep your eyes on the flower.* It was like turning a lock. *I can do this*, she thought.

Closing her eyes, she rotated the performer with her finger the necessary quarter turn to reach the outstretched hands of her catcher. What must have felt like an eternity for both Lara and the performer was measured in mere seconds. The missed handoff was probably unnoticeable to everyone else.

Sure she'd done the task correctly, Lara opened her eyes and stretched her neck to get a different view. The aerialist was floating, her arms and legs almost in a swimming motion while Lara turned her finger. The girl stretched so the catcher could meet her and take another attempt. This one was successful, and he gripped her tightly. Regaining their rhythm, the team finished. Only at the end of the act, after they'd descended the ropes, could Lara visibly see the young girl's legs shaking. Lara glanced over to find Audrey watching her intently, an eyebrow raised.

She had made a correction in full view of everyone. This was forbidden. While she felt guilty defying Audrey, this wasn't refashioning a wedding dress. In a second, with a focused command, she'd saved a woman's life. Surely a little public magic was worth it to avert a disaster. While it had only been a few seconds, Lara knew the amount of skill that had been required to hold the woman in midair for even that small length of time, especially in a panic. Her abilities were increasing. She had little doubt that she could go back to the field now and pull the carousel through—and even re-create the tent—with little effort.

The performance continued with clowns, another trapeze act, three elephants, and finally the trick rider, Audrey's favorite. The white steed came charging out outfitted with an elaborate headdress, the horse's long, flowing mane whipping furiously as it rounded the arena. While Audrey had been an experienced horsewoman, Lara had never been encouraged to ride. As she'd gotten older, she'd learned it was because a fall could rupture the one remaining kidney she had.

Standing on the horse's back, anticipating the rhythm of the animal's gallop, was the equestrian, a red-haired girl dressed in a green leotard with spangles and fringe. She took in the audience with two full rotations around the tent before contorting herself into a backbend as the horse went around in a smaller circle. Then she performed a forward flip and launched herself from the animal's back, landing in perfect unison as they traveled. Then, in one swift movement, she slid down and hung with one leg as the pony kept a sure and steady gallop. And then, as if it couldn't get more daring, a second horse entered the ring and she flipped from one horse to the other, finally riding them out as though she were a gladiator heading home from victory in the ring—and that's essentially what she was.

While her mother should have been exhilarated from the act, as the lights came up, Audrey appeared distracted. "What you did back there. It was risky."

"I couldn't let her die."

Audrey didn't answer.

"Mother?"

"I know," said Audrey, finally, her voice tense. Lara saw her jaw tighten. "What you did took skill. You just reacted. It's not like taking twenty minutes to pick a lock."

Lara gave her a quizzical look.

"Of course I knew you were the reason why none of the locks in the house worked, Lara. Do you think my magic never came in? I fiddled with the stove and turned the gas on. Nearly blew up the house. At least you didn't do that."

"If I hadn't helped her, you would have."

Audrey didn't answer her. She motioned toward the big top for emphasis. "That stunt back there means you're getting stronger."

"Stronger than what?"

"Stronger than *me*."

As they walked in silence, Lara mulled over her mother's words. Why was she getting stronger? She knew that Audrey claimed to not practice her magic out of principle, but Lara didn't believe it. Yet her mother was rattled by what she'd just seen.

They wandered out to the concessions area where T-shirts and mugs were sold and performers were posing for pictures. Lara noticed a fortune-teller's booth. Madame Fonseca was nowhere to be found. Instead a young boy stood in front of the only empty booth in the circus alley. "Oh, look at him standing over there. I feel bad for him."

"Then go get your fortune told," said Audrey, fumbling with her purse. "We've got time until the crowd thins…getting out of here will be a nightmare. If anyone needs her fortune told, it's you."

Lara made a face and approached the boy, who couldn't have been older than eighteen.

"You don't look like a Madame Fonseca." Lara pointed to the sign, which depicted an old woman looming over a crystal ball, her hair in a turban—so cliché it was comical.

"She died two days ago." A hint of a deep Southern accent in the boy's voice—Alabama or Mississippi, Lara couldn't quite place it.

"Oh." Lara hadn't realized Madame Fonseca had been that old. "So I guess you're Mr. Fonseca?"

"Hell no." The boy bowed. "Shane Speer at your service, ma'am." He was dressed in a blue robe with green piping that looked too big for him, like a choir robe.

"I like your robe," said Lara, lying.

"I have a green one, too." Shane's expression was deadpan.

"I bet you do."

She followed him behind the curtain into a small area lined with dark-blue velvet. It felt like they were in a closet, and the room smelled like SweeTarts. Shane sat down opposite her and turned on a table lamp. "Cards or hands?"

"Dunno. Which is better?"

"For me?" The boy considered this. "Hands."

Lara flipped over her hands. He touched her palms and frowned.

"So how'd you get into this line of work?" She thought she'd start with small talk.

The boy kept studying her palms. From somewhere under the curtain came a small brown monkey dressed in a little green tuxedo. "Hello, Mr. Tisdale." The boy leaned in. "I swear he likes to eavesdrop on my all sessions." The boy picked up the monkey, lovingly placing him on his knee. "I guess you could say I have a gift.

"When it comes to the dead, I see things other people don't." He fiddled with his fingers on the table. Lara could also feel his leg shaking with energy, the little monkey bouncing. "It was like they were hidden behind my mama's dirty curtain that had once been clean and sheer. So for a while, people gave me money to visit the places where people had died. Loved ones—you know, to see if I could feel their energy and talk to them."

The kid was like a windup toy. He wouldn't stop chattering. Lara thought he must be nervous filling in for Madame Fonseca. She was a fucking legend. He seemed not to have stopped for a breath.

"At first, my work was limited to local folks who knew about me— mothers who'd lost their kids. It's always parents looking for answers." He went back to her hand, turning it over then scrutinizing her fingers.

"Why, that first summer, I spent a lot of time standing along the bad dip in County Road 68 down in Alabama where those makeshift crosses were crafted at the hairpin turns, or out on Interstate 10, walking the brim of the highway while the big rigs blew by me."

He looked up like Lara should know Interstate 10. "But then Madame Fonseca found me when they were in Montgomery and she helped me hone my 'craft' as she called it. She taught me the cards, too."

Lara exhaled. The story was done. Shane turned Lara's hand back around. The monkey reached over and touched the lines on her palm. With his expressive brown eyes and human face, he seemed to regard her gravely.

"I know, Mr. Tisdale," Shane said, nodding. "I see it, too. It's crazy, but this little guy can pick out exactly *the* thing about each reading."

"My fiancé left me at the altar nine months ago," blurted Lara sardonically. "Did he pick up on that?"

Shane Speer studied her face, squinting as though he was trying to bore holes in her. She could see an enormous zit forming on his adolescent nose, and she wondered if Mr. Tisdale would point *that* out, too.

Shane closed his eyes, more for show than anything, Lara was sure. "Nothing."

"Nothing?" It was the same thing Audrey had said the afternoon of her wedding.

"It happens," he said, like he was apologizing for failing to get a boner. "Sometimes, they just aren't there . . . this fiancé. He's gone."

"Well, hell, I know that," snapped Lara. "Gone to where?"

"He's nowhere." Shane shrugged. "That boy is not your destiny."

"What did you just say?" Lara leaned in, her voice rising. It was the same thing the man had said to her in the field all those years ago.

"*He* is not the point."

Lara thought he was exactly the point and the reason she was spending money for this goddamned kid to fondle her hand. "Who are you?"

In a swift motion, Shane Speer grabbed Lara's wrist and slapped it down. The cheap table shook and nearly toppled. The boy leaned in so close that Lara could tell he'd been chewing cinnamon gum. She was worried he was trying to kiss her and the thought of it repulsed her. The prospect seemed to repulse Mr. Tisdale as well, because the monkey slid off Shane's knee and scurried out of the room chirping.

"I see the dark magic . . . the Dark Circus in you, girl. It is your destiny." His voice wasn't a boy's anymore; it was deep like an opera baritone. And was that a Russian accent? "You're part of the Devil's Circus. You're the key—the one. But you must beware. She knows and she is coming for you. She wants you dead."

Shane shook his head and peered up at her through greasy bangs. "What did I say?"

"You don't know?" Lara cradled her sore hand in the other one, studying it to see if anything had been bruised.

"It comes on that way. It's why I prefer the hands."

"Well, you were gibbering on about a Dark Circus. And you sounded Russian, too."

"The Secret Circus?" The boy's eyes widened. "I was?" The boy looked off, sick almost. "I bet Madame Fonseca is channeling me again. I hate it when she does that. I can do this on my own without her meddling in all my fucking sessions."

"You called it the Dark Circus, not the Secret Circus," said Lara, looking up at the ceiling and expecting the ghost of Madame Fonseca to be hanging up there.

"Same thing." Shane shrugged. "Some call it the Secret Circus, others the Dark Circus."

"So how does this circus relate to me?"

"Dunno. Depends on what I said." The boy looked around, distracted, like he needed a cigarette. "Hey, what happened to Mr. Tisdale?"

"He fled when your voice got weird."

"Oh fuck, really? He ran out?" Shane dipped his head and raised it, looking for the little monkey. "Oh no, I gotta find him. He gets into mischief when he's loose."

"That's just great," said Lara, rolling her eyes. She could see he was sweating. "You also said that I was in danger and that *she* wants me dead. Who wants me dead?"

The boy was still distracted, but he swallowed hard. Lara could see his Adam's apple rise and fall. "Ma'am. If I said that, then you are in very grave danger. I'm sorry to tell you I'm never wrong about these matters. Madame Fonseca said I had the gift and I do." He reached under the table and pulled out a gray cashbox, thunking it between them. "That'll be twenty dollars."

Lara left Madame Fonseca's booth feeling a bit dizzy. What on earth was happening? From the corner of her eye, she saw the curtain move. A tiny hand, followed by a small face, peered out at her.

"Mr. Tisdale?"

The monkey looked around as though something had spooked him. Tentatively, like a shy dog, the little creature walked over to Lara. In his hand was a package. He held it out in front of him.

"Is this for me?" Lara bent down. This circus was getting weirder by the minute.

She took it from his hands and he scampered away. Studying it, Lara saw it was an elaborate flat envelope made of a heavy, shiny gold paper. The envelope was addressed to *Mademoiselle Lara Barnes*. She slid her finger across the top to open it, but the paper didn't give way. Trying again, she got a nasty paper cut. "Shit." A drop of blood hit the envelope's flap, and it loosened instantly. Sucking the blood from her finger, she opened the envelope with her other hand. There Lara found an old composition book, its beige cover so weathered that it was brown.

"What on earth is that?" Audrey found her sucking on her cut finger and holding the envelope at an odd angle. Her mother reached into her purse and handed Lara a tissue before taking the package from her hands.

Lara shrugged. "A monkey gave it to me."

"A monkey?" Her mother looked at her, curious.

"Trust me, that's not the weirdest thing that's happened to me tonight." While her mother held the envelope, Lara reached inside and pulled out the composition book.

Eyeing the package suspiciously, Audrey turned it over and examined the flap. "Odd. It was addressed to you. It must be from one of the old circus people. I didn't know any of them were still around."

Lara began scanning the pages as her mother looked over her

shoulder. The writing was from another time period, the script looping and artistic, unlike the cursive of Lara's generation that seemed intent on speed. The faded brown lettering was sharp and precise, with heavy loops on the capitals, but time had made the ink nearly the same color as the paper. It was written entirely in French. Lara could make out names like *Sylvie* and *E.* Once a fluent French speaker, Lara was surprised to find her skills rusty, but she was itching to open it and begin translating.

Her mother took the book and squinted at the cover. "I need my reading glasses."

"What do you think it is?"

"I'd say it's a journal." Audrey looked at it strangely. She looked more closely at the writing on the cover. "It's from 1925."

The journal read: LE JOURNAL DE CECILE CABOT.

Lara touched the pages tentatively, like they could disintegrate under her fingers. "You don't think it's odd?"

"Well." Audrey took her keys out of her handbag. "I wouldn't be telling anyone a monkey gave it to me. It's just…"

"What?"

"I never knew Cecile to keep a diary."

"From the looks of this, she was a young woman when she wrote it."

"To me, she just wasn't particularly reflective in that way. I lived with her a long time and I never once heard her mention a journal," said Audrey with a shrug, "but who knows. Maybe she was a different person when she was younger. See if you can translate it, then you'll know for sure. Anyway, it's a nice gesture; a piece of history that someone thought you should have."

As they walked out of the big top, Lara held the cloth spine of the book in her palm. A sense of dread tugged at her. She wasn't so convinced this had been a nice gesture at all.

11

There was a slow drizzle falling and the air was cool. Lara was sure there would be fog in the rest of the valley. The June morning breeze had a lingering smoky scent from plants and trees that had been cooking for days in the heat before finally getting relief from a cool, hard rain. These were the kind of mornings when people stayed in, so the streets were spare, allowing the rain to gently wash the cobblestones. By noon, the sun would beat down and the place would feel like a swamp.

In the past few days, her father had been out touring with the Dangerous Tendencies reunion band. The first show had been last week in Charlottesville, followed by Durham then Clemson, but last night they did a practice concert in Winchester.

Lara placed the journal on her desk and sat back in her chair. "How'd it go?" She was settled in for an hour of the play-by-play on the set changes, troubles with the new drummer, and crowd size and energy. She'd toured with him for a year, playing rhythm guitar, but she'd nearly been electrocuted by a faulty wire on a guitar and Jason never invited her back on the road. For years now, his taste had been shifting toward blues and he was seeking out musicians who shared his vision. To the dismay of old fans, his concerts only played a few old Dangerous Tendencies tracks, allowing them to focus on new material. All his Son House, Bukka White, and Hound Dog Taylor records were out in prime positions near his phone.

Jason sat on the edge of his desk. He was all movement, his face flushed, fingers tapping. "I loved it." He'd even gotten a haircut for the gig, his auburn curls clipped tightly to his scalp.

"Really?" She cocked her head. "You never love it."

"It was perfect," he said, looking away with a smile, like he was savoring a memory.

Jason was a creature of the road. Lara hated caging him up in a desk job, even if it was one that had him playing records like a teenager.

"I've got something new," he said. "We were jamming a little in the bus. Lots of good vibes among the guys."

"You didn't just say *vibes*?" She put her hands on her face.

He put his finger up and picked up his Gibson. "We've been working on some stuff. I think this band is actually gelling."

"The word *gelling* is only moderately better." She grimaced pitifully.

Jason had wanted to form a new band and make another studio album. Although he denied it, she knew part of the reason he'd agreed to do the syndicated radio show was to find a new audience and catch the attention of a record studio. After his third album, there had been no request for a fourth. Ten years later, she knew it was still a sore subject.

Her father started with a few bars. It was a nice song. All of his songs were nice, but they had simple, straightforward melodies. They didn't take on a layered edge until they were in the hands of a good producer. Lara had heard the tracks "before" and "after" a producer, and they were almost unrecognizable. While not the greatest balladwriter, Jason was a brilliant cover musician, so his live performances were usually four-to-five-song segues where each one blended seamlessly into the next. They weren't the faithful reproductions of a less talented cover band. Jason took them to another level, weaving an overlay of a similar blues style through everything from Creedence Clearwater Revival's "Run Through the Jungle" and "Effigy" to the

Beatles' "Hey Jude." Like a good mix, you could hear bits of the melody on cue, bleeding through the one he was singing.

"Hey, can I ask you something?" She twirled a pen between her fingers, her legs perched on her desk.

"Sure." He continued strumming, working something out with the new arrangement.

Lara sprang up and grabbed the acoustic Fender—her favorite. "You didn't backmask anything on the *Tending* album, did you?"

"No, why?"

"I didn't think so," she said, grabbing for the guitar and perching it on her knee, checking to see how out of tune it was and tightening the strings quickly. "There was just this weird thing that happened the other night with your album."

He stopped strumming, the note fading until he quieted it with his finger and shot her a puzzled look.

"I decided to play 'The One I Left Behind.' As I was cuing it up, I heard a song."

"You need to stop doing the late shift." He laughed, stroking his beard. "You can hear lots of shit when you're cuing a record in a studio. You know that."

"This was different," she said. "It was a song, not a noise." Grabbing the scrap paper with the notes she'd put on her desk, she played a few chords, then started singing.

"Stop!" His jaw was clenched, and he gripped her guitar so tightly that it seemed like he would snap it in two.

Lara's eyes shot up to see he was shaking and pale.

"*Where* in the hell did you hear that?"

"I just told you," she said, her eyes wide. She wasn't expecting this type of reaction. "I was cuing your album—"

"Not that song, Lara." He cut her off, his voice raised and edgy, like it had been when she was a child swimming out too far in the pool. "That song doesn't exist, not anymore."

Lara stopped strumming. "I...I...told you. I cued up 'The One I Left Behind' and when I did, I heard *this* several times." She pointed to the tabs on her paper for emphasis. "I tried to get a tape recorder, but I'd forgotten to get fucking batteries. I thought I might be able to get the notes down on the guitar, so I hauled this into the studio. The weird thing is that when Melissa came to relieve me at ten, the song was gone."

Jason ran his hands through his hair. "It can't be."

"Can't be what?" Lara put the Fender back in its cradle. "What is it?"

"Peter." He lowered his eyes. "You've been hounding me since Todd split, asking me all the time about Peter Beaumont. Well, if you heard that song, then you heard Peter Beaumont. We didn't record *that* song, Lara. That song lives only in my memories." He pointed to his temple. "At least it did." Jason shot up and pulled a copy of *Tending* from the record library. "Was this the album?" There were multiple copies around the studio, but she'd specifically used that library copy.

Lara nodded.

"You sure?" He tapped the album cover frantically.

"I always grab the library copy, never your personal one."

He walked over to the spare turntable that sat in their office. This set had a smaller channel mixer hooked up to it, nothing like the elaborate one in the studio. She watched her father flip the turntable dial into cue and place the record on the platter. He guided the arm over track three, pulled the lever to lower it, then pushed the START button, stopping the record as the beginnings of a song formed. Twisting the record slowly, he began to rewind it on the turntable.

The room was quiet as they both waited to hear.

Lara didn't know what to expect. She didn't know if she wanted the song to be there as proof that she hadn't—hadn't what? Made it up? But a part of her didn't want it to be there, either. That would mean a dead man was speaking through an album.

The familiar sound of warbled, heavy chords came through the speakers. Jason stared at the turntable, blinking.

Something stirred in Lara. She got up, placed the Fender on her desk, and walked over to the turntable. Jason moved away to let her at the controls. Touching the vinyl disk at the twelve o'clock position, Lara began to spin it counterclockwise. Before she even heard the first chord strum, she knew the song was there, beneath her fingers. Unwinding the record, spinning it, she found what she knew was the proper tempo. The melody flowed through her as if she were weaving it from the fabric of memory and history. She stopped, knowing what she had was not a full song, but a tasting of something, clipped from time.

She turned to find her father looking at her like he'd seen a ghost.

He stood and walked over to his collection of guitars that were hung on walls and scattered around displayed on stands. Leaning down, he carefully selected the oldest, most battered maple-neck Fender Sunburst in his collection. Pulling a cord from another guitar, he plugged the Fender into the small amp. Jason quickly tuned the battered Sunburst by ear, adjusting old strings that sounded to Lara like they hadn't been played for thirty years.

"It should be played on this," said Jason. He started on the first chord but shook his head, stopped, and started the first few chords again. Knowing the confidence that her father had when combining chords and notes for his songs and set, Lara could tell this song was one he hadn't played in a very long time. His fingers fumbled chord changes, and his voice broke. Shivers ran up her arms and the back of her neck as Lara recognized it as the song she'd heard haunting the *Tending* album.

"I'm sorry," she said after she'd finished.

"After all these years, I waited for a sign—anything from him."

"Why now?"

"I'll be damned if I have any idea." He avoided her eyes. "And why you?" Jason walked over and put the Sunburst back on the wall.

Lara felt terrible. He'd been so animated fifteen minutes ago, excited about the show. And now he had that look, like he was seeing her for the first time. It unnerved her. She shouldn't have said anything. This revealed something magical, and Audrey had always cautioned her to hide it. Now she understood. Her father looked at her like she was a stranger.

"I'm going to go," he said, nodding toward the door and grabbing his keys.

"Yeah," said Lara. "Get some sleep; you've been on the road." She smiled, hoping to lighten up the conversation.

He walked toward the door and didn't look back, not even bothering to shut it behind him.

While Jason had asked why it was Lara who got the message, she didn't question this. He'd never known about her magic. Like a strange rite of passage, Lara felt as though Todd's disappearance had set certain events in motion and she was now a conduit to strange happenings. Things were swirling around her and she couldn't connect them yet, but she had a feeling that nothing was a coincidence—her magic, the disappearances of Todd and Peter. She just didn't know how all these pieces fit together.

Rattled, she went home and took a long, hot bath, then slid into her sheets. Perched on the edge of her nightstand was Cecile Cabot's journal, almost beckoning to her. Instinctively, she knew that this diary wasn't just a random gift. Maybe it held some answers. She reached for it and flipped it open to page one.

The Journal of Cecile Cabot
Book One

April 3, 1925

Had our mother lived, I know things would have been different. A photo of her sits in the circus's wardrobe office. It's a side profile of her, a stage still, but I can tell from it that she has blue eyes like Esmé and me. Her coiled platinum hair resembles mine—a mixture of snow and silver. I cannot tell you how much I cling to this small detail that I resemble our precious mother more than Esmé does. Other than Father, Madame Plutard, Mother's former costumer, is the only person at the circus who knew her when she was alive. Yet despite her knowledge, Madame Plutard is silent.

The story is that our mother died giving birth to us. Everyone who was there is quite sober about the circumstances, so I fear we were a gruesome birth. Whenever I ask, Madame Plutard looks down at the floor or changes the subject and begins furiously ripping seams from costumes, her wrist flicking as her lips draw a line so firm that words dare not escape. Esmé has never asked. That we are twins shocks most people since there is such a sharp contrast between us. I'm the quiet one. The pensive one. Madame Plutard calls me the shadow twin.

I think she means that I am always following Esmé like a silhouette.

Yesterday after the performance, Esmé and I sat side by side at our matching ivory vanities. She was putting on and taking off makeup. "Who is older?" I asked. "You or me?"

It's one of those things I've always wondered but never asked. There is no doubt in my mind that she knows the answer.

Esmé turned to me with a coy smile then sharply inhaled, like she was honing her reply. "I am. Why on earth would you ever think that *you* would be older?" Through her mirror she glared at me, a measure of disbelief at my apparent stupidity. Immediately she began busying herself, opening gold tops on ornate crystal bottles, dabbing things at her neck and face with a fury before finally emerging from this frenzy to steadily apply her lipstick—a garnet shade, nearly black—to her small, full lips. She smacked them and ground them together, then cocked her head and ran a nail along her upper lip to correct the errant border.

"I don't know why you're always so mean," I said, sighing and pulling my long hair from its pins, then pulling it forward and picking at it before brushing the long silver strands.

She turned her body toward me, the nude bodysuit with black webbed piping she wore doing little to hide what was underneath. "No one wants to tell you, so I will. You shouldn't even exist, you know. You are like an extra arm. Unnecessary." She reached over to her vanity and handed me a tube of lipstick. "Here," she said, holding the exquisite piped metal case out in her hand. "You need it." Turning back to her mirror, she dabbed at her brows with a lace handkerchief. "I don't even know why you have a vanity in my dressing room. It's not like you have an act."

Stung by her comment, I had no retort, so I leaned into my own mirror, busying my hands and studying my pale face. She wasn't wrong. I was the only person in the circus without something to do, other than being "his" daughter. All my life—well, all of the life that I can remember—my sister has been tossing these barbs at me, hinting she knows more. In my heart, I have come to believe what she says: *I am nothing.* No wonder I lurk in the shadows.

"You still don't remember, do you?" She brushed her silky hair, making the dark bob line up with her chin.

I didn't answer, which was answer enough. The great shame of my life is that I've retained no memories of my childhood. It had never occurred to me that everyone didn't suffer from this form of amnesia. A few years ago, I learned that even the performers serving out their sentences here recalled their childhoods quite fondly, even when it was obvious those memories were washed over and revised in their minds. I'd love to have this type of nostalgia, but it is as though I emerged from a clamshell at the age of eleven. The first memory etched in my mind is of a birthday cake, a pink tiered monstrosity with the words ONZE ANS written between layers. I was bewildered that day, not recognizing the celebrants around the table. Like a muscle memory, I knew to blow the candles out after the verse of *"Joyeux Anniversaire"* was sung, but I did not immediately answer to the name Cecile, as though it were foreign to me. Worse yet, I had no memory of the girl with the chin-length black hair who sat beside me.

This same girl sat beside me. Her words had a way of twisting around me and cutting off the circulation around my neck, causing me to feel breathless. In my head, I've kept a ledger of each insult. Without memories to anchor me, her accusations have begun to define me. She was beautiful, confident, and talented, yet I was nothing—a creature with no past and no purpose. I swallowed hard, having nothing to lose. "Quit hinting like a coward. Just tell me, for once. Why do you remember, but I don't?" I faced her, ready for the confrontation. Or at least I thought I was, but her knowing smile struck fear in me.

The smile didn't last long before her face twisted. I could tell calling her a coward had emboldened her, just as I knew it would. "He didn't think you were strong enough, so he took your memories."

I felt my world tilt. This comment was pure madness and yet it made all the sense in the world. Illness or injury was not the cause of my emptiness. My memories—my life—had been *taken* from me. That they'd been stolen was the only answer that made sense. And the *he* was most definitely our father. Gripping the vanity, I processed the knowledge for a moment. "Why?"

She was about to speak when we were interrupted by the sound of a loud yawn coming from the velvet chaise, where a fat tabby named Hercules watched Esmé's movements intently. As though I were an afterthought, she focused on the cat and began to pet him. No one would have guessed that Hercules, himself, was resting after his own performance. Along with his feline partner, Dante, a sleek black short-hair, they were the entertainers in Esmé's cat act. Instead of the majestic lion and hungry black panther they saw bounding around in the center ring, the audience never suspected that what they were actually witnessing were these two fat, pathetic house cats. On Esmé's command, the two pounced and roared about the stage, dangerously close to their tamer. But like a magician sliding a card into a jacket sleeve, she conjured this illusion entirely. Each night, the audience held their breath as she maneuvered around the ring, never realizing that the thing that she manipulated was *them*.

And now the thing she manipulated was me. "Esmé? Answer me."

She frowned, like it pained her to speak. "Because he felt the truth was too horrible for you to bear."

"What truth?"

There was a knock. Sylvie, our trick rider and Madame Plutard's daughter, stood in the doorway, clutching her purse. Since she'd been young, Sylvie had tagged around with us, acting as the glue between us as well as the occasional buffer. An expert at reading us, Sylvie knew that she'd stepped into another spat. With Sylvie standing there, I knew that Esmé would never finish the story. While we were all friends, she considered the costumer's daughter "the help" and never discussed family matters in front of outsiders.

"We're going to be late. I don't want to miss Le Dôme tonight," said Sylvie, tapping her foot. Normally, she preferred the Ritz, but this week the circus had moved to the Bois de Boulogne, so Montparnasse was now closer.

Esmé's words ringing in my head, I wearily stood up from my chair and began to change into a silk aqua-colored, drop-waisted dress with platinum piping and beading at the hem that I'd draped across the chair. I spied my T-strap heels under Hercules.

"What about you?" Sylvie turned to Esmé, who was making no move toward getting dressed.

"What about me?" My sister's voice had a raised tone. She was irritated; the coward remark had stung her. I smiled at the thought that my words could affect her as well. How could a shadow hurt anyone?

Sylvie and I exchanged looks, but we knew that despite her petulance, Esmé wouldn't miss a night out in Montparnasse. This was all an act. She would make us wait, but she would be at the gate when the door opened. "Are you coming?" Sylvie folded her arms.

Esmé stood and pulled on her stockings and then slid on a black lace dress with a bow at the shoulder. She frowned and pulled the entire thing off, rolling it into a ball on the chair, and grabbed a blush dress with an aqua bow at the hip. Turning, she frowned and slid the dress off, kicking it under the chair. Next she grabbed a plain beige-and-black lace dress. Sylvie and I held our breaths, hoping this one would stay, but soon it was discarded for an elaborate tulle and gold-beaded dress with a small train that brushed the back of her calves. It was a new creation that Madame Plutard had made especially for Esmé, her muse.

Madame Plutard loved contrast and texture, and often our performers resembled desserts. Last night, Esmé was dressed in her newest costume—a gold military jacket with tails. Her wardrobe featured bold shades of gold and red. As Esmé rushed around the room, she passed the dressmaker's form that had been fitted with her newest costume: a blood-red brocade jacket with gold-and-black shoulder epaulets made of peacock feathers. I had no costumes because, as my sister rightly pointed out, I was the only person in this circus without an act.

All of the performers in our circus were once famous. They've chosen to be here to serve out their punishment. While this circus is a prison for them, from the looks on their faces, they are still grateful, so some prisons must be better than others.

As we approached the door, I spotted Doro, the clown. It was always heartbreaking when he stood so near the entrance, so I hung back to wave to him. It wasn't a chance meeting: He always seemed to know when we were about to leave for the evening and positioned himself near the door for one glimpse at the world beyond these walls. None of the performers could leave. This was a peculiarity of our circus. As we are full or part mortal, Esmé, Sylvie, and I can come and go freely. Oddly, Madame Plutard, although living, shows no interest in leaving.

"I have no need for the outside world," she often says, irritated at us as we prod her to go to the markets or the gardens.

Knowing it's futile, we've stopped inviting her, leaving her to her sewing.

As the entrance opened—its shape resembling the large mouth of the Devil—Sylvie and Esmé started through, but I stood at the mouth. Despite the fact that I could see Esmé's hands folded in disgust on the other side, I held the door open just a beat longer.

"Come on, Cecile." That she made Sylvie and me wait while she dressed then undressed into four outfits was now a distant memory to my sister.

Sylvie's face looked tense, always concerned that someone would see us deposited out of thin air into the Bois de Boulogne. From the mist outside, her blond bob had begun to curl. "Cecile," she called, motioning. "*Dépêche-toi!*"

I turned back to see Doro, straining for one last peek at the world beyond the gate. Before I emerged on the other side, I saw Sylvie's breath and knew the April night in Paris would be cold even before I'd stepped onto the grass. I always felt the entrance close before I heard it. And always I'm amazed when I turn to find the door—and the circus—gone, replaced with the stillness of night.

April 6, 1925

Today the performers were buzzing because Father had returned. The best place to find Father was in the gardens. Our circus patrons also love the gardens. They would enter our doors at night and were shocked to find an outdoor setting within the walls, wondering what trick has allowed the sun to still shine. Father says that pacing through the Great Maze gives him clarity, so he can spend days traversing the hedges. As a result of his devotion, the garden was quite fragrant at his request—fresh sprigs of lavender and rosemary mixing with perpetually blooming magnolias and linden trees. As I raced through the meticulously tended shrubberies, I discovered Doro drinking tea with the Crimson Sisters, their red curls shaped into geometric shapes like the surrounding greenery. As if he instinctively knew who I was looking for, he pointed inside to the Grand Promenade, where I could see Father was surveying something intently.

Deep in conversation with Curio, the mortal who serves as the Architect of Rides, he considered the newest creation—a Ferris wheel that went underneath the circus. He frowned and folded up the plans, tossing them back at Curio. *Backward* and *upside down* were two concepts that fascinated Father; this ride accomplished both according to Curio, who was hurriedly explaining the features of the ride now being built below us. Neither noticed me standing there.

"It doesn't travel deep enough," barked Father, stroking his chin.

Curio's face twisted like he was sitting on a pin. "But I can't make it go any deeper, my lord."

"I can't see Styx," said Father through gritted teeth at the mention of his beloved river. "You promised me that I would see Styx. That was the purpose of this ride, Curio."

"I've tried, my lord." Curio's face was reddening. "There isn't enough magic to get that far and hold the circus together. You need to give me more magic." Just then, Curio did a peculiar thing. As though he'd just discovered me, his gaze traveled to where I stood as if something brilliant had just occurred to him. "Of course," he exclaimed. "We can use Cecile, too. Why didn't I think of it sooner. Perhaps there is a way—"

The architect never finished his thought. With his left hand, Father silenced him with a clenched fist. Curio's face appeared to pucker, like he was chewing on something unpleasant, his eyes wide. His rounded body traveled to the floor, convulsing.

"Never," said Father, leaning over him. "That will never happen, Curio. Find another way." The architect's head rotated and he writhed in pain. With his boot, Father gave him a little tap, then held out his hand. "Now give it to me. This is what happens when you speak before thinking."

"Curio." I fell to my knees, holding his fleshy head in my hands, and looked up at Father. "What have you done to him? Make it stop, Father!" Frantically, I tugged at the man's suit, trying to find a reason for his distress. The portly architect's head shook back and forth furiously, pushing away from me like my touch burned him.

"This is not your concern, Cecile."

"Father!" I put myself between the man and Father's gaze, hoping it would break whatever magic was flowing from Father.

Father sighed wearily and stared up at the chandelier above us, his voice bored. "Curio. Would you like to be the entrée at tonight's Dinner of the Daemons?" Father leaned over and held his hand out. "Now."

Reluctantly, Curio spit something red and raw into Father's outstretched gloved palm. To my horror, I realized that Curio had severed his own tongue. Foamy drool and blood ran down the man's feverish face and drizzled over his gray chin stubble.

"Oh no!" Immediately, I scrambled, peeling off my sweater to wipe at the little man's face. With a fury, I turned to Father, the anger coursing inside me. "How could you *do* this? How?" My voice was now a shriek, and I could see heads poke up from chairs to see what the fuss was about.

Ignoring me, Father put his face close to Curio's. "You must find a way to dig deeper toward Styx using the magic you have. Let this be a lesson to you. It will be your arms next." Father opened the window and tossed Curio's tongue into the garden, where a pair of crows immediately seized upon it with a loud racket.

"Cecile," said Father. "You must *not* interrupt me when I'm doing business."

"This man is in pain!" As I spat the words out, I could see a smile form on Father's face, which only infuriated me more. He was so much like Esmé that I could feel my hands shaking. I patted at Curio, whose eyes were now bulging as he choked on his own blood. Attempting to sit him up, I was surprised when the man violently pushed me away, sending me tumbling across the floor. By then Doro and the Crimson Sisters had surrounded him, the entire hallway a mad rush of activity. Curio grunted and squealed something to Doro in a strange language that the fellow mute clown seemed to understand innately.

"Cecile," said Father. "Come." He stepped over Curio's quaking torso toward the door that led to the Great Maze.

"No," I said, my voice deepening so much that he regarded me curiously.

Doro's eyes met mine. The Crimson Sister with the single pyramid hedge of hair placed her hand on my shoulder. "We'll take him back to his room. It's not safe for him with you here," she whispered.

My eyes moved from Doro to the sister and back to Curio, who all stared back at me with dread. I wasn't wanted here. Composing myself, I stood and followed Father through the doors and into the gardens.

"What was so important that you came charging out to find me?" The sun was shining high as it always did in the maze, our gardens never requiring rain. As though nothing had happened, Father calmly placed his sunglasses on and tapped his cane, his long black duster coat far too heavy for such a warm walk. Pausing, he noticed something on his ruffled collar and picked at it, annoyed. It was blood. "Curio," he spat before starting toward the Great Maze.

I followed behind him with heavy footsteps. "What on earth did Curio do to deserve that? You cut out his tongue like a barbarian."

He spun in the narrow aisle between the hedgerows to face me. "I assure you, Curio ate his *own* tongue."

"Hardly," I snorted. From my position at the entrance to the maze, I could see Curio's shiny patent shoes still trembling.

"Cecile." Father tapped his cane. "Get on with it."

Swallowing hard, I found fury at every word he spoke. This creature had stolen my memories, my childhood. Thanks to him, I was a ship with no compass. As I watched Doro lift Curio to his feet, I became enraged. They'd both lost their voices at Father's hand. My fists tightened and I didn't mince words. "I understand that you felt I wasn't strong enough to remember my own childhood."

By habit, Father's cane tapped impatiently, but when it stopped abruptly, I knew that I'd made a grave miscalculation. I wanted to pull my words back immediately, but it was too late. So quiet was he that, somewhere in a distance, I could hear a single croquet ball connecting with another; laughter ensued, followed by the sound of a porcelain teacup returning to its saucer.

"Who told you that?" I could see the features that he tried to hide slide through his mask.

"No one," I said defiantly. Yet as I spoke, I wondered what it would feel like if he made me bite my own tongue off right now for talking to him so harshly. Would he do that to his own daughter? With his handsome visage and witty humor, I find he is often underestimated, but I know better.

"Of course, *someone* told you these things, Cecile." The calm lilt of his voice was disarming.

"Is it true?" Taking a deep breath, I fumbled with the piping on my skirt, trying to refocus the conversation.

He faced me, and the corner of his lip turned up. Father is a vain creature, having perfected his mortal look—handsome, ageless—yet small traces of his true essence peek through, the white tuft of chin hair, the hint of dished ears. His soft curls nearly touch his collar, and his amber eyes are wide and child-like but have a hint of his horizontal pupils. When he was weary or, in this case, livid, his mortal "coat" often slid off. "Was it Plutard?" He spat her name.

"No," I said, recoiling in fear for our costumer.

"Sylvie, then?"

"God, no." But the mention of her name was confirmation that, as I had suspected, she knew more than she let on.

"Then it was your sister." His voice was less urgent now, so sure that he had identified his culprit. Now he could cut out the rot and restore order in his circus.

Even though she has taunted and humiliated me, I suddenly feared for Esmé. This had been a terrible, terrible mistake. I had been angry at Esmé for years of gibes and innuendos. Like a child, I'd wanted Father to intervene, to make her stop. In a way, I wanted a little revenge on her. The idea of him doling out a fitting punishment to her—like no outside trips for a few weeks—felt justified to me. Just the thought of her watching Sylvie and myself leave through the door was strangely satisfying, but from the pulsing vein on his temple, I had been a wicked fool. Despite the fact that she was his daughter, I sensed her punishment would be severe. I had not figured on this.

"It doesn't matter." I tried to match his calmness, measure for measure, allowing him to think the information she'd given me was trivial and that I was not affected by it.

"But it does, my dear. It most certainly *does* matter. She knows better."

This was a curious thing for him to say. While I have thought my sister cruel for her hints, it had never occurred to me that she was not *permitted* to tell me about our own shared childhood. *What happened to me to cause this secrecy?*

April 7, 1925

Esmé disappeared this morning.

Her bedroom door was ajar, her beloved perfume bottles shattered, the bedcovers pulled violently from the mattress, and the slipper chair overturned. At the doorframe, I spied marks where her nails had dug into the wood in an attempt to fight off whatever had taken her. Next I ran from room to room, alerting everyone to what I'd found. Frantically, I searched the dressing room, the mazes, the horse stalls. Nothing. The realization came to me that I was the only person hunting for her. The other performers lowered their heads in affirmation that they already knew she was gone. Charging down the hall, I pounded furiously at Madame Plutard's oddly locked door, but she refused to let me in.

It was as though the entire circus had shuttered up tight and left me outside.

April 10, 1925

After three days with no word of Esmé, I was almost feverish. I'd scratched my arms raw from worry until they bled. Father had gone again and refused my requests to be summoned back. Finally, I tried one more attempt at Madame Plutard's room, banging on the door wildly until she finally opened it. "Yes?" Her tone was cold, distant.

"When will she be coming back?" I realized that I hadn't bathed in days and my hair was matted.

"She may never be coming back, you little fool." The older woman's face registered such a look of disgust that I almost didn't recognize her. "Your mother would have been so disappointed in you." With that, she shut the door in my face.

And at that moment I knew that she was correct. With a mixture of fury and stupidity, I'd likely led my sister to her death. Esmé had been right all along. *I was nothing.*

This evening, just hours before Saturday's performance, I smelled them before I saw them. Minotaurs. A swirling stench of filthy fur and rot wafted down the Grand Promenade even before they materialized. Two beasts each held one of an unconscious Esmé's arms around their necks, her feet dragging behind her. Tailing the minotaurs were two enormous, growling hellhounds, giant inky curs with coats so shiny they resembled glass figurines. Nipping at the air around them, the beasts snarled at nothing and then began clawing at each other until the head minotaur grabbed one by the scruff of the neck to settle the animal.

In the hallway, I stood speechless. Their entire entrance was designed to be pure spectacle. They could have easily carried her back without the added histrionics, but the show was for the rest of us and it was pure Father. That he was away was also no accident. As the duo turned a sharp corner with Esmé's limp body, her leg snapped against the wall, nearly breaking as the hounds bit at her bare feet. Esmé, drooling with her head resting on her chest, never stirred.

I put my hand to my mouth in horror. Never had I imagined that this would be Esmé's fate.

Following behind them was Madame Plutard like a priest trailing an executioner. From outside her room, you could hear Esmé's body hitting the bed with force. Then the door opened and shut again.

Hoofbeats pounded back down the hall as the lot headed to their next assignment. Our costumer entered my sister's room and shut the door.

Quietly, I crept down the hall and put my ear to the wall. I could only make out the sound of Madame Plutard sobbing.

April 15, 1925

Her door remained shut for several days.

I had time to contemplate my actions.

I wasn't alone in my hatred. Since Esmé's disappearance, the performers nearly fled when they saw me coming or when I attempted to sit next to them—a silent allegiance to her that I understood. It was yesterday—the fourth day—before Doro allowed me to sit next to him.

"I know I did a terrible thing," I admitted to Doro.

He placed his hand over mine. Whatever path had led him here, Doro was always kind to me. There were rumors he'd once been an opera singer who was quite the lothario in life, leaving a string of broken hearts throughout Paris and Rome. This version of Hell, our circus, had re-created him as a mute clown. Father's punishments stung. In Father's version of Hell, a great beauty in life was reimagined as a monstrosity. If his story is true, Doro, once a vain and proud tenor, would never hear the sound of his voice again. Doro's white face paint and red smile are like a permanent mask. Often I've wondered what he looked like in his life, but the performers here were always in costume now as though they were dolls that could be removed from a shelf.

Doro did, in fact, have a doll. It was a miniature Doro that never left his side. The two were exact replicas—and I can't say that I knew which version was the original. Our circus was dizzying that way. Perched on his lap, the miniature Doro puppet seemed to wake from his sleep to speak.

"You didn't know," said Doro's puppet. He said these words carefully, like he was giving me the benefit of the doubt.

I hung my head. I *had* hoped that Esmé would be punished. I just didn't expect it to be this extreme. "What happened to her?"

Doro's puppet sighed. "She was taken to the White Forest."

"How bad is that?" There were always threats of banishment to the White Forest, but I'd never seen one carried out.

"It is the worst possible fate, Cecile." Doro the clown looked down. The puppet continued, his voice smooth and bright like he was speaking from somewhere far away. "She may never recover. Many people do not." At this, Doro the clown began to cry. "Your father sent us there once." I realized it was there that his tongue had been cut out.

"My father sent you there?"

The puppet bobbed his head.

Squeezing the big clown's hand, I did not blame the other performers for hating me.

I hated me.

April 16, 1925

Yesterday I tried to see her, but Madame Plutard refused to let me through the door. "She has nothing to say to you." From Madame Plutard's manner, I could tell that she preferred not to talk to me, either.

To witness the scorn on their faces is almost unbearable. I took to my room, not bothering with the fireplace, wanting to feel the discomfort and pain that I deserved. A dampness set in, causing my bones to ache, particularly my leg. After a few hours, Sylvie came and brought me soup. I knew that she had to smuggle it because no one sought to feed me right now. As she handed me the bowl, she glanced over her shoulder and I knew that she didn't wish to be seen with me. I took the soup and despised myself for needing to eat it. I'd considered wasting away here, but I found that I could not do it. I closed my eyes as the spoon touched my mouth and the broth warmed me.

There was a show that evening. Even without Esmé, it went on. My role in the circus was to help the performers get into their different costumes. I stood at the side door, holding props for the performers while they shot me looks of contempt or, as usual, ignored me.

After the Wheel of Death, I rotated the bull's-eye back to its original spot. I thought that I could stand on the bull's-eye while Louis threw knives. As I filled the water for the horses, I wondered what it would be like to stand astride them, like Sylvie.

In the past, I'd tried to learn to ride, but Father has not permitted it for fear that I get hurt. Even Esmé was not permitted to ride the horses, a rare refusal from him.

So this morning, I walked out to the trapeze ladder for the first time. I don't know what possessed me to do this, but I believe it was the soup. Sylvie's small act of kindness exposed my desire to live, but I won't exist without undergoing a metamorphosis. The old Cecile, the one who tattled on her sister and lived as a shadow, is gone. No longer will I be the object of scorn or pity. I may not know what happened before the pink cake, but I can control what happens now. Weak from lack of eating, I forced myself on as I started up the ladder. A hush fell over the rehearsal. A few snickers and a "What does she think she's doing?" erupted from the floor below me. Because it moved, the ladder was more difficult to climb than I'd anticipated, but I wasn't giving anyone the satisfaction of saying that I couldn't cut it. If I plunged to my death here, it would be an honorable death, so I kept climbing. It was true that I was the weak twin, but I was also light, like a ballerina, which would be to my advantage on the trapeze. When I finally reached the top, I looked down. My knees nearly buckled from fright, but I held the bar in my palms for the first time, determined to change my fate.

It was morning practice, the one no one paid attention to, and half the performers barely showed up for it, but I looked down and all eyes were on me: Arms were on hips, hands over mouths, and Doro was motioning for me to come down. I'd never held the bar before, but I'd longed to feel it in my hands. It was heavier, thicker, and smoother than I'd imagined. From the other side of the trapeze, Hugo, the catcher, tried to shoo me down. I shook my head. "Let me try."

Hugo did not seem thrilled to have me on his trapeze. I didn't blame him, but I wasn't budging. I held on to the bar, pulling it toward me defiantly. Reluctantly, he shouted for me to keep my thumbs tucked under. If I was going over, he appeared to be trying to make it not cost him a limb. I nodded at his direction. With his finger, he drew a net that appeared below us. As it materialized, I breathed a sigh of relief.

There are no words to describe the first time that I swung. It isn't even the swing, it's the decision to step off and let go. I recalled my sister's limp body being dragged through the hall as I jumped, and I left the old me on the platform. Hugo sat on the opposite side, not moving and not trying to catch me.

I fell that first time.

I could hear rumblings around the circus and a few laughs and an "I knew it" from somewhere. Hugo was taking a big risk. The aftereffects of Father's wrath on Curio were still being felt. I crawled to the edge of the net and twisted myself down like I'd seen them do. I was awkward and got tangled in the net, but I walked right past the performers and up the ladder again. The second time at the top, I faced Hugo and nodded, ready to go again. He sent the bar over to me and I missed it, causing him to have to send it again and a roar of laughter from the performers below. My legs were shaking at the spectacle I was creating but also the fear. This time, I was prepared for the way the bar felt against my hands, and my weight was no longer a surprise. I knew what the leap would feel like and the missing strength I needed to do more than cling to the bar.

I fell again, but I knew how it felt to drop into the net. Landing on a net isn't soft. It's rough and scratches you as you crawl across to the edge. My knees were scraped up, but I felt joy for the first time. Even as meager as my attempts had been, I had made myself useful—I had *performed*. I finally understood that it wasn't just the applause each night, but a sense of accomplishment from the act itself that drove the performers—the very heart of the circus. Tomorrow I would be better. I made a promise that even if I never got to perform under this big top, I would earn my place.

I climbed the rope again.

Hugo never left his position, instead choosing to swing on the other bar, watching me. We faced each other and I could see it in his face: He was wondering if I had the determination to keep coming back. As if to answer, I grabbed the bar one more time.

Sweat beaded on my face and I wiped it. It was my third attempt and I was getting tired. The lack of strength caused my arms to shake a bit. Sensing this, Hugo shouted.

"Try to get your knees on the bar this time. Your legs are stronger. Let them get you over here if you can."

I'd seen the move hundreds of times, so I knew what he was talking about, but the strength to hold on to the bar while my legs hooked around it seemed nearly impossible. I took too long to execute the motion and dangled until the trapeze bar came to a stall at the bottom.

"There's a rhythm to it," Hugo called. "One swift movement quickly, then turn your body to look up for me. One movement." He held up a firm finger. "*Un.*"

He came down and met me at the bottom after I'd fallen. "Come back tomorrow. Now go rest."

April 19, 1925

My arms ached, but I returned the next day. The second day went much like the first. It was yesterday, the third day, when I finally felt comfortable enough with the swing that I could focus on my legs. On the fourth attempt, I hooked them. I remember the sheer fear I felt in letting my arms go, net below me or not, but also the delight. I had done it. And if I'd done it once, I could do it again. As I came up to meet Hugo, who was waiting for me on the other bar with outstretched hands, I'd never felt so free. And the look on Hugo's face—and the faces of everyone—was something that I'd never seen directed at me— the look of admiration.

As Hugo patted me on the arm encouragingly, the crowd parted, and I heard the tapping of the cane before he materialized. Father had gotten word of what was happening and was furious. There was always a commotion around him, people trailing after him, seeking favor, like he was a king. Immediately he focused on Hugo, threatening him with all kinds of dreadful things, including the White Forest. A hush fell about the circus, and I could see the troupe looking to me. I wasn't sure what had happened with Curio, but I felt that I was the cause. I would not let this same fate befall Hugo.

"I wanted to do this," I said, stepping in front of Hugo protectively. "I am not a doll."

"You are too weak." I could see his face shift, the varnish giving way to the real him.

"Let her try, Althacazur," Hugo said, wiping his hands on a cloth. He held firm, calling Father by his real name. Everyone kept their heads down, hoping Father's wrath wouldn't extend to them after he'd finished with Hugo. "I'll be responsible for her. It will keep her out of your hair. Yours and Esmé's."

His comment stung: *I needed to be kept out of people's hair.* To my dismay, it seemed to be the exact thing that Father needed to hear. His face softened and I knew he was working up a proper response in his head. Father sized up Hugo a moment.

"Let me do this. Please," I said. That I was being treated like a nuisance who needed a babysitter was hurtful, but I would prove them all wrong.

To my relief, sweet Hugo remained in one piece and Father went back to his office shouting to my catcher behind him, "If anything happens to her, you won't have any arms or legs to swing from that trapeze. Do you understand me?"

"Yes, sir."

And I could see that Hugo was visibly frightened.

May 9, 1925

Over the weeks, I became stronger. My arms went from skin and bone to a delicate curve below the muscle.

Beyond my body, I felt I finally had a place here at the circus. Hugo and Michel, the other aerialist, took me under their wings, allowing me to play croquet with them in the gardens when we weren't practicing. Until this point, I hadn't realized how much I'd been an outsider in my own home. I had no mother, an absent father, and a sister who detested me, and so Hugo and Michel quickly became my family. Given the nature of what we did, I found that I grew to trust them, and they, me.

After weeks of being locked away in her room, Esmé emerged and stood with her hands on her hips, watching my entire practice. The rest appeared to have restored her. Her shiny black bob had been newly trimmed against the jawline, her skin glowed again, and those bright, round blue eyes took note of every connection that I made with Hugo. I could see that as the small audience clapped for me, she was shocked.

Later, I got up the courage to make several attempts at a knock on her door. After wiping my sweaty hands on my skirt, I rapped on the wood. She cracked it open a bit, but she kept her arm braced across the door, the sleeves of her purple kimono fanned dramatically in front of me like a shield. "What do you want?"

"I've heard you don't want to speak to me." My face was feverish. The words came tumbling out and I grabbed my throat, waiting for her reply.

"You've heard correctly." She cocked her head.

Flustered, I didn't know how to respond. I'd prepared for her to shout out at me, even strike me, but she was defiant and showed no emotion at all. "I'm so sorry. I never thought he would send you to the White Forest." I burst into tears. "I didn't know."

"You knew he would punish me." Her voice raised; an accusing tone hung on it. "You wanted it."

I balked. She was right. I had known—hoped—that Father would make her stay home for a Saturday night—some childish punishment wished for by a child. My head lowered in shame.

She laughed. It was a biting cackle. "Of *course* you did. You're spoiled."

"I was so tired of the comments, the constant barbs, but…" I couldn't finish my words and began to shake and snuffle, finally wiping my eyes on my dress. "I'm so sorry, you have to believe me."

She sighed and looked out in the hall, like the act of speaking to me taxed her. The White Forest had changed her. At first glance, I thought that she had returned to normal, but up close, I could see that she was thinner, gaunter. The Esmé standing in front of me was now hardened and hollow, a shell of my sister, not the real thing.

"What's happened to you?" I yelped, placing my hand over my mouth. From inside her room, I could smell sweet, fragrant flowers, like linden blooms. The scent was strong, as though it was needed to mask a rot forming within.

"*You* happened to me, Cecile. With your childish tantrum, you made Father choose between us."

"Doro said—"

"Doro shouldn't speak of the White Forest to someone who hasn't been there. Surely he's learned his lesson. If he's not careful, Doro's puppet's tongue will be removed as well."

And she meant it. The hollow spaces in Esmé had been filled with evil. In her purple kimono, she even resembled Father when he wore his signature robe. Shaking my head furiously, I said, "I'm so sorry, Esmé. You must believe me. Had I known he would send you there, I would never have done that foolish thing. It was awful. I was awful. I didn't know, Esmé. I'm sorry." I began swaying back and forth and repeating the words "I didn't know." I wasn't sure that I could ever forgive myself for my part in this. She was right. I had been so young and it was clear that she had been hurt.

"I know you didn't know," she said coolly after letting me babble for an eternity. "Father wants it that way. He's made that clear." She began to close the door. "Oh, I've requested my own dressing room. You can share our old one with Sylvie. While the circus is small, I don't want to see you, Cecile. If you're truly sorry, please do me the kindness of staying out of my way."

The door slammed in my face.

I found my way back to practice that afternoon and missed all my handoffs as I attempted to twist into a roll out of my bar into Hugo's waiting hands. It was the best trick I had, but it wasn't a move that I could land each time; I plummeted to the net below if my timing was off.

"You're missing your transitions." Hugo met me at the bottom.

"It's my sister—" I stopped. My sniveling was exactly the thing that had sent Esmé to the White Forest. I needed to grow up. "It's nothing." I lifted my head. "I'll do better."

As I climbed the ladder again, Hugo called to me, "I'd like to use you in the show tonight."

"I...I can't." I was overcome with a creeping sense of dread. Practice was one thing; a performance was beyond my skills.

"Of course you can. You're ready to do the basics." With his hand, Hugo drew a net under me. "Just do what we practice. The net will be there to catch you. We'll just enchant it so they can't see it's below you. Don't worry. They'll love you. Michel and I can handle the rest of the tricky parts." He moved around under the net and climbed to the other side, facing me, then clapped his hands and rolled his muscular shoulders. His voice was sure and steady as he barked, "Come on, Cecile. This is the very thing that you need to do tonight, and you know it."

And he was right. Hugo was always right when it came to me. Almost innately, he understood my fears and my motivations before I could even begin to comprehend them. I suppose, as a catcher, he needed to hone that fine sense of his target, just as I could tell when he and Michel were out of sorts. From across the trapeze, I don't know how, Hugo knew what had happened between Esmé and me. He could tell that my confidence was shaken and that I didn't like myself very much.

I've often wondered about Hugo. Who had he been in his life? What on earth did he do to earn a lifetime serving his penance on a trapeze with Althacazur's daughter?

Later, seeing the patrons all dressed in their finest dresses and coats made me nervous. In past performances, I just stood and watched. And I guess I'd thought that performing was easy. I'd envied everyone their jobs but didn't realize that performing was a responsibility. I needed to deliver a solid performance tonight.

Esmé went on right before us.

There had been an inspiration for Esmé's act. While walking on Boulevard Saint-Germain, she'd seen a postcard that featured a German lion tamer named Claire Heliot. Dressed in a silk gown, Miss Heliot had assembled a rather sophisticated dinner party complete with bone china and eight of her lions, who sat dutifully at attention as she sipped tea and fed them horsemeat from her fingertips. Esmé was entranced with this act, but Father refused to let her bring real lions onto the stage with her. My sister had shown an interest in illusion, so she began to toy with her own pets, changing their appearances. The first time he saw her ragtag act, even Father was fooled into thinking she was about to be devoured by Hercules, so good was her magic. But Father adored her performance, so he spared no expense for props and costumes.

She'd copied Claire Heliot's act, the one where she walked a tightrope opposite her lion. In this case, the cat is the lithe Dante. It's a rather difficult illusion to achieve because there is no tightrope and there is no panther, simply she and a cat walking on the arena floor toward each other, but the audience thinks she is balancing on a thin piece of twine opposite a six-hundred-pound animal. As the audience jumped to their feet, it was clear why she was the star of our ensemble.

Next, it was my turn. As I climbed the ladder, the spotlight followed me. My hands were sweating, which was not a good start. Gripping the chalk, I wiped my hands on my legs and looked at Hugo standing on the perch opposite me. Unbeknownst to the audience, he'd enchanted an invisible net under me.

To the patrons, it looked like there was nothing between me and the ground. If I fell, however, they'd see that something had, indeed, caught me and realize they'd been duped. Whether they'd admit it or not, our patrons would be disappointed that we'd cheated and tipped the risk in our favor. That is the thing about the circus. Our potential for death is the entertainment, whether by fire, knife, lion, or trapeze. From my time of watching from the side stage, I could tell that each successfully performed trick allowed spectators to believe, for an instant, that magical things *could* happen and death could be held at bay, if only for an evening.

I set out and the first handoff went a little shakily, but Hugo's sure hands gripped me. Even for him, it looked like it was a struggle to hold on to my sweaty palms. The chalk had turned pasty. I slid a little out of his grip, but we held on. The problem was that we were on a rhythm with Michel, who was waiting to grab me on the other side. Michel's hands weren't as sure as Hugo's. I would have liked another second or two, but I turned and switched with Hugo grabbing the bar. I never trusted the bar on the return since we didn't practice our returns with as much frequency. As I went into the roll, I teetered, losing the propulsion needed to reach the angle that would allow me to meet Michel's hands. Worse yet, the audience knew it. I could hear the sound of dull moans mixed with excitement as they anticipated what would come next. In a split second I felt myself sink in the air and my face became hot—almost feverish—as I waited for what would come next: the humiliation when the net below me was revealed to the patrons.

My thoughts raced. "No," I cried, loud enough that Niccolò's orchestra paused.

And as though I'd issued a command to my own body, I floated in midair. With the lights dimmed, I couldn't see them, but I could hear the gasps from the audience. As I felt myself sink, I recalled the feeling of humiliation and found that my body rose with the intensity of my emotion. Knowing the timing necessary for the performance, I began rotating my torso in a vertical turn, like a corkscrew, so I could stretch enough to meet Michel's waiting hands. To my surprise, as I focused on his hands, my body traveled. What was now clear to this evening's ticket holders was that I spun without the aid of any prop in my hands—no bar, no Spanish Web, no hanging silk. I was floating. Then I met Michel and he pulled me over to the perch.

With the lights drowning out the audience, I could only hear their applause. As I bowed, Hugo held my hand tightly. "You've got to do that corkscrew move again tomorrow," he whispered. "That was the performance of the evening."

At the end of the show, all of us—the horses, monkeys, elephants, bearded ladies, knife throwers, and lion tamers—took our final bow and walked around the arena. Standing in the center for the first time, I was surprised to find that I couldn't actually see the crowd with the spotlight. Each performer stepped forward, and the noise from the crowed lifted and lowered. Hugo grabbed my hand and pulled me out from the line, and it was as though time stood still. As I bowed, I could feel the perspiration on my forehead and hear the whistling and roaring above me in the stands. When I returned to the line, I saw them— my fellow performers, imprisoned as oddities, but from the gratified looks on their faces, their eyes glistening with tears as the crowd clamored for them, I realized that when you've had a lifetime of adoration, you still crave it. Even if it required transforming into a bearded lady, a clown, or even a steed, adorned with a crown of plumes, they were given the ability to perform again. As I took a bow, I finally understood Le Cirque Secret.

In the hallway where I used to stand with buckets of water for the horses—a place I would never stand again—I saw the outline of Father standing there. Applauding.

And then to my surprise, tears began to roll down my face.

After the performance, Sylvie and I headed to Montparnasse. We'd had some famous guests at the show that night: Hadley and Ernest Hemingway, Ezra Pound and his wife whom they all call Shakespear, and Marc Chagall. I heard these artists were all the rage. Rage or not, after the performance, they clamored to meet us.

Even late into the evening, the cafés were packed. Montparnasse on a busy night was a symphony of sounds: conversations in French, English, and German; the clinking of cups against saucers; the street music of American jazz mixed with old-world accordions, both played with deft hands. Depending on where you turned your head, a different Montparnasse filled your ears.

We moved around all night, finally settling at Le Dôme Café, known as the American café. Inside, I could make out the drawl of the Americans' accents, which sound remarkably different from those of their clipped British cousins. Halfway through my second glass of champagne, Hadley Hemingway tugged on my arm.

"That is the modernist French painter Émile Giroux." She pointed to a man in the corner. "He wants to meet you." The painter looked embarrassed and blushed. Then he turned his head and was fully absorbed in a conversation with the painter Chagall.

"I'm not sure what a modernist painter is?" I had been to the Louvre several times, but painters were Esmé's territory.

"He's defying convention," she said brightly.

When my expression didn't change, she laughed. "The legs are long and out of proportion," she said. "The colors are crude."

"So he's not very good?"

"Oh no." She motioned for me to come closer. "He's quite good. In fact, he's the best here. It doesn't take much to copy something—he sees it differently."

"Painters are my sister's weakness." I nodded over to Esmé, who came to the café on her own. She and a painter had struck up a conversation near the bar. With each drink they'd begun leaning into each other like rotting trees.

While champagne flowed, couples circulated, coming in from the Ritz, the Dingo, and the Poirier. Everyone raved about the circus.

"So was it real?" Ernest Hemingway lit a cigarette, and I could barely make out the words. I leaned toward him, straining to hear.

"Yes, I was wondering—how did you make the building appear out of nowhere? Was it lighting?" This question came from the bearded Ezra Pound.

Sylvie and I exchanged glances. We couldn't reveal what went on inside the circus. Ever. People wouldn't understand. Moreover, Father forbade it.

Esmé answered from her perch on the bar, "We can't say." She smiled mischievously, knowing the comment only made her more alluring.

"Ahh, you aren't being good sports." Hemingway pointed his cigarette at her and ordered a beer. "Just one secret, come on." A big man, he pounded the table a lot when he spoke, quite confident that people wanted to hear what he had to say.

"A French magician never reveals secrets." I looked up to see Émile

Giroux standing above me. "To the French, the circus is sacred. Your question is like asking you to unfurl your current story for us while it is being written or for me to unveil a painting before it is ready. You don't ask too many questions about the process. It is bad luck. Am I right?"

He looked down and I saw that he had large green eyes, like the spangles on that night's costume. Those eyes were in stark contrast to his dark-brown hair and hint of brown beard. I sipped my cherry brandy and nodded, grateful for his intervention. Hemingway quickly moved on to another topic, this time poetry. In my short time with them, I realized that just as they preferred to flit through bars, rarely did this group stay on a topic for long, moving from politics to art and finally bullfighting in anticipation of Hemingway's upcoming trip to Pamplona. Ernest was talking about Spain when two women joined us who were introduced to us as the Steins.

At the bar, my sister held court. With her coal-black bobbed hair and contrasting light eyes, Esmé had a circle of admirers and had caught the attention of a short Spanish painter who had just joined the group. "Picasso," they yelled to him. I could see that he was revered by everyone, particularly Hemingway, who shouted at him in Spanish from our table. With one glance, Picasso determined that Esmé was the prize of tonight's group and began positioning himself to speak to her. As if she sensed his interest, Esmé, who had taken to smoking long cigarettes, turned her back on him and struck up a conversation with an unknown artist. As she faced away from him, I observed the Spaniard laugh, then down his drink as though he was leaving. With his popularity, I knew that Esmé would never let him go. As he was passing, as if on cue, she pretended to drop her cigarette in front of him. Dutifully, he picked it up and returned it to her lips then lit it.

I'd seen it enough to know what would happen next. Esmé would go home with this Picasso gentleman. After ending up in bed together and because she is a great beauty, he would insist—*demand*—to paint her. The world would not be complete until her sketch was realized on his canvas, and no one—*no one*—could capture her or understand her better than him.

She would finally acquiesce to be interpreted on his canvas and would then strip for him. For her, it was the ultimate form of attention that she craved, and yet, for her, the need for attention was bottomless. After he had agonized over the flesh colors of the insides of her thighs and the perfect hue of her nipples, like foreplay, he would finally fuck her. And in the morning, she would leave him. After she'd gone, the artist would go to the canvas expecting to admire his work, only to find it blank.

At first, he would think that she had stolen his greatest work—for the missing work is always the finest in the artist's mind—but upon closer inspection, he'd see that it was, indeed, his same canvas. Only now it was bare.

By early afternoon, the crazed artist would have made his way to the last known location of the circus, claiming magic or witchcraft.

It is always the same. Always. The painter's name is just different.

You see, Esmé and I cannot be captured, not in photos, nor in paintings. In the morning, the canvas will always revert to white and film remains blank. But it's the painters who are bothered the most. They labor, connecting lines into form to create Esmé's upturned nose, her small cherubic mouth, only to find that by dawn she has faded into the canvas like she was never there at all.

Within the hour, though, Esmé and the Spaniard had gone. Émile Giroux took a chair and wedged it between Hadley and me. She was amused by his audacity and widened her eyes. He was wearing brown corduroy pants with a sloppy jacket—all the men in Montparnasse seem to wear brown corduroys and sloppy jackets. He told me that he has never gotten a ticket to my circus. I nodded. So this was why he was trying to converse with me. Now it all made sense. I sighed, a little disappointed. "Let me guess. You haven't gotten a ticket, but all your friends have?" The brandy had gone to my head a little.

"I hear it's quite a spectacle," he admitted, leaning back in his chair. "I never much liked the circus, though." He studied my face, causing me to look away. "Why do you do that?"

"Do what?"

"Turn away." He reached over and turned my chin toward him, adjusting it up to the low lighting. "I should paint you."

I smiled. He could, but my likeness would be gone before the paint dried.

"Are you hungry?"

It was an unexpected question, and I realized that I was famished.

"Let's get out of here." He didn't move, but his eyes motioned toward the entrance.

"Let me guess?" My eyebrow rose. "Back to your flat to paint me?"

He shook his head, finally standing. "No, to Les Halles."

Hadley overheard him. "The market?" She made a face.

"Come," he said, taking my hand.

I looked at Hadley for her opinion.

"He's honestly the best of all of them." She winked. "And he knows Paris better than anyone. I'd go."

Her earnest smile made me warm to her. Unlike the flappers, like Esmé, who had dyed and cropped their hair and painted their faces with sapphire and black eye shadow and dark-red lips, Hadley kept her face pristine. There was little pretension to her, and I'd liked her instantly. My own silver hair flowed down my back in ringlets like hers. As it is the fashion, I know that we have both been under pressure to bob our hair. She and I looked like we belonged in another time, like two American Gibson girls.

Sylvie, in a cozy corner and deep in conversation with an American socialite, eyed me warily as I made my way to the door. "Can you get home all right?" I could feel Émile's impatience at the door. I'd never been alone with a man before and I was hoping that Sylvie wouldn't spook me.

It was the woman who teased, twirling a strand of Sylvie's hair. "She's not going home tonight—at least not with you."

Her eyes traveled to Émile pacing outside, and a wicked smile formed on her face. My face felt hot. I pushed through the door into the night.

During the taxi ride across the Pont Neuf, I could see that he was trying to impress me and that the price of the cab would likely cause him not to eat for a day, so this gesture was touching. We arrived at the First Arrondissement and the entrance of Les Halles, a hint of the bone-colored stones of the imposing Gothic Église Saint-Eustache shining above the pavilions of the central market. Even though it was two in the morning, the market still buzzed with activity.

Men were steering carts—trucks and black cars were weaving among horse-drawn carriages—all with buyers and sellers either loading or unloading crates of apples, cauliflower, meat, potatoes. Boys held empty baskets on their heads while weary women wandered around with full ones tucked under their arms. And throughout the crowd, men in evening coats guided women in ball gowns and furs, smoking long cigarettes, through the halls.

When I normally left the circus, I did so with Sylvie or Esmé. I had never ventured this far on my own. From the expert manner that he turned past the carts and wove through the crowds, I could tell he came here often. We cut through the opening of one of the marts.

"Have you been here before?" I could see hints of his breath in the cold air.

I shook my head.

"My mother had a flower and fruit cart," he said. Counting off on his fingers, he walked backward like a tour guide. "There is a flower and fruit pavilion; a vegetable, butter, and cheese pavilion; fish and poultry and then charcuterie, of course." He pointed to the farthest structure. "My father was a butcher. He was in that pavilion over there."

Looking up at the ceiling, I could see the moonlight shining down through the windows. I couldn't imagine growing up so free, running around the different markets under the iron-and-glass pavilions all day and night.

"I never…" I stood there in the center of it all, amazed.

"It's my favorite part of Paris," said Émile, grinning. "It *is* Paris, to me." His hair had just a touch of curl in it, like he'd missed a few weeks' worth of haircuts. "Here." He pointed to a restaurant at the end of the block. The sign read: L'ESCARGOT.

Tucked inside the market, the restaurant was a gem. Its black ironwork facade recalled the Belle Époque period. Inside, the restaurant was warm and cozy. We took a seat in the corner.

"Their onion soup is the best. They use red, not white onions." Émile ordered two glasses of champagne and a heaping single order of soup.

The wood ceiling with its low chandeliers as well as the intimacy of sharing this bowl of soup with this man had been such an unexpected pleasure. This curious order had me wondering if he couldn't afford two, but when the soup arrived, I understood. The waiter carried a giant pottery bowl with bread and melted cheese spilling out. The cheese was stubborn; it clung to the bread, so I wound my spoon until

I got a good chunk of it. The country bread was more than a thumb's width thick. The soup was too hot, but the first taste of the salty-sweet broth on my lips was heaven.

The last bowl of soup, the one Sylvie had sneaked out of the kitchen and into my room, had been the genesis of my metamorphosis. As Émile took his first spoonful and shut his eyes in ecstasy, I considered that this broth just might possibly change my life as well.

What is it about soup? "*Magnifique,*" I said, smiling.

Émile wound his own ribbon of cheese. "You have not seen much of Paris, have you?"

I ignored him. "I hear you paint long arms and legs on women."

He laughed. "If you let me paint you, I promise that I would paint normal legs on you." The soup was messy and our spoons and hands were entwined. That we had both eaten the same thing, tasted the salty broth and red onions on our tongues, was an intimate gesture. He inched closer to me, and I began to notice details—his upper lip was thin, yet his lower lip was full. It was incongruous, making him look like he had the beginnings of a child's pout. I saw the gold glint of stubble on his upper lip and I knew I was not meant to see these accidental sprouts of hair. Those details were personal, but we had now slid into intimate hours when such things were revealed. The day had gone on too long.

"Why don't you talk about your circus?"

I hesitated, but there was something about him that seemed so honest that it felt wrong not to tell him the real reason. "We can't." I thought about my response for a moment and how lacking it was. I tried a different approach. "Hadley tells me that you could paint an exact replica of an arm or a leg, but you don't. Is that correct?"

He smiled. "I have the skill to do an exact replica. I could give you an Auguste Marchant painting if that is what you prefer."

While I had never seen a painting by Auguste Marchant, I think I understood the point he was making. "Like you, I see the world differently, but I cannot discuss it because you wouldn't understand how I see it."

"You're a surrealist, then. Your mind is unknowable?"

I considered his question. "Not all of me, but yes. What I do is unknowable and mysterious, not unlike you."

As I said this, I knew it was a lie. We were not producing art—although many people have accused us of being performance artists, like Kiki or Bricktop with their songs and dances, or illusionists, given to elaborate trickery like carnival fortune-tellers or mesmerists.

The performers of Le Cirque Secret were more than that of course, but I couldn't—I wouldn't—say what we were.

We both reached for the last bread and our fingers bumped into each other. I took in his muddy-green eyes, like the Seine when it hadn't rained in weeks. I was frozen. After a moment, he insisted I take the last bit of bread.

At the end of the night, I told Émile that I could get myself home. Despite the intimacy, the evening with him made me feel as though I could never be anything other than alone. Once in the cab, the driver took me back to the empty space. "Are you sure?" The driver looked puzzled; they all do when we ask to be left off in abandoned spaces. "This part is not so safe."

"It's fine," I said. I waited for the cab to leave and found myself standing at the edge of the woods at Bois de Boulogne. The breeze across the trees felt good against my skin and I closed my eyes and thought of the circus door. The door came first, followed by the grand stone steeds that guarded it; finally the round building appeared. I waited for a moment for everything to assemble, and then I walked through the doors that shut tightly behind me.

May 11, 1925

This morning, Sylvie and I went to the markets on the Rue Mouffetard. I saw Émile Giroux there buying tomatoes and my heart leapt.
He looked different in the daytime—or perhaps I had just constructed
the image of him in my head all wrong. But my heart beat faster and I
found myself at a loss for words.

He smiled when he saw me, but he kept his eyes on the produce. "So
you *can* appear in the daylight."

"Dracula?" This statement hurt me. Was he comparing me to Bram
Stoker's undead count? I considered that it was closer to the truth than
he knew.

"I was thinking Cinderella."

I blushed and looked down at my shoes.

"Picasso was in quite a state the other morning over your
sister."

"Really?" I feigned surprise. The painters always showed up at the
last known address of Le Cirque Secret, expecting it to still be there,
holding their blank canvases, claiming it was witchcraft. But by then
we'd moved on to another part of the city—north to Saint-Denis or
nestled in the trees or the Rue Réaumur.

As he handed me an apple, I could see that his hands were stained
with aqua and brown paint. I bit into it and felt some of the errant juice
drip down my chin. I wiped it.

"After seeing your face, Cecile Cabot, I believe I am done with landscapes forever."

It now made sense—the weathered look of him—painting hills and lavender and sunflowers. I was about to respond when Sylvie came to show me something: this morning's edition of *Le Figaro*.

"Look." She pointed to the article. "The reporter Jacques Mourier has written an entire article about you."

"Me?"

Émile scanned the article. "I know Jacques," he said. "He's quite influential."

Sylvie read and summarized: "He's never seen more artistry displayed than the smooth way you take to the air and slide down the Spanish Web like a silk snake." She raised her eyebrow.

"That's some endorsement," said Émile, his voice almost musical with excitement.

"Any mention of the cats?" I was afraid to look at it.

"One line, at the very end. He says they're lovely, but every circus has cats." Her voice fell and she folded the paper.

I winced. This would infuriate Esmé.

With Sylvie's arrival, however, the spell between Émile and me had been broken. He gathered two more apples and paid for all three.

"Monsieur Giroux," I called out.

"Please, call me Émile."

I paused before saying his name. His glorious name. "Émile, where do you live?"

"Why? Are you coming for a visit?" His hair glinted in the morning sun. No one had ever looked at me with such desire.

I blushed and I heard Sylvie snicker. She was observing me flirt— something I had never done before. "Your ticket."

"Rue Delambre." He began to tell me about floors and numbers and I waved him away.

I do not need house numbers or floors. The tickets to Le Cirque Secret don't work that way. The admission is enchanted. The circus thrives on the energy of people who desire it. The surest way to get a ticket to Le Cirque Secret is to wish for it—blowing on birthday candles, wishing on stars, or tossing pennies—those devotions work well.

And the tickets have minds of their own. They're wicked little things, preferring patrons who barter their soul for admission—say, someone who says or thinks "I'd sell my soul for a ticket" will most surely find one on their doorstep, if for no other reason than to tempt them.

As one of the mortal residents of the circus, I possessed a certain amount of sway with the tickets, but they were moody little things and you have to ask them respectfully, and not too often, for a favor. I simply had to wish him a ticket, as I did the circus door, and one should appear for the next performance. Yet I nodded politely while he made me repeat his street number and address back to him.

May 16, 1925

Today was the unveiling of our new act. The clown Millet delivered a bouquet of blush peonies, cream roses, and green hydrangeas to me before the show, a gift from Émile Giroux, who would be watching me from the second row, center.

After the article, audiences expected the corkscrew, so they got it. While I'd seen Esmé performing her illusions, I didn't appear to have that same talent. The ability to levitate was my gift, so I threw myself into perfecting my signature move. While Hugo's act had been a straightforward trapeze performance, it needed to change with the enhancement of magic. Over the next week, Hugo and I began directing several clowns and women in a performance that started on the ground and moved to the air.

Madame Plutard balked when I asked for coordinating leotards in the same striped pattern in hues of aqua, soft pink, and moss green with elaborate gold-and-cream piping. All the performers donned white wigs to look like me. The baroque effect was something similar to the colors you'd imagine of the fashion of Versailles.

The dancers took to the center stage, and their movements resembled a waltz in the court of Louis XVI. The sea of them parted and I appeared in my blush-and-gold version of their outfits, emerging from a troupe of jugglers and synchronized tumblers to ascend the Spanish Web. As I rose above them, the audience was so quiet that I could hear champagne glasses tinkling while the orchestra hushed. Then Niccolò matched his orchestra to my moves, and the song pounded through the hall in a furious, twisting rhythm.

At the end, when I took my final bow, I could see the outlines of him as he rose to his feet.

I was a shadow no more.

13

Kerrigan Falls, Virginia
June 23, 2005

L ara had a reminder message from Audrey to pick up the tickets and a stern warning that the office was only open for two hours today, from ten in the morning until noon.

Throwing on jeans that were not covered in dust, Lara twisted her ankles into her black Chuck Taylors and raced out the door. She had fifteen minutes until the offices of the historical society closed.

It was Saturday, so she usually slept in a little later, but this was unusual. All night, armed with a French dictionary, she'd been up translating Cecile's journal. At first, she thought she'd just work on a few pages, but by two in the morning Lara had found that she'd been able to read most of the composition book without the help of her dog-eared and coverless Bantam French dictionary. Some of the handwriting had been faded or stained with what appeared to be a watermark and some phrases had to be looked up, but she managed to finish most of the translation.

As she read, she'd tried to equate the woman with the silver bob and heart-shaped face that she'd known with the young girl trying to learn the trapeze. Something about it didn't fit, causing Lara to wonder if Cecile had tried her hand at creative writing. Perhaps the journal was just some made-up story.

She ran the last block, sliding through the doors of the historical society offices at eleven fifty. Marla Archer had her back to Lara, and she wondered if she should feel weird about this. Tonight, she was going to the gala with this woman's ex-husband.

The radio was playing classical music, a baroque piece, likely Bach. Lara had majored in music, so she'd generally spent more time playing classical than anything modern until she'd graduated. The music suited the place. Looking around, Lara realized she'd never come in here before. All around the office were old photos of Main Street and Jefferson Street; "before" and "after" photos of schoolhouses turned into grocery stores, factories into housing developments; and of course the posters of Zoltan's Spicy Brown Mustard and Le Cirque Margot.

Above the counter was an old circus poster featuring the blond likeness of her grandmother Margot Cabot draped over a white steed, her famous leg clutching the back of the animal. It was an unreal position—anyone normal would have fallen from that angle—but it sure made for a great illustration.

"She was a beauty, wasn't she?" It was Marla.

Lara looked up, surprised that she'd been so lost in the artwork, she hadn't seen Marla turn around.

"She really was, but no one can stay on a horse perched like that."

Marla chuckled. "Well, I think that pose was more to draw the teenage boys to the circus than anything else."

Lara walked up to the counter, where books like *Virginia's Battle-fields* and *Kerrigan Falls in Photography*, which Lara noticed was written by Marla, were stacked in neat piles. "I need to pick up tickets for my mother." Lara paused. "Audrey Barnes."

Marla smiled. "I remember you from Gaston's." She thumbed through a small box of envelopes, going forward and backward until she found the one she was looking for. "Barnes." She opened it. "Two tickets?"

Lara nodded.

"I hear you are Ben's date tonight." Marla held the tickets out for Lara.

Lara stammered, not sure how to respond.

"It's okay," said Marla. "He told me. I warn you, though, he doesn't dance. I tried for years. Took him to Arthur Murray for salsa lessons and they refunded my money after one session. Said he was hopeless."

Lara clutched her tickets. "He also has terrible taste in James Bond films."

Marla leaned against the counter and folded her arms. "Can I ask you something?"

"Sure," said Lara, a bit wary.

"I have something for you." She paused. "It's complicated. It was for Todd, actually. Do you want it?" Marla put her finger up for Lara to wait, then opened a drawer and pulled out a parchment envelope of photos.

"The truck," said Lara, remembering that Todd had been looking for old examples of Le Cirque Margot's livery. He'd shown her some photos that night in the garage. *That night.*

She spread them out on the counter. There were eight photos of the old truck from its day, most black-and-whites showing people posed around it. In one, Margot stood next to it with a feather headdress and sequined leotard. "This is the best one." Marla slid the smaller photo from the pile. Lara noticed that the woman's nails were meticulous with shiny beige polish. She tapped a color photo. "I think this one is from 1969." She picked it up, studied it, and then, satisfied, pointed to the date stamped on the side of the photo paper. At this point, the truck looked old, but the logo was still visible. The photo was in color, and it appeared that the black lettering was actually royal blue. The woman paused, her clear blue eyes shining. "I didn't know if I should give them to you, or if you knew about the truck. I'd tried to find other examples of the logo for him."

Lara studied the photos and had trouble catching her breath. "I did know," she said, almost croaking her words. "He showed it to me before..." She let the sentence hang. Gathering up the photos quickly, Lara slid them into the sleeve of the envelope. "Thank you. Do I owe you for these?" Lara didn't look up, trying to scurry out of the place.

"Of course not." Marla waved her hand.

Lara nodded and turned toward the door, clutching the two envelopes in her sweaty hands. As she got to the front of the office, the door opened and Kim Landau stepped through.

"Am I too late?" she called, realizing that Lara was blocking her from the counter.

"Just under the wire," said Marla, her head back down in the file box, searching for Kim's tickets.

"Lara," said Kim, rather surprised to find her there, her big blue eyes wide. "You're going to the gala tonight?"

"I am," said Lara, turning toward the door in an attempt to pass her. It wasn't that she didn't like Kim—she really didn't know her. It was just that the articles Kim had written about Todd after his disappearance always had a bite to them, like there was some underlying reason that Todd had left Lara, but she was too polite to spell it out.

"I...I was hoping that maybe you'd be up for an interview."

"An interview?" Lara leveled her eyes at Kim. Her brows furrowed.

"You know," said Kim, pulling strands of dark, nearly red hair away from her face. "How you're feeling since the whole Todd thing..." She tilted her head from side to side, like she was selling jeans at the mall.

Lara felt her stomach twist. "How I'm *feeling*?" she snorted. "Are you kidding?"

Kim looked blank. "No...I—"

"I feel awful, Kim," said Lara, cutting her off. "How do you think I'd feel? He's missing...dead, maybe. I feel like shit. And you can quote me."

"Here you go," called Marla, holding Kim's tickets in her hand. She turned her eyes to Lara conspiratorially. "It was so good to see you. I know you're in a hurry. Thanks for stopping by to pick up those photos."

Lara smiled, grateful for the rescue.

Kim went to say something to Lara, but she'd already pushed through the door.

14

That was ghastly," said Audrey, her eyes wide. "She wanted to *interview* you?"

Lara fell back on the bed, closing her eyes. "She said she wanted to know how I was feeling." Reaching out, Lara's fingers felt the edge of Cecile's journal, right on her bed where she'd left it.

"I hope you told her," said Audrey, sitting back in Lara's chair, her posture perfect. "The *nerve* of that woman. I ought to call Avery Caldwell myself to complain. You're Simon Webster's granddaughter for Christ's sake. All the articles that they printed about you..." Audrey stared out at the window. "I should have called him earlier, instead of just having Caren get them from the mailbox. You know Ben Archer would get that paper first and would call me if there was something he thought you shouldn't see in it." Her mother kicked off her sneakers.

"Ben." She hadn't known the great *Kerrigan Falls Express* newspaper conspiracy had so many participants. Sensing the tone in her mother's voice, she asked, "Do you approve?"

"It's not that I don't approve of him escorting you tonight. I just hope it's for the right reason on your part." Audrey picked up the photo of Lara and Todd that sat next to the lamp on the side table.

"You think it's too soon," said Lara, eyeing her mother.

"That's not it." Audrey placed the photo back on the table and strummed her long, pale fingers over it, considering her words. "As you well know, I was never a fan of Todd's."

"Then you think Ben is too old for me."

"Well," said Audrey. "He is ten years older than you? At least I can't sense other women on him, like I used to do with Todd." Her mother closed her eyes tightly at what appeared to be a painful memory, then realized that she was speaking out loud. "Sorry…"

Lara put her hands on her face, hoping this would all go away. "Todd was certainly no angel."

"He wasn't worthy of you, but I'm your mother, so…Just make sure that you really care about Ben Archer, that's all. Don't rebound. Trust me, I know about that. Take the time you need to recover."

Lara lifted her head from the bed and looked at her mother suspiciously. "Rebound? What would you know about rebounding?"

"Are you thinking an updo?" Her mother changed the subject, swirling her finger in the general direction of Lara's tangled mess of hair.

An hour later, those same locks had been tamed by a curling iron into smooth, long waves. She let her mother zip her into the blue gown that made her waist look tiny. Perhaps she had lost more weight than she'd thought. One of the things that hadn't made it into her new house was a scale. Once zipped, she tugged on the gown, which fit her like a glove.

"You've lost weight since your wedding gown," confirmed her mother.

Lara studied her collarbones, which were far more pronounced than they'd been. A wave of nausea gripped her. Maybe it was too soon to be doing this. The gala…Ben. He had been her lifeline for information about Todd, but they'd become entwined over the last nine months. Complicating things with him risked losing her closest ally. Often, knowing Ben was home alone in his apartment, she'd strung together a bunch of songs for him—"Lovesong" by the Cure (only off the *Mixed Up* album), "Go Your Own Way" and "I'm So Afraid" by Fleetwood

Mac, "When I Was Young" by Eric Burdon and the Animals, "Invisible Sun" by the Police, and "Rumble" by Link Wray. It was reassuring knowing that he was on the other side of the airwaves listening to her well into the night. As the months wore on, Lara couldn't imagine not talking to him. She valued—and needed—his opinion on everything. The subtleness of this shift struck her. How had she allowed this to happen? She had sworn she wouldn't care about someone again. *And yet.*

Lara felt flushed and sat down on the edge of the bed.

"Are you all right?" Audrey was pulling her own dress down over her head, a platinum strapless beaded number with a plunging back and a slight mermaid cut. She turned for Lara to zip her.

"I don't think I can do this?" Lara fell back on the bed.

"Sit up. You'll crinkle the dress," said Audrey. "I need to be zipped."

"I might be fainting, Mother."

"Doubtful," said Audrey. "Zip, zip."

Lara sighed deeply and raised herself high enough to zip Audrey into her gown. Her mother looked stunning. "I know something that will change your mind about this whole evening." Audrey dug into her purse and held out a box. Lara opened it, knowing what was inside: Cecile's pearl choker. "Someone needs to see you in this."

A pang of sadness overtook her as she touched it.

"That choker is yours," said Audrey. "It has no connection to him."

"I'm afraid everything has a connection to him," said Lara under her breath. She looked up. God knows, the woman was trying. "You are the world's most thoughtful mother." She reached out and took her mother's hand.

Audrey leaned over and kissed her daughter on the forehead. "I'd give anything to take your pain away."

"I know you would." Lara stood and shook herself. She felt very conflicted now, torn between her past and present. Oddly, as she was embarking on her first date, Todd seemed closer to her tonight than he had been at any point in the past months. Lara pushed those thoughts away and focused on her mother. Her hair was gathered in a French twist, and she had chandelier earrings dangling to her chin. If she was involved with Gaston Boucher, he was a lucky man.

"So, Gaston Boucher?"

"Look at the time," said Audrey, handing Lara a mask. "I need to find my shoes."

"They're on your feet," said Lara, laughing before she turned and headed down the long hallway. "Someone's in love."

Mother and daughter made their way down the street toward City Hall down past the old Kerrigan Falls cemetery. As the sun set, the alabaster slabs, obelisks, and weathered cherub statues shimmered with a gold glow. Cecile and Margot were both buried on the southern side—the newer wing of the cemetery.

Lara peered through the tall iron gates. "Do you know if Peter Beaumont has a gravestone?" She was surprised to find herself thinking about him tonight.

Audrey stopped walking and opened her bag, pulled out a lipstick tube, and took one final swipe across her lips. "He does," she said, pointing. "The grave is empty, of course, but his mother needed somewhere to go to honor his memory."

So far, Fred and Betty had resisted any memorial for Todd. Lost in thought, Lara stared at a marble bench under the weeping willow tree, its branches overgrown and heavy.

"Peter's grave is on the south side, near the back entrance of the church. It's a small stone, easy to miss if you aren't looking for it," said Audrey, snapping her evening bag shut and walking on, like she couldn't bear the sight of the graveyard.

A scatter of pale stones in all sizes and shapes bordered the chapel.

Lara wondered how it was that her mother knew the exact location and details of Peter Beaumont's grave.

"Something strange happened the other night," said Lara, nearly running to catch up. "When I told Dad about it, he was upset."

Audrey stopped again. "What did you do?"

Lara frowned at the accusation. "I didn't *do* anything. I was cuing one of the Dangerous Tendencies albums, and there was a song when you ran the album backward. I mentioned it to Dad, who said they hadn't done backmasking on the *Tending* album, so to prove his point, he cued the record up and there was nothing. But then I tried…"

"And—" Audrey's voice fell like she knew where Lara was going with the story. "The song was there."

"He said it was Peter Beaumont's song."

"Peter?" The look of alarm on her mother's face caused Lara to step back.

"And the song I heard had never actually been recorded." Lara started to hum a few bars.

Audrey turned pale.

"You know the song?"

She nodded and turned, walking down the street, holding her stomach.

"Dad believes Peter was sending him a message."

Audrey stopped walking again.

"The way he looked at me," recalled Lara, observing the change in her mother's face. "It was like he'd seen a ghost. You know, like you're looking at me now."

Audrey's voice was low, yet no one was around to hear them. "It was magic, Lara. Just like the enchantment of a gown or the turn of a lock." She backtracked a few steps, her expression weary. If it hadn't been for the pink lipstick, she would have looked sickly. "You must remember to hide your magic, my dear. It has the potential to hurt others who don't understand." Audrey gathered her gown and walked down the cobblestones past the cemetery gate. The discussion was over.

The pathway leading to City Hall was lit with hurricane lanterns with tall white candles burning. At the stairway, the Rivoli jugglers were tossing fire and a small group stood to watch them. As they ascended the steps, Lara saw a sea of black and white formal wear in front of her. The lobby of the two-story building with its curving staircase had been converted for the gala. Other than the Victorian Christmas celebration when the twenty-five-foot tree stood here, this was the biggest event in the town. The Rivoli Circus had loaned out their orchestra for the occasion, and the sound of stringed instruments tuning themselves could be heard around the block.

While most towns wouldn't have focused as much on their historical societies, Kerrigan Falls played it up. With Monticello and Montpelier nearby, the town was nestled among some of the most historic locations in America. Over the years, the carnival gala had grown, thanks largely to the fundraising efforts of Marla Archer. Before her, Marla's mother, Vivian, had been the executive director of the Kerrigan Falls Historical Society. Under Marla's leadership, the once tired dinner had become the social event of the season. It was a lovely tradition, and the fete only grew more crowded with each passing year. Along with the homes tour, it was also one of the biggest fundraisers.

The color scheme used the Rivoli colors of blue and green. In the grand foyer, chartreuse and indigo fabric panels streamed down in a dramatic maypole sweep over the two stories to mimic the circus's big top. At center, a giant chandelier, surrounded by cascading green garland vines, dangled. Pots of green, blue, and white hydrangeas were interspersed with hurricane lamps. The room shimmered.

Audrey was immediately drawn into a conversation with a clump of masked revelers whom Lara recognized as some of the local vintners and stable owners. Passing her, waiters carried silver trays of smoked salmon and goat cheese puffs. Far off, Lara heard the sound of glassware clinking and the smell of meat on a grill.

Even with a mask, Marla Archer was easy to spot. She was wearing a peacock-blue mermaid gown with long sleeves and a plunging neckline with a matching green-and-blue choker necklace. As Marla turned, Lara noticed the gown was backless to her hips. Surrounded by board members and the mayor, who was drinking up the attention, Marla held court, placing her hand on the mayor's forearm for emphasis in their conversation. Off to the side, drinking a glass of champagne, was a maskless Ben Archer. If there was any awkwardness between Marla and Ben, they put on a very good public display. He exchanged a quick hug with his ex-wife before the rest of their group began to squeeze together for a party picture. While Ben stood outside the frame of the camera, Lara watched as Marla coaxed Ben into the shot, pulling him in to replace her at the last minute. Ben looked sour before switching to a wide smile for the impromptu pose.

Lara was about to head over to him when she glanced up at the stairs that led to the second floor. Lara froze.

Waiting for her on the landing at the top of the stairs was Todd Sutton.

She blinked, making sure that she was seeing clearly, then closed her eyes firmly and opened them again. He was still there, a crooked smile on his face, like he knew what she was doing. The room spun and she planted herself, looking down at her feet before looking up at him again. Her heart began to pound, and then, like the morning realization that a restless night had been nothing but a bad dream, a sense of relief washed over her. She had been too afraid to hope he would ever come back. Whatever reason he had for not showing that day, she was sure it was a good one. He was here now.

Like a popped cork, feelings that she had been too afraid to tap came flowing out of her—the despair at the loss of him, the anger, and finally the fear she couldn't even admit to herself, yet she knew lurked underneath, that bitterness would eventually seep in until it gripped her fully. Lara had been so afraid of who she would become after the grief and the loss had permanently altered her and bitterness set in. Yet none of that mattered now.

Gathering the full skirt of the navy dress up in her hands, the tulle like foam under her fingertips, she climbed the stairs toward him, slowly at first, savoring each moment of eye contact with him again. With every step, she realized how much of a lie it had been—that she'd moved on—that she was strong—that she could go on without him. She'd told everyone what they'd wanted to hear. There was a crackle in the air. The truth was, she'd longed for him—his body— his voice—the firm feel of his hand in hers. In those hands were two glasses of champagne. Before climbing the final two stairs, she was about to take off into a run when she spied it.

The wedding ring on his finger.

She stopped on the step and looked down, holding on to the rail for a moment. That ring was still in Audrey's jewelry box where she'd placed it that day. *That day.*

Gazing up at him, Lara realized after a moment that the tuxedo he was wearing was the one he would have worn to their wedding, the one that had been left on his bed. She placed her hand on her stomach and tried to compose herself.

This was nothing but an illusion. A cruel manifestation of her own mind, like the chandeliers in the old circus tent or the turn of a lock. This is what she'd wanted to see. This was *all* she'd wanted to see.

As he beamed down at her, she allowed herself to see this moment for what it was. Had he been at the church, this was the look he would have given her at the end of the aisle where he'd have stood waiting for her before they said their vows. She took the champagne glass from him. The stem was thin, and she could feel the chill on her forefinger as she held it. She slid her hand in his. It was warm, like a real one. She clung to it for a moment, pulling the illusion of him toward her.

"You look beautiful." It was that voice, deeper than you expected from him, that always surprised her. The timbre of it. She'd never erased his voicemails, saving them for the day she could bear to listen to them again.

"Don't leave me," she whispered.

The knowing smile he gave her was heartbreaking. "You'll be fine, Lara."

"I don't want to be fine." Tears so easily began to run down her face, the grief hitting her in waves.

As she blinked, her tears seemed to fade him, like a watercolor in rain. And he was gone.

Wiping her face, Lara felt something stir, a breeze, giving her goose bumps. Despite the fact that she was at the top of the stairs in a crowded room, everything and everyone in the room fell away. Standing in front of her on the other side of the staircase, wearing a black tuxedo and gold mask, was the man with brown ringlets who had stood in her field all those years ago. Even with his mask, he was unmistakable, dashing. Like a wicked fairy-tale villain from childhood, he flashed the same devilish smile. With him was the woman with the parasol, only now she was wearing a gold dress that matched his mask. Margot—her grandmother.

This entire scene was impossible and yet they stood before her, just as Todd had a minute ago.

"You're getting so much better with your illusions, my dear. I almost believed he was here with us."

"Aren't you another one?" She didn't have time for games. Lara wanted to run down the stairs and out the door like some princess in a Grimm fairy tale.

"Hardly." The man slid his arm around her as if he instinctively knew that she was unsteady. He whisked her down the stairs like a Victorian lady and into the foyer below. His arm felt real and people seemed to part for them, as if they saw him, too. "I assure you, I'm as real as you."

"What did I just do?"

He led her through the double front doors and onto the street. "You created the illusion you wanted the most." Everything about him looked normal—human. "But you need to be careful, my child. Sometimes illusion has the power to destroy us. Best to snuff it out like a single flame before it catches."

He pulled away and looked into her eyes, taking her in with his strange horizontal pupils. "You look lovely in that choker."

"It's an heirloom." She wanted to touch it, but he held on to her firmly, not allowing her shoulders to move.

"I know," he said. "I created it for my Juno, so many years ago." He slid a finger across the necklace, causing a chill to travel up Lara's spine. "It was my gift to her. Those are the finest pearls found in Styx."

"The river?"

"Well, certainly not the band, my dear," he said with amusement. From the vantage point of the City Hall entrance steps, he scanned Main Street like a cat in a window. "We are alike, you and me. There are some days the desire to glimpse Juno again—even the shell of her—is still so overpowering that I would risk everything to conjure her. And yet I know it would be only the manifestation of her. It would be hollow, like a waxwork."

Lara met his eyes. "Why are you here?"

"Excellent question." He started down the steps with surprising grace, like a Bob Fosse dancer, his shoes tapping against the concrete. Lara followed after him. At the bottom, he stood with his hands in his pockets, smelling the night air as an animal does. "I have a proposition for you, my dear. That fiancé of yours."

"Todd?"

He looked bored at the specifics, like names. "You just conjured that tall drink of water up as your date for this evening's soiree, so you must want to know what happened to him?"

"You know what happened to him?" There was desperation in her voice. She heard it crack.

"Of *course* I do."

"Well?" Lara rubbed her sweating palms on the dress. She wasn't fifteen minutes into this gala and she'd seen three surprising guests. Why did she always feel faint when she saw Althacazur? Her breathing was growing shallow and she tried to remember everything she could from her research on him. If he was, in fact, the daemon Althacazur, then he was Lucifer's favorite...ruled the greatest layer of Hell...was vain and often underestimated...had horizontal pupils. As she did the checklist in her head, she thought she should probably sit down before she passed out. Eyeing a bench near the bus stop, Lara steered him there. At the entrance to the gala, Lara watched Margot flirting with two young men. While she seemed to be enthralled with their conversation, she kept a watchful eye on Althacazur's and Lara's movements.

He took a seat next to her, like it was something novel. "Is this what it's like to wait for a bus? I've never done that before."

"You know what happened to Todd?" Lara felt the need to repeat herself now that they were seated.

"Tsk. Tsk." He wagged his finger at her. "I require something for that information. If you want to know what happened to Tom."

"Todd."

"Whatever." He shrugged and kicked at a cigarette butt with his shoe.

"What do you require?" She put her hand to her forehead, which was covered in sweat. They sat side by side like the spies in thriller films, speaking conspiratorially.

"Oh, don't look so frightened. I'm not asking for your soul, if that's what you mean. At least not yet." He chuckled. "I simply need for you to come to Paris. You are needed there." He seemed uncomfortable. "I need you there."

"Why?" She looked over at him. "Is it because of the Devil's Circus?"

"An inaccurate nomenclature, I assure you." He slouched down. "But yes. Le Cirque Secret requires you. In return, I'll tell you everything you want to know—the fiancé, great-grandmother Cecile, all of it—if...*and only if*...you come to Paris. But it must be our little secret. Do you understand? That mother of yours cannot know."

"Why are strange things happening to me?" She hadn't meant to blurt it out, but maybe he would give her some answers or at least admit which of the strange happenings he was behind.

"If you do not come to Paris, it will keep getting weirder, my dear. The fabric of this quaint little community your family has built for you is beginning to tear apart. Without my help, I fear it could be the end for you all."

At his confirmation of the threat against her, Lara found she could not speak. She recalled what Shane Speer had said: *She is coming for you.*

He smiled slyly as though he read her thoughts. "She is, indeed, coming for you, you know. And make no mistake, she is dangerous." There was a tiny hint of pride in his voice.

"Who is she?" Lara nearly shouted.

"A very powerful creature."

"What on earth would a *powerful creature* want with me?" She was getting tired of him talking in circles.

"Well, that's a rather complicated tale. Let's just say that you pose a threat to her."

"How on earth would I pose a threat to anyone?"

"I fear it's my fault." He wasn't looking at her; rather, he focused on each detail around them with a sense of wonder—the mailbox, the streetlamp, the *Kerrigan Falls Express* newspaper stand—as though he was witnessing such details for the first time.

"Your fault?"

"When you were little, Margot and I came to visit you in the field. Do you remember that?"

"I do."

"Then you remember that I said you were *the one*?"

"I still don't know what you meant." Lara folded her arms.

"It meant that I've made you powerful. I'm sure you've noticed that your abilities are now increasing."

"You've done that?"

"Well *you* certainly haven't done it." He laughed and sat up straight on the bench. "But as you grow more powerful, you become a threat to her." Staring up at the stars, he cocked his head. "This little world really isn't as awful as I recall."

Lara stumbled over what to say next. Suddenly, in the night air, she was cold, so she began rubbing her bare arms. This was all too much. These disappearances, veiled threats, and strange visions. "If I come to Paris, you promise to help me?"

Facing her, he gave a slow and deep nod. "I will."

It felt like a contract forming between them.

"Do I have an address to meet you? Do I call you when I land?"

He nearly bent over with laughter. "How precious you are. I assure you, that won't be necessary. You'll hear from me." He stood and bowed dramatically, like a Versailles courtier.

"I don't know your name."

He winked before he began to walk up the street toward the cemetery gates. "That, my dear, is the first lie you've ever told me. You know exactly who I am." He turned back. "Oh, one more thing. Did you get my little present the other night at the Rivoli Circus?"

"The journal?"

"Hopefully it was an intriguing read." His eyes widened dramatically, like a stage actor's. "There will be more of them...call it a little scavenger hunt."

As he walked into the night, she noticed that his steps were now silent, as though his feet never touched the cobblestones. He first floated, then faded as if walking into a thick mist. Immediately Lara looked up to find that the two men who had been standing with Margot were now alone and quite perplexed.

Lara felt a hand on her shoulder and turned to see Ben.

"Is that Lara Barnes under that mask?" He leaned down and gave her a kiss on the cheek. Ben Archer was one of the rare men who could go from a uniform to a tuxedo with ease. His caramel-colored hair looked a little stiff with gel, the glaze of it glistening under the streetlamp.

"Did you see that man?"

"No," said Ben, eyeing her suspiciously. "You were sitting here alone." He looked up at the sign. "You catching a bus?"

"I was alone?"

"Yes." He laughed, eyeing her peculiarly. "Are you okay? Why were you sitting out here alone?"

"I'm fine. Just nerves going into a party, I guess," she lied. "Why aren't you wearing your mask?"

"Marla just scolded me about that as well. I'm likely to fall with this damnable thing on. It's terrible." He held it out like a child. "Look at it; it's sweaty like a kid's Halloween mask and it's giving me a headache."

Lara took the mask and tried to loosen the elastic before sliding it on his head. "There."

She followed him back through the front doors and stood there while he went to the bar. While the wait staff buzzed, she downed a mini chicken kebab and goat cheese puff that made her footing feel solid again. As she stood gazing out at the oblivious partygoers milling about and laughing, she had a strong urge to flee. She didn't belong here with carefree people. Getting up the courage to look at the top of the stairs again, she found the space empty. It was like reopening a wound. This had been too soon.

Lara saw Kim Landau make a beeline toward Ben. While Lara didn't want to have another exchange with Kim on how she'd felt about Todd's disappearance, Ben looked equally uncomfortable with their conversation and seemed to be itching to gather his drinks and go, but the bartender was taking his time. Whatever Kim was saying made Ben pull at the neck of his tuxedo. Finally, he snatched two glasses and quickly sidestepped her in mid-sentence. Kim watched him all the way across the room until her gaze landed on Lara. A chill went up Lara's neck as the woman frowned, like Lara had won a round, then smirked, before turning and heading into a sea of partygoers.

Lara was shaken by the reporter's boldness, like there was some competition between them.

"Here." Ben handed her the second glass of champagne she'd held tonight, only this one wasn't an illusion.

Taking a sip, she pointed her glass at the bar. "I see Kim Landau cornered you."

"Unfortunately." He clinked her glass.

She took a long sip of her champagne and wondered how it was possible that she'd thought Todd was real tonight, had ached for him as though he'd never left, and yet she could still be curious about the nature of Kim and Ben's relationship. Her thoughts were beginning to scramble. She no longer trusted them.

Just then a doorbell sound rang through the room—the xylophone being played by the wait staff to let everyone know that dinner was about to be served.

The sea of people began to move into the back courtyard for dinner. Overhead was a tent; this time, white fabric streams hung overhead. "This is stunning," said Ben as they got their first look at the color and texture of the silk, flowers, and candles.

Instead of traditional "rounds," Marla Archer had set up the event with several long tables, like a Tuscan dinner. Green garland vines and chandeliers hung over each table. The chartreuse tablecloths featured bunches of hydrangeas in blue, green, and cream with cream roses. Other groupings were accented by tall gold candelabras or tall vases with gold cane chairs and chargers. With votives lighting every few inches, the event shimmered. In the last year, Marla had become the go-to photographer for Virginia wineries, so each course this year was paired with a local wine that had been donated for the cause.

"She was nice to me today," said Lara, recalling how Marla inserted herself so Lara could flee Kim Landau.

"Not always nice to me, though." He finished his champagne in a single gulp.

Lara found their place cards: Audrey and Ben were seated across from each other with Lara to Ben's right and Inez Favre, the wife of Rivoli Circus director Louie Favre, to his left. On the opposite side of the table, Audrey sat between Gaston and Louie.

Watching Audrey and Gaston clearly flirt with each other was charming. Lara couldn't figure out *when* this relationship had blos-somed between them, but now, seeing them together, they were clearly a couple. During the salad course, Gaston leaned in frequently, whisper-ing something to her mother, and Lara saw Audrey light up. She hadn't seen this much joy on her mother's face, ever. Lara had a pang of sadness for her father, who had always seemed to hold a soft spot for his ex-wife. Jason had taken the night shift at the station tonight. He'd avoided her all day after the song yesterday and she felt guilty. While Jason wasn't much for events like this anyway, Lara wondered if he knew about Audrey and Gaston and had decided to stay away. Or was he just avoiding *her*? She recalled the way he looked at her last night, like he'd seen a ghost.

And what if the man from the field was nothing but an appari-tion? What if she had manifested both him and Margot tonight, just as she'd done with Todd? While the man had assured her he was "as real as her," it would be exactly the kind of thing a figment of your imagination *would* say to you. Recalling the look of horror on Cecile's face when she'd first told her about the man's visit, she wondered if her great-grandmother had just been afraid that Lara was going mad like Margot. Is this what her mother meant by warning her to hide her magic? Did using it cause madness? Hallucinations? She was deep in thought when she felt her mother kick her back to attention from under the table. Lara hadn't realized it, but she'd been rubbing her neck and staring off into space.

"They say four people from Washington, DC, bought second homes out here this month," said Audrey, twirling her earring. "It's a trend." She met Lara's eyes with a warning to pay attention.

"A good one?" said Ben, shifting in his chair and touching one of the flower centerpieces. "I'm not so sure."

"Must be the low crime," said Lara under her breath, seeing the opening to tease Ben.

"Smart-ass," said Ben, not looking at her, but grinning.

As the waiter poured more wine, Audrey leaned in, her face illuminated by the votives. "Also, Gaston has news of the painting, don't you?"

"*Oui,*" he said. "I sent an email to Teddy Barrow." Gaston's tuxedo was clearly one that he owned. His normally messy hair was now secured into a smooth, low ponytail. This change from day to night looked effortless for him, like he'd donned tons of tuxedos in his life.

"Barrow the Fourth?" Lara's eyebrow raised. She was trying to show Audrey that she was focusing on the conversation at hand.

Gaston chuckled. "Yes. *Barrow-le-quatrième.* I sent him a photo of the painting. He called from Paris this morning, waking me up from a most wonderful sleep. He is very excited."

"Gaston's friend thinks a painting we had might be a real Giroux," Lara turned to explain to Ben. She was enjoying this wine. It was a full-bodied red, and she took another sip to make sure it was as good as she'd thought.

"Yes," said Gaston, lowering his voice so as not to be overheard. "Barrow thinks that it might, indeed, be one of the long-thought-missing Giroux paintings—The Ladies of the Secret Circus, as they were called."

"The Ladies of the Secret Circus?" Lara leaned in to listen, truly interested in the conversation now. "That sounds mysterious."

Gaston nodded before taking a sip of wine. "It is. This entire series of paintings has been missing for more than seventy years."

"What is a Secret Circus exactly?" Ben seemed amused. "I gather the Rivoli Circus is not a Secret Circus?"

"Most definitely *not,*" said Audrey, wiping the corners of her mouth with her cloth napkin.

Louie Favre, the Rivoli director, perked up. "What's this about the Secret Circus?"

"Have you heard of it?" Audrey turned toward him.

"Of course. Everyone in the circus world has heard of it; I'm surprised you haven't, Audrey." Louie Favre was a barrel of a man with a large, full mustache as thick as a paintbrush. "It's legendary." He swirled a glass of what looked like bourbon.

"No," said Audrey. "I've never heard of it until tonight."

"My friend Barrow has written quite a bit on the subject and considers himself an expert," said Gaston, leaning toward Audrey so that he could hear Favre. "It is one of his obsessions. It's quite something to hear him go on about it. He was rambling something about a mysterious circus that had no physical building."

"*Oui*," said Favre. "It was rumored to have existed in Paris in the 1920s. Guests received tickets and were told where to go and voilà— a building would appear—out of nowhere." Favre had once been the ringmaster of the Rivoli Circus, and he could tell a good story. "But"—he held out a finger—"only to the ticket holders. If the person next to you wasn't holding a ticket, they did not see a circus in front of them at all."

"Sounds a bit like Willy Wonka and the golden ticket." Ben was playing with the stem of his wineglass. While she had been excited to be here with Ben, the illusion of Todd hung heavy over the evening, dampening what would have been her first date. And is this why she'd manifested Todd? Was she secretly afraid of moving on?

"We French are a little mad," said Gaston with a wink.

Lara spied one of the boys who had been talking to Margot. As he went past her table, she reached for him. "Can I ask you a question?" She was up out of her seat, the momentum of his movement taking her several steps.

The man turned around to face her. From the smell of him, he'd had quite a few drinks. "Sure, darlin'...anything."

"The woman I saw you with tonight. The one in the gold dress."

The boy smiled and Lara could see the overlap in his front two teeth. "Margo. Yeah, I don't know where she went to. I love those retro-looking woman, all Bettie Page." He winked at her and Lara was nearly toppled by the whiskey on his breath. "She a friend of yours?"

"Something like that," said Lara.

"I'd love to have her number."

Smiling, Lara started back to her table, calling over her shoulder, "I don't think she has a phone."

When she turned back toward her own table, both Audrey and Ben were staring at her. Gaston was still talking and it didn't sound like she'd missed much, but she was relieved. Someone else, drunk though he was, had seen Margot tonight. She *wasn't* hallucinating.

"It was quite the destination for the rich and famous at the time— particularly your 'Lost Generation,'" said Gaston, still on the subject of the painting. "According to Barrow, Josephine Baker, Gertrude Stein, Ernest Hemingway, Man Ray, and F. Scott Fitzgerald were all guests of Le Cirque Secret. Giroux was the only artist permitted to paint it, though, and that was significant."

As the dinner plates were placed and everyone focused on their surf and turf of salmon and filet, Lara considered her next question carefully. "Was it ever called the Devil's Circus, Mr. Favre?"

Mr. Favre met her eyes. "It was...and an accurate description of it, too, from what I've heard. Very bad things happened with that circus."

"Like what?" Ben was cutting his filet.

"Murders," said Favre between chews. "Men going missing."

"Well, that's right up your alley," said Audrey to Ben. "And you believe this legend, Louie?"

"I do," said Louie gravely. "I once knew people who had gone to it. They said it was quite a spectacle. Gruesome acts—much like the art of that time. But those who saw it said it was the most beautiful circus that had ever existed. Ah, what I wouldn't give to have seen it."

From what she'd read in Cecile's journal, Lara thought that Louie would have been a prime candidate to receive a ticket, especially if he would give anything to get one.

"You think Cecile was part of this strange circus?" Audrey laughed. "That's madness, Louie. You knew her. She wore khakis, for God's sake."

"Perhaps not." Gaston turned to Audrey, raising his finger. "I'm sorry, Audrey, I didn't have a chance to tell you. When I removed the frame and turned the painting over, the title was written on the back. It did not, in fact, mention a Cecile. Instead what was written was: SYLVIE ON THE STEED. Perhaps, Audrey, your grandmother was also called Sylvie?"

"No," said Audrey. "Never Sylvie. Always Cecile."

"Then perhaps this painting is not of Cecile Cabot."

Audrey and Lara looked at each other. Both of them were thinking the same thing. The painting resembled Cecile. *It had to be Cecile, didn't it?*

But then Lara recalled there had been a Sylvie in Cecile's journal. She was the trick rider and the daughter of Madame Plutard. Had they been mistaken?

Gaston shrugged. "Barrow would love to see the painting for himself. He is suggesting we visit." He leaned in close so that even Louie Favre could not hear. "This painting could be quite valuable. It could be worth eight or ten million dollars?"

"Really?" Lara met her mother's eyes. Like a lot of people who had Virginia farms, business was spotty and often funded out of old money that was drying up. Ten million dollars could change everything. She quickly considered what they could do with that sum. Quit running the station on a shoestring budget. Buy some new horses for her mother.

"He wants us to come to Paris?"

Audrey hesitated. "But she can't—"

"Paris?" This was the second time today that she was being summoned to Paris. This was no coincidence.

"Change of scenery…Paris…a little art mystery for us to solve. It might be fun, *non*?" Gaston raised his brow.

"Wine…almond croissants…ten million dollars." Lara nodded. "I'm in." She noticed that her mother had suddenly become very uncomfortable, shifting in her chair and tugging at her hair. "Are you okay, Mother?"

"I'm fine." Audrey looked anything but fine.

"*Bon*. I will email Barrow tonight," said Gaston.

After dinner, the Rivoli Circus Orchestra performed in the foyer of City Hall. The expansive stairs and balcony were lined with people sipping cocktails and dancing.

Ben and Lara were perched on the stairs watching partygoers. "Can I get you champagne?"

"I would like that," said Lara. She followed him down the stairs.

He put his finger up for her to wait one minute at the bottom and Lara watched him walk to the bar.

He returned with two glasses, and instead of handing one to her, he placed both glasses on a highboy and took her hand, leading her to the dance floor. She wrapped her arm around his neck and felt his body press against hers. Oh, how she'd wanted this night to be different. Ben was her closest confidant. Had she been confused by her feelings for him? Was she rebounding as her mother had suggested? No. Even now, dancing with him, there was a space for him. She just wasn't sure that it would be enough for him. Even now, he looked at her expectantly.

"You look far away tonight," said Ben.

She smiled. It was hard for her to hide anything from him. "I heard you're a terrible dancer."

"No," he said. "I'm a terrible waltzer and I cannot do the tango. I see you've been talking to Marla. She delights in telling people that I can't dance. And quit evading the question."

"I'm okay," she said. "Stop interrogating me."

"You look beautiful."

She closed her eyes. It was what Todd had said to her earlier, on the steps.

He leaned in, and Lara could smell his aftershave. "Can I tell you something that I've never told you? I mean, I wanted to tell you this so many times, but I just didn't know how to broach it."

"Sure." Her cheek was nearly touching his, and she whispered into his ear.

"It's a shame no one saw you," he said. "That day." He turned his lips, and she could feel the warmth of his breath in her hair. He didn't need to elaborate on what day he meant. She knew it was the day of her wedding. "You were breathtaking."

She recalled the scene as she marched out through the Gothic church doors. She pulled him close and just held him. It was such a raw admission from him. And that day was still such a wound to her that it was like a glue between them.

"Thank you," she whispered, more genuinely than she had ever said anything in her life. They danced that way for two songs, holding each other tightly, feeling the rhythm of each other's breath.

Finally, he took her hand and guided her out the door, down the steps, and up the block to her house. While she was glad to be leaving, Lara felt a weight tugging on her. She'd have to tell Ben Archer that she wasn't ready for this. They walked in silence, his hand placed in the small of her back. When they got to her gate, she could still hear the echoes of big-band sounds coming from the gala on the street below.

"'Moonlight Serenade.'"

"You know Glenn Miller?" There was more than a hint of admiration in the question.

"I am a true Renaissance man, Lara Barnes. You aren't the only one who knows music." He slid his hand in hers and led her through the gate, up the stairs to the porch swing.

"You most certainly are," she said, taking a seat. As they swung, the band's clarinet sound from another time competed with the sound of the breeze shuffling the leaves, the moths hitting the light, and a wind chime clinking off-key somewhere in the distance.

"I love the sounds of summer," she said.

"Lawn mowers," he added.

"Ice in glasses."

In the moonlight, she could see his eyes light up. She studied his face, loving the angle and the way the moon cast shadows on him.

"Can I tell you something?" She placed her fingers under the swing's seat to steady herself.

He gave her a disapproving look. After months of telling him everything, however minuscule, about Todd and her feelings, she knew the answer already.

"I thought I saw him tonight," she said, looking down at her dress, which was sweeping the floor with each swing. "In the crowd."

He was silent, then sighed. "Him?"

"Him," she confirmed.

"You saw him, like, I should call Doyle and investigate it?"

"No," said Lara sadly. "It wasn't real. I was mistaken."

"But you'd *wanted* to see him." His voice fell and he leaned back on the swing, groaning. "I knew this was too soon."

"I'm conflicted," said Lara. "I shouldn't have told you."

"Well, I wish you hadn't been thinking of him tonight, but no, I'm glad you were honest with me."

"I thought I was over him...and ready for this. I really did." They weren't saying his name—Todd—as though he wielded a power over both of them that his name would intensify.

"Oh, Lara," he said, pulling her to him. She leaned her head on his shoulder. "I don't think it's like a bout of the flu."

She put her hands over her face. "I'm so sorry. I wanted this night to be different."

After a few moments of silence, he got up from the swing, the sudden absence of his weight sending it sideways until she put her legs out to stop it. "I should go," he said.

Rising, she followed him to the edge of the porch, both wanting him to go so she could be alone to process each detail from tonight and yet not wanting him to leave, because she truly loved his company. "I had a lovely time with you tonight," she said. "I really did. It's just going to take me some time."

He took her hand and drew her near.

"Don't give up on me," she whispered. It had been so long since she'd touched anyone like this. "I get butterflies whenever I see you."

"And I with you." He kissed her softly on the side of her head, near her temple.

As he walked down the steps, Lara touched her neck, feeling it flushed, then placed her hand near her hairline.

No one had ever kissed her on her temple.

She watched him walk until he'd passed the Miltons' hedge. A few hours earlier and he might have crossed paths with Althacazur on the same street. Ben lingered near the hedge like he was going to turn around but seemed to change his mind, and then, he was gone.

15

Lara wasn't surprised to find Audrey on her doorstep the next morning. She'd watched her mother's face through dinner as Gaston discussed the painting and spoke of taking it to Paris to be evaluated by the historian. By the end of the dinner, she'd looked distracted and tense, tugging on her hair and adjusting a pretend crick in her neck.

She plowed through the door holding a paper grocery bag with a baguette sticking out of it. The groceries were a ruse, of course, her mother's way of easing into conversation over almond croissants and coffee. Hugo, Oddjob, and Moneypenny all came scampering leashless behind her, their nails clicking and sliding on the wood floors. Lara thought she heard one of them, likely Hugo because he always had to be first at everything, lose his footing on the newly polished wood and slide into the wall.

Lara followed her through the foyer and into the kitchen. Hers was an old kitchen that likely held a lot of memories of lavish parties in the 1920s and '40s. At the entrance to the kitchen was a door with a transom window, which Lara kept propped open, a throwback to the time when the house had a kitchen staff and no air-conditioning. Well, the house still didn't have air-conditioning, but the kitchen staff was long gone. The wood cabinets were dramatic floor-to-ceiling, with secret nooks like bread drawers and flour bins. Having the cabinets repainted a color called "limestone" had been one of her few splurges, along with replacing the old countertops with granite as well as updating the cabinet hardware and lighting. This was one of the finished rooms that gave Lara hope that the rest of the house could look glorious again. After refilling the water bowls, she placed them in front of the dogs, but they looked up like they expected more.

"Haven't you fed them?" The three were a perfect group of beggars.

"Of course I have," said Audrey, rustling through bags. "They know you harbor biscuits."

Lara opened the flour bin and pulled out the dog biscuits. They chomped loudly before settling to sun themselves in the bright morning sunlight streaming through the open windows.

"They had the most wonderful cherries at the farmers market today." Her mother placed various paper containers on the kitchen island that Lara had built herself. "I'm thinking pie."

"What did you think of the gala last night?"

Audrey looked around. "Well, I wondered if I might find Ben Archer still here this morning."

"No," she said, blushing. Lara walked over to the refrigerator and pulled open the door, grabbing half-and-half.

"So, this little idea of Gaston's is nuts. You aren't actually thinking of going to Paris, are you?" Audrey braced herself dramatically on the island. "That painting is worthless, Lara. I mean, I was going to tell him myself, but..."

There was a long silence while Lara poured two cups of coffee and slid one across the counter to her mother, like the last offering of peace before battle.

"But you decided to start with me, instead." Lara took a sip of her coffee. The brew was a little hot and she put it down on the counter to let it cool. "I *am* planning on going to Paris. If that painting is valuable, then a representative from the family should be there with it. Don't you think? Plus, I still have an airline ticket from my honeymoon that I need to use before October. The stars are aligning."

"Well, frankly, I'm concerned about you going to Paris."

"Why would you be concerned?" Lara laughed. "I'm thirty years old."

"It's not safe."

In the months since Todd disappeared, Lara continued to harbor suspicions that her mother knew more than she was telling. Now those suspicions were beginning to feel confirmed. "That painting could be worth millions."

"Or it's worthless." Audrey dismissed Lara with her hand.

"Gaston doesn't think so and he's an art expert."

"Then I'll go to Paris with Gaston, not you."

Lara inhaled, putting her hand on her hip and straightening her body. She decided the best approach was to say nothing.

After a good minute of silence, her mother finally spoke. "Say something."

Lara shrugged. "I have nothing to add. As much as it pains me to tell you, Mother, you've kept things from me." Her mother began to protest, but Lara put her hand up to stop her. "You'll deny it, of course, but we both know it. I'm going to Paris. End of discussion. If this is about Gaston, I don't need him to go with me. I can meet with Edward Binghampton Barrow the Fourth myself. It's our family's painting."

Audrey's nostrils flared. "What on earth have I kept from you? I...I told you that I don't know—"

"Nothing," said Lara, cutting her mother off sharply. "You've told me nothing."

"Because there is nothing to tell, Lara," said Audrey, taking a drink of her coffee, then setting the cup down on the counter with a thud. "You're beginning to sound crazy."

Audrey wasn't manipulative. For her mother to keep something from her this long, and to protest this much, meant that Audrey was frightened. And for Audrey to be frightened, it had to be something big. Combining this hunch with what Shane Speer had said to her at the circus and what the man had confirmed last night, Lara thought she'd try to bluff. "I know that she's trying to kill me." She stared confidently into her mother's eyes, not blinking.

Audrey nearly yelped, causing the dogs to lift their heads instantly. "Who told you?"

Lara's knees went weak. While she thought she was being clever, she really hadn't anticipated being correct. "The man at the circus."

"What *man* at the circus?" Audrey's eyes widened.

"The fortune-teller." In exchange for information, Lara had promised Althacazur that she would not tell her mother about him. She thought it wise to keep that promise.

Her mother visibly relaxed. "Oh, my dear, you cannot possibly think that poor teenaged boy was correct about *anything*. Hell, he wasn't even through puberty yet."

But Lara's bluff had worked. Someone *was* trying to kill her, and the comment about "the man" had upset her mother terribly. Lara just hadn't mentioned the right man: Althacazur.

"Of course he was correct. That's why you're here telling me not to go to Paris. Cut the bullshit, Mother, and start talking. You've never told me the truth about Todd. We both know it." Lara shrugged.

"Like what?"

Lara shrugged again, noncommittally, but didn't answer.

Audrey slid onto the counter stool, placing her hands down in front of her, as if steeling herself for what she was about to say next: "There is a spell that we must maintain to keep us safe."

"A spell?" Lara cocked her head. And then it occurred to her: All the unnatural perfection of the town. *It's a spell.* That made sense. It was the only thing, frankly, that made sense, and she couldn't believe that she hadn't realized it before.

"The women in our family have been enchanting a protective spell since 1935. When she was nine years old, my mother, Margot, was the first to cast it."

"Margot? Not Cecile?"

Audrey shook her head. "Apparently not, although I don't know why. After Mother was gone, I needed to keep it going. Cecile taught me how to do it. She'd seen Margot chant it enough times."

"I don't understand. Why does the town need a spell?"

"The *town* doesn't need a spell. *We* do. Kerrigan Falls simply benefits from the protective cloak we place over it. Cecile said that what she'd run away from in Paris would always hunt us without this spell. I have to reaffirm it every year."

Lara recalled what Althacazur had said to her last night: *The fabric of this quaint little community your family has built for you is beginning to tear apart. Without my help, I fear it could be the end for you.* This was the fabric he'd been talking about. "Let me guess. You do the spell on October ninth?"

She nodded gravely. "And it goes along fine, except one night every thirty years when the spell seems to come down for one night. Cecile stressed that the spell had to be done at eleven fifty-nine on October ninth...the words must cross over to the tenth, and you must be finished by twelve oh one."

"That's why you didn't want us getting married on that day."

Audrey closed her eyes, like she was thinking of something painful. "I simply wanted you to move the wedding to the spring. That is a dreadful date and I couldn't believe you chose it, but I swear that I don't know what happened to Todd, my dear. You need to believe me.

I just know that whatever happened to him, happened on *that* date, so it may have something to do with us, but I can't be sure. Cecile wasn't specific. *Ever.*" Audrey seemed annoyed at the thought of Cecile. "I always thought she was hiding something, so I guess I can understand your frustration with me."

Lara remembered how stubborn and secretive Cecile could be, but she knew there was more that Audrey was hiding from her. And it was about Althacazur. "Can I ask what drove grandmother Margot mad?"

Audrey took a sip of her coffee. "It was around the time her magic came in. Cecile said she was turning on radios, lighting the stove. My mother always wanted attention, so she'd often go out of her way with mischief to scare people. Then she announced that she'd seen a man standing in the field. He spoke to her. Mother was never the same after that."

Lara leaned back on the counter. "Have you seen him, too?"

"Have *you*?" Her mother's voice was pointed. She locked eyes with Lara.

Lara wasn't about to start confessing first, so she bent over the counter toward her mother, waiting for Audrey to reply. She'd endured a lifetime of her mother's secrets.

When Audrey realized that Lara was waiting for her, she began to speak. "I saw him the first time when I was seven years old. My magic had just come in, and Cecile was terrified that he'd come looking for me. He did, but I told him to go away," said Audrey with the sad, faraway smile that a distant memory brought her. "Cecile said magic had killed my mother, driven her mad. I saw the anguish on both Cecile's and my father's faces when they spoke of my mother, so when it began to happen to me, I wanted nothing to do with this legacy of madness, of magic. Althacazur visited me twice. Both times, I refused to speak to him. On the second visit he even brought my mother along with him."

"Margot?" Lara realized how cruel this must have been.

"She wasn't right, even then. Talking crazy." Audrey wiped her eyes with her hands and tried to clear off her mascara. "I was a child, Lara. I saw my *mother*—the woman I most wanted to see—and I ignored her. Do you know what that was like for a seven-year-old girl with no mother?"

Lara placed her hand over her mother's, thinking of Audrey as a little girl and the pair of them—Althacazur with his glasses and Margot with her parasol. "I'm so sorry."

"I'd never known her and yet, I let her go," said Audrey, "because I was so afraid of what she was—what I thought that I was becoming as well."

"What *we* are." Lara finished her sentence.

"Yes," said Audrey, clasping Lara's hands. "What *we* are."

"And what are we?" Lara recalled the Ouija board moving at the slumber party, opening locks on her grandfather's doors, and enchanting her wedding gown.

"I don't know," said Audrey. "I suppose the answers were there, I just didn't want them at the time. After Cecile died, it was too late, but she never wanted to talk about Paris. You might have more information in that journal than I ever wrangled out of her."

Lara went over to her briefcase and pulled out the journal. "You could be right about that." She handed her mother the translation. "There are a couple spots here where my French isn't so great, but it could be indicative of slang of the time that I don't understand."

Audrey pointed to the journal entry date as she reached into her purse and pulled out her reading glasses, studying Lara's notes. "This is incredible, Lara."

"I know you didn't think she'd kept one, but I do think it's Cecile's diary from when she lived in Paris," said Lara. "There is this rivalry between Cecile and her twin sister. There is also a third girl, Sylvie. She's the trick rider."

"*Sylvie on the Steed?*" Audrey considered it, then let the idea go. "Cecile never mentioned she had a sister, certainly not a twin."

"I think Cecile didn't mention a lot of things." Lara flipped through the pages. "Don't you think it's strange that of all the professions that Cecile might have chosen, she started a circus?"

"It certainly wasn't a business that a woman ran back then, but circuses *were* places where women thrived, especially after the war. Still, I get your point: It's not a business you'd seek out."

"Unless she'd grown up in one," said Lara, handing her mother the book. "The woman in this book lived and worked in a very, very strange circus."

"Le Cirque Secret," said Audrey. She reached over and touched Lara on the cheek. "I hated keeping things from you."

"I know you did," said Lara, and she understood, because she hated not telling her mother that she'd also seen Althacazur, but the stakes were too high. "Something about this diary is off. The Cecile in this diary is not a trick rider, she's a trapeze artist—rather magical, too—a bit like us. The answers we need are in Paris."

"If you're going to leave Kerrigan Falls, then you need to learn a few protection spells."

"I've traveled a lot without needing a spell," said Lara, laughing. "I went to Europe, on the road with Dad."

Audrey looked guilty. "No, my dear, you did not." She twirled her cup intently. "I know that everyone thinks that I didn't want Le Cirque Margot, so it closed. That isn't the truth. I *did* want the circus, but Cecile had gone through so much with Mother's madness, claiming she was being tormented while on the road by a pair of daemons— a man and a woman—the woman threatening to kill her and the man trying to help her. It got bad—really bad—in Gaffney, where Margot claimed that an angel with white hair had given her a protection spell. Well, of course Cecile thought it just another of Mother's crazy ramblings, until Mother said the incantation. Cecile said the birds stopped singing immediately and the wind began to stir, leaves fell from trees, flowers wilted—you get the idea. Then, in some crazy attempt to test it, she walked into traffic."

Lara's eyes were wide. "And?"

"Traffic parted for her." Audrey shivered. There was a soft breeze coming through the kitchen and the Airedales raised their heads to sniff at it. "Margot claimed that she was told to recite the spell each year on October ninth for her protection, but that it worked better if she stayed in one place. Something about Mother's tales of a white-haired lady unnerved Cecile to the point that she believed it. When I came of age, she made me recite it to stay safe. But Margot was right. It didn't work as well outside Kerrigan Falls. It offers some protection, but it needs to be administered daily if we're not here. When Cecile was getting up in years, she began to think this 'angel' didn't want us on the road with the circus, especially after the accident that I had with my horse."

"What accident?" Lara had heard all the tales from the old performers at Le Cirque Margot. There had been no mention of an accident involving her mother.

"My horse, Belle, stepped into a strange divot that came out of nowhere during one of my shows; I toppled over her and nearly broke my neck. Belle broke her leg and had to be put down while I watched."

"So *she* closed the circus."

"I didn't want her to, but she insisted. I think the old circus folks took my horse business as a sign that I'd turned my back on my legacy, but that wasn't true. I promised Cecile that I wouldn't rekindle any talk of a troupe, especially after you were born. When you went on the road with your father, I showed up in every city you toured. You just didn't know I was there. I said the spell every night, faithfully. Even then, you still had the accident with the guitar wire that nearly electrocuted you."

"Oh, that was just a freak occurrence, Mother." Lara could still see the frayed wire and the puddle of water, which had no real origin—it couldn't be chalked up to rain or to any leak from the amphitheater's ceiling. Still, the charge had gone through her hand. When she turned over her palm, it was still there, like a stigmata scar.

"No." Audrey shook her head. "You were nearly killed onstage in front of five thousand people. Even Jason was spooked—that's why he's never invited you on tour with him again."

"What about my summer in France and Italy?"

"I can work wonders with hair and sunglasses. Even then, you were nearly struck by a moped in Rome."

Lara leaned heavy on the counter. "That was—"

"—another accident?" Audrey cut in. "We're safe here. Mother claimed it was a daemon of some sort trying to kill us—a woman."

"Do you know who?"

Audrey shook her head. "But you are constantly reminding me that you're thirty and you can take care of yourself, so it's time I teach you what we really do."

They walked into Lara's living room and Audrey took a seat on the floor, settling herself in front of the fireplace on the area rug. "I just need one candle, but you have to make sure that you have one with you always. Each night, you must do this."

Lara found a candle and handed it to her mother.

"Perfect," said Audrey. "You don't have to be picky. The fire binds the spell."

Watching her mother run her hand over the flame again and again, Lara worried that the hand would burn, but it appeared to take on a sheen. "Yours will do this, too," said Audrey.

Bracatus losieus tegretatto.
Eh na drataut bei ragonne beate.

The door blew open and a gust of wind hit them. Her mother smiled.

"Done," said Audrey. "Now sit. I have some chants to teach you."

PART 2

THE TRIP TO PARIS

16

While they waited at the gate for the flight to Paris, Gaston kept a tight grip on Lara's carry-on suitcase, which now contained the wrapped painting *Sylvie on the Steed*. He had chosen not to use an art handling service, preferring to keep the painting with them during the flight. Freed from its heavy frame, the painting was now small enough to fit into an international carry-on bag. Gaston had used acid-free packing paper to fill the hard-sided suitcase along with a healthy mixture of tissue and then bubble wrap.

Lara hadn't been to Paris since the summer after her sophomore year in college. Now she knew that she hadn't been alone—her mother had traveled along with her that summer. She'd written down the incantation to keep her safe and purchased two small candles, which were now stored in her bag. While she hated to admit it, she was nervous—and a little frightened—knowing she might be in danger. In the end, Audrey had toyed with joining them, and Lara had hoped her mother could make the trip, but she had an expectant mare and decided to stay behind. The trip would be short—only forty-eight hours. They'd see Edward Binghampton Barrow soon after landing and give the scholar a day to decide whether it was a real Giroux or not.

As they boarded, Lara took the suitcase from Gaston's hand, pushing her carry-on toward him to take instead. It was *her* painting, her family's potentially *valuable* painting. Gaston made a move to take the handle from her and she shot him a look. "I've got it."

They landed at Charles de Gaulle Airport the following morning. Knowing their hotel rooms wouldn't be available, they took a taxi directly to the Sorbonne's Institut National d'Histoire de l'Art on Rue Vivienne on the Right Bank, Second Arrondissement.

It was strange traveling with Gaston, a man she barely knew. He drank a steady stream of espressos and was prone to pacing while on his phone, securing art with the intensity of a stock trader.

As she rode through Paris, Kerrigan Falls felt so far away, and her thoughts turned to Althacazur. He had told her that she wouldn't need to contact him—he'd find her. So far in her life, he'd been able to do just that. Lara realized how much she'd needed this diversion. Althacazur had compared Todd to his lost love, Juno, and described them as mere illusions. While he indicated that he held the answers she was looking for, in her heart Lara felt the answer had been inside her for nine months now. She'd just needed to be somewhere else for a little context to be able to admit that Todd wasn't coming back, because he couldn't.

She was deep in thought when the taxi slowed in front of a tall cement building and Gaston reached into his wallet and paid the driver.

In the French Arts Section, they found room 313 belonging to Edward Binghampton Barrow IV. The man who answered the door was not gangly, out of shape, and dressed in tweed, as Lara expected, but rather a man with brown skin and close-cropped hair that was graying at the temples. He was slight and thin and dressed in black pants with a crisp white shirt, horn-rimmed glasses, and Gucci loafers. That's where the fine detailing stopped. Much like fossils, all of his plants were dead and seemed to have been trying to flee out the window in search of sun or rain before they petrified in their terra-cotta pots. His office held hundreds of books organized in haphazard, thigh-high stacks, several with deep curves that threatened to topple, like dominoes. Any visitor wanting to avoid disaster walked sideways to the lone chair.

"Teddy," said Gaston, referring to Barrow's mother's embarrassing moniker of Teddy Bear-row.

"Boucher! You haven't changed a bit." Barrow pulled Gaston into a tight, almost violent embrace that seemed to rattle the slight Frenchman.

"Nor you, my friend." Gaston turned to Lara. "This is Mademoi-selle Lara Barnes. Lara without a *u*."

"My mother was a fan of *Doctor Zhivago*," said Lara, feeling the need to explain the odd spelling.

"Lara," said Barrow, emphasizing the *a* in her name in a clipped upper-crust English accent. Barrow's smile was quick, and his hands were warm and large. "It is wonderful to meet you. Let me guess, I am not what you expected?" He turned his head expectantly, waiting for her response.

Lara wasn't quite sure how to answer. "True, I expected more tweed."

"She said your name was ridiculous," said Gaston wryly, rubbing his chin as he studied his phone.

"So when did you two last see each other?"

Barrow looked at Gaston, and they both seemed to blank. "What has it been? Twenty years?"

"Nineteen eighty-five, I think," agreed Gaston.

"And *neither* of you say you've changed?" Lara raised her eyebrow. "Liars."

The two men looked at each other and laughed. "*Un peu*," said Bar-row, bringing his fingers together.

"We are great liars," agreed Gaston.

Dismissing the small talk, Barrow rubbed his hands together. His worktable was in disarray, and he began clearing it. "I have been waiting all week to see the painting." He looked at them, disappointed to see only luggage trailing behind them. "Did you bring it?"

Gaston lifted the suitcase onto the table and unzipped it. Removing the wrap, he slid the canvas out and presented it to Barrow like a swaddled newborn.

Lara leaned over the portrait while Barrow donned gloves and began to carefully unwrap each layer. If Lara closed her eyes, she could almost hear the audience whispering and murmuring to each other while the horse galloped around the arena. The sophisticated dress of the seated patrons was a reminder that the circus in Paris during this time was not the same as its traveling American carnival cousins, like the Margot or even the Rivoli. Here women wore pearls and furs. Circuses in France were considered art and were treated as such. While not as prestigious as a trip to the opera, a night at the circus was still considered a glamorous evening out.

"Beautiful job removing the frame, Gaston," said Barrow, taking the painting in his gloved hands.

"It was a later frame," said Gaston. "Likely the 1940s. Monstrous bastard."

"Ugly, too," added Lara.

Barrow spun around to another table with a lamp, just missing a stack of art books that sat on the floor. He pulled out a loupe and began to study the painting carefully, examining every edge and adjusting the light in places. Lara held her breath. If he didn't think this was a real Giroux, then her Paris adventure was over barely thirty minutes after it began. Lara blinked, trying to keep her heavy lids open after the flight. The room was silent as Barrow turned the light as he went.

She wondered if they should have dealt with the painting tomorrow, allowing themselves to rest for a day while they held on to the magical idea that they might be in possession of a famous missing masterpiece.

In the corner was a box of hardback books. Lara picked up the top one. *Émile Giroux: A Perspective* by Edward Binghampton Barrow. While Lara had been a music major in college, she'd minored in art history. Yet until she heard Gaston talk about Giroux, she couldn't recall seeing any of his works. Then she spied *The Vampire*. There wasn't an art student in the world who didn't recognize *The Vampire*.

Thumbing through the book, the photos of Giroux's work showed a range of styles. His early paintings right out of school were classic and traditional. Then Giroux migrated toward cruder paintings, longer legs, elongated heads. The work was rich and vibrant—the colors leaping off the page—yet Lara didn't care for them as much as Giroux's earlier work. She kept flipping the pages as Giroux shifted to an attempt at cubism. Here, Lara thought he excelled. His portraits were deeply angled, exaggerated, yet displayed perfect perspective. The subjects were close-up. The deep angles were shaded with objects. Inside a cheekbone or a crease of the eye were tiny symbols that represented the moment, the time, or the subject. The paintings were intricate, textured, yet beautiful. Lara could see that his color choices were either tightly coordinated or elegantly contrasted. The final folio of photos showed Giroux—a striking man with long brown hair in a style that looked like he couldn't be bothered to cut it. He had light round eyes and small pursed lips; his skin was pale. The photo of him, slouching in an uncomfortable chair, head cocked and resting in his hand, was taken by Man Ray. The date: April 8, 1925.

The artist was dressed in brown, his clothes warm and worn. For a poor artist, Lara imagined how cold April could be in Paris. A smile formed at the corner of her mouth as she recalled the journal entry where Cecile described all of the men in Montparnasse wearing brown jackets. Her description of the man in this photo had been so accurate that he could have stepped right out of her journal.

Seeing him, Lara wanted *Sylvie on the Steed* to be his creation. He looked dreamy and romantic, worthy of painting Cecile. She'd brought the journal with her, finding it hard to be away from it. Now that she was in Paris, she felt it was almost guiding her, Cecile's voice beckoning her on. With her free time, she'd planned on retracing her great-grandmother's steps—touring the cafés of Montparnasse, the markets at Rue Mouffetard and the Bois de Boulogne—places where Cecile had stood and lived.

A steady tick of the clock was the only sound in the room. Barrow took a long time studying the EG signature before he turned the painting over to look at the back, running his hand over the wood frame that shaped the canvas. He tilted *Sylvie on the Steed* under the light, scanning each inch of the edge of the picture.

Gaston had begun to whistle, and both Lara and Barrow looked up at him, annoyed.

"Well?" Gaston leaned over the table, joining Barrow.

"You were right. The signature looks correct, although it is not perfect, but the canvas and the painting style are pure Giroux. I've seen this exact canvas type and paint in every one of his other works."

"But?" Lara dreaded what was coming next. There was something in his voice.

"Well, while there were rumors that in the year before he died, Giroux had been a frequent guest at Le Cirque Secret and that three paintings had been commissioned, the problem is that all of them *are* missing, so sadly I have nothing to compare this painting to. The lore around these paintings is high, so the scrutiny it would face will be great. Without another verified painting from the series as a reference, I'm purely going on dating and the materials used. *But* on first glance, those things match up. If this were to be one of the missing paintings, I cannot tell you what a huge find this would be in the art world. It will just take time to verify it."

"*All* of the paintings are missing?" She put the biography back in the box where she'd found it.

"You haven't told her?" Barrow looked at Gaston, shocked.

Gaston patted his friend on the back. "You, my friend, are the expert on Giroux and the occult. I thought you could do it greater justice."

"I'll start at the beginning," said Barrow, his voice animated. "Le Cirque Secret is a longtime legend in Paris. From oral history, we think it existed for two years—1924 through 1926—but no physical evidence of the circus's existence remains."

Lara recalled the elaborate posters, tickets, and memorabilia of Le Cirque Margot that still hung in the Kerrigan Falls Historical Society office. "Surely *something* exists."

Barrow shook his head gravely. "It has been the material lacking in my research on Giroux. The lore was that guests would receive a special ticket by delivery for the night's performance. People went to the location printed on the ticket, only to find that nothing was there— just an empty field or abandoned courtyard." He paused dramatically. "Until there *was* something. The circus would appear out of nowhere. If you had a ticket in your possession, you saw it in front of you. Legend has it, however, that if you were standing next to someone without a ticket, they couldn't see anything and thought you were mad."

At the dinner table the other night, Louie Favre had told roughly the same story. From reading Cecile's diary, she felt that the *wicked tickets* Cecile had described were the culprit. Elements of what Cecile had written matched this story.

Gaston shrugged. "Well, it *was* the Jazz Age, Teddy."

"He means they were all drunk," said Barrow, rolling his eyes. "This one here is a nonbeliever."

"They were also trying to outdo each other, so it could have been some cheap carnival in Bois de Boulogne," said Gaston. "You have to admit, it might have just been some stage magic."

"You think they were exaggerating?" Barrow looked over at Gaston, offended.

"Things just don't appear out of nowhere," said Gaston.

From experience, Lara knew that they did. Suddenly a wave of exhaustion hit her. While Gaston had slept soundly on the airplane with an eye mask and earplugs, she had tried to read, then watched the movie, and then ate the morning croissant with a paper cup of coffee, never sleeping a wink due to the excitement of this adventure.

Barrow took off his glasses. "Normally, I agree with you, Gaston, but there were enough people who said they attended the circus. Something *was* there. They all described the same thing, yet there is no actual, *physical proof* of its existence. No promotional posters, tickets, or photos. There were no permits for it to be in the city. The thought was that the circus moved so as not to pick up notice from the police. No records whatsoever other than word of mouth and small snippets written in passing in biographies—and I have collected *every* one of them."

"No photos, really?" Lara knew she had seen countless photos of Ernest Hemingway and F. Scott Fitzgerald in Paris. If this circus had been so famous, surely someone had snapped a picture of it.

Barrow pointed his glasses at *Sylvie on the Steed.* "When I was writing Giroux's biography, many scholars told me the paintings had never existed at all. Your painting may be the greatest proof of the existence of Le Cirque Secret yet."

But it wasn't just the painting. Lara reached into her messenger bag and pulled out the envelope with the old journal. "I don't think the painting is the only proof of its existence."

Gaston looked puzzled. Lara hadn't told him about the journal.

Barrow touched the envelope tentatively, sliding the book out.

"Here." Lara handed him her written notes. "It's what I've been able to translate, but some of the pages are in bad condition. It's a journal. I think it may be my great-grandmother's journal. It tells the story of a strange circus, similar to what you just described." She pointed to the warped and faded paper. "It might be nothing."

"Looks like water damage of some sort," said Barrow. "I have some software that can enhance this." He touched it tenderly. "Where did you get it?"

"My family owned a circus in America called Le Cirque Margot. After it closed, a lot of the people went to work for the Rivoli Circus in Montreal. The other night, I was at one of the Rivoli's performances and someone handed this to me," said Lara. That the "someone" had been a monkey named Mr. Tisdale was information that Lara decided to omit. "It appears to be from 1925. It matches the story that you just told me."

"The Rivoli Circus out of Montreal?" Barrow's eyes lit up.

"You've heard of it?" She leaned forward.

"I have," said Barrow. "I know it well. I've attended their performances over the years."

"Take it," said Lara. "You might be able to confirm that it is from 1925. I have my copy of the notes. You might be able to translate a few of the things I couldn't." She opened up the diary and showed him a few notes on the pages.

"Why don't we finish this discussion over lunch?" Gaston looked over at Lara and seemed to read her mind. She was starved. "Hopefully our hotel rooms will be ready after that."

Barrow made a copy of Lara's journal translation before sliding the original back in the envelope and placing it in the locked safe along with the wrapped painting. "I know a great spot for lunch," said Barrow. "We can finish our discussion there."

As the trio walked up Rue de Richelieu to a little restaurant tucked behind Opéra-Comique, Lara was so exhausted that she felt like she was staggering. With its cozy red velvet banquettes and low chandeliers, the restaurant looked like it had remained frozen in time from the Belle Époque period. Any moment, Lara expected women to arrive in velvet dresses with their hair pinned up and men in waistcoats. Vintage opera costumes and photos of opera stars decorated the walls. With its atmosphere, Lara imagined the place was a delight in the winter.

The waitress walked by with a chalkboard displaying the lunch specials. Barrow ordered the carpaccio de Saint-Jacques followed by the côte de boeuf, and Gaston the snails and the turbot. Lara chose a "tiramisu" of tomatoes with Parmesan and chicken ravioli, which consisted of two large pasta sheets formed into one giant raviolo containing shredded chicken smothered in an onion-and-cream sauce topped with the floral taste of thyme. All three had wine—something Lara didn't typically drink at lunch. Barrow chose a Bordeaux, Gaston a Sancerre, and Lara a Meursault, the rare, oaky wine produced by a commune in Côte de Beaune.

While they waited for the wine to arrive, Barrow skimmed the copy of Lara's journal translation. Pushing the paper aside, Barrow took off his glasses and rubbed his face.

"So, what do you think?" She sensed that he couldn't wait for her and Gaston to leave so he could devour the journal and her notes. He kept coming back to it, pulling it over to refer to it and then pushing it away toward the salt and pepper shakers.

"I am speechless, Ms. Barnes," said Barrow. "You don't know how long I have searched for answers on these missing paintings. I believe it is not an exaggeration to say that I am the foremost scholar on Giroux's work."

"Modest," said Gaston, chuckling as he tore off a piece of bread and pointed it at Barrow. "But true."

"In my book, I was forced to write that while the paintings might exist, they could also be hearsay; stories people told. This could be the final, missing chapter of Giroux's life and work. His life—and my scholarship, frankly—is not complete without The Ladies of the Secret Circus. Jacques Mourier, the writer at *Le Figaro*, was the only journalist to attempt to investigate the existence of Le Cirque Secret. He received a ticket to one performance and wrote the only existing article about the circus for the paper."

Lara recalled the article in Cecile's journal. Sylvie had read the article to her while they were at the market at Rue Mouffetard. Taking the notes from Barrow's side of the table, she shuffled them to find the entry. "Here." She pushed the notes at him. "They reference his article in the journal."

He read the pages, rubbing his neck in disbelief. "Poor Mourier drove himself crazy trying to get another ticket just so he could see it again. The performance had left him with more questions. Who ran it? How did it work? The police didn't know. The city of Paris didn't know. Mourier said that he saw the ladies of the circus out in Montparnasse frequently, but they would never discuss the circus with him or anyone else. And then, of course, there were the disappearances."

"*Disappearances?*" Lara's throat caught and she drank some water. At the gala, Louie Favre had mentioned the disappearances. Peter Beaumont and then Todd had gone missing. Was there a connection?

"Each time the circus showed up somewhere, dozens of men

went missing. Mourier thought that is why it kept moving, avoiding authorities. He even considered that a serial killer was working at the circus—either that or a ritual killing—but without proof of the circus, they couldn't connect the disappearances to it. In the end, Mourier might have been onto something, because the disappearances stopped when the circus did." Barrow lifted his glass and looked out at the street. "I have to tell you. Part of me is apprehensive about getting my hopes up again. The pursuit of this circus can drive you mad."

The wine arrived quickly, followed by their entrées.

"Do you remember what Zelda Fitzgerald said about the Secret Circus?" Gaston sipped his wine. "That after the performance she left through the mouth of the Devil. She turned around to take one last look and there was nothing but the cold night air." He raised his eyebrow. "I read that somewhere?"

"My book, you bastard," laughed Barrow. "You read it in *my* book. Patrons entered through a giant Devil's mouth—it was all high theater. There were rumored to be animals turned into humans and vice versa, spell casting, devils. But you have to remember, magic and the occult shows were all the rage in the 1920s. Harry Houdini would die right around that time, having spent his last years debunking other popular occultists, from spirit painters to mediums."

"But you have to admit, my friend," said Gaston. "It all sounds crazy."

"Look, I'm not saying that it couldn't have been a tall tale," admitted Barrow. "Liquor flowed freely then. The first war had left a city full of old people and women. So many young men had been killed. Paris had changed. Montparnasse was near the Sorbonne, so rent was cheap there, and the run-down first-floor apartments were easy for sculptors to get their art in and out, but Picasso was the first *real* artist to leave Montmartre and come to a studio on Boulevard Raspail. Then the Americans flocked here...jazz...writers and artists and even more alcohol. Prohibition was alive and well in America, but not here, and it was relatively cheap to live in Paris. The elements that created the Second World War were a slow drumbeat in the background. A Devil's Circus? Yes, I could see how it could be a lovely romantic notion for a city such as this one had become."

"You've got to admit, Teddy," said Gaston. "It could have just been a surrealist performance circus. They used mirrors or mesmerized them all. The joke could have been on the audience. I mean, I don't know how they pulled it off, but you have to admit it *is* possible. Even the journal could be a fictional account." He pointed toward the notes.

Barrow shook his head violently. "I've considered that. Mourier didn't believe it was performance art, like so many of the artists did at the time. In fact, he was the one who coined it the Devil's Circus in his article." Barrow pointed a fork at Gaston. "When Giroux died mysteriously after completing the final painting of the circus, Mourier was convinced that it had been his association with it—and the ladies—that killed him."

Gaston grinned at Barrow, conceding. "It's a real fucking Giroux, isn't it? You finally found one of the missing Giroux paintings, my friend!"

"In my estimation, yes," said Barrow, leaning in. "The canvas on your painting is the same, down to the wraps and the hardware of the other ones from that time period. I could set that painting next to another one and you could see the blue he used. He loved muted turquoise and it wasn't an easy color to paint, but he used it in all his works. That it isn't finished is also an intriguing detail giving credence to it being one of his final paintings."

"To think it was hanging in the hallway next to the powder room all these years," said Lara.

Barrow laughed. "So many valuable paintings were in barns or in attics, especially after the Second World War." He leaned in. "If you leave the painting with the institute, I will give you a definitive answer. I don't know your plans for the painting's future, Ms. Barnes, but I do know that the Musée d'Orsay would be a fine home for it should we all agree that it's authentic."

While Lara had thought about parting with the painting, she wasn't prepared to make a decision this fast; plus, she'd need to consult with Audrey. Gaston, sensing her unease, tapped his fingers on the table. "I don't think Lara has thought much about the painting's future yet. This is all so new."

"Well, Gaston," said Barrow. "I'm not sure carting it around is exactly the best plan for what might be a French national treasure."

The weight of this hit Lara suddenly. "How valuable is it, really?"

Barrow shrugged. "In one of the auction houses, ten million, especially if it is proved to be one of his final paintings."

"You might consider keeping it locked in the institute's vault, not that the Tumi you're carting around isn't doing a wonderful job of securing it." Barrow winked at Gaston.

During a breakfast of croissants and café au laits, Barrow had called saying another Giroux specialist was excited at the prospect of seeing the painting and would be driving up from Nice that morning. Barrow had also been working most of the night enhancing Lara's translation of the diary, adding to and fixing missing entries.

"I wonder if there are more journals?" Gaston settled into reading her notes.

"I don't know," said Lara, lying. While Althacazur had promised her a scavenger hunt where she'd find more, so far there had been nothing.

After he'd finished reading, Gaston flagged the waiter for another espresso. "I am going to see a few art contacts up in Saint-Denis. The art is cheap up there. Would you care to join me?"

"Nah, I'm going to try Père Lachaise instead." The last time Lara was in Paris, she'd failed to see Jim Morrison's grave. Her father wouldn't forgive her if she didn't make the pilgrimage on this trip. After that, she'd thought about going to the Rue Mouffetard and the cafés that Cecile mentioned in her diary.

"Jim Morrison is so touristy." Gaston frowned. "Maybe go see Sartre's grave instead?"

"Wrong cemetery," said Lara. "But I may do that when I'm over at Montparnasse. I know, I'm *so* American." She looked at him gravely.

"There is hope for you yet. At least see Proust while you're at Lachaise."

"That," she said, grabbing a *pain au chocolat* on her way out, "I will do."

As she rode down the boulevards in her taxi, she could smell the linden trees blooming above her, the sweet smell reminiscent of honeysuckle. The driver let her out at the Père Lachaise entrance gate on the Boulevard de Ménilmontant. After consulting the map, Lara walked up the hill on the cobblestone path through the thick canopy of trees, weaving among old stones with their layers of moss and untended tombstones covered in weeds. After winding around, she made a hard right and followed a group of people who were clearly Americans and about her father's age, so she took a bet which grave they were visiting. Within moments, she found a group gathered in front of the modest headstone of James Douglas Morrison, lead singer of the Doors. The site was overflowing with a number of trinkets, flowers, and photos of the musician in front of his concrete slab, causing the cemetery to require a barricade.

The Lizard King was one of her father's great music idols, and that legacy had been passed down to her. Jason Barnes was one of the true anchors of her life. While her mother was a reminder of who she was—the daughter of a famous family of circus owners—her father was the catalyst to show her who she could become. Without him, she never would have had the courage to buy a radio station. For both of them, music was always the door to where they could go next. It still pained her to think of the way he'd looked at her the other night as she'd played Peter Beaumont's song.

As a kid, Lara recalled riding around with him in his old pickup truck to see a widow about a vintage guitar. Jason was always on the hunt for something, usually related to music. In those days, Lara followed him around like a bad shadow. This particular widow greeted them at the door in her housecoat and curlers, then led them through a maze of boxes and too-big furniture. As they navigated the tumbledown house that smelled of piss and old newspapers, Lara stuck close by her father, clutching his hand until her fingers went numb. At a clearing in the clutter, the woman presented Jason with a battered black guitar case.

While everything about the house was decayed, her father popped the case, and tucked in the worn red velvet was the most beautiful and well-tended guitar that Lara had ever seen. Lacquered and black with a big silver shield on the front, this instrument—as Lara would learn—was known as a resonator guitar. What she was looking at was, in fact, a 1937 Dobro. Her father seemed to sway at the sight of the instrument before he rubbed his hands together and coaxed it from its velvet cradle. He placed it on his lap, adjusted it briefly, and borrowed a worn finger pick from inside the case—one the guitar knew well. Jason didn't even need to tune the guitar first, just wanting to hear what the instrument sounded like. When her father played the first few notes, Lara fell in love. It was a deep metal sound, rich yet spare, and she could hear the physical transitions from the strings and the melancholy sound of the minor chords. Her father's smile told her the guitar would be going home with them that day.

As they drove down the dirt path out of the house, her father looked back at the guitar case. "You know about Robert Johnson?"

Lara shook her head.

"Robert Johnson had been an okay guitar player in Mississippi, getting gigs in juke joints and bars, but he was nothing great until he went away to Chicago and came back like a year later with skills he didn't have before."

"Maybe he practiced." Lara was sure of things in those days, and practicing had been drilled into her head from her mother and Cecile.

From riding horses to playing the piano, they believed in the power of practicing.

"Maybe so," said Jason. "But the legend said that he'd gone to the crossroads in Clarksdale, Mississippi, and sold his soul to the Devil to play so well. Guitars are mysterious things, Lara. The strings hold things; so does the instrument. The man who owned that guitar—well, his energy is still in that instrument. I only want to try to honor it."

"So it's haunted?" Lara's eyes were wide. She chewed on the end of her ponytail, an occasional habit to quell the nerves.

"I guess so, in a way," he said, pulling down his aviator sunglasses and adjusting the truck's sun flap.

Like an artifact in a museum, that guitar still sat in the radio station, along with ten others, including Rickenbackers, Gibsons, and Fenders.

Morrison's own father had purchased a headstone for his son. Lara read the Greek inscription—KATA TON DAIMONA EAYTOY—which means "according to his own daemon" or "true or faithful to his own spirit," depending upon how much lore you wanted to attach to it. Much like the music legend of Robert Johnson, another idea that circulated for years was that, having faked his own death, Jim Morrison was still alive somewhere. These were great stories, but she wasn't sure either of them had much truth. It was funny really; if anyone should have been a believer after all she'd seen, it should have been her. She took a picture of the grave, for her father.

From there, Lara walked up the hill toward section 85 to see Marcel Proust's grave, noticing the broken columns of people who died violently, usually young. As she turned left on Avenue Transversale, one of the main tree-lined boulevards of the cemetery, she saw something moving out of the corner of her eye. Turning slowly, she pretended to be consulting a paper in her hand. There standing fifty feet behind her was a woman with a low blond ponytail, bangs that looked to be a wig, and cat's-eye sunglasses. When Lara turned, the woman immediately attempted to look occupied. Lara glanced to her right, but there was nothing behind her. Something about the woman's stance suggested purpose, not a leisurely stroll. Lara thought she must be getting paranoid, so she continued to walk up the hill toward the crematorium at a faster clip, winding around the random headstones, then the writer Molière's grave, before ducking into the row early and making a fast right turn that led in a circle down the hill and took her back to Jim Morrison's grave.

Tucking behind a tall obelisk gravestone, Lara discovered that the woman had also made the same hard right turn and appeared to be searching for her along the trail. The peacefulness of the cemetery was now broken as Lara started down the hill, climbing among the gravestones, staying low so the woman wouldn't spot her. She was sorry she hadn't gotten a better look at her, but wasn't sure it was worth the risk to try to do so. At the bottom of the trail, Lara was dumped back out onto the main boulevard. She made an immediate left, heading back toward the front entrance, using the rows like a maze. When she got down to the front entrance, she turned to see that the woman was about two hundred yards behind her and walking at a near run. She wasn't going crazy. This woman *was* following her, and she now knew that Lara was aware of her. This realization only seemed to embolden her.

She is coming for you. Was this the woman Shane Speer and Althacazur had warned her about?

Once she was through the gates, a sudden adrenaline rush kicked in and Lara ran down Boulevard de Ménilmontant. As she stopped for breath, she could see that the woman was trying to keep pace, but she'd had a good head start. Ignoring her pounding lungs, Lara started up again, picking up her pace in a steady run down Avenue de la République, dodging and ducking around crowds of people. She stopped and bought a hat and T-shirt, changing into them as she ran, and tried to blend in with a flock of tourists. Craning her neck, Lara could see that the woman was still on her trail, but the quick costume change had worked—at least for now.

She ducked into the kitchen of a café. Catching her breath, Lara realized that everything Audrey had said was true. The faulty guitar wire, the scooter in Rome—all of it had been designed to kill her. A tightness started in her throat, and recalling the words her mother had made her memorize, Lara began to chant them, almost choke them out:

Bracatus losieus tegretatto.
Eh na drataut bei ragonne beate.

It was just as Audrey had described. Despite it being a sweltering day, a heavy breeze rolled down the boulevard. Trees began to shed their leaves, the lindens sending a sweet perfume past her. Rather than relying solely on the magic, Lara searched for an escape.

She ran to the traffic circle. Coming down the hill, she saw the woman spy her and pick up her pace to catch Lara. Remembering what Margot had done, Lara considered the cars circling then took a deep breath before darting in front of traffic. As her foot left the curb, she realized just how risky this was, but she trusted the magic. The cars had to stop. She took off running, drivers swerved and slammed on their brakes to avoid her, and she was able to cut across four lanes. From over her shoulder she saw that the woman had gotten caught in the tangle of traffic. Lara turned down another street and ran past a tall iron gate, chanting quietly under her breath as she looked around for the woman. She stopped so suddenly she could hear her shoes squeak. Her lungs were burning, and she wasn't sure she could run much more without a break.

An old man with Coke-bottle glasses looked up from sweeping an empty courtyard. He noticed that she was breathing heavily and looked panicked. Quickly, he motioned for her to come toward the gate, opening the door a crack. Looking behind her, Lara didn't see a taxi; nor were there any Métro signs in the area. The man's offer was as good as any. As she heard the gate clank behind her, she wondered if this was another illusion she'd just conjured, but the gate felt real, so she shut it tightly behind her.

Wordlessly, the man pointed toward a converted railcar that sat parked in the otherwise vacant courtyard. A railcar? Lara quickly stepped up into the car and shut the door behind her, crouching down near an open window, a cool breeze rustling the white curtain. The woman ran past the gate as the man continued to sweep. From her vantage point, Lara could see the ponytailed blonde double back to ask the man something in French. Lara's heart sank. Had this been a trap?

The man nodded, saying "*Oui*" to something. Lara's breath caught. She looked around the cramped railcar, wondering where she could go if she needed to escape. The windows might open wide enough to send her out the back, since both doors opened to the front. Crouching down by the table, she began chanting again in a whisper. She watched as the man pointed across the street, indicating that Lara had cut through the park. Satisfied, the woman ran in that direction.

Sinking into the seat, Lara closed her eyes and exhaled. So it *was* true: She really wasn't safe outside of Kerrigan Falls.

Inside the railcar, Lara noticed it was a museum of some sort. Lining the walls were black-and-white photos, all of vintage circuses. She spun, realizing the entire car was a shrine to the Paris circus, featuring vintage photos of Cirque Medrano's famous Boum Boum the clown, the curious wig shaped into two points on his head making him resemble a rabbit. Another showed Jumbo, the famous elephant whom Lara knew eventually ended his career in the United States. In a case near the door hung a gold-and-red vertical-striped leotard. The inscription read: LEOTARD OF MISS LA LA. It was the costume from the famous Edgar Degas painting. She studied each photo—together this had to be the largest collection of circus memorabilia in the world.

"Vous êtes un fan?" asked the man, who had come in through the door. Now Lara could see he was older—perhaps in his seventies. He was tan and wiped sweat from his brow with a hankie that he kept in his back pocket. His glasses were so thick, she wondered how he could see anything.

"Oui," said Lara. "What is this place?" She motioned around the room.

"Ah, the Musée de Cirque Parisian." He pointed to the sign behind him. "You are American, *oui?*"

"Oui."

"My English is not so good." He sat down rather heavily in one of the wooden seats that was part of a booth. "This is the rear entrance of Le Cirque de Fragonard."

Lara looked out the window to see the famous hexagonal building of Le Cirque de Fragonard's Paris location. She was so busy running that she hadn't noticed it earlier.

"The woman?" He pointed outside.

Lara shook her head. *"Je ne la connais pas. Elle m'a suivi de Père Lachaise. Merci."*

"A pickpocket, perhaps?" the man asked in better English than Lara expected.

"Oui," said Lara, not believing that the woman's intentions were that innocent. She turned to the photo. "Is this from the 1920s?"

"Earlier." The man stood up and walked toward the photo. "This was the famous clown Boum Boum. *Le musée* has photos and paintings from all the circuses in Paris, not just Fragonard. The circuses were very competitive, but le musée is for all." His hands gestured around the room. There was a pride in his expression, like this was a personal collection.

Lara studied some of the photos, looking for anything that might resemble a secret circus. "My great-grandmother performed here in Paris in the 1920s. They called it Le Cirque Secret. Have you ever heard of it?"

The man's face fell. "Le Cirque Secret? Are you sure?" He motioned toward the door. "Come with me." He breezed past her and back down the stairs. Before she exited the railcar, Lara looked to make sure the ponytailed lady wasn't standing outside the gate, but the street was empty. The man was insistent, motioning for her to follow him, his keys and chains rattling as he walked. So fast was his pace that Lara nearly had to run through the door to the main circus building, past the bathrooms and down the hall marked EMPLOYÉS SEULEMENT. As she walked through the door, she found herself in a hall lined with empty animal stalls. The man was ahead of her in the long hallway and was already unlocking the door when Lara got to him. She assumed he was a maintenance man, but she wasn't sure that he—or she, for that matter—should be in this room.

Once the door opened, he motioned her in and turned on the light. Inside the tiny, windowless office, Lara saw that the walls were littered with more circus memorabilia, but unlike the railcar, *this* was a private collection. Women spinning by their teeth or riding horses, sad clowns, happy clowns, clowns with umbrellas, horses diving, women walking on tightropes with umbrellas. There were nudes and disturbing fetish photos as well. She felt uncomfortable looking at some of these with the man staring at her, but then there was one picture—a small painting—that caught her eye and seemed to beckon her. It was the painting's size that stood out as well as the now familiar color palette, the muted baby blues, aquas, and browns. This painting showed a woman with long white-blond, almost platinum hair that was gathered at the nape of her neck. The woman was about to step onto a ladder. The artist had chosen to paint the subject with the trapeze above her, tilting her head toward the ladder before she ascended. It was the moment before the performance was to begin, the excitement and fear visible on her face in her clenched jaw and the firm lines of her mouth. This was a more intimate portrait than the other one, now called *Sylvie on the Steed*; more time had been spent on this subject's face. While the finish on this small painting was smooth, it bore the initials EG. Émile Giroux.

She inhaled sharply. "May I?" Lara turned to the man to see if she could remove the painting from the wall.

He nodded.

Lara pulled the painting from the nail on the wall and turned it over. The crude charcoal wording read CECILE CABOT TAKES FLIGHT.

Cecile Cabot.

She turned the frame over and studied it carefully, trying to take in every detail she could so she could describe it to Barrow and Gaston. Holding it in her hands, she found they were shaking. This portrait appeared to be smaller than *Sylvie on the Steed*, but it could be an optical illusion since this frame was much smaller. From Barrow she knew to look at the canvas—which, after she flipped it over, seemed identical to the one that Barrow was now studying. "Why did you bring me here?" Lara looked up at the man.

"This painting was of Le Cirque Secret. The owner keeps it in here. It is his favorite."

"This is a very valuable painting, you know."

The man shrugged. "It does not matter to him." He pointed to the desk that seemed to belong to the head of Le Cirque de Fragonard. "He calls her his tragic muse."

"Tragic?"

He nodded. "The woman in that painting died right after she posed."

"But that's not possible..." Lara leaned in to study the woman's face. If Cecile Cabot had died, then who was the woman claiming to be Cecile in Kerrigan Falls? Looking down at the painting, Lara felt a connection to this woman. *This* Cecile Cabot. The platinum hair. *This* was the woman who had written the journal.

Lara put the frame back up on the wall. "Thank you. Is there anything more? Archives or anything?"

"*Oui.*" The man nodded and led her back to the railcar. As Lara stepped up into the car again, watching for the ponytailed lady, she saw the old man bent over, pulling out boxes of papers. "All circus memorabilia."

Lara knelt down. "Is it okay if I look through this?"

The man nodded. "I have more cleaning to do." He motioned around the courtyard.

All she wanted to do was run back into that office, pull that painting from the wall, and take it away to the institute.

Furiously rummaging, Lara discovered about ten other boxes containing photos, costumes, programs—everything from the French, British, Spanish, and German circuses before World War II. Two boxes labeled FRANÇAIS seemed the best bet to find anything on Le Cirque Secret. The first box contained a bunch of tickets to other circuses as well as photos—many of them of haunting oddities, like clowns making themselves look like otherworldly creatures with makeup and wigs.

The second box contained circus programs. She was midway through the second box when she spotted them: familiar aged composition books, two of them, with weathered, almost leathery beige covers bearing the name CECILE. Flipping through them, she recognized the familiar handwriting.

She smiled. "A scavenger hunt, huh?" She looked around the rail-car. This entire day had been one big scavenger hunt.

The man returned thirty minutes later to find her on the floor sur-rounded by circus memorabilia.

"Success?" He wiped his forehead with his hankie.

"*Oui*," said Lara, holding up the two books.

"Would you like to borrow them?"

"Yes," said Lara. "*C'est possible?*"

"*Oui*." The man scowled. "These are rotting. They were to be..." He motioned, looking for the word, flicking his hand toward the curb. "Tossed."

Lara looked down at the composition books, her heart sick at the thought that someone might have thrown these away. What if she had not come to Paris? They would have been lost to history. What if her mother had never brought the painting over to her? What if Gaston hadn't noticed the EG? There were so many things that nearly led to her not being on this quest.

"Did it help?"

"*Merci*." She nodded. "I should probably head back."

The man walked toward the door. "Taxi?"

Lara followed him back to the office. Her pulse quickened as she got a last look at Cecile Cabot while he dialed the phone on the desk.

Barrow had said there were three paintings: The Ladies of the Secret Circus. Now she knew the location of two of them. She was closing in on the mystery. One more painting to find, and she had a good hunch it was of Esmé.

An idling taxi waited for her at the front entrance.

"*Merci*." She shook the man's hand. "For helping me." She held up the composition books. "And for these."

He bowed. "I'm at your service, mademoiselle."

Arriving back at her hotel, Lara kept her ball cap low and her blond hair pulled into a low bun. The lady with the ponytail was nowhere to be found, but she quickly got into the elevator and hit the button for the fourth floor. The elevator was old and came to a creaking stop on the second floor. Lara held her breath as the door opened, but there was no one there. The whole scene reminded her of the eerie elevator with a mind of its own in the Doris Day film *Midnight Lace*. At the fourth floor, Lara hurried to her hotel room and slammed the door behind her. Turning on the lights, she checked the bathroom and the closets, even ruffling the drapes.

The phone was blinking with a message from Audrey. She was frantic.

Lara, It's your mother. You used the protection spell. I could feel it. Are you okay? Let me know as soon as you get this message. I knew that I should have come with you. I knew it. Call me!

Picking up the receiver, she got out a calling card.

Audrey picked up on the first ring. "Are you okay?"

"How did you know?"

"I know when you use magic."

"That answers so many questions for me now," quipped Lara.

Audrey wasn't in a humorous mood. "What happened? Tell me."

"A woman chased me in the Père Lachaise Cemetery. I think it might have been the *she* that Shane Speer meant in the *she wants you dead* prediction."

She could hear her mother gasp. "Did you get a good look at her?"

"No. She's about my height, but she was wearing a wig. Oh, and she's in great shape; she chased my ass all over Paris. I used the spell and found a place to hide. A circus of all places."

"Where are you now?" Audrey was clearly ready to pepper her

with questions. "Are you safe?" She was nearly shrieking. "I can't get ahold of Gaston, but you need to call the police. I knew I should have come with you."

"I'm fine. I'm back in my room."

"Don't leave. Call Gaston if you go anywhere." Audrey was speaking rapidly. "You need to come home. Barrow has the painting now—"

"Mom." Lara cut her mother off, trying to sound composed, but her heart was pounding. She really wasn't safe here, but she couldn't go home yet. As she held the phone, Lara checked under the bed and behind the closet, then pulled back the shower curtain and even the heavy drapes that led to a balcony—all empty. "Barrow thinks it's a rare painting. I also saw its twin today. A painting called *Cecile Cabot Takes Flight*. Our Cecile—I don't think she was the *real* Cecile, Mom."

"What do you mean?" Audrey seemed to struggle with what to say next. "Who was she, then?"

"I don't know," said Lara, twirling the phone cord. "But I can't come home until I find out. The spell protected me today. It will keep protecting me." It wasn't just the spell. While she couldn't admit this to her mother, Althacazur knew she was in Paris. He'd orchestrated this entire day, she knew that. He'd promised her answers, a "scavenger hunt," but he'd also protected her today. That was one of the reasons she wasn't banging on Gaston's door right now.

Her mother audibly sighed. "Do you have enough candles?"

"I do. I feel such a connection to this woman and this mystery. I *need* to do this."

She hung up and contemplated her next call. Finally, she picked up the hotel phone and punched in the numbers.

The voice picked up on the second ring. "Archer."

Oh, that voice. Lara felt she could breathe again, and she closed her eyes, sinking into the pillow. She'd missed him. "It's me."

"How is Paris?" He had taken on an intimate tone. She could imagine him turning away from the door so Doyle couldn't hear him. The last time she'd seen him—on their first date—she'd told him that she'd imagined Todd at the gala. Sinking a little from the memory of it, Lara thought she must have been an idiot to tell him that.

"Weird things are happening." Flicking off her shoes, she grabbed the remote volume to turn down the oddly comforting atmospheric music that had been playing when she'd come in the room. Lara couldn't believe that she'd just blurted that out to him.

"Like what?" His voice took on a concerned note.

"I was chased through the Père Lachaise Cemetery today by a woman."

"Really?" The register in his voice rose.

"You think I'd make that up?" She sank into the pillow and crossed her legs.

"Did you call the police?"

Lara sighed. Of course he'd tell her to call the police. Perhaps she *should* call the police. "No. I was rescued by a man at the circus."

"You really need to start at the beginning." He was clicking a pen; she could hear it snapping.

"I ran, like, two miles."

"You can run two miles?"

She loved that he could calm her down with his banter. "Yes, Ben. I can run two miles. Anyway, there was a man sweeping a courtyard. When I ran by, he saw that I was scared. He motioned for me to come into the courtyard and I hid in a railcar that was also a circus museum. Here is where it gets *really* crazy. This man showed me a painting of the *real* Cecile Cabot, not the woman from the painting that I have. This Cecile Cabot died in the 1920s here in Paris. Now I don't know who it was who helped raise me. After that, he let me rummage through old circus memorabilia and I found something."

"What?"

"Two more journals from Cecile. Hopefully, I'll find out more answers there." She was scanning them as she spoke to him, picking out sentences here and there. It was the same voice, the same writing. Checking the date, she saw that it picked up where the other book left off. She had the next volume. These books were in worse shape than the first one, so she'd definitely need Barrow's help reconstructing some of the damaged pages. She couldn't wait to show them to him.

"Is the dead bolt on your door?"

"It is."

"Have you checked the closets? Do it while I'm on the phone."

"I checked them while I was on with my mother."

"And you're okay?"

"I'm fine, just shaken up."

He inhaled like he was about to speak, but then hesitated.

"What?" she pressed. When he'd done this in the past, there was always a kernel of wisdom in his next comment.

"You don't think it's odd that you ran right into the place where you found the journals?"

"You think someone led me there?" Of course Lara realized the chances of running randomly into Le Cirque de Fragonard were slim.

"It's exactly what I think. Where was Gaston? Why wasn't he with you?" There was the same edge to his voice that she'd heard from Audrey.

"He was shopping for paintings today. And I'm not a child, Ben."

"You're not a child, but you might be in possession of a valuable painting. Maybe the woman was after that?"

It hadn't occurred to her that it might be the painting that had spurred the woman to follow her. Barrow might have told someone about it and how much it was worth. It might be worth kidnapping

Lara for. More than likely, though, it was the powerful woman she'd been warned about. There was no point in giving Ben that piece of information. He'd think she was crazy since the warning came from a circus fortune-teller. Either that, or he'd insist she get the next flight home. And she wasn't going home just yet.

"Promise me you won't be wandering the streets of Paris alone tomorrow." He was silent like he was piecing something together.

"I promise no more wandering around Paris unchaperoned." She twisted the cord of the old phone. "Anything going on back home?"

"The *Washington Post* is sending a reporter tomorrow to do a story on Todd's and Peter's disappearances. Apparently, with all the success of the *Ghostly Happenings* episode, there is a renewed interest in Todd's case."

"Oh," said Lara, suddenly feeling the tug of Todd again. As scared as she had been running through Paris, she had felt alive again—it was an adrenaline rush. This whole mystery had given her a purpose, something she hadn't really felt since her wedding. "That's good, right?"

"It might open up a lead, you never know." He sounded tired. "When are you coming home?"

"Day after tomorrow. We pushed our return flight back because the painting looks to be real. There is another expert reviewing it now." Sadly, she wasn't sure an article would lead to any information on Peter or Todd. If there were leads, it would come from Althacazur, not some hotline set up by the police.

"I miss you." His comment hung in the air. She knew he was testing her, seeing what she would say.

"I miss you, too." Hers came out in a whisper, a final breath. Through a little time and some distance, Lara realized that she missed him terribly.

There was a pause on the line. "Be careful, Lara."

"I will." She hated to hang up. "It was really good to hear your voice." The ache for him, the distance was palatable now.

The mood was interrupted by a rustling noise that had Lara sitting up like a shot. She heard something slide under her door. At first, she assumed it was a bill, but after everything that had happened today she wasn't taking any chances. She rose from the bed and saw that there was a half-inch space under the old door. Lying on the floor in front of it was a white envelope that had been pushed through the opening. Snatching it from the floor, she quickly tossed it on the bed. The envelope had been too heavy and bulky for the hotel bill.

Plucking it off the bedspread, she could feel the heaviness of the object. It was rectangular, like a—

Like a ticket.

She opened the envelope by unwinding one of those old-fashioned cords over a button. Plunging her hand deep inside, she pulled out a cream ticket with gold embossed lettering—the very invitation Mourier had gone mad trying to secure a second time. Yet here it was, on her bed, beckoning to her. *The wicked ticket.*

Admission pour une
(Mademoiselle Lara Barnes)

Le Cirque Secret

Trois Juillet
Vingt-trois heures

Palais Brongniart
(Rue Vivienne et Rue Réaumur)

Crouching down, she looked under the door to see if someone was still standing there. Seeing no shadow, Lara walked over to the door and looked out the peephole and found the hallway empty.

The ticket was lying flat on the center of the bed. "I've heard about you," she said to it. After a few minutes, she picked it up. It felt heavy in her hand, not like any paper she'd ever touched. She tore at the end of the paper but found the parchment didn't give. Again, she tried, and it seemed that a liquid came from the very end of it. She looked down at her fingers. Was it blood? Lara sniffed at the garnet-red smudge on her finger and dropped the ticket back on the bed, horrified. The ticket was bleeding. "You bleed?"

None of the tickets to Le Cirque Secret remained. Except this one.

Althacazur had said he'd find her. And it appeared he had.

The Journal of Cecile Cabot
Book Two

May 25, 1925

Father did something entirely unusual a few days ago. In a big show in front of all of the performers, he announced that he has *permitted* Émile Giroux to capture the circus on canvas for three paintings of the artist's choosing. Since it is impossible for us to be painted, I pressed Father as to how he was going to achieve this, but he said it was not my concern. This led to my questioning him why we couldn't be painted like normal people in the first place. He said that my tongue could be cut out if I asked another question. We have enough mutes in the circus that I'll take him at his word. Hours later, I overhead him telling Esmé that he would be enchanting the three paintings. Even though I have earned the respect of my fellow performers, he still treats Esmé like an equal and me, a child.

I don't entirely trust this development with Émile. Rarely does Father do anything without wanting something in return. He says everything is point and counterpoint. Balance is required.

After being permitted to attend our practices, Émile chose me as his first subject.

For the first sitting, I posed in my aqua costume with the brown beading. I prefer the blush one, my signature costume, but Émile fancies the aqua one because he says it makes my eyes come alive. Sitting for him was a maddening chore, but the idea of him studying me so intently stirred something in me. Now I think that I finally understand Esmé's love for painters. Feeling Émile's eyes on me was such an intimate act. The honesty in his depiction of me; the way he's chosen to both scrutinize and rearrange me in paint. Each night, as he unveiled the progress of his work, I found that we were both so vulnerable: him for the artistic risk that he had taken and me for opening myself to how he truly sees me. While I am not the great beauty my sister is, in the way Émile has pinpointed my most intense moment, the one *before* I've ascended the ladder where I'm anticipating the crowd and the performance ahead of me, he has captured not just my likeness, but my true essence.

While he worked, he often gazed at pieces of me—a hand, a foot— but I noticed everything about him: his white shirt with paint stains on the forearms, the ones that he rolls so I won't see; the quiet way he can work for hours without talking; and his strong chin, which is the telltale indicator of frustration when he is unhappy with some detail. And those eyes—the sad, dirty-green eyes that gaze up at me, hungrily. Toward the end of my sitting our eyes lingered until the end, when we found ourselves sitting in silence simply taking each other in, watching each other breathe.

May 30, 1925

Tonight Émile asked me to accompany him to Le Select. Outside the café, it was a warm night, so there were hordes of people sitting on cane chairs. Inside, patrons were packed like in a crowded cafeteria. This is not the romantic notion of Montparnasse anymore. I heard the American and German accents and saw that what they said is true: There are more tourists than artists here now.

For dinner, we were meeting with Man Ray and his girlfriend, Kiki, but the photographer's French was as terrible as my English, so we talked at each other, gesturing and requiring Émile to translate, until we both nearly fell over in our chairs with laughter at our wild arm movements. Man Ray had a hook to his nose and the most intense eyes I have ever seen on a man, yet I found him handsome. When you spoke, he focused intently on your voice—even if he could not understand a word of my French. It's a heady, sensual thing, as though I am the only person in the restaurant. I think Émile's gaze has opened something up in my soul, like the breeze that flows from the window after a stuffy summer night. While Man has made a living as a portrait photographer, he longs to be a painter. There was something about Émile's work that inspired him. At first, I was intimidated by both Man and Kiki, but to my surprise, they'd had a ticket to Le Cirque Secret recently and were in awe of *me*?

While they don't know it and would completely disagree about it for hours, Émile and his friends were not unlike circus performers—each night they displayed their works and read their poems to the grow-ing crowd of admirers outside places like Le Dôme Café or Café de la Rotonde, never seeing that they, too, were contained under their own big top. They are too close to observe that there is change coming to Montparnasse, subtle for now, but I fear it will soon loom large. The artists and intellects have *become* the attractions. The tourists go back to their Right Bank hotel, then back home to America, Germany, or England to regale their friends with their proximity to the writer Hemingway or the photographer Man Ray like they bought tickets to see them. As an outsider to this world, I've observed that the sea of expats with extra pocket money don't care about Dada versus cubism nor understand the art of the unconscious mind as dear Salvador Dalí does. Émile's friends, so wrapped up in their own conversations, haven't seen the shift that has occurred around them, but I fear this special place is coming to an end. I can almost smell it around me, like that most fragrant scent of the ripest fruit just before it begins to rot.

From across the table, Émile glanced at me. He was excited that he'd been permitted to do what no other artist has done—paint Le Cirque Secret. There were two more paintings to complete, and Man was telling him how to frame the next one. There was a part of me that felt a sense of dread for Émile, like he had agreed to something before he was fully aware of the consequences. As always, with Father there is the fear he has struck some terrible, mortal bargain. Émile doesn't know how the world—my world—works. *There are always consequences.*

While our dinner companions dined on oysters, I chose *boeuf.* Overhead, I heard the fan cycling above me and felt its cool waves of air as they hit my forearms.

"You need to push yourself." Man lit a cigarette and dismissed him with the shrug of his hand. "You are an old romantic."

Like in a tennis match, they volleyed ideas back and forth, trying them on. What is surrealism? Who is a true surrealist? What role does art play in a mad world?

I realized the idea was to shock or subvert with art. To my horror, it occurred to me that this is what they think we do with Le Cirque Secret. What we do isn't a performance—what they see each night is not some *dream* of Hell. It *is* Hell. That I come and go freely makes it seem like I'm an actress who dons a part and shakes it off cleanly each night. But for Doro and the others, their Hell is hardly metaphorical, and their costumes are not so easily tossed.

Halfway through drinks, Man began to chastise Émile for being too much like a man named Modigliani, saying he hasn't pushed against the vein enough. At the mention of Modigliani, Émile became quiet, almost forlorn.

When they were talking among themselves, Émile leaned in to whisper to me. "Amedeo has been dead for five years, but I feel as though it were yesterday."

I must have registered confusion on my face because Kiki leaned in and whispered, "Amedeo Modigliani was Émile's mentor. Terrible shame about him. He died of tuberculosis. His pregnant wife, Jeanne, leapt to her own death two days later. Her family won't even let her be buried next to him." Kiki touched my arm for emphasis, her blood-red nails lightly tapping my forearm.

From across the table, Émile picked up the saltshaker and rotated it with such intensity, that the little glass shaker hit the table, causing it to vibrate.

June 2, 1925

Today I found Émile painting Sylvie. I stood behind him to admire the many sketches of her standing by the steed—an old horse who might have been a king in his previous life. Naturally, the horse couldn't tell us anything, but Father has alluded to his true identity several times.

This was not the pose that Émile wanted, so I called to Sylvie for her to try an easy stand on the horse's back since she would need to re-create it several times in order to capture the sketch.

Émile looked puzzled at the required pomp to mount His Majesty. So the horse would cooperate, Sylvie was required to address His Majesty by bowing to him before she began her routine. To an onlooker (and everyone but His Majesty), it is a comical gesture. After the bow, Sylvie walked him around the ring and stroked his mane and neck as she fed him carrots. If Father's hints were to be believed, this horse was once a particularly randy king who seduced his entire court, so the idea that he is ridden for show is a rather interesting punishment.

Sylvie mounted His Majesty and they began their routine. Using her leg, Sylvie hooked onto the horse's back, dangling on the side, her arms outstretched, the only thing holding her to the horse being the power of her legs. Next, as the horse galloped, Sylvie, in one swift move, stood on the horse's back then flipped midair, landing in a perfect stand. In this simple stand, both horse and rider were completely one, Sylvie's body rocking in time with His Majesty. While Émile could have chosen a more complicated flip, it was the face of the horse and rider so perfectly in sync that made this sketch so compelling.

"You try." Émile handed me a charcoal. I gave him a quizzical look. I wasn't an artist, but while Émile stood to the side watching Sylvie perform, I sketched the curves of the horse for him, the bob of his head rocking in perfect unison with Sylvie.

From my life in the shadows, I knew every corner of the circus. This intimate knowledge has provided me with a watcher's eye, an artist's gaze. "You want this pose," I said to Émile, motioning to Sylvie in the moment just after she finished a flip when she was flushed like she had been happily ravaged. If you saw her up close, there would be sweat on her upper lip and forehead.

Immediately he sat down and began to sketch the outlines of Sylvie and the horse, attempting several versions to get the right amount of space on the canvas.

"The painting is so small." I'd imagined the three paintings on large, dramatic canvases.

"I hate those giant things. My last painting was a hulking thing called *The Vampire*. I want to try something different. Honestly, I never know where the circus will be from week to week and I need to be able to carry everything." He pointed to his case of paints.

Sheet after sheet of poses littered the floor. As quickly as they fell, he called on Sylvie to try the flip two more times. As she maneuvered on the horse, Émile altered the sketch until he had the final pose. It was an angle from above them in the stands. The composition was clever, and I remembered Man Ray suggesting an exaggerated angle for one. Smiling, I realized he had taken Man Ray's advice. I feel that I am in the center of the creation of something brilliant.

June 9, 1925

Émile has nearly finished Sylvie's painting. He let me tinker with the bronze shade of paint, instructing me how to layer it on and wipe it off. I was amazed at the skill he possessed. I couldn't quite get the technique that he could do with one hand.

"You have some talent." Over my shoulder, he brought his lips close to my neck, so near I could feel the warmth of his breath.

"No," I said, shaking my head.

"Use it to sign." He pointed to the brush tinged with the brown shade.

"I couldn't." I pointed the brush at him but turned it, positioning it over the lower right corner of the canvas. He took my hand and crouched down beside me and guided the E and the G. Nervous, I saw my lines quiver. I made a face. "It's terrible."

"Marvelous," he said, but he was not looking at the canvas; he was staring at me.

Last night, I met him in Montparnasse. Paris was stifling and dinner was late, which was wondrous because some of the heat had left for the evening. The air filled the city like a bath with too-warm, stagnant water—none of us could breathe, and yet with the heat came freedom. Women used it as an excuse not to wear stockings for the night and raised their skirt hems above their knees. Parched and sweating, men ordered more drinks than they normally could tolerate. All the restaurants with overhead fans were crowded—so we headed to Le Dôme Café, which sat in a wedge between Boulevard du Montparnasse and Boulevard Raspail. We stood at the bar, envious of those who had secured early seats. I ordered a cognac and water. The café was overrun tonight so Émile suggested that we go to his apartment. I found myself sweating with nerves. Both Esmé and Sylvie routinely left with people, leaving me the one traveling back to the circus alone in a taxi, and I admit that I had no idea what to expect.

Émile's studio was one block from Le Dôme Café on Rue Delambre. The old staircase creaked as though it would pull away from the wall as we climbed. As he shut the door behind us, I was aware that we were alone for the first time. He cracked open the only two windows in the stuffy little apartment and pulled the biggest chair he had in front of them. I looked down and noticed that the two plates he'd placed in front of me were from the Café de la Rotonde. He appeared to have stolen a set of everything for our meal tonight. From Kiki, I know that all of the artists steal plates and cutlery from the Café de la Rotonde, but I find it charming. We sat together on the chair and listened to the sounds of Paris below us as we ate Gouda with some fresh bread and apples.

Surrounding us were paintings in various stages of completion. The lights were off so we relied on the outside illumination from Montparnasse. Émile was a master of manipulating light, so I felt like he'd arranged this scene and I wondered how he saw me now. The moon was full and shining, giving me a good view of a stack of his paintings. Curious, I perused the canvases.

A few of his paintings were interesting attempts at cubism, the shadows of a man's face perfectly drawn, yet angular. Where the shadows fell in the hollows of the cheekbones, he'd created landscapes using an elaborate crosshatch technique. The scene wasn't entirely visible until the eye was close. There were also several nudes of one woman— a woman with golden hair—and I found that I was struck with a pang of jealousy, certain that while the oil was drying on the canvas, he was making love to her in the threadbare sheets on his tiny bed. My calves brushed against the bedspread and I was imagining myself tangled in the sheets, our bodies sticking together in the heat.

"She's beautiful," I said. He'd come to stand behind me.

"*Oui.*"

I was struck by his honesty, yet he gave nothing away, no hint that she was a lover past or present. I wanted to run out, fearing that I was not built for this vulnerability.

"I wish every one of these paintings were of you." I felt his presence behind me, then his hand resting softly on the center of my back. "Then I might not miss you as much."

I turned to see his face in the moonlight. It was the sincerest look. "I want to be surrounded by you, Cecile."

I shook my head. "You could paint me every night. And every morning your canvas would be blank."

"I do have the one painting of you."

True. And his painting would be the only likeness of me ever created. Somehow the thought gave me a great wave of melancholy.

"For my final portrait, I will paint you again."

"*Non*," I said. "You must paint Esmé. She is the natural third painting."

"But I don't want to paint Esmé. Everyone in Montparnasse has painted her."

"She is a phantom, like me. Only your painting of her will survive," I said. "It will make you famous—rich even." I glanced around his apartment, realizing he probably struggled to buy paints and pay the rent each month.

"Why am I the only one who can paint you?"

"Because we are of the circus," I said, rubbing my arms. "It is magic, Émile. True magic and not some trick of light."

"My mysterious Cecile." He took my hand and led me over to the bed.

"What did you do before you painted?" I asked, changing the subject.

He sat down on the bed heavily. "I was in the war and then I came back and worked in a building, the Sacré-Coeur. After that had finished, I worked at the factory painting cars."

Our legs touched, and I felt the heat of him. When he kissed me, I tasted cognac on his breath.

"In the morning will you disappear?"

"*Non*." My hand touched his lightly.

"Promise?" He slid on top of me and his kisses were erratic, frantic, both short and long, like he would devour me if he could. I unbuttoned his shirt and felt the beads of sweat on his chest from the sweltering apartment. He pulled me up and unfastened my dress. It pooled around my feet. I unbuttoned his trousers and slipped my hands between his shirt and shoulders and let the shirt fall into a pile next to my dress; then I returned to his trousers, which he had already begun to lower. We spun against the wall next to the open window and the breeze hit me. I didn't tell him as he entered me that I had not done this before with anyone, but his face changed when he realized there had been no one before him. As he moved, I also saw the realization alter him. He took my face in his hands and kissed me until he came with rough, erratic thrusts. When we were done, our sweat combined and we were dripping.

"You are not like the other girls I have known." He caught his breath so this came out in short bursts, so much so that I struggled to hear him.

I was not sure what this meant, nor was I sure that I wanted to be reminded of other girls he has known.

The church bells clanged and reminded us that, outside, life would start again soon.

"We could go to Jardin du Luxembourg today. I could paint you."

I frowned.

"I know." He looked down. "But I could change a detail so it wouldn't be you exactly. It would stay; I know it would."

"I need to get back to the circus." I met his eyes and saw they were hungry for more. I scrambled, gathering my clothes. His shirt was open as I left, and I looked back at him with such longing. Realizing now how light my life was before him—how easily I moved through each arrondissement in Paris with Esmé and Sylvie each weekend, drinking champagne with socialites, musicians, and writers until we caught the door at Le Cirque Secret. But now it is as though I have caught an illness that will addle my brain and weigh on my heart until it bursts.

It is sad that in this moment of what should be carnal joy, I am aware that we are already doomed.

19

Paris
July 3, 2005

You should have called me," said Gaston, first adjusting his sunglasses, then his cane chair, his hair still wet from the shower. "You have no idea who might have been lurking in the hallways. Audrey would kill me if something happened to you."

Lara smiled; that was definitely the reason he was in such a panic. She took a first sip of her cappuccino. "I'm sure you got a bunch of safety instructions for me before you left."

He rolled his eyes and sipped his espresso but didn't disagree.

"Ha." She pointed her finger at him. "I knew it."

Gaston made a face as he watched the morning commuters rush past dressed in their sneakers and business clothes. "Let's just say if anything happened to you, I would not be going back to Kerrigan Falls, so please help me to go home again. Just stay with Barrow and me today so we know you will be safe."

"I agree." Barrow's spoon clinked against the porcelain cappuccino cup.

The three of them were seated outside the café at Métro Quatre Septembre, named for the day the Third Republic was announced upon the death of Napoleon III. The trio faced Rue Réaumur.

Although it was only ten, Gaston was alternating between a glass of champagne and his second cup of espresso. As she recounted the story of her day, both men were speechless.

Pulling the two composition books from her messenger bag, she began to tell them about Émile and Cecile. She'd spent all night translating the second journal and had made a copy of her English translation for Barrow, indicating where she couldn't decipher the manuscript. Also tucked away in her bag was an *actual* ticket to Le Cirque Secret. While the ticket had appeared to bleed last night when she'd torn it, this morning the paper was perfectly mended as though it was a living thing that had healed itself overnight.

She was undecided whether she was going to tell them about the invitation but was leaning toward not. From a purely academic standpoint, it made sense to show them, so they could lay their lands on an authentic ticket from Le Cirque Secret. Yet if she told Gaston and Barrow, they'd never let her show up tonight. She couldn't risk them trying to stop her. This was the opportunity of a lifetime. Looking at them both, she knew if *they* had tickets in their pockets, they would go.

"I cannot believe another Giroux painting has been hanging in the office of Le Cirque de Fragonard for years?" Barrow's hands were on his face in disbelief, his eyes wild. "I need to see it. Today if possible."

"Oh, Teddy, it's so beautiful. Even more beautiful than my painting." Lara cut a piece of her duck confit as Barrow skimmed the notebook. "It's in the owner's private collection. And I do mean private; there is some creepy stuff in there."

"I'll call someone at the institute to see if I can get Fragonard to let us see it." Barrow was distracted, furiously scanning through his phone contacts. After leaving two voicemails, he settled back into his seat and focused on the journal, smoothing the pages. "The writing is so faded. We should be wearing gloves."

"I've only managed to translate the second journal." She met his eyes. "It tells the story of two of the paintings—Cecile's and Sylvie's. I'm convinced that my grandmother—the woman who helped raise me—was not Cecile, but Sylvie. I think the answer is the third journal." She handed the second journal to him. While it might have been faster for him to read the third, she kept it, preferring to be its first reader. After all, this was *her* family, *her* legacy. She needed to be the one to read Cecile's words. While Barrow was fixed on Giroux, she was getting drawn into Cecile's world. "Any word about the painting?"

"I'm seeing Micheau right after this," said Barrow about Alain Micheau, the Giroux specialist who'd driven up from Nice. Earlier, Barrow indicated that two scholars needed to agree that it was a Giroux before raising the discovery to the larger art community. "Last night, Alain was at the institute until I had to force him to leave. The paints used on *Sylvie on the Steed* match an order Giroux placed with Lefebvre-Foinet on Rue Vavin in Montparnasse right before his death. They would have custom-blended the pinks and aquas for him. Giroux got his canvases there as well. He'd ordered three smaller ones for The Ladies of the Secret Circus a month before his death. The size on the first painting is a match. The journals also provide a wonderful first-person account of the creation of these works." Barrow looked at the notes and the second book in disbelief. He reached out and touched Lara's hand. "I want to thank you for this gift."

She smiled. "It's quite a story, isn't it?"

"The paintings need to be together," said Barrow. "I can't believe Fragonard has held on to it all these years. They were an urban legend in Paris. Fragonard would have known that, especially being in the circus community. It was selfish...irresponsible."

"So how did the first painting measure up?" asked Gaston, changing the subject. "I'm sure it was different in your mind."

Barrow did not shift his gaze, and it seemed as though he didn't hear the question at first. "*Sylvie on the Steed* was smaller than I'd thought it would be, a bit like the *Mona Lisa*—it lives large in your mind but is rather small on the wall. It was also moodier than his earlier work, the colors more vivid, and he used a technique that made them look like they're dripping, yet it was not an impressionistic work. So I guess I would say I was underwhelmed by the painting's size but overwhelmed by how it spoke to me. After seeing one of the series, I believe they are the crown jewels of Giroux's works."

"Why Giroux?" asked Lara.

"What is this? The question-Teddy *petite dejeuner*?" Barrow laughed and tore off a piece of country bread and studied it intently. "I was ten years old when my mother took me to the Louvre for the first time. She was often on location for photo shoots, and by this time she and my father had divorced, so I was raised by the nanny. Time with my mother…well…it was precious to me, and anything associated with it was heightened, special. At the Louvre, I spied this hulking canvas in front of me with these green skin tones and this yellow-orange haze. It was his painting of the Devil, but the Devil as Giroux saw him was not the standard depiction with horns and pitchforks and hooves. Instead it was the most magnificent woman in red, blood dripping from her fingertips and from her chin, but she was stunning and ravenous. It was a violent painting, yet sexual. The Spanish painters did works like this, but not the French. Giroux used some kind of melting technique with it that became his signature; the work just looked like it was dripping. He returned to this technique for your painting. I had never seen anything like it. That I was so attracted to this dark work seemed to unnerve my mother, who steered me away from it. And so I forgot about it until *years* later, when I was in Milan and it happened to be on loan there. To see it again, I felt a destiny with both the painting and the man. It had stirred feelings in me and made me want to know more about art—about him. Of course, I was to learn that the painting was not of the Devil."

"*The Vampire*," said Lara.

"Indeed." He smiled. "The most beautiful painting I had ever seen."

On cue, Gaston started. "You have to understand, Lara, that artists in 1925 had largely rejected painterly, beautiful art. Art was political—they believed that the colonial, bourgeois tastes had led to the events surrounding the Great War, so the entire *premise* of art was being challenged. Paris at the time was surrounded by Dadaists, surrealists, and futurists all trying to set the course for what art would be next," said Gaston. "And yet here is Giroux sitting in the cafés beside them still painting largely beautiful paintings."

"And getting away with it," Barrow chimed in, not wanting Gaston to have too much expertise. "Had he lived, he would have been as famous as Salvador Dalí or Picasso. I'm sure of it."

"And he wasn't using everyday materials like pens and doors to create art, like Man Ray," added Gaston, his espresso cup hitting his saucer loudly.

"No," agreed Barrow, "the bastard just created beautiful paintings that were rather out of fashion at the time. He did challenge ideals of art—but even those are quite exquisite. He once remarked that being in the war, he'd seen many forms of hell in his life, and the one thing it had taught him was to value beauty.

"After I'd learned what happened to him—that his death was shrouded in some mystery—that added another layer for me," said Barrow. "No one had ever really solved what had killed him or where these paintings had gone. There were various theories, but no one had taken the time to study it. That, and my mother took me to all of the circuses when she was on photo shoots—Paris, Rome, Barcelona, Madrid, and Montreal—the Rivoli."

She hadn't thought he was a fan of the circus, but it made sense. "So it was the scholarship," said Lara. "I'm curious. You said there was a mystery about his death? What killed him?"

"Bright's disease," said Barrow, distracted.

Lara looked puzzled.

"An old term for kidney failure," said Gaston, clarifying.

"That's hardly mysterious," said Lara.

Barrow shrugged. "The disease came on rather suddenly. His friends said that he'd cut his hand at Le Cirque Secret and never recovered. They attributed it to Bright's disease, but the feeling was that it might have been some strange blood disease. He just seemed to waste away within a week's time. The circus lasted another eight months or so after Giroux died. And just like that"—Barrow snapped his fingers—"it was never heard from again. Its last performance was held sometime in 1926. Mourier looked for word about it anywhere... Barcelona...Rome...London, but it never appeared again."

Lara couldn't imagine spending a lifetime researching one person's work. She understood that these men liked their little art lectures—liked to listen to themselves. Yet as they talked, the ticket burned in her bag. She took a little joy in knowing that she had a secret that wasn't being tossed around by the two of them for discussion. If they knew she had the ticket, she'd be irrelevant in the conversation about it.

"And you both believe Le Cirque Secret is responsible for his death?" If she was going to go to Le Cirque Secret, she should know what she was getting into. She hadn't finished the third journal yet. So far, there was nothing indicating that Giroux was about to meet a mysterious end. On the contrary, he seemed to be a man very much in love.

"I believe Mourier," said Barrow. "He was a well-respected journalist and he was convinced there was something very odd about Giroux's death. In fact, it remains one of the great mysteries of the art world. After he died, the landlady took his canvases out back to the trash. Man Ray and Duchamp—who happened to be in Paris at that time—pulled some of them out of the garbage. Oddly enough, Duchamp—who was never a fan of Giroux—ended up curating and selling most of his work."

Barrow stopped for a moment while his entrée was placed in front of him. "The exciting thing about these journals is that they really correspond to the final weeks of Giroux's life."

"There was much discussion a few years back about going to the Père Lachaise and exhuming his body to find out what had actually killed him," said Gaston.

"I was hoping they'd do it," added Barrow.

"Wait! Émile Giroux is buried in the Père Lachaise? Why didn't you tell me that yesterday?" Lara couldn't believe she'd been right near the artist's grave yesterday.

"I forgot," said Gaston, shrugging, his face blushing.

Barrow shook his head. "Gaston was never much for cemeteries."

"Couldn't it have been something as simple as alcohol poisoning or poison from the paints he used? Pneumonia from a nasty chill?"

Both men grumbled. She wasn't being a good sport. They were all fans of Giroux and it seemed like she was challenging them.

"Based on Cecile's diary, I now feel sure the circus also had ties to the occult," said Barrow. "There were even rumors that it was a gateway to Hell itself. But *we* found it—you found it. After all these years of searching, we actually fucking found it, Lara. Do you know what it was like? I feel like I've sold my soul for this damned circus, believing in my heart that there was always more to the story. I pored through every biography of anyone who had ever known or spoken to Émile Giroux or anyone—I mean anyone at all—who had gone to the circus. I even met people who claimed they'd gotten a ticket, but they were all frauds. I had nothing until Gaston called me and told me what you had in your possession. I am forever in your debt."

Lara looked up and saw tears in Teddy Barrow's eyes.

20

Kerrigan Falls, Virginia
July 3, 2005

W *ashington Post* reporter Michelle Hixson stood in front of the battered chalkboard looking perplexed.

"I'm surprised you're working on a Sunday," said Ben.

The reporter gave him a puzzled look. "The story is due to my editor on Tuesday morning. It's hard to get way out here during the week."

"Yes, the July Fourth holiday." Ben noticed she returned her gaze to the board. He had dragged it up from the basement in an attempt to frame out the details about the disappearances of both Peter Beaumont and Todd Sutton. Embarrassingly, it looked like those time lines he'd seen the TV cops use and he felt like he was playing at being a real police officer, like he'd done when he was a kid when his father would set up a small desk for him beside his own, complete with nonworking phone. He could imagine that, as a *Post* reporter, Michelle had seen real police work at the First Precinct in DC. Given he had little experience with true crime, he was ashamed by how it looked when people walked into his office and found notes taped to the board. Did he look too eager to *finally* have a real case?

Yet the reporter seemed engrossed, taking in the information. She was tiny, elf-like, with short brown hair. In heels, she came to Ben's shoulder. "This is quite helpful," she said, her head following his scribbles. Since Doyle couldn't be trusted not to blab key clues on the case, Ben had never included details on the board that needed to be protected. He looked at the time line written in pink chalk—the only color he could find at the supermarket. It made the board look like some sidewalk hopscotch game.

"It's a strange story for sure." She turned, pushing up her glasses. Everything about her was neat—even her small handwriting in the notebook that he'd glimpsed.

"And your father was also the chief of police here, is that correct?"

"Yes, he retired in 1993," said Ben. "He died two years ago."

"I'm sorry to hear that." Talking with her was damned awkward and unnerving. She allowed pauses between sentences and made no attempt to fill up the silences with words.

"Yes, well..." Ben motioned for her to sit. He was already uneasy. He wiped his palms on his pant legs. From the details in his father's files on Peter Beaumont, the older police officer had taken the disappearance seriously. Whoever had placed Todd's car in the exact same location either had seen this file or had firsthand knowledge of Peter Beaumont's case. Given the thick layer of dust that had covered the locked file cabinet, Ben didn't think that anyone but him had looked through it in years.

"What is your current theory of the case?" Her voice had no inflection. Ben thought she was a real no-bullshit type of reporter, quiet but deadly.

Seasoned cops, real cops, didn't dish out details. They held back clues and "refused to discuss the case." Ben inhaled sharply, not wanting to appear a fool in the pages of the *Washington Post*. "Well." He tried to think what Steve McQueen would do if he were playing Ben in this scene. Steve McQueen would look pensive and in control. Shifting in his seat, he leaned back and folded his hands on his lap, like they did in *Bullitt*. "It's possible that the same person committed both crimes. The other thought was that Todd Sutton knew about Peter Beaumont's disappearance and staged the entire thing to look like it. I don't think that the latter is likely, but it can't be ruled out."

"Was Sutton having money problems?" The reporter thumbed through her notes. Her nails were bitten to the quick.

"Not that we've found."

"He disappeared on his wedding day. Perhaps cold feet?"

"Possibly, but then why leave his car behind?"

She seemed to consider his explanation but gave nothing away. "The site, Wickelow Bend." She straightened herself in her chair. "People are calling it the Devil's Bend."

"Sadly, yes. The *Ghostly Happenings* show has made it a tourist attraction." In the nine months since Todd Sutton's disappearance, Ben knew what everyone was saying about Wickelow Bend, but he wasn't about to believe in something otherworldly, not yet. Something evil may have befallen both Todd Sutton and Peter Beaumont, but Ben had to think that it was more likely some mortal person, not some Witch of the Wickelow Woods. Unfortunately, reporters, ghost hunters, and tourists were still crowding the Shumholdt Bridge, causing something that Kerrigan Falls had never had before: traffic.

"But you don't think there is anything...odd about it?"

"You mean *supernatural*?"

She shrugged but jotted something down. "Your word."

"No," he said, letting the simple answer hang between them for a moment. Her eyebrow rose as if she wanted him to elaborate. "I think someone out there knows what happened to these men. Stories like yours are helpful to bring new leads to light."

"Y'all are a legend around here with no crime. That means you also don't have a lot of experience with missing persons cases, Chief Archer. No offense." At this, she smiled.

"None taken." He smiled back coolly, channeling Steve McQueen once again. He'd expected a bit of a dance, but he hadn't anticipated that she would be trying to paint them as Mayberry. This was a very different feeling than he'd had with the *Kerrigan Falls Express* reporters, especially Kim Landau. "Your paper wrote about our phenomenon a few years back. It ran in your Style Section."

"Oh yes, I read that one. It was cute," she said. "Yet the cases you have involve two men who've gone missing on the same exact date."

Her tone was sweet, curious even, yet her questions were precise... sharp. He knew what she was hinting at. "We are certainly exploring some ritual aspect to the case."

"By *we*, you mean you and your one deputy?" She did this thing where she looked at her notes before she fired a shot across the desk.

Yes, he thought, they *were* a small police force. Just the two of them. "And help from the Virginia State Police." He played with a frayed hem on his uniform so his hands had something to do. Inside, he was steaming. They were a small force, but they weren't inept. He could see the outline of her article forming. "Would you like some coffee, Ms. Hixson?"

"No, thank you," she replied. "Yes, the Virginia State Police." She was thumbing through her notes. "Yes, here it is. Todd Sutton's car—the 1976 Ford Mustang. According to them, it was wiped by a professional. You don't think that's strange?" She looked up at him.

He leaned forward, smiling again and hating himself for smiling. "May I ask where you got that information?" Behind his calm exterior, Ben was seething. There had been no prints of any kind found in or on the car. It had been wiped clean. Not just wiped; the state police admitted that the lab hadn't seen anything like it. No fiber, hair, or

DNA of any kind. That information was supposed to be confidential. How did *this* woman find it?

"You may." She smiled. "I have my sources."

Of course. "Then you also know that the state police thought it was a professional job." At this point, since she knew what was found in the car, it didn't matter. "By professional, they meant it could have been some type of hit, but they couldn't rule out that Sutton himself just wiped the car clean and fled. After all, he did restore cars for a living. In the end, the state police's report was inconclusive, but like I said, you know this already."

"You don't agree?"

He ignored her question. "The conclusion from them is that people sometimes simply disappear. Often there are underlying issues that you didn't know about."

"Drugs?" So, she had read the notes from the state police.

"Yes. If he had gotten in bad with the wrong people—owed them money, perhaps—then they'd send professionals...that could explain the car."

"But you don't believe that?"

"No," he said. "I do not believe that Todd Sutton was cooking up anything in his garage." Privately, Ben agreed with the state police that there was a logical explanation for these disappearances. It just required good, old-fashioned police work to solve it.

"But it doesn't explain the other case. Was that car wiped clean as well?"

Peter Beaumont's car was, indeed, wiped clean, but Michelle Hixson did not appear to have that information and he wasn't going to enlighten her further. "I think they are connected cases, Miss Hixson, but I don't think they're supernatural. Beyond that, I cannot say more. Anything else that you need?"

"I need a good photo of both Todd Sutton and Peter Beaumont."

"I can get you those."

"We're also having a sketch artist draw an aged composite of Peter Beaumont. Maybe someone has been living next door to him for thirty years."

"Anything that I can do to help." Ben nodded.

She stood up and gathered her things. He was pretty sure that she'd already been to see Kim Landau. As she shut the door behind her, Ben stared at the time line on the board. He felt like an idiot. A small-town police chief, he was in over his head with these cases. She knew it and he knew it; he just didn't want to read about it.

As he always did when he stood in front of this board, he studied the details to see if there was something he'd missed. Todd Sutton had gotten up around eight that morning and then played nine rounds of golf with Chet. After golf, he bought a chicken sandwich at Burger King at eleven forty-one A.M.; the receipt was found on the floor of the car. Although he'd eaten and drunk in the car, no DNA was found there—a near impossibility. Sutton returned to his house around eleven fifty A.M., placing his golf clubs in the garage. Before getting ready for his wedding, he did an odd thing: He told his stepfather, Fred Sutton, that he would be heading to Zippy Wash to clean his beloved Mustang. Lara Barnes had rented a vintage car for the wedding, so the couple wouldn't be using Sutton's car for the ceremony, making the trip to Zippy Wash seem like an excuse to get away for some time. Was it nerves? Did Sutton meet with someone? When Fred and Betty Sutton departed for the church around three thirty P.M., Todd's tuxedo was still draped on the bed. Assuming he was running late, they took it with them to the church. At four thirty P.M., when the ceremony was about to begin and there was no sign of Todd, they began searching for him. His car showed up the following morning at five o'clock on Wickelow Bend.

If Sutton did go to Zippy Wash, there was no evidence of it. Assuming he did go, he paid with coins and was not spotted by the cashier on duty. While the car had been wiped clean, it was messy, wrappers strewn all over the seats. Sutton had probably never made it to the car wash or he'd never intended to go. The last people who admitted to seeing Sutton were his mother and stepfather. Over the next two days, there had been "sightings" of him—Dulles Airport being the most famous, but it had not been credible. Ben had seen the security tapes himself and the man had not been Todd Sutton.

Next to Todd's time line was Peter Beaumont's. Peter Beaumont had practiced with the band the night before, then failed to show up at a concert at the Skyline Nightclub. Jason Barnes noted that they delayed the band's start for an hour and finally had to go onstage without him. Jason and the bass player had to alternate as lead singer for the night. Unlike Todd Sutton, Peter Beaumont's whereabouts the day of his disappearance were a mystery. No one admitted to having seen him for twenty-four hours. He lived with his mother, who was on vacation in the Finger Lakes with her boyfriend at the time.

But there was one specific link between the two cases that had been nagging Ben for months now. Jason Barnes had been the bandmate and best friend of one victim and the prospective father-in-law of the other. Physically, Jason Barnes could have committed a crime in either scenario. He was a young man when Peter went missing and older, but still physically able to dispose of a body, at the time of Todd Sutton's more recent disappearance. Ben hated to think of Lara's father this way, but it was the only connection he could find between the two men. He sighed. That wasn't a satisfying theory. Why would Jason Barnes harm the man who was his possible ticket to stardom?

"Oh, Lara." He sighed and ran his hands over his face, hoping, for her sake, he was wrong.

His phone rang. It was Doyle in the next room. "Kim Landau is hot to find you. She wanted you to call her when the lady from the *Post* left."

"Did she say why?"

"Nah, she said to call her." He paused. "That you'd have the number. Do you?"

"Do I what?"

"Have her number?"

He sighed. "I do." He was sure that if he could see Doyle's face, it would have a smirk on it like a sixteen-year-old boy.

He picked up the phone and punched in Kim's number.

"Doyle said Michelle Hixson was already there." Kim didn't even wait for hello.

"She was."

"A bit tenacious, don't you think?"

"*A bit* is being kind."

Kim laughed. "In preparation for her interview, I think I found a clue that might help you. I didn't mention this to Michelle Hixson. Meet you at the diner in five?"

"Sure." He wasn't sure if he was going to regret this or not. Right after he and Marla had separated, he'd made the mistake of sleeping with Kim Landau one time. It had been nothing short of a disaster. Recently, she'd sent him signs that she was interested in being more than a onetime fling. At the gala last week, she'd cornered him at the bar and pressed him about him spending time with Lara. He'd been trying to steer their relationship back to the professional, but he groaned every time he saw her phone number pop up on his mobile.

He walked the two blocks to the diner to find Kim scanning the lunch menu in a prime booth near the window. An institution since 1941, the historic Kerrigan Falls Diner was known for its red velvet cake and wide array of pancakes, which it served all day. One of Ben's great pleasures in life was eating buttermilk pancakes at eight in the evening. While the food wasn't always great, the location across from City Hall ensured it was always bustling.

"Don't get the croque monsieur." He slid into the booth.

"That's exactly what I was going to get." She looked up, perplexed. Kim Landau was a beautiful woman with dark-auburn hair, blue eyes, and an upturned nose. She reminded him of Ginger from *Gilligan's Island*. There was an intensity about her, though, that had always unsettled him. The day after they'd slept together, she'd called him six times. He'd felt trapped, pursued, and as a man who was just getting out of one relationship he wasn't in a hurry to tie himself down to another—at least not then.

He turned the menu toward her and pointed. "Stay away from the tuna, too."

"What are you getting, then?" She folded her arms in front of her.

"Cobb salad, maybe the onion soup if it's good today."

She glanced down at the menu. "Grilled chicken sandwich?"

He shrugged. "It's okay, not great. So, what was so urgent?" He didn't mean to sound harsh, but he also didn't want to lead her on. Getting to the point was the best strategy.

She gave him a sly smile. "I hear Lara is in Paris with Gaston Boucher."

He put his arm up on the booth. "Yes, they went to see someone at the Sorbonne about a painting that's been in her family for years."

She raised her eyebrow and gave him a pitying glance. "Is that what she told you?"

What was going on today? He laughed, loudly, placing his folded hands on the table. "She didn't tell me anything, Kim. I talked to her last night. And Gaston is dating Audrey."

Cocking her head, she looked at him like he was pathetic. "Oh, Ben."

This was going to be a short lunch. Flagging the waitress down, he ordered drinks and food together with encouragement to hurry because he had a meeting in thirty minutes. The waitress winked at him. Within minutes, she'd brought them a Heinz Ketchup bottle, a Diet Coke for Ben, and a sweet iced tea for Kim as well as a soup spoon and some crackers.

He crushed the cracker pack in advance of the soup. "Kim, what was so was urgent?" To his delight, the waitress plunked the onion soup down in front of him.

"Well." She leaned in. "In preparation for Miss Hixson's visit, I was looking through some old files on Peter Beaumont's disappearance."

"She thinks we're hillbillies, by the way." Ben opened the crackers and then dumped them in the soup. He tasted it. As expected, it was tepid. "She kept talking about my *one* deputy. We'll be made fools in the pages of the *Washington Post* again; I just know it."

She rested her hand on his. He stared down at it before sliding it away. "Do you remember Paul Oglethorpe?"

"The old guy? The one who covered the town council meetings?"

She tugged at her black twinset, arranging herself. "The one. Back in 1974, he was the main news reporter. One of the notes he left in Peter Beaumont's file was for your father."

"Really?"

She reached in her pocket, pulled out a weathered piece of paper, and slid it across the table. It was the kind of paper that came from a tablet they issued to kids at school, now turned a caramel color from age. Written in pencil was: *Tell Ben Archer to look into the other case. Connected.*

"It was in the Peter Beaumont file. On top." She tapped the table with a perfectly manicured fingernail. "No one had been in that file since the 1970s."

"Thank you," said Ben, sliding the paper across the table. "I'll check my father's files again."

"So." Kim leaned in, whispering. "Since you're alone this week, you could take me to dinner to thank me. Maybe the fireworks tomorrow?"

"I'm on duty tomorrow." It wasn't a lie. He and Doyle would be working the Fourth of July parade on Main Street.

"Well," she said. "I didn't tell Michelle Hixson about the lead, you know... out of loyalty to you."

"Kim—"

She cut him off. "Is this where you tell me it's not me, it's you?" She was a beautiful woman, there was no doubt, but there was something off about her that had always unsettled him. It felt like a feral neediness that he just wanted no part of. He took four bites of the Cobb salad and began itching for the check, trying to catch the waitress's eye.

"Look," he said. "We've known each other a long time. What happened between us was nice, but..." And then he stumbled over what to say next.

She leaned in like she was expecting him to finish the sentence.

"I'm with Lara now." This wasn't entirely true—in fact, it was a damned lie—but he wished it were true so that had to count for something. The other night on her porch when she'd told him she thought she'd seen Todd Sutton, he felt like an idiot to wish for anything more. He wasn't sure when things had changed for him from Lara just being a case—a phone number he called because it was part of the job—to someone whose voice he couldn't wait to hear. That wonderful rough, gravelly voice. And the way Lara laughed, a full laugh. "I'm sorry if I led you to believe anything else. Truly, I am."

Her face fell a little, but she tried to cover it up. "It's a little soon after Todd, don't you think?"

Ben contemplated her question and the suggestion made him furious. "It's been nearly a year, Kim."

"Has it?" she said, gazing off into space like she was adding up the months. "And here I was hoping you'd save me from another boring Sunday night with my cats."

"I'm sorry," he said.

She shrugged. "Are you sure I can't change your mind?"

"I don't think so."

"Lara Barnes is a lucky girl." Her tone had changed abruptly, and she picked up her purse. "I think you've got this, right?"

"Yeah," he said with a weak smile. "I've got this."

Kim Landau was out of the booth in one swift motion; only her perfume lingered.

Ben pondered what she'd said about Lara. In his mind, Lara Barnes was far from a lucky girl. What had happened to her had been cruel and devastating.

"I think I'm the lucky one," he said to the empty booth.

When she'd called last night, Lara had sounded shaken. Immediately, he regretted not having gone with her...not that she'd invited him. When he heard she'd been chased through the Père Lachaise, he had the urge to get a ticket and fly to Paris, but she'd assured him that Gaston Boucher and this Barrow gentleman were taking no chances. Still, he found that Lara often thought she could handle things and sometimes got in over her head without realizing it. He thought of her house and how she'd just leapt at the chance to buy it with no idea how to fix it up, as well as the radio station that she'd plunked down a fortune for. Lara was impulsive. And if she was thinking she saw Todd Sutton, then she was certainly stressed. Had he pushed her toward seeing things by moving too soon and asking her to the gala as his date?

When he got back to the office, he pulled out the Peter Beaumont case files again. There were four thick files that appeared to be in chronological order. Ben sat down with a hot cup of coffee and began slowly scanning each piece of paper, looking for a note or scrap of paper that referred to another case. Looking at his father's handwriting after all these years, he felt a pang of nostalgia.

There was more background in his father's files on Peter. Attached was a photo of Peter Beaumont—the bad 1970s film exposure gave his features a yellow wash, but you could tell he'd been tan. It was a summer picture. Peter was laughing, his sun-bleached long hair contrasting with darker-blond sideburns. Ben studied the photo—something about the man looked familiar, but he couldn't quite place it.

In another pen from another time, a phone number had been quickly jotted down. Looking it up in the file, Ben saw that the number belonged to Fiona Beaumont; his dad had added *Kinsey* to the name, along with *got remarried.* Ben checked "Fiona Kinsey" in the old Kerrigan Falls phone book, finding an F. Kinsey listed at 777 Noles Street. He called the number, trying to do the calculation on Fiona Kinsey's current age. She had to be seventy-four, seventy-five years old now. It was a long shot that she was still alive, though according to the 1997 phone book, she was.

On the sixth ring, Ben was just about to hang up when a woman answered. "Hello."

"Is this Fiona Kinsey?" Ben was sorting through the small pile of photos of Peter Beaumont. He spied a snap of Peter's high school graduation ceremony. It showed a woman with long blond hair and an ultra-mini skirt that was the fashion of the day. The woman was older than Peter, but she looked more like an older sister than a mother. A cigarette dangled from her right hand as she mimed moving the tassel on Peter's cap with the left. Flipping it over, he saw FEE AND PETER written on it.

"Yes," said the woman. Her voice was nasal and suspicious.

"My name is Ben Archer," he said. "I'm—"

"I know who you are," said the woman flatly. "I knew your father."

"Yes," he said, caught off-guard by her bluntness. He could hear what sounded like a grandfather clock ticking in the background. "I was wondering if I could come and talk to you about your son?"

There was a long pause. "I'd prefer that you not."

Ben cleared his throat, trying to buy time to figure out what to say next. "May I ask why?"

"Mr. Archer," she said, like it was too painful to expend the energy to speak. "Do you know the number of people who have stood on my doorstep asking to *talk to me about my son*? And do you know what all the talking has gotten me? Nothing. I'm an old woman. I'm blind and I have liver cancer. Terminal. Peter is dead and I will see him soon enough. At this point, there is nothing that you can tell me or that I can tell you. Peter's gone. Where or why doesn't matter anymore, at least not to me, so please do me the courtesy of staying away. I liked your father. He did what he could, but he failed my son. We all did. Some things, Mr. Archer, are just too late."

The weight of her words fell heavy on him. Ben tapped on the photo with his forefinger. From his father's notes, he could see that he'd tried every angle on the case, but she was correct. His father—and the police department—had failed.

Until now, Peter Beaumont had simply been a name to him—a bookend to Todd Sutton, but this woman's pain was contagious. It came through the phone lines and wrapped around him like a kudzu vine.

"Can you at least tell me what was he like? I didn't know him."

The woman sighed. He could hear the groan of an old chair being pulled across the floor—what he imagined to be a kitchen floor—then the heavy sound of someone settling into it, both bone and breath.

"Honestly, Mr. Archer, there are things that I remember as clear as day. Him dragging that old Fender guitar with him everywhere, knocking it against doorframes and car doors. He had an old strap, never a case for it, and just slung it over his shoulder. An old boyfriend of mine had given it to him—the thing was already battered when he'd gotten it and it didn't get any better. Beautiful guitar, too; it's a shame. Peter hated getting his hair cut, hated wearing shoes as a kid, and until he left us…" The last word hung on her. "…well, he was always barefoot. He had beautiful feet. I know that's a strange memory, but it's one of the things I remember about him that final summer, tan and running around barefoot, getting stung by bees with that beautiful tumble of long, shaggy dirty-blond hair, just like his father. Every week, I recall me telling him to get a haircut, even giving him money for it, which of course he pocketed, but then he and Jason Barnes would spend it on records. I also remember trying to look young enough to be his sister and never being a good enough mother to him. Those are things I remember, Mr. Archer."

"Did he have a girlfriend?"

"He had a harem." She laughed and it turned into coughing, the deep, wet cough from unhealthy lungs. "Even my girlfriends liked him. I think one even dated him, but they kept that kind of thing away from me." Her voice was straining at the end, and she erupted into another series of coughs.

"Anyone special?"

"Not that I recall, Mr. Archer," she said, clearing her throat. "Maybe. Certainly no one came to my door after he went missing claiming to be the love of his life or anything like that. I even wished at one point that someone would. It was sad he'd died with no one. Only Jason Barnes." She laughed. "Those two boys loved each other like brothers. I'm not sure there was room in Peter's life for anything other than his dream. And sweet Jesus could my boy play that guitar."

"The band."

"The band. Always the band. And they'd have made it, too." She paused. "Had he lived long enough." With that, the phone clicked and the line went dead.

21

Paris
July 3, 2005

At the foot of the grand Palais Brongniart at the corner of Rue Vivienne and Rue Réaumur, Lara looked down at her watch. Five minutes until eleven. The imposing building in front of her was too large to be so quiet. Moonlight illuminated the fronts of the pillars. The waiter at the bistro across the street was stacking chairs in an effort to close. During the day, this part of Paris was buzzing with offices and businesses, but at night, it was nearly abandoned. Other than the waiters and the occasional couple on their way home, there was nothing here. She looked down at the ticket and confirmed the streets. The courtyard in front of her was empty and dark.

She paced, her heels clicking on the cement. Turning, she thought she heard something behind her. Footsteps. She kept pacing. If anyone was watching her, she'd pretend like she was waiting for someone—she *was* waiting for someone. She regretted not telling Gaston what she was doing tonight, but she didn't want to worry him or Barrow. After the woman had chased her, she should have been more careful, though she'd cast the protection spell again tonight before she left the hotel. She looked down at her watch again. Three minutes until eleven. All she had to do was hold this woman off for three minutes. Althacazur would find her.

The night air in Paris was sticky and warm, giving little relief. Feeling the need to dress for the occasion, she'd worn a black dress with strappy sandals like she was going to dinner or a concert. Slung over her arm was a denim jacket.

And she heard it again, the clicking of heels—a woman's heels.

Lara spun. The noise was coming from the corner near Rue Vivienne where the streetlight was out. She felt a chill run up her neck. "Come on…come on." She looked around for something to change. Silently, she began the chant.

Bracatus losieus tegretatto.

From a distance, she heard a church bell begin to clang. It was eleven. As if her vision were bending, she saw the pillars in front of her warp. At first it was small, like a ripple when you throw a small stone in the water. Within seconds, the smooth waves became more pronounced, like something was trying to tear through the scene. The streetlights dimmed, making a charged noise as the scene in front of her—the massive building with pillars—gave way. In its place emerged a giant round arena with an opulent gold entrance complete with a Devil's open mouth.

Lara gasped. *The Devil's mouth.* It was just as Cecile and Barrow had described. Looking back toward Rue Vivienne, she thought she saw the outline of a woman standing under the dead streetlamp, waiting. She stared in that direction, letting the woman know she wasn't backing down. Straining her eyes in the dark, Lara couldn't make out if this was the same woman from the Père Lachaise.

There was a steady hum, as if a fluorescent light had just been turned on after a lengthy recess. Four sets of pillars led the way to a door, gaslights illuminating the path. Like a picture coming into focus, the circus with its MATINEE sign became clear. Lara looked down at her ticket.

If she threw the ticket down now and ran, would this scene disappear? Tempting though it was to flee, she stared out at the figure of the woman standing in the shadows. If she didn't go through the doors to Le Cirque Secret, then she had to face whoever was out there, knowing it was *the woman*. No, it was safer to be *inside* this circus.

Blinking, she took in the scene in front of her. An entire circus had just materialized in front of her eyes, supplanting a Parisian landmark. Lara looked around. The waiter at the nearby café continued to stack chairs as though the entire square had not transformed in front of him. Without a ticket, perhaps it hadn't.

"For goodness' sake, get in or get out."

Lara looked around the pillars to find a clown holding a miniature version of himself—a ventriloquist dummy. *Doro.* From Cecile's journal, Lara felt like she already knew him.

"Yes, you." The clowns were dressed identically—all in white, from the face paint to the fez hat to the costume.

Above her, a horse whinnied. Was the statue alive as well?

Amazed, she spun around, not unlike Dorothy who had just entered Oz.

"Ms. Barnes." The dummy's hand pointed to the door. "This way, *s'il vous plaît.*" As the clown walked, the dummy peered around him. "I am Doro. Or, he is." The little wooden hand pointed up to the clown, who held out his hand to claim her ticket.

She was reluctant to give it up.

"The ticket does not belong to you," snapped the dummy.

It was the same dread she'd felt entering a fake haunted house for Halloween. She expected to be entertained, yet there was a foreboding sense in the background. Lara nodded and handed the larger clown the ticket and watched as it melted into his hand. As she stepped onto the carpet, it rolled up behind her, giving her the sinking feeling that perhaps the ticket was one-way. She gulped, regretting she'd been so impulsive. She should have told Gaston. But what would he and Barrow have done? This building wasn't real—or at least wasn't real in this dimension. And they hadn't been invited.

Entering through the giant mouth, she then stepped through a set of ten-foot-tall arched doors that snapped shut tightly behind her. Unfurling in front of her was a hallway—not any old mundane hallway, but a corridor lined with windows, light shining in brightly through them. Which was an impossibility, because it was now night in Paris. For a moment, Lara wasn't sure if this was a circus or Versailles, as the walls were adorned with gold reliefs. As she continued through the hallways, she found a series of adjoining rooms with doors positioned in the center of each room. In front of her were nine more sets of matching white lacquered arched doors, all open; their elaborate gold-leaf inlay and handles looked like something out of a rococo dream—the colors like a macaron shop window. Below her, the floor was a black-and-white harlequin pattern, followed by a dizzying beige spiral floor past the next doorway. The walls of the arcade were painted white, gold, and aqua. White and gold reliefs adorned the walls, and heavy crystal chandeliers dripped from the ceiling—she tried counting and there had to be a hundred of them, reflecting light and making the place drip and sparkle.

It was then that she noticed it. The colors were like a 1960s Technicolor film—the blues and golds more pronounced and everything bathed in a kind of glow, almost a soft focus. This world didn't look real, as if she'd stepped into a Claymation puppet show. Perhaps Giroux had tried to mimic it with his dripping technique. In each room she saw a different attraction: a fortune-teller, shooting games, cakes and food trays, even the smell of popcorn. While elegant, the gauges and machinery were old, like they'd been installed during the Belle Époque period, causing her to feel like she was walking through a time capsule.

The place also smelled like a stale house that had been shut up for the winter before enduring a furious spit-and-polish attempt at freshening.

Each room was painted in hues like macarons. As they entered the next room, another scent greeted them at the doors. It was sweet. "What is that smell?" She looked down at the small puppet for an answer.

"Melting chocolate, I'd say, although I cannot smell."

Lara inhaled sharply. "God, that was amazing."

"We have the almond room next." The clown pointed. "This way," said the dummy, leading her through the doors as the sweet smell of almonds and sugar engulfed her. "We call this hallway the Grand Promenade." While she'd entered the building at night, outside the windows the sun was streaming down on elaborate hedges and mazes in the lawns outdoors.

At the fourth room, they stopped at an old carousel. With its double-decker platform, it was the grandest carousel that Lara had ever seen.

He motioned for her to get on.

"You're kidding?" She cocked her head. This carousel looked familiar. When the dummy didn't reply, she reluctantly grabbed the pole. There was a carousel horse in front of her, and its tail began to swish. Surely it didn't move? As if to answer her, the tail flicked again. The dummy said, "Get on."

Lara took a moment to think. She was in what appeared to be another dimension, talking to a clown's dummy, who was trying to get her onto a carousel with what might be live animals. "What the fuck. This can't get any weirder." She shrugged and placed her foot in the stirrup, sliding over the horse's back. Lara felt the animal move under her, as though it were breathing. Its neck began to move up and down of its own accord like it was waking up from a long sleep. On cue, the organ music started and Lara began to feel dizzy as she lost sight of the clown and matching dummy.

She definitely felt a little fuzzy—as if she'd had two glasses of champagne. Then something unexpected happened. The carousel began to move *backward*. The first image struck her hard. The carousel lights became brighter until all she could see were images of Ben Archer's face. She was sitting on the stool at the bar in Delilah's listening to him telling her about the widow hitting on him. Gripping the edges of the chair, she felt the bar's cushion squeeze beneath her fingers even as she realized that this image could not be real. Still, she felt the sensation of jealousy wash over her again as he vaguely glossed over the details of what had happened with the widow.

The next image felt like a slap: her dinner with Ben Archer months before. The illusion was so real that she slid her arms around the carousel horse's neck to stabilize herself and found that she was gripping smooth, silky hair. With a rhythmic beating noise, the horse was cantering backward on the platform with its head down. The strange sensation made her sick to her stomach, like when she'd ridden on a train with her back to the front car. She looked around to see that all the animals—the lion, the tiger, and the zebra—were also running in reverse and in unison, like a herd stampede being rewound on film.

The carousel lights flashed again and Ben's face morphed. Now she saw him on the steps of the old stone Methodist church, shaking his head. She wore the ivory lace dress.

Lara gasped loudly at the next scene. Todd stood in front of her, hazy like he was in the sun; she squinted to see him. *Todd*. She gasped when she saw his face again. He was like the illusion she'd seen at the gala, but this Todd was in a memory—the scene familiar to her. Up close, after all these months, she'd forgotten so many details about his features—the lines next to his mouth and the blue flecks in his hazel eyes. Perhaps her pain was so bad that she'd had to erase him. And now it felt as though a weak seam had begun to rip again at the fabric of her insides. The carousel lights flashed and the music was loud, but inside the image it was just them. They were in his Jeep with the top down; he was looking at her and smiling. The wind was blowing in her face, stray hairs of hers getting snagged on her recently applied lip gloss. She stared at Todd's face, so grateful to be seeing it again and ashamed that she'd forgotten the way he brushed his brown hair back with his hand. He was so beautiful.

"Don't go." She put her hand out to touch him.

He looked over at her and laughed. "What are you talking about?"

She remembered this drive. Two weeks before the wedding they'd been on their way to Charlottesville. She'd stared at his profile as he drove, but in this exact moment, they hadn't said this to each other. He lifted his sunglasses and pulled the Jeep over, then leaned in and kissed her. These images were beautifully assembled, like lines of poetry. To touch Todd's face again—knowing in her heart that he was lost to her—had such a purity and beauty that it took her breath away. This had been her wish: to see him again knowing the significance of the moment and the loss that was to follow. She held his face in her hands, studying every line and stray hair.

The carousel began to slow. She could see flickers of light showing through him. Todd was fading.

"I love you." She choked the words out quickly, her hands still holding on to his face, a little hard so his face shook as she spoke.

"I love you, too." He dissolved in front of her, his voice echoing.

Lara began to sob, hugging the horse's neck tightly. It, too, had changed, returning to a smooth polished wood. Its tail gave one final flick that brushed against her thigh.

When it stopped, it wasn't the pair of clowns waiting for her anymore. She recognized the familiar blue-and-green uniform of Shane Speer, the fortune-teller from the Rivoli Circus.

Had she been transported back to Kerrigan Falls? At this point, anything was possible. She climbed down off the horse, dizzy and slightly sick. Her head and stomach were not in unison. She'd never been one for rides.

"Hello, Miss Barnes." In this wild French circus, his American Southern accent was terribly out of place.

Oh Jesus. This was like those dreams where strange things in her life merged—her kindergarten teacher replacing her father onstage at a Dangerous Tendencies gig and not knowing the words to the set list they were about to play.

"I know." Shane was leaning against the control booth, smoking a cigarette. He took a final drag before extinguishing it on the ground with a black Puma sneaker. "You're thinking, *What is* he *doing here?*"

"You?" She was wobbly and pointed to him as she stepped onto the ground. Well, her hand was trying to point at him, but she stumbled.

"I really work here," he said, catching her, "but I had to make sure you had the desire to join us inside our little circus, so I was forced to come to you."

"All that stuff you said to me. Was it bullshit, then?"

"Hardly." He stood her up and then walked backward down the Grand Promenade, nodding toward the merry-go-round. "What do you think of her?"

She followed behind him, staggering a bit and looking back at the carousel, taking in the ride. The carousel was aqua with a seascape scene painted on the top marquee, surrounded by ornate gold livery and round lights. She remembered her old carousel that sat rotting behind the barn and all her attempts at getting it to move with magic. This was the carousel that Althacazur had tried to teach her to pull through to her world; she'd caught enough glimpses of it when she'd come close to conjuring it up.

"It goes back in time. Trippy isn't it? Most people can't stay on here for long. If they do, they go back to before they were born and then they kind of..." He snapped his fingers. "...go poof."

"They go poof?" Lara nearly shouted.

He shrugged. "I guess it should come with some kind of warning...like one of those YOU MUST BE THIS TALL TO RIDE signs." He gestured to his navel with a flat hand.

"Or that it kills you?"

"Well, I think that's a bit harsh, Ms. Barnes. It just makes you evaporate, which is quite different from killing you, I assure you. But we could stand here and quibble all day." He kept walking. "Come on." They passed the fortune-teller room. "Now, here I can give you a really accurate fortune. I can even change it up if someone asks. That cheating husband that I see in your palm? He'll be as faithful as a nun on Sunday...but it'll cost you."

"Let me guess." Lara straightened her skirt. "Poof?"

"Nah, just your soul. You'd be surprised who takes me up on it." He stopped for a moment, then spun around like a real estate agent walking her through a showing. "This," he said, "is the Room of Truth. No one ever wants to go in there."

"Why not?"

"The room is filled with mirrors that strip out all illusion, so all you see before you is the truth. As you can imagine, no one wants to see things as they really are. People have gone mad in that room." He shook his head gravely. "Oh, we say we want to know the truth. But do we really?" Like a stage magician, he produced a stick of aqua, pink, and white cotton candy that appeared out of nowhere. He held out the stick. "Cotton candy?"

"No, thanks," said Lara, her stomach still settling from the ride.

Shane shrugged and began tugging at the fluff. At the end of the hall was an even bigger set of aqua doors, which opened as they approached. Through the doors was the big top, labeled LE HIPPODROME. The sun was shining in the Grand Promenade when Lara stepped into the big top. Unlike the sunny rooms in the hall, the night sky and stars peered through the glass-and-gold ceiling of the hippodrome. Baroque carved box seats with gold reliefs lined the inside walls, with large baroque chandeliers dripping down from the ceiling, the largest in the center dome; additional clusters formed over the seating groups closest to the ring. It was like the inside of a jewelry box. To Lara's surprise, the seats were all elaborate velvet chairs. In the center ring, the wood floor had an ornately carved and polished chevron pattern. She'd seen this circus before, in the painting *Sylvie on the Steed*.

"The seat of honor." He motioned toward a teal velvet chair—what looked like a throne—located in the empty front row.

Shane walked over to the center of the ring and stood there. The room went dark, and then a spotlight appeared on him. "Ladies… and, well, Lady…may I introduce your ringmaster tonight. The creator of this circus…"

There was a drumroll, followed by the smash of cymbals—the spotlight searching, circling until it finally focused on a set of double doors that opened. No one emerged.

"Oh fuck," said Shane. "I'll be right back. Time for a costume change."

The spotlight went dark and the doors shut tightly. Then the spotlight flashed again and this time a man emerged from the doors. He was dressed as the ringmaster in a gold top hat and tails. His black boots and jodhpurs shimmered. He greeted Lara as a late-night comedian does his studio audience. *It's him! Althacazur.*

"Welcome, my dear." His voice echoed in the empty arena. "I know." He looked down at himself; his brown curls touched his shoulders. "I like this form much better, too. You've seen me not only as Shane Speer but also as the janitor from Le Cirque de Fragonard. You see, I can hop circuses pretty easily." He put one of his polished boots up on the wooden banister that separated the front row from the circle. "Tell me, which one of me do you like best?"

The man who'd rescued her from the lady at the Père Lachaise and had shown her the painting of Cecile Cabot? That had been *him*? "You said you'd find me," said Lara, in awe of the entire spectacle in front of her. This world was beautiful. She stared around the big top. It was magnificent!

"And so I did," he said with a wink.

"Why?" At the gala, he'd said that he'd made her magic strong, but none of this made sense.

"Ah yes...we'll get to that in a moment." He bowed deeply, as if Queen Elizabeth stood in front of him, his brown curls tipping over in cascades before he secured his top hat. "I'm so pleased you could join us tonight, Lara Margot Barnes. Allow me to introduce myself properly. I am your host, Althacazur. We're a little out of practice at Le Cirque Secret, so please bear with us tonight. It's our first show in front of an audience in seventy-some years. We have some new members of the troupe as well, and they're excited to perform just for you."

As he circled—or rather pranced—around the floor, Lara saw a small monkey scamper to him. *Mr. Tisdale?* As if he could read her mind, Althacazur smiled. "Oh yes, you've met Mr. Tisdale. Tis, it seems Miss Barnes remembers you. You made quite an impression."

Mr. Tisdale waved his small hand at her.

She found herself waving back at the little creature.

"Mr. Tisdale says that it would be very rude of me not to explain ourselves to you first. Well, welcome to Le Cirque Secret. Perhaps you've heard of us." He stopped as if on cue, waiting for Lara to reply.

She nodded.

"Good. Try to interact with us a bit, Miss Barnes. It helps." He circled the ring like it was a stage and he, a modern-day rock star.

The little monkey's head followed Althacazur's every move, seemingly as mesmerized as Lara was.

"So other than the complaints you expressed earlier about including *warnings* on it"—he rolled his eyes—"did you like my carousel, Miss Barnes? If you recall, you tried to pull it through to your world once?"

Lara nodded. "I did."

"Oh, it's one of my greatest creations. It goes back"—he stopped, like a comedian waiting for a punch line, then laughed like a teenager telling a dirty joke—"in time."

Mr. Tisdale clapped as if on cue. It was then that Lara noticed that he and Althacazur were wearing matching outfits.

"Forgive me, I should explain because the internet doesn't do me justice. I am the premier daemon of...well, *fun shit*. Let me be clear. First, please be sure to put the *a* in *daemon*. We hate it when it is left off, makes us look like barbarians. The *a* is so elegant, don't you think?" He waited for her reply. "I'm also known as Althacazar"—he emphasized the *a*—"and Althacazure." He focused on the very French pronunciation of the latter.

"Quite elegant," said Lara, finally agreeing.

"Do try to keep up." He put his hand to his chin like he was considering something. "So, what was I saying? Oh yes, I am the daemon of lust...wine...music...sex...everything that makes the world go 'round is in my purview."

Althacazur looked down at the adoring monkey. "I know. Mr. Tisdale here was once quite famous himself." The monkey gazed down at his foot modestly. As if performing a Shakespeare aside, Althacazur leaned in, placing his boot on the ledge again directly in front of her, and whispered loudly, "He might have led a country in his previous life." He turned to the monkey, who cast his eyes down toward the ground. "Is that fair to say? Well, he doesn't like to talk about it too much, but let's say he ruled a country some years back that's famous for its gelato. Am I right, Tis?"

The monkey looked ashamed, embarrassed at having his identity revealed in this current form.

"Oh, don't mind him. He's been a great manager of the circus. He gets a little nostalgic for his old being, but, well…that isn't to be anymore, is it, Tis?"

The defeated monkey shook his head. Lara was mortified to think that if the clues were correct, the monkey standing in front of her was once…*Benito Mussolini*?

As if he could read her mind, the poor creature looked up at her, squeaked, and sulked off, his head hanging.

"Oh, Miss Barnes. A little rule. Please don't say or think the actual names of my creatures in their previous lives. It reminds them of who they once were. You can hint at it, but never *say* it. Tisdale, Tisdale, come back…she didn't mean it."

Althacazur turned to her. "You must understand…everyone in my collection was once a famous performer of some type or another… opera singers…rock stars…politicians. Ah…politicians are the best, by far. Such egomaniacs. I *adore* them!" He gave a jaunty jerk of his head in Tisdale's direction. "They've all, well, ended up…" He pointed toward the floor. "Down there, as you all like to call it. But I said, 'Fuck no, we're going to get a troupe together and allow these poor damned souls to perform again.' So here we are for one night only—Le Cirque Secret." He pointed to her. His delivery was over the top, like a vaudeville performer.

The doors opened and hordes of performers emerged—clowns,

trapeze artists, bearded ladies carrying house cats in cages, followed by horses and elephants.

Althacazur took the house cats from the bearded lady. He opened the door, and the cats jumped out. "Make sure Tisdale is out of sight." He turned to Lara. "They try to eat him when they change."

Lara was confused until Althacazur snapped his fingers and the tabby and the black house cat morphed into a lion complete with a full mane and a black panther, respectively. Lara remembered the passage in Cecile's diary. "Hercules and Dante."

"Oh, Miss Barnes, the cats will be so happy to hear that you know them. Come, come..." He motioned for her to join him in the ring. Was he really suggesting she go into the ring with a lion and a panther?

"Yes," he said, answering her thought. "I am suggesting it. Move your ass, Miss Barnes."

Lara got up from the velvet throne and stepped gingerly into the ring. The lion noticed her first and walked over to her, like it was sizing her up. Gripped with fear, Lara stood still until the animal paced around her, finally stopping in front of her. Lara reminded herself that in all likelihood this cat was no taller than her shin, but damn, the lion looked real.

"I assure you," said Althacazur, considering his fingernails. "He's a house cat. A tiny little thing." As if on command, the lion roared loudly, causing Lara to scream.

"Hercules," commanded Althacazur. "Up." The lion jumped onto a pedestal and sat watching the ringmaster for further commands. "Dante." The man turned and raised his arms; the sleek black cat stood up on his hind legs. Althacazur patted the cat on the head as he walked past. "Go to Miss Barnes," he commanded.

Lara could hear his front paws as they landed heavily on the wooden floor. Like Hercules before him, the cat circled Lara before sitting in front of her like a dog. He was so large that in the sitting position, his head was near her throat.

"Don't give him ideas. Just give him a treat."

Lara looked confused.

Althacazur sighed, bored.

She could see that his amber eyes with flat pupils stood out vividly. Was that eyeliner? Thick black eyeliner.

"In your pocket, Miss Barnes."

Lara reached into her pocket and pulled out a Pounce cat treat.

"Give it to him, Miss Barnes. Before he gets pissed. Tell him he's a good boy."

Lara extended a shaking hand out to the cat. He turned his head to remove the treat gently with his tongue.

From the pedestal above her, the lion roared loudly.

"I know, I know," said Althacazur. "But you haven't done anything for Miss Barnes to earn a treat, have you, Hercules? You lazy animal."

The lion jumped to the floor and lay in front of Lara like the Sphinx. As if he was waiting for a dramatic point in the routine, he executed a perfect roll. Lara reached into her pocket to find another treat. She held out her hand, and the lion, who now stood before her, took it gently.

"Snap your fingers, Miss Barnes."

Lara looked at Althacazur, who made a snapping motion like she was an idiot. She snapped her fingers, and just like in an episode of *Bewitched*, the panther and lion sat perched in front of her as two small cats, their tails flicking back and forth. She reached into her pocket again and found two more treats. She bent over and gave each cat one more.

"You liked that one, didn't you?"

Lara smiled and petted the animals.

The bearded lady came by and swatted them lightly, sensing their reluctance to go to their cages.

The show continued as two clowns entered and began to screw off their limbs.

Lara watched in horror as they exchanged left arms and right legs, then one took the other by the head and rotated until his head came off; in turn, the headless body held on while the other clown rotated around him until his own head came off. They tossed the heads back and forth as the heads continued to chatter to each other. Then each took the opposite head, placed it on top of his neck, and rotated it back on.

Althacazur clapped as the clowns bowed and exited. "I just love that one. You'd never guess who that was in a million years. The irony of the heads coming off... you just can't design this stuff any better." Althacazur circled in front of her, still clapping. "Now, this one is just for you."

The door opened and a figure came out—a large one—a towering figure with eight fucking legs. Jesus. Lara had a thing about spiders. A bad thing. Ever since Peter Brady had the tarantula on his chest on *The Brady Bunch* vacation episode in Hawaii, Lara had *hated* spiders. Worst thing about buying an old house? Spiders. Now bounding toward her was one that stood at least eight feet tall.

"Seven," corrected Althacazur, his eyebrow raised. "Seven feet tall. Your inner voice exaggerates."

Lara felt sweat beading on her lip. "I suppose this little guy is actually the size of a postage stamp, too?"

Althacazur leaned against the bandstand and lit a cigarette. "Nope. She's fucking huge. Am I right?"

The spider slowly approached and then lifted her front legs, exposing giant furry fangs. From the countless books Lara had read about spiders—from the Sydney funnel-web spider that chased down your ass to the black widow that lurked in woodpiles—she knew this was bad, very bad. But underneath the arachnid was—a woman. *Was a woman pinned to the thorax?*

Lara felt bile rise in her throat. She was definitely going to vomit.

On second glance, the woman was not *attached* to the spider so much as she *was* the thorax—her arms and legs transformed to spider legs. When the spider got close, she could see that the woman looked just like her. Lara felt her blood drain, then her body became heavy.

The next thing she felt was Tisdale's leathery fingers touching her. She had passed out in the ring.

"Did I faint?"

The monkey nodded. The arena was now empty, and Althacazur was chuckling.

"That is my biggest nightmare," Lara said, gulping.

"You should have seen your face." His eyes were wide with excitement. "Wasn't it groovy, though, staring down your fear." He peered down her. "I mean, you *literally* stared it down."

She looked toward her left at Tisdale, who seemed sympathetic.

"Get her up, Tisdale, shake her off a bit."

The monkey patted Lara, who got to her feet and looked behind her to make sure her giant spider-self wasn't lurking in the entrance.

"I'll stop toying with you now, Lara," said Althacazur. "You can take your seat."

Lara returned to the giant throne in the front row, checking her watch to see what time it was, but the display still showed one minute after eleven—the exact time she'd come through the doors. At this point it could have been minutes or days.

The pin spotlights came on, and the orchestra roared to life. Althacazur sashayed out from the pit. "*Mesdames et messieurs,* welcome to Le Cirque Secret—where nothing is as it seems." He cocked his top hat and the lights came up, revealing a full house of people—actual patrons.

Men and women dressed in their finest—dresses and coats and hats from another time. She saw top hats resting on laps; in front of her where it had not been a few moments ago was a silver plate with a glass of champagne.

"Popcorn?" Lara turned to find a small black bear wearing a tulle collar of aquamarine with bronze sequined beading and carrying a tray.

"I know," said the bear, moving his neck uncomfortably in his collar. "It's a bit much. Itchy, too."

"Thank you." Lara slid the popcorn bag from his outstretched hand. He scanned the rest of the rows like a flight attendant with a beverage cart.

Lara looked at the man next to her. Was he real? He appeared to be real, but his coat was wool and it was July. The women wore their hair up or severely bobbed. If she had to guess, the clothing placed them in the early 1920s. Lara caught the man's eye, and he winked at her. Immediately she turned and looked forward, sinking into her seat. He looked so familiar, and it took Lara a moment to realize that he was the man in the audience from the *Sylvie on the Steed* painting, the one who was pointing. Quickly she turned her head to sneak a confirming look. Yes, it was definitely him.

A steady beat came from the bass drum, followed by strings. It was a familiar opening—Gustav Mahler's "Vampire Song." Everyone in the ring scrambled.

In the center, women in white skirts and top hats over Raggedy-Ann-red hair juggled. The jugglers parted and two women were spun on separate wheels while jesters in matching blue, red, and gold costumes threw knives at them.

The act was familiar to anyone who had attended a simple street carnival. In a whoosh, a dozen women rotated a giant wheel in place at the center of the ring. The women were a strange sight, their other-worldly crimson tresses trimmed to resemble yard hedges—one with a tidy single cone above her head, like a tipped ice cream cone; the other with two cone peaks projected above her ears; their faces ghostly white with exaggerated Cupid's bow lips to match their hair.

After a flurry of set changes, the spotlight panned and a woman and man emerged holding hands before taking their places.

As Edvard Grieg's "Hall of the Mountain King" began, a man donned a blindfold while a woman stepped onto the wheel. Without much fanfare, the man gathered his arsenal into a leather satchel that he slung from his left shoulder and in one movement both turned and emptied his collection of knives and axes at the tall, smirking blonde. Metal scraped as the blades left the leather bag and then thunked as each hit the intended target. Rather than savoring each throw, the thrower dispatched his blades much like bullets from a gun. Lara watched as the audience, so sure they knew what was to happen next, settled back in their velvet chairs. Anyone standing in the alcove could hear the clinking of glasses as the bored patrons in the darkened hall took sips of their champagne. In the dimly lit seating area, Lara could make out the faces of the audience—they were bored, as if this act was nothing spectacular. Hell, the opera was better.

The thrower removed his blindfold and admired his handiwork, allowing the dramatic moment to hang for an intended beat too long. Somewhere near the top of the stands, a man coughed as if to prod the thrower to get on with the next reveal—which of course had to be the unveiling of the woman, stepping off the wheel without a scrape on her.

Except it wasn't.

Like an adjustment the eye makes from light to dark, Lara saw the woman on the wheel come sharply into focus. The patrons in the front row nearest to the spectacle sat forward in their seats, sure their eyes were playing tricks on them. Next came audible gasps, Lara's included. The scene came into focus, spreading backward and catching the throats of the audience, until the full horror reached the very top. Lara swooned with them, bile rising again in her throat.

The woman had, in fact, been severed like a felled tree trunk. All her limbs, as well as her neck, were chopped with manic precision—a bloodless upper thigh rolling off the board and settling at the feet of the patrons in the front row, causing a delicate lady to scream and then faint. Back on the wheel, the woman didn't bleed, but rather seemed to separate, her severed head resting at an odd angle with her eyes open.

Lara felt the room spin. Shit, she was going to faint again.

The thrower, upon securing her thigh back in its place, spun the wheel, letting it come to a halt on its own. He then turned his back to the woman and put his hand to his chin, like he was waiting for something to happen. Only then did the woman step off the platform entirely whole to take a deep bow.

The ringmaster entered the ring, his hand sweeping proudly toward the performers. "*Louis et Marie.*"

The delighted audience roared and jumped to their feet, the sound of their shoes hitting the stands like thunder echoing through the big top.

Lara looked around the arena, horrified. Guests were gripped, staring at the spectacle, pointing and laughing.

Next came a group of synchronized tumblers dressed in aqua-and-gold leotards and pink-and-gold leotards, all striped the same pattern with gold beading.

Through the tumblers came a white horse. The animal was magnificent with a flowing white mane. On the horse's head was a plume of aqua feathers. From the description in the journal, Lara knew it could only be His Majesty.

Doing a backbend on the horse with her shins on His Majesty's neck and her hands on the saddle was Margot Cabot of Le Cirque Margot. The entire floor of the circus turned into flames and His Majesty continued his steady gallop as Margot lifted her legs into a graceful handstand and then dipped under the horse, into the roaring flames. Both rider and horse seemed unfazed, but Lara could feel the heat rising from the floor. Like a graceful ballerina, Margot hung off the animal with one leg while swinging her other, then stood up on His Majesty's back on one leg as he simultaneously leapt in the air. Finally, the flames engulfed both horse and rider until the pair broke through a wall of fire, completely unharmed. The horse made a bow of sorts as Margot jumped off his back to curtsy.

In a flash, the flames were gone and Althacazur was back announcing the next act—the Dance of Death. Twelve androgynous clowns began to waltz, their elaborately beaded costumes a muted color of blush and their hair white. They looked ghostly, but the dance was beautiful. Three elephants made their way onstage and lifted the clowns onto their backs in perfect unison. From the ceiling emerged three Spanish Webs.

While this spectacle was unfolding, the other clowns wheeled out guillotines. Lara began to get apprehensive about this act, ominously called the Dance of Death. In perfect unison, the guillotines lowered as the clowns leapt from the backs of the elephants... and it was revealed that the Spanish Web ropes were not ropes at all, but nooses. As the orchestra played on, heads rolled and necks snapped. Lara put her hand to her mouth. She heard one woman sigh and appear to faint. The entire circus was a macabre spectacle of death played out inside a ring. No wonder some of the artists in Montparnasse had thought it was performance art. And yet, Lara knew it was entirely a dance of the damned.

As the clowns dangled from the ropes, they began to wake and crawl back up, their legs swinging in perfect unison. In the same manner, the headless clowns picked up the waltz and resumed the dance, spinning and turning. The music picked up the pace until it crescendoed into a frenzied flurry.

The stage went dark. As the lights came back on and the clowns were back in their original positions, the waltz grew tame again until they circled out of the arena.

The drum began to beat, followed by a Gregorian chant.

From the group emerged a woman with platinum hair. Lara had seen her likeness hanging on the wall at Le Cirque de Fragonard.

It was Cecile Cabot, the one from the painting.

The Spanish Web she was using was a rope with a bell at the bottom. As she waited, it lowered from the center of the ring. Cecile leapt onto the bell and quickly began to contort herself around the object as it rose higher and higher above the audience. When she reached the top, the audience realized there was no net below her. Cecile began to spin on the golden rope faster and faster, finally slowing and lowering herself back down from the rope to the bell-shaped end. Hanging off the bell, she spun her legs under it like a propeller, her body spinning like a plate faster and faster—and then she let go of the bell.

The music was otherworldly. It reminded Lara of eastern European composers, as haunting and tragic as a Russian funeral march.

The crowd, realizing that Cecile was suspended entirely on her own, leaned forward, expecting her to fall at any moment, but she didn't. Instead she slowed her rotations so the crowd could see that she was, indeed, hovering in the air. She gathered herself and spun horizontally, picking up speed like a figure skater, moving through the air as if she were a human drill bit. Cecile had the grace of a rhythmic gymnast or ballet dancer, her moves fluid. As the rotations ended, she rolled slowly to the floor and landed softly before she lowered herself and bowed.

It was hard to describe the corkscrew. Certainly the journals didn't do the move justice. To watch a woman fly so gracefully across the stage like a spiraling bird was one of the most stunning performances she'd ever seen.

The crowd jumped to their feet, giving Cecile Cabot a standing ovation.

With a swipe of her arm, Cecile Cabot made everything—the audience and the entire spectacle—disappear.

Turning to Lara, she bowed. "That, my dear, is Le Cirque Secret— where nothing is as it seems." This woman in front of her seemed so different from the shy, sheltered girl from her journals. As she walked toward Lara, she commanded the room, confident and sure, but wasn't she dead? Lara couldn't understand how a woman long dead could be standing in front of her.

Cecile smiled, apparently knowing Lara's thoughts. "I'm not the naive girl I once was. True, I have been dead a long time, but this circus is primarily performed by the dead."

Lara kept forgetting anything she thought here was basically broadcast on a goddamned Jumbotron. "I'm sorry. I didn't mean…"

But Cecile shook her head. "Lara Barnes. I've been waiting for you a long, long time."

22

Kerrigan Falls, Virginia
July 5, 2005

Ben had been through most of the notes in Peter Beaumont's file and hadn't turned up anything he hadn't seen before. From a stack of photos held together by a paper clip, he took one out and studied it. Whoever had taken the picture seemed to cause Peter's face to light up, so Ben assumed it was taken by someone he'd loved, and yet his mother had said there had been no one special.

The only person Peter's mother mentioned was Jason Barnes, who had been interviewed twice and said it was inconceivable that Peter had just up and left. The two had been planning to go to LA that November and try their luck. Yet Jason Barnes had not gone to LA after his best friend disappeared. Ben wondered about this detail. Why? Surely Jason could have made it on his own—eventually, he did succeed as a musician. Looking at the date, Ben did the math and realized that part of the reason Jason probably never went to LA was due to the fact that Audrey had been pregnant with Lara at the time. Jason and Audrey were married two months after Peter died. As much as he hated to do it, he would need to talk to Lara's father.

He turned the photo of Peter over, and there was on old note attached to it. Well, *attached* wasn't quite the word; the tape had almost melted into the photo paper from years of being stored in humidity. Nothing here was preserved in storage, and the photos looked like they were beginning to warp. While he'd spent hours studying his father's notes, he hadn't looked at the photos. There it was. The little detail he'd missed.

Other case connected? 1944.

No one had ever mentioned another case. He searched his father's drawer, where he'd kept Peter Beaumont's file. There was no other case. Ben inspected the writing more closely. This wasn't his father's penmanship. Given that it was stuck on the back of a photo, he wondered if his father had even gotten this message. The police files from the 1940s were all archived in the courthouse basement, and he wasn't sure what he should look for. None of the archives were online. There had been no murders since the 1930s, so it was safe to limit his search to missing persons cases. He could call Kim and see if it was easier for her to check the newspaper archives on microfilm from that year for any missing persons case. He lifted the receiver to call over to the newspaper and then, remembering their lunch Sunday, thought better of it. He grabbed his keys and walked the block to the courthouse.

On the way, he stopped in for a black coffee at the Feed & Supply. He wasn't sleeping well these days, and he found it hard to stay awake in the early afternoon. A coffee might be exactly what he needed. Caren Jackson was restocking pastries after the morning rush.

"Moving from croissants to cupcakes, I see." Looking around the coffee bar, he was impressed with what Caren had done with the old hardware store. Every business in Kerrigan Falls was housed in a building that "used to be" something else. The old floor still had that heavy sound as your feet moved over the solid planks. He'd once come here with his dad, poring through the drawers and drawers of screws and nails. Now they housed tea bags and coffee beans. The rich jewel tones of the velvet sofas and chairs mixed well with the weathered leather Chesterfield chairs and sofas Caren and Lara had found.

Caren laughed. "Can I interest you in an almond croissant? It only has about an hour of good life left in it. I usually order them for our mutual friend, who is probably enjoying the real thing in Paris."

"Sure," said Ben. "I usually only see her for dinner, so I wasn't aware of her croissant habit."

"Have you talked to her?" There was a hint to Caren's voice that she had inside knowledge of his budding relationship with Lara. If you could call it that.

"I talked to her a few days ago," he said. "She should be home today, shouldn't she?"

Caren smirked as if this only reaffirmed her suspicions.

"Have you talked to her?"

"I got an email," said Caren. "They extended their trip a few days. Something about an art expert."

"Did she tell you she was chased by some woman down through the streets of Paris?"

"What?" Caren's voice rose. "She did *not*." He'd wanted a to-go cup, but she poured his coffee into a porcelain mug and placed the warmed croissant on a matching plate. After sliding both across the counter, she leaned on the glass display. "Does Audrey know this?"

"I don't know," he said. "I told Lara to call the police. She's got a valuable painting. Someone could be trying to steal it or kidnap her to get it. If you talk to her before I do, make sure she calls the police." He took a sip and was pleasantly surprised that it was a fresh pot— something that usually didn't happen in the afternoon. He carried the mug over to the nearest seating area.

Caren came around with the warm croissant on a plate. "I worry about her." She leaned on the back of a low leather chair. "I've seen that painting hanging across the hall from the guest bathroom all my life. Who would have thought it was valuable."

"So it was the across-from-the-guest-bathroom painting?"

"Exactly," said Caren, laughing. "Usually it's some Parisian champagne advertisement poster or dogs playing poker. It's the most disrespected wall space in any home."

Ben laughed. "And Audrey *gave* the painting to Lara?"

"Yeah," said Caren, folding her arms. "Lara wasn't really a fan of it. The thought that it might be valuable was a real shock to her." She paused.

"You look like you want to ask me something?" He took a bite of the almond croissant, realizing he'd never had one before. The flowery, vanilla taste of the center was a surprise.

"Is it that obvious?" she hesitated.

He was wondering if she was going to ask him his intentions toward her best friend. "What do you think *really* happened to Todd?" Caren looked down, her long spiral curls bouncing anytime her head moved.

He was uncomfortable with this question. Michelle Hixson had asked the same thing, and he hadn't had a good answer then. In the interest of the case, he couldn't get into the specifics with Caren any more than he could with the reporter—*especially* not Caren, who out of friendship would feel some obligation to tell Lara whether advertently or inadvertently. Carefully, he weighed his response. "What I can say is that I don't think Todd abandoned Lara."

She actually looked relieved at his answer. "There are just so many theories out there—some of them crazy. I heard there is a coven."

"I've heard most of them, but the coven is a new one," said Ben, amused, sipping his coffee. "The Dulles Airport thing was wrong. I saw the guy on the security tape, definitely not Todd Sutton."

"Seriously," said Caren, sounding a little surprised. "You need to get a phone line for tips." Just then the bell rang and a customer came through the door. Caren excused herself and went back behind the counter.

Placing his cup on the coffee table, Ben noticed there was a Ouija board—an old one. He touched the curved edges. It doubled as a tray. It was vintage, but the wood on it was pretty and it had been well kept. He pushed the planchette with his finger, causing it to move a little. It seemed to move a bit farther than his effort implied, and he jerked back a little. "What the—"

Smoothly, as if it were skating, the planchette began to slide across the wood. Instinctively Ben looked up to see if it was hooked to a wire. He looked under the table to see if there was a remote. That would be a funny gag, he thought. The planchette stopped, like it was idling, waiting for him to focus on it. Then, slowly it began to move again, stopping on the letter D.

"Okay," said Ben nervously, still glancing around to see if anyone was watching him, playing a trick on him. This would be the kind of prank his college buddy would play…then he realized that Walker was dead.

The planchette traveled across the board, landing on E.

Ben picked up his coffee and sniffed it. It smelled like coffee and it didn't seem to be spiked. "Okay."

As though it was waiting for his affirmation, the pointer moved again, settling on the letter z.

Z? Ben looked confused and waited for another letter. A minute went by and nothing. "Dez?"

Nothing.

Caren appeared behind him and Ben jumped. "Oh my God, you scared me." He put his hand on his chest.

"Are you okay?" Her brown eyes were wide. He noticed how long her eyelashes were and that one eye was actually green. Heterochromia, they called it.

"Is this some trick board?" He pointed to the Ouija with the planchette still resting on the z.

"No," said Caren. "Why?"

"I swear it moved."

"Oh God," said Caren. "Not you, too."

"Huh?" Ben looked confused.

"Lara hates Ouija boards. In all fairness, years ago, at my sister's slumber party, one went nuts in front of us. There was a house full of screaming girls. Lara thought it was her mind that had done it. To this day, she still thinks it was her doing. My dad said it was likely static electricity."

"Static *electricity*?" Ben was a huge skeptic, but even he wasn't buying that answer. But then what was the alternative? He picked up the coffee cup and empty plate.

"Just leave those," said Caren. "I've got them."

He stood up, surprisingly a little dizzy. Ben didn't *see* things. The world had order as far as he was concerned. "Thanks, Caren."

Once outside, he realized how shaken he was. It had to be lack of sleep.

At the courthouse, Ben had offered to let himself into the file room, but Esther Hurston assured him it was her job to open the door. She led him down the hallway...well, *led* was a strong word because Esther waddled very slowly on her bad hips. After she got him to the door, Ben could do what he wanted.

Esther opened the old-fashioned door with a large frosted-glass panel adorning the upper half. It reminded Ben of those old ones from Philip Marlowe. PRIVATE DETECTIVE could be etched on the glass. Ben felt a little like one today. It was tough being a police chief in a town where nothing happened. This mystery held more excitement than he'd had in a long while.

Something about the endless stack of 1944 cases made Ben a little discouraged. The place wasn't air-conditioned, so he cracked a few windows and a nice breeze made its way in. Dust particles swirled as they hit the sunlight. The files were in chronological order by the date the case was opened, starting with December 1944 and working backward. Opening the first file, he had a hunch and found the October batch. About ten files in, he found what he was looking for. He didn't even have to go through the pile any further. This was it. "Ah shit."

Desmond "Dez" Bennett, 19. Missing on Duvall Road on October 10, 1944.

Bennett's car was found abandoned with the engine running and the driver's-side door open the morning of October tenth. There were no photos of the scene in the file, but Ben didn't need any; he'd witnessed the same crime scene twice and bet the car was found at an angle. Yet, he'd never heard of Duvall Road. What was it about this date that was so important? Was there some type of ritual killing happening every thirty years? That had to be it. He even had to admit that Caren's coven theory was beginning to have merit.

And the Ouija board. As much as he wanted to write it off as lack of sleep, it had spelled out *Dez* on its own.

God, he wished his father were still alive. He was in over his head with three cases. These disappearances went back sixty years now. Assuming the same person was responsible for all three incidents, that person would have to be eighty years old. Not that it was impossible, but it wasn't likely. So what did that mean? There was always the supernatural theory, but he still couldn't accept it. So were these ritual killings or serial killings committed by multiple people? Those ideas frightened the hell out of him.

He closed the file and tucked it under his arm, shutting the file room door behind him. As he walked down the same hall where he'd danced with Lara the other night, Ben realized that if some miracle happened and Todd Sutton returned to Kerrigan Falls, he would take his chances and fight for Lara. He glanced down at the file in his hand; Desmond Bennett's case was still open, which meant that Bennett had not returned as of 1965 when the file was sent to archives. Given the history, it was unlikely that Todd would come back, either.

He returned the keys to Esther. Something was bothering him. He thought he knew everything about this town, but obviously that wasn't so. "Do you know where Duvall Road is? I've never heard of it."

She snorted. "You mean *was*." Her knotted hands were busy stapling papers together with a fury that made Ben glad he was neither the paper *nor* the stapler.

"*Was?*"

"It was the road that ran over the old Shumholdt Bridge. It was a terrible one-lane thing. You'd have to honk your horn and listen to hear if someone else was coming over the bridge in the opposite direction, especially at the bend before they widened it. You'd pray that you wouldn't meet another car. If you did, one of you would have to back up on a horrible narrow bridge."

"Wait!" Ben leaned over the desk. "You're saying that Duvall Road was renamed?"

"Yes, when the new bridge went up they renamed it Wickelow Bend Road. I thought *everyone* knew that." As she spoke, the metal stapler vibrated like an instrument every time her hand came down. "Young people today just don't know their history."

"Thank you." Ben turned and leaned against the doorframe. "Hey, you don't remember a man named Desmond Bennett, do you? Went missing in 1944."

She looked at him, and her face lit up. "The derby driver? Oh yes, I remember him. He was quite handsome. All of us girls would line up for tickets when the derby came to town. He'd come back from the war...injured I believe...then he got on the racing circuit. Famous around these parts as well as North Carolina, Georgia, and Tennessee. A heartbreaker if I don't say so myself. Saw him once." She raised her eyebrows at the memory.

"Thanks, Esther." He turned the knob on the door.

"Oh," said Esther, catching Ben just before he left. "Funny thing about Dez Bennett. He was the boyfriend... well, rumored love interest, really... of Margot Cabot. You know, the blonde from all the circus posters around here. Legs like Betty Grable."

"No," said Ben, suddenly frozen in the doorway. "I didn't know that."

Ben stepped out of the records office and into the hallway. Not only did he have three missing men, but they all seemed connected to Lara's family.

When he got back to the station, Ben found Doyle playing a video game. Ben dropped a file on his desk. "Anytime when you're finished."

"I'm about to lose a troll." Doyle pushed away from the chair, defeated. "I just got killed."

"Do you really think you should be playing this in front of me, Doyle?"

"Dunno." He shrugged. "What else do we have to do?"

"Funny you should mention it." Ben pointed to the file he'd just placed on the desk.

Doyle picked it up and started leafing through it. "Holy shit. How old is this thing?"

"Nineteen forty-four. It's on a man named Desmond Bennett. Nineteen years of age. He disappeared on October ninth, 1944. They found his car on Duvall Road the next day."

"That's fucking weird."

"Even weirder is that, according to Esther Hurston, Duvall Road was the former name of—" Ben let the sentence hang to see if Doyle was paying attention.

"I'll take a guess and say Wickelow Bend?" Doyle smiled.

"You got it."

"So we've got three men, missing on the same day, in the same manner, at the same location, every thirty years?"

"Yeah, I'm starting to think it's a ritual killing of some sort. Do we have any known witch communities?" One thing that Ben had been relieved about was that the appearance of another killing thirty years earlier seemed to rule out Jason Barnes as a potential suspect.

"I don't think so." Doyle looked at his computer.

"Can you find out more about Desmond Bennett? Maybe ask over at the paper?"

"You can't make a call to Kim Landau yourself?" Doyle chuckled.

"I'd prefer not to."

"I see." Doyle winked.

"No, you don't see, Doyle. You see nothing."

"Uh-huh." Doyle shrugged, noncommittal. "You had a call by the way, some real estate agent."

"Shit," said Ben aloud as he looked down at the note on his desk. Abigail Atwater had called him back and she was on her way to the house.

Five Victorian houses separated his house from the one where he'd grown up, each sporting some oversize American flag for the July Fourth holiday. Ben ran past them all, spying the magnetic sign for ATWATER & ASSOCIATES on a black Cadillac SUV. He was too far away to see if Abigail Atwater was in the car or not.

All the houses on Washington Street looked as though a child had gone through a Crayola box to paint them. Next to Ben's house stood Victor Benson's stately old two-story lemon-yellow Victorian with periwinkle-blue accents and a wraparound porch. On the weekends, Vic and his wife would sit on their porch swing and drink wine. Ben's was a natural brick home, but Marla had painted it two years ago so that both the brick and grout were now a vibrant fire-engine-red color.

"It's really a showplace, isn't it?" called Victor Benson from his own porch. "Your wife..." He paused, realizing his mistake. "...well, she really has a green thumb."

"I guess so," said Ben. The house was Marla's domain now. Every corner of the porch had a pot with flowers spilling out of it.

Victor Benson's gray-white hair was styled like a game-show host's. He was perpetually tan and talked about golf courses like Torrey Pines that he played regularly, as if Ben knew what he was talking about. "Thanks to her, your property value just shot up," said Victor. "I see Abigail Atwater just went in." He let the comment hang. He was Kerrigan County's Century 21 Realtor and seemed more than a little irritated to find his biggest competitor going into his neighbor's house. Ben hadn't thought of using Vic, thinking his neighbor was too close to them.

"I need to have you over for an estimate," said Ben. "I'll call you."

"You know my number." Victor waved, giving Ben a look like he didn't believe him.

Since he'd last been to the house, Marla had turned her attention to the garden. Last year, he had offered to hire a landscape architect, but she'd looked irritated at the suggestion. As he went to open the screen door he saw ten firebush plants and a small stack of flagstone tiles waiting on the front porch for her attention.

He had never spent much time in the garden, but from the porch he could see that the small patch of land between their house and the Benson's Victorian was now thick with flowers, rows and clusters of boxwood topiaries, geraniums, black-eyed Susans, blue salvias, and azalea bushes, blooms and bulbs in clumps of greens and reds and yellows and purples. The flowers were in full bloom, and he was sure that the bees would soon follow.

As he got to the door, he saw Abigail Atwater standing in the foyer, punctuating her conversation with her pink nails. "You have my card," she emphasized.

"I do," said Marla from inside the house. He could see Marla flicking it. "I'll talk with Ben and we'll get back to you when we're ready to sell."

"This really is a stunning home," gushed Abigail. "It'll go in a minute."

He heard Marla's laugh. It was a laugh that told him he was in big trouble.

As Abigail opened the door she said, "Well, *look* who it is."

"Yes," echoed Marla. "Look at him."

"Sorry," said Ben. "I should have warned you."

Marla raised her eyebrows in silent agreement.

"Well, I told your wife here that I'd be thrilled to get this baby on the market." She leaned in. "I'm not surprised you're not going with Victor Benson." She motioned with her head in the direction of the neighbor's house. "I hear he's a little..." She took a fake drink with her hand.

"Oh," said Marla. "Is that so?" She waved her fingers in an effort to herd Abigail along.

Like parents waiting for children to clear the room before arguing, Ben and Marla were quiet until Abigail was out of earshot.

"How could you?" snapped Marla, her voice still low. "You're such a coward, Benjamin Archer. Sending a real estate agent...and not even *our neighbor*, for God's sake."

"I didn't think she'd actually come down here," said Ben. "I was away from my desk. I'm sorry, Marla. Victor Benson did say the value of the house has skyrocketed due to your green thumb."

"Did he?" Marla put her hands in the pockets of her white jeans. "It was all for the homes tour."

How could Ben have forgotten? There had been hundreds of people traipsing through this house for the Summer Festival that had ended nearly two weeks earlier. Thanks to Marla, their house—and now their garden—was always included on the tour. She was also the official photographer of the festival, although most of those bookings still weren't paying. "Might be a good time to sell, then."

"We've been over this before. I'm not selling." She put her hands over her face in exasperation and walked down the hall. While he didn't feel he should notice such things anymore, he did think she looked great, refreshed even. He sank a little when he realized that it was probably because she was rid of him. She had on jeans with a flowing pink top. As she shuffled to the kitchen, the sound of her bare feet whooshed against the floorboards, her long, chestnut-colored ponytail bobbing behind her. "You aren't coming in if you're just here to talk about selling. This house belongs to me."

Technically the house belonged to *them*—both Ben and Marla— but he wasn't going to push it. Before them, it had belonged to her mother and had been in her family for years. Marla had been working as a photographer in Los Angeles when her mother had gotten sick. She'd moved home to care for the woman until she'd died, then found herself living in a dilapidated eight-room house.

The repairs needed on the house were bad, so Ben had refinanced the house before they'd gotten married and had fixed it up with money he'd been saving for years. They'd only dated about four months before he'd asked her to marry him, but Ben could feel the time on her running out for a place like Kerrigan Falls, so he'd made grand gestures like proposing and taking on the financial responsibility for the house, just so she'd remain there. He recalled walking into the house for the first time and thinking it was like a collection of old-fashioned mourning rooms with the curtains drawn.

And now it was like something out of a *Southern Living* spread. On the light-lavender walls in the dining room were examples of her work, black-and-white photographs with intricate compositions and striking uses of light. They were thoughtfully grouped, with smaller photos on the outside and one large photograph of an old roller coaster as its centerpiece. She'd been known for taking photos of abandoned places—malls, theme parks, airports. The entire collection was framed with dramatic white mats and thin platinum frames. The white woodwork and matching fireplace mantel were lightly glossed. It was a tranquil room that she'd agonized over.

In the ten years they'd been married, the house had become one of the most well-known houses in the Falls. They'd become a bit of a power couple, yet Ben masked the fact that Marla's business had never done particularly well, and the historical society salary was more honorary than lucrative. He felt guilty making her stay here when she could have gone back—should have gone back—to Los Angeles and taken pictures of movie stars for magazines, like she'd dreamed of doing, so he hadn't pushed her to sell at first.

"Maybe you could turn it into a bed-and-breakfast."

"I've had enough of people," she snorted.

"How so?"

"I took a group of twelve-year-olds white-water rafting."

"Why on earth would you do that?"

"Someone had to." She just shrugged and poured herself a cup of coffee and didn't offer him one. Instead, she leaned against the counter holding the oversize mug with both hands. Ben wasn't even through the front door and already they were rubbing each other raw, like a rug burn. This is what they did.

"Look, I appreciate what you did for me with this house." She took a deep sip of coffee. "You know that."

"You're welcome. Now I'd like to be free of it."

"It? Or me?"

There was no way that Ben was stepping into this. She was twisting the business into something personal between them. It wasn't. "You were the one who left me."

"I threw you out." She shrugged in reluctant agreement, like it was no big deal.

"I went of my own accord, Marla," said Ben.

"You blubbered." She picked at something on her cup, avoiding his eyes.

"I was emotional, yes." He felt like a door had opened, yet this whole conversation felt like a trap. "Look, don't you want to start over?"

"With *you*?" She seemed horrified at the question.

"No," he said, a little too quickly.

She placed the mug on the counter and folded her arms in front of her. It was a power stance. "I do want to start over in *this house*. Tell me. Would you really take it from me?"

"Oh Jesus, Marla." He perched on a counter stool and noticed that her eyebrow was raised a little, like he shouldn't be making himself at home in a house he was still paying for.

"Well? Would you?"

"No, but I'd love for you to *buy* me out, just like our divorce agreement said you'd do."

"I can't do that yet. Business isn't that good right now. I just need a little more time."

"You keep saying that. How much more time?"

She looked like she'd been slapped.

He sighed. "We'll talk about it later." But it was always the same. She wanted the house. Solely. It was to be divided, but she kept stalling on repairs so it couldn't be listed and now she was saying she was strapped, but from the look of the plants she was buying he wasn't sure that was the case. He supposed that he could push the issue, but given the public nature of his job, he hadn't wanted to do that. And she was banking on his silence.

"I have to go."

"You just got here." Marla's expression was unreadable. Over the years, he'd found that he could never predict what she'd do. She was always cold, aloof, a stranger. Truth was, they'd jumped into a quick marriage and both felt compelled to make it work when it had become clear that they were different people. He was shocked that it had lasted ten years.

"Jesus, Marla." He lowered his voice, not sure why. "I'm ready to move on."

"So I see—the entire town sees." Her voice was cool. "Lara Barnes. Interesting choice—a little young for you. But then you *do* love a damsel in distress."

He turned and waved goodbye to her, knowing that she was still leaning against the counter feeling victorious that she'd driven him out—again.

As he walked back to the police station, he thought that there hadn't been any one thing that had broken them up. They'd just grown apart and moved like strangers through the house with nothing to say to each other. The last time they'd had sex, he noticed she kept her eyes closed—she wasn't there, or at least she didn't want to be there. And he found he didn't want to be with a shell of a wife.

That began a slow move to the spare bedroom, starting with him sleeping on the sofa, then the spare room so as not to wake her as he researched all night. Marla seemed to have the same thought, because she asked him to leave the following month. It had been a shock to him that his stuff was leaving first in suitcases and then black trash bags. The first night in his new apartment, he didn't even have a sofa or a mattress, and he'd ordered a free pizza from a coupon he'd gotten with his phone hookup.

But then Todd Sutton went missing and he'd thrown himself fully into the case. To see someone like Lara aching for Todd made him realize that he could have that kind of love, too.

Lara. Was Marla right in that he liked a damsel in distress? He dismissed the thought, but he remembered Marla in the months after her mother died and him piecing together her life. Then he did it again with Lara.

He'd just walked back into the office when his office line rang. Ben picked it up. "Archer here."

There was a pause and a crackle. "Ben?" The voice sounded far away. "This is Gaston Boucher. I'm with Lara Barnes here in Paris."

"Hey, Gaston." Ben started tearing open the morning's mail, sorting the junk from the essentials while he cocked the phone on his neck, but he stopped. Something was wrong or Gaston wouldn't be calling. "What is it?"

"Well..." The man stammered.

"Well, what?" Ben felt his stomach lurch and his blood pressure drop. He almost didn't want to hear the next thing out of Gaston's mouth.

"Lara's gone missing."

"Gone missing?" The police chief in him knew the importance of the next question even if Gaston didn't. "How long?"

"Twenty-four hours now."

23

Ben booked the first flight he could get out of Dulles to Charles de Gaulle and hadn't slept at all. The worst had been the waiting. He'd carried only a duffel bag with the few things he grabbed—an extra pair of jeans, two shirts, a polo, and underwear, but then time slowed and he waited at the gate, on the airplane, and in the taxi line. Now that he was here, he needed to be doing something. Expecting to be furious with Gaston and Barrow, he found that both men appeared not to have slept or showered in days.

"Espresso?" Gaston suggested.

Ben shrugged him off. "No. We need to get out and find her."

"You'll never last without it." Gaston pushed the tiny cup toward him. "And you need to last."

"We've tried to find her." The other man, Edward Binghampton Barrow, removed his reading glasses and pushed the composition books toward him. "We think she may have been contacted by Le Cirque Secret. If that is the case, then she isn't 'in' Paris anymore in the literal sense."

"What does that mean?" Ben took a sip from the tiny cup after stirring sugar in it with a tiny spoon.

"The circus is in another dimension," said Barrow.

Ben laughed. "Seriously?"

"Seriously," said Gaston. "We searched her room. There was an envelope with her name on it, but it was empty. We think she had a ticket." It seemed to Ben that this was a well-worn discussion between the two men.

Barrow shook his head. "She knew we'd never let her go alone. Lara had no intention of telling us. If history repeats itself, there was only one ticket—and it was for her, alone."

"I never would have allowed her to go *alone*." Gaston rubbed his face, his gray stubble showing.

"There was no 'allowing' Lara to go. No one controls her. She had to go," said Barrow, who now seemed to be an expert on Lara after just a few days. "You can't get a ticket to Le Cirque Secret—not after all these years—and *not* go."

Ben could tell that tensions were high between the two men, but he wasn't sure the argument was helping Lara.

"You'd have let her go, if you'd known?" Gaston had sunk back into the chair, but now he leaned forward, like he was readying for another round.

"Yes," said Barrow. "The scholarship required it."

"There is no fucking scholarship here, Teddy," said Gaston, his voice rising. "We've left her alone in a daemonic circus."

"Daemonic?" Ben hadn't heard anyone use the term *daemonic*.

"Yes," the two men said in unison.

Barrow's voice rose; his clipped English accent grew more pronounced. "You can sit there all day and think that you could have held her back from going, but you couldn't have. And you wouldn't have."

"That fucking painting isn't my only concern, and neither is that circus. That is all I'm saying." Gaston folded his arms, the veins in his neck prominent. "That was *your* dream that you've chased all these years."

Barrow looked like he was about to speak, but Ben interrupted. "Maybe it was a deranged killer—a real physical person and not some otherworldly circus run by a devil. Have either of you considered that?" He was trying to cool the situation down. In his experience, you only pieced things together when you were coolheaded. For Lara's sake, he needed to be that now. "You have them here in Paris, too, don't you? We need to call the police. She was chased by someone the other day—from her account it was a *physical* person. You can't just assume that she's gone and joined a daemonic circus."

Barrow narrowed his eyes. "We have psychopaths here in Paris as well, monsieur. But the concierge saw her leave around ten forty-five."

"So?"

"So," said Barrow slowly, like he was trying to remain patient with a child. "From everything we know about Le Cirque Secret, performances began promptly at eleven. Always." Barrow had given up his desk chair to Ben, who was sipping his espresso. "The empty envelope and the time being so close to eleven is a good indicator that she had a ticket."

"This isn't the doing of a madman or an art thief, Ben," said Gaston. "If we went to the police, we would sound crazy. Anyway, we did call the police. We called you."

"What did she say when you talked to her last?" Barrow directed his question to Ben.

"She assured me she wouldn't be wandering around Paris without you both. That she wouldn't take any chances—" As he recalled the conversation, Ben's body felt heavy; he couldn't speak for a moment. What if Lara disappeared as well? He was furious with her for taking chances. He nodded toward the composition books and couldn't believe what he was about to ask next. "So this circus, if it is real, it has no *physical* location?"

"It does not." Barrow tapped on the desk. "Nothing about the circus was physical. That was the problem. When Gaston called about the circus painting that Lara had, it was the first real lead that the paintings were real and that the circus, itself, had ever existed. But these books." He laid his hand flat on them as he would on a lover. "These books are the first real indication of what went on behind the scenes. Cecile Cabot's journals explain everything. The legend has the circus appearing only to the ticket holders who were given an address. And we know that it sounds crazy, but that's what happened to Lara. I'm sure of it. The circus had been reaching out to her." Barrow took off his glasses and rubbed his eyes. The man appeared not to have slept for days. He was unshaven, his shirt untucked and stained with coffee.

"Why?" Ben knew he had to be open to all possibilities.

Gaston nodded. "We're aware it sounds crazy. If her great-grandmother was, indeed, Cecile Cabot, then she has a true connection to Le Cirque Secret."

"But so would Audrey," said Ben.

"I think Audrey is in the dark about Le Cirque Secret, or perhaps denial," said Gaston. "There must be something special about Lara, but I don't know what it is."

Ben almost snorted. "And you both believe this fantastical tale?"

Gaston straightened his back. "Tell me, Ben," he said with more than a hint of sarcasm. "Back home, do you have a case right now that defies explanation?"

Ben sighed, recalling the Ouija board and the three men who had gone missing every thirty years. "I do."

"It's either this or a deranged lunatic." Gaston sank back in his chair. "I'm hoping for this."

"I'm not sure they're mutually exclusive," said Ben, skimming the composition book notes. "From what you've translated, the facts seem pretty weird. Are you sure someone wasn't drinking too much absinthe?" There was a painting lying on the worktable.

"The Giroux, you mean? *Oui*," said Gaston.

Ben walked over and lifted the canvas off the table. He could hear Barrow stirring like he was going to chastise him for not wearing gloves, but they knew Ben was furious with them for failing to keep Lara safe. Ben turned. "So this is what all the fuss is about, huh?"

"Yes," said Barrow, looking itchy. "That was in the safe here all night. You might want to wear gloves." He motioned to a pile of gloves next to the loupe.

"It hung on Audrey's wall near the bathroom for decades," said Ben, irritated. "I think it can withstand my hands."

"Lara said she found a second one at Le Cirque de Fragonard." Barrow seemed excited about this information, a point Ben thought was out of place given Lara's disappearance. "I've been wanting to see it."

"Is this when she was chased?" Ben placed the painting back on the table and leaned against it wearily. "And you two don't think that's odd? She happens upon a painting that no one else has seen, then she goes missing? Where is Le Cirque de Fragonard?"

"Near Marais."

Ben grabbed his jacket. "Let's go." The espresso had jolted him awake, but his eyes were burning and he longed for a bed. That would have to wait, though.

"Here," said Gaston, handing him a thick pile of handwritten notes. "We found this on Lara's bed in the hotel."

"What is it?"

"She translated the third journal. You might want to read the translation from all three journals before you say that you don't believe any of this. She did."

The Journal of Cecile Cabot
Book Three

June 9, 1925

While it was my suggestion, I was stopped dead in my tracks when I saw them together. He was smiling, and it felt like a small betrayal. But what was I expecting? That he'd dread spending time with my sister? Surely I wasn't that naive.

As I walked to the trapeze, a sly smile crossed Esmé's lips. For the painting she was posed dressed in a black-and-gold-striped jacket with a short front and long tails, gold shorts, and stockings with a light netting. To indicate the pattern of her stockings, Émile sketched a cross-hatch pattern over her thighs. Despite trying not to watch them, I felt the attention to my sister's stockings had dragged on quite long.

Grabbing the Spanish Web, I began to climb but thought better of it and came back down. I'd perfected the corkscrew move to where I could float in midair for several minutes. It all began innocently enough. Fatigued after practice, I didn't want to climb the ladder again. Standing at its foot, I closed my eyes and wondered what it would be like to move through the air, landing at the top. It was effort-less, really, the lifting. My body felt light, as though it had longed to take flight.

Now I can take to the air at will—the ladder and rope are quite unnecessary. Yet for my audience, props are required. To simply soar to the top would have felt like I was performing some cheap magic trick with mirrors. Instead I lured them into an act they recognized and then slowly I pulled the rug out from under them, challeng-ing everything they thought they knew about circus acts. I loved the sound of the gasps in the audience when I shed the ropes and bars and it was just me and the air. Those moments have provided me with the greatest sense of peace I have ever known, like a mermaid returning to water.

Until I'm warmed up, however, it's dangerous for me to be dis-tracted. Lack of concentration is the *only* dangerous part of my magic. If I'm caught unawares, my flying powers might not be there exactly when I need them. While I'm good, my flying powers are not yet perfect.

To know that I am a magical creature like Esmé has filled me with purpose here. The other performers, like Doro, have begun to treat me as an equal. It's still tense when Esmé is in the room, as she demands loyalty from our troupe. Any act of kindness toward me is taken as an affront to her. Yet I see how this act of choosing between us has weighed everyone down and a silent resentment toward her has formed. We're already existing in Hell; why make it worse?

Walking back to my room, Doro passed me and nodded to Esmé. "Looks like she's got a fly in the web," said Doro's puppet. He raised his eyebrows in what he thought was a private joke between us, yet he couldn't have known how this comment would affect me. I stormed back to my dressing room in a jealous rage, leaving Esmé and Émile to themselves. I hadn't felt this way when he'd painted Sylvie, but then I hadn't been to his apartment when he was painting her. Some part of me feared he would make a fool of me.

Back in my room, I peeled off my leotard and dress, deciding to head into Montparnasse instead. If I stayed, I feared I might storm out there and rip the canvas in two. Where was this anger coming from? Placing the back of my hand on my forehead, I didn't think I was feverish, but I've been in a constant state of agitation lately.

At Esmé's request, we now have separate dressing rooms and most of the space is empty, but I've kept the old velvet daybed, my vanity, and the rug. A new mirror arrived for me a few weeks ago. While I assumed it was from an admirer, there was no note attached. It was rather beautiful, a heavy gold, baroque full-length thing, but I've begun to fear it's enchanted. As I stare into it, I almost don't recognize the vengeful creature staring back at me. It isn't just my reflection in the glass that disturbs me, but the mirror itself. There are angles where I've caught a reflection of myself that is not possible. I've asked Doro if there was a fun-house mirror missing from the arcade with some poor spirit trapped in it, but he gestured no. At times, the image that has peered back at me is one of a young girl with only one arm and one leg—her left limbs missing entirely. Knowing it must be my head play-ing tricks on me, I've taken to covering it with my robe and I've asked for it to be removed, but no one has bothered with it, claiming it's too heavy and bulky.

Father was back today. Moving the circus always required him, so I figured that we will be leaving the Bois de Boulogne. I broached the topic of the mirror and how no one had moved it, but he brushed me off like I was a silly girl. "Turn it around, for goodness' sake," he said dismissively. So I did. Still, it has made me hate my dressing room, so I've begun staying in Sylvie's.

June 10, 1925

Today Émile sketched more of Esmé's face detail, so she was sitting close to him. He'd tried to catch me earlier, but I retreated to Sylvie's dressing room. The sight of them together sent me into a fury. "You cannot just hand him over to her," said Sylvie, her face sympathetic. "Get out there and fight for him. It is *you* that he wants, Cecile."

While I've thrown things in my own room and ripped up my own costumes, I don't know how to fight Esmé. I'm afraid of her. Sylvie was wrong. Everyone wanted Esmé, so there wasn't much point to fighting for Émile when I'd surely lose.

As I entered the big top, Father was observing Esmé telling Émile a joke that had them both roaring with laughter. "You're distracted?"

"*Non.*" I didn't want Father to know that I cared about Émile or that I was bothered by the camaraderie between them.

"Tell me. Has Esmé gone and stolen your candy?" He motioned over at the painter and his subject, so close they were almost touching.

Father has always known how to choose the precise knife with which to stab you in your weakest spot. I glared at him. "I have no idea what you're talking about."

A thin smile appeared on his lips, and he deduced that he was correct. "Or did you just hand it to her as you did when you were younger?"

"You're enjoying this," I said, chalking my palms and wiping them on my thighs.

"I have no opinion one way or the other on the matter, although you know how I do enjoy chaos." His tone changed, low and grave, like a warning. "This is a lesson for you, Cecile. Where your sister is concerned, one day you will need to fight for what is yours."

His comment lingered long after he'd left.

After practice, Doro found me. "The painter was looking for you," said Doro's puppet. "They left."

"They?"

"Esmé and her fly."

My heart sank. "Together?"

"He said that you'd know where to find them."

Buoyed by Father's words, I decided that today I *would* claim what I felt was mine. I threw on my best dress, a blue chiffon drop-waisted number, and allowed my hair to cascade down my back in ringlets. As I left, I found Doro standing by the door again. Once, on a dare from Esmé, I tried to take him with me, absorbing his essence. It nearly killed me, sending me to bed for weeks with a raging fever.

When I stepped onto the street, I realized that the circus had, indeed, moved. It took me a moment to orient myself. No longer on the Left Bank, but now in Montmartre. I caught the omnibus to Boulevard Saint-Germain and then walked to Montparnasse. It had been a nice stroll, but it had taken me nearly two hours.

When I reached Le Dôme Café, I didn't see them sitting at the bar or in the café. An uneasy feeling set in. I walked the two blocks to Émile's apartment. As I opened the door in the landing, I heard Esmé's voice coming from the rooms upstairs. Then the beginning of a song from Émile's phonograph, "Oh, How I Miss You Tonight." My instinct told me to turn around and return to the circus, but I'd led her to him, insisting he paint her.

I ascended the stairs and knocked on the door. Inside, I heard a furious scrambling and giggling. They were drunk. Placing my ear to the door, I heard the sliding of clothing as it was arranging back on bodies. My heart sank. I was too late.

Not long ago, I had been in that room; *my* clothes had been on that floor. I'd been a fool to think he cared about me. Tears began to flow down my cheeks as I turned and began down the stairs, my legs hurting from the earlier walk.

Finally, Émile cracked open the door, just a hair. From the look of horror on his face, it was clear that he had not been expecting me. His face had a conflicted look, like I had interrupted something that he'd wanted in the moment but now was ashamed of.

At least he looked sorry, that was something. A real cad wouldn't have shown even that much emotion.

"*Qu'est-ce?*" I heard Esmé call from the bed. I couldn't see her, but from my angle on the steps, I could see the tangle of bedsheets through the crack in the door.

My eyes met Émile's. I'm sure I looked frightening with my red, swollen face, but I didn't care.

"Cecile." He moved toward me, but I shook my head and placed my finger to my lips.

I wouldn't give her the satisfaction of knowing that I'd caught them together. Turning, I continued back down the stairway.

June 24, 1925

Émile never returned to the circus.

I have no idea if Esmé's painting was ever completed or if they took to working on it at his apartment, away from me.

After last night's performance, Sylvie and I stopped by the Closerie des Lilas. We'd ceased going to Le Dôme, to avoid seeing him. As we were leaving the café, I heard his voice calling to me from across the street.

"Ignore him." Sylvie touched my hand protectively. There has been a change in her recently. She was always the third person in our mortal trio, but she has taken greater care with my feelings over my sister's. This hasn't always been the case. When we were younger, Sylvie vacillated between Esmé and me, choosing sides and tipping the scales as it suited her. From the memories I have, I know that Sylvie could be fickle. Often, I'd be left out of the maze while she and Esmé played, deciding that I couldn't follow them for silly reasons. But like her mother, Sylvie was also a political creature. While she has been a friend to me, she is not unaware of my increasing stature within the troupe, and it has tipped her loyalties a bit.

"Cecile." Émile's voice was pleading. I heard cars honk as he crossed to me. When he finally caught up to us, he was out of breath from running down the street.

I was stunned by what I saw in front of me. In the two weeks since I had found Esmé in his room, there had been a startling change in him. Dark circles hollowed the area under his eyes. Normally thin, his frame was now skeletal and his clothes hung on him. "Émile? What has happened to you?"

"I have been looking for you," he said, breathless. "You are not easy to find."

"You could have found her at the circus," said Sylvie sharply. She looked beyond him down the street toward our destination, hoping this was a momentary diversion.

"Can I walk with you alone?" His doe-like eyes pleaded with me.

Sylvie tensed. I motioned to her to go on.

"I'll be at the Closerie des Lilas waiting for you." She gave Émile a final, disapproving glance before placing her hands in her pockets, spinning on her heels, and starting toward Boulevard du Montparnasse at a pace that let me know she didn't agree with my decision.

Émile and I ambled down the street in the opposite direction, in silence.

"Why did you need to see me?" I stared straight ahead at the crowd in front of me, not meeting his eyes.

"I hated that you saw me with her," he said. His tone was desperate. "I needed to explain."

"You don't owe me an explanation, Émile." Clutching my purse tightly, I had a vivid recollection of that night. I was humiliated that he saw me in such a state, my bloodshot eyes, tearstained cheeks, and swollen face.

"But I do." He stepped in front of me. The soft breeze blew at his hair, and car headlights illuminated him as they passed. "I don't want her. I don't know how that could have happened."

"Oh, I'm sure you do." I raised my eyebrow.

He placed his hands on my shoulders to stop me from moving on. "I tried to find you, but I could not get back into the circus."

That was a curious development. Father had shut off Émile's access to us.

"Then you didn't come back here, either. When I couldn't find you, I painted you, again and again. Each night. I would paint you and stare at you, telling you all the things that I am telling you now, and I would wake every morning—"

"And I would be gone," I said. Am I terrible for admitting that I smiled at him then? It was just a small upward tilt of my mouth, but the idea that he had been in agony over me seemed fair. Now we were even.

"Each time, I tried to change something...your nose or your lips... anything so it wasn't exactly you."

"It isn't like that, Émile. You can't paint my essence, even by memory.

It has nothing to do with changing my nose or lips." I could smell the alcohol on his breath. "Have you eaten?"

He shook his head. "Oh, Cecile. I am so in love with you. After you left, I sent Esmé away. Nothing happened between the two of us, I swear! The look on your face. I could not believe what I had done and how stupidly I'd behaved." He grabbed his head, like it was pounding. "We'd had too much to drink then we got dancing; that's all. It was hot in my apartment. You must believe me."

"Can I ask you something?" I stood close to him, looking up.

"Of course, anything," he said. He began to wind up for another wave of protestations of his innocence, but I held up my hand to silence them.

"Even if what you say is true, had I not come to your door when I did, what would have happened between you and my sister?" The question lingered. I could see the guilt on his face. "I see." Having my answer, I turned and walked down the street. Two blocks ahead, I could still make out Sylvie's shape ahead of me.

"I'm sorry. Please forgive me," he called, running after me, catching my arm. "I will do anything that you require to make it right. I will give up painting. We can move away together."

I shook free of him. How dare he touch me when he just admitted to me that he'd wanted my sister. There was a cruel streak in me that longed to tell him there was nothing to be done, his choice had been made when he'd invited her to his apartment. The desire to see him twist for what he had done to me was great. Before I'd met him, my life had been lonely, but simple. Surely this spiteful inclination comes from Father. I took a few deep breaths in through my nose, trying to calm myself. I took him in and softened, for the man who stood before me looked to be days away from his own death. He had not eaten nor, it seemed, slept for days.

"Please," he pleaded with me. He began pacing the street like a madman, tugging at his hair.

I was startled to see my own internal storm of emotions physically manifested in him. He looked like I felt. Waves of both worry and relief washed over me as I saw that his feelings for me had been very real, but then I realized that he was causing a scene on the street. Women were stepping away from him as they passed us.

"Let's get you something to eat." I took his hand and led him to Closerie des Lilas. As we approached, Sylvie, who'd found a two-seat table, frowned.

"Why is *he* still here?"

"Shut up, Sylvie," I said, muttering under my breath as I attempted to locate another chair in the crowded café.

The three of us sat in the corner table while Émile ordered the duck. In this light, I saw the deep cavities that had formed under his eyes and cheekbones. The skin around his lips had taken on a dusty color. His face recalled the painting that Man Ray had done of Marcel Proust on his deathbed.

The dinner was deadly silent. Sylvie glared at him as he ate, her hands at her sides and her posture as straight and still as a dressmaker's form. When he'd swallowed the final forkful of duck, Sylvie clapped her hands and announced, "Well, that's done. You've eaten. Can we go now, Cecile?"

I was taken aback by her rudeness. "Sylvie!"

Scowling, she pulled out a cigarette and met my eyes, her face defiant.

After we left the restaurant, Émile reached for my hand. "Please come back with me."

The idea of going back to that apartment where I'd stood outside listening to them was unthinkable. As though Sylvie read my mind, she said, "We can *all* go."

This was not the response that either Émile or I wanted. Since dinner, I'd longed to talk with him alone, but Sylvie tagged along behind us, making it clear she wouldn't be leaving without me. As we ascended the stairs, the memories of that evening came flooding back to me and I paused. Émile, who was opening the door, looked stricken. It was the same angle—him at the door and me on the stairs. A dreadful déjà vu overtook me.

If the memories were so bad that I was unable to even walk up the steps to his apartment then I could not go through that door; I could not laugh with this man again, kiss him, certainly not make love to him again. Sadly, I knew it was impossible for me to forgive him.

Émile's dire condition, however, prodded me on up the stairs, Sylvie in tow. While the color had returned to his face, he was clearly not well. Tentatively, he opened the door and I walked through, Sylvie following. The room was in complete disarray: canvases broken in two, their wooden frames splintered all around the bed; empty and broken liquor bottles littering the floor; records smashed into sharp pieces.

"What on earth—?" Sylvie was so shocked by the state of the place that she grabbed my hand.

"Go, if you cannot bear it." His tone was sharp. "I will understand, Cecile. I deserve it."

"You do," agreed Sylvie. Her heart-shaped face and pursed lips fixated on him.

"Sylvie." I shot her a look. Never had I seen her so hostile to anyone.

Sensing my disgust with her, she turned and walked out the door, shutting it hard behind her. Next I could hear her heavy steps, and then the door at the foot of the stairs opened then shut.

We were alone.

Despite Émile's appearance, his pride returned and he composed himself, straightening but unable look at me. "Can you forgive me?"

"I don't know." I shrugged.

"Could you *try*?"

I wanted to say no and then turn on my heels and follow Sylvie out the door and return to my life and my trapeze. There would be other admirers, I knew that now. Émile Giroux was too much trouble for a simple girl like me. The words were on my lips. But then I recalled the last two weeks without him; the emptiness. Some moments, when I pictured him out there in the world, without me, I'd wanted to retch. Until him, I hadn't been aware of the hollowness inside me. How quickly he'd wormed his way into my small life and heart. "I guess I could try." It had been so simple to say.

"That's all I ask." There was no satisfaction on his face. I got the sense that he didn't believe me.

"What did you do with her painting?"

"I threw it in the trash." He ran his hands through his hair, considered the shamble of a room around him.

It was a lie. "You shouldn't have done that. It might be valuable one day."

"I want nothing to do with her." I could tell that he longed to punish Esmé for his moment of weakness, but it was no more her fault than his.

"I will come when I can, Émile." I stepped over the broken glass pieces and turned the doorknob, leaving him standing amid the ruin.

June 27, 1925

A strange illness has plagued me for days. This morning I decided to leave the circus to determine if it is the circus that is making me sick. The longer I stay on the other side, the more I wonder if I wouldn't be better over there. To my dismay, I am sick on that side as well, throwing up all over the sidewalk in Montmartre.

When I returned, it was late and I met Esmé at the door. I was surprised by her appearance. The dress she wore was quite revealing, enough to see that she was not wearing a bra. Her eyes were glassy from crying and heavily lined with kohl. If I did not know her, I would have thought she was a prostitute.

"Get out of my way." She nearly knocked me over. Her voice gave her away—she was surprised to see me.

"Are you okay?" I reached my hand out to touch her.

She stopped and peeled my fingers from her arm. "I will never be okay again." She choked the words out as little heaves emitted from her body.

"I don't understand—"

"Émile," she said, cutting me off. "You have everything." When she turned to face me, it was not the usual veneer. Her face was gaunt; her eyes glassy and dead. "Why him, too?" Those few words seem to have drained her. Spent, she turned and pushed through the front doors of the circus and into the night.

After Father had sent her away to the White Forest, I'd sworn that I would never harm my sister again. Whether she accepted it or not, we were connected in body and spirt. To see my twin so broken has made my decision easier. I will not be the cause of her suffering any longer.

June 28, 1925

I went to Émile's apartment. Thankfully, the place was cleaner. He looked at me standing outside the door and pulled me in. "What is wrong?"

From his face, I saw that Émile had hoped that we were reunited so he could focus on things like his canvases again. In the corner there was a new painting, a nude of a woman. While she was not a beautiful woman, he had discovered the spark inside of her and drawn it out and onto his paintbrush. I could only wonder how he had achieved this. He was an artist, after all. If he seduced his models, it was only part of his craft, perfecting it as he did his brushstrokes. While I had come here with the sole intent of saying goodbye to him, it was at this precise moment that I knew for certain my decision was the correct one. Though I'd longed to be, I would never be the woman for him. I could see clearly that, as the years passed, I would become a shell, measuring myself against each model. Without malice, his talent and passion along with their consequences would chisel away at me.

He was wiping brushes, his clothes spotted with errant paint strokes, but he placed them on the table and took my head in his hands, kissing me deeply.

I pulled back. "It's Esmé." I found that I could not take my eyes off the painting, the woman's eyes staring at me in pity.

"What about her?" He believed that he had won me again, making her irrelevant.

"She loves you." My breath was shallow. As I spoke the words, I knew that I was doing the right thing, yet in my heart, I had never wanted anything more than this man.

"That is ridiculous," he said, laughing, and yet there was a flicker across his face, perhaps some part of him flattered. To be adored by a beautiful woman such as Esmé was a conquest, whether he loved her or not.

"It's not possible for us to be together, Émile."

Starting in his eyes, which dimmed like the chandeliers in the circus just before the performance begins, I watched the light leave him.

The fade of his normally bright smile came next, once my words had fully reached him.

"But I only love *you*, Cecile. I don't love her."

"I won't destroy my sister, Émile. I do love you, but I love her more." A flush came over my body, causing me to become sick again in one swift wave. Searching for something, I ran to the window, reaching for the washbasin and throwing up in it.

Émile led me to the bed, where I gripped the bedsheets with my fists in anticipation of the next wave that I could feel forming. He touched my cheek lightly. "You don't have a fever."

He slid next to me and placed his arms around me. "Cecile."

"Yes," I said, briefly allowing myself one last moment to fully embrace the warmth and weight of him as he pressed against my body.

"Are you pregnant?"

July 1, 1925

I visited a doctor. Everything was strange to me, from the small office where Sylvie and I waited to the entire process of discovering that I was, indeed, pregnant. For me nothing has changed. I have decided to raise this child in the circus world. It would be the little piece of Émile that I could keep.

I found Esmé in her dressing room. She was about to bar the door with her arm again, but I would not be begging her to talk to me anymore.

"What do you want?"

"He is yours," I said, spitting the words out. "I have told him that I will not see him again." Pulling my sweater around my neck, I turned to leave. As I walked down the hallway, I knew that I'd left her standing in her doorway both speechless—and elated.

True to my word, I refused to see Émile, despite his pleas. If my sister wanted him, then I would step aside. I was sure it would only take a modest bit of coaxing on her part to change his devotions from me to her.

August 8, 1925

Before tonight's performance, I was sick again and went to the animals' stalls where I wouldn't be discovered vomiting. I was near His Majesty's stable—an elaborate, lavish corral with a velvet curtain fit for a king—when I spied Esmé, covered in blood, scrubbing herself in a nearby empty stall.

I had always suspected there was a pattern to our circus. Tomorrow, Father was planning to return, and we would likely move our location again, finding ourselves back at the Bois de Boulogne for the month. As she dried herself with a towel, I could see bloodstains on it. She stood there shivering in the hallway, her silk slip illuminating the outlines of her nipples and the tops of her thighs.

Later, Sylvie and I were at Le Select, where no one made room for us at the bar. I heard whispering about two men who went missing near the last known location of our circus. Hemingway looked up from the table and asked me if I knew anything about it. All eyes turned to Sylvie and me, cigarettes puffing wildly.

"She doesn't know anything," said Émile from a corner seat at the bar. Even Sylvie was touched that he defended us. Seeing him sent a charge of pain through my body like an errant current.

When I returned to the circus, Father asked me to accompany him on the Ferris wheel ride that Curio had completed. I was hesitant because I knew that this ride led to the White Forest. I climbed into the car, and with a swipe of his hand, we began to descend.

"They're saying that our circus is responsible for several men's disappearances."

He looked far away tonight. I knew what he was—a great general in the Army of the Underworld—yet he has been the only parent I have ever known. Although I have seen his cruelty, I felt the tug of sadness and love for him.

"Who has said this?" He was preoccupied, looking down at the River Styx to the right of us. "Giroux?"

"No," I said. "It is all the gossip in Montparnasse. It's in the newspaper as well."

"It isn't your concern, Cecile." Father's response was firm.

"Why?" Leaning forward, I touched his leg. "Earlier tonight before the performance, I caught Esmé in the animal stalls washing blood off herself. Then I heard of men going missing, and now you are here and I know what that means. The circus will move. There is a pattern here."

He gazed over at me, like I was a much-loved doll. "You look so much like her . . . Juno." He closed his eyes at the memory of my mother; the vision of her still cut him. How hard to be a powerful being and yet be denied the only thing you've ever desired. It was the first time I saw the imprint of his own prison on him. "But both you and your sister have cost me dearly." He spoke slowly and deliberately, so that I absorbed each word. "When you were born, I should have thrown both you and Esmé into the Styx and let it have you."

My eyes slowly traveled up to meet his. Those flat pupils stared back at me, unflinching.

Terror swept through me. I gripped the handle of the ride.

"I could do it now, in fact," he said, his tone measured like he was discussing the weather. "Start with you, right here, then her next." He tapped his cane, then stroked the arm of the gondola seat.

Tensing, I sat back in my own seat as far away from him as I could get. He had a strange sense of humor, but this wasn't one bit funny. I felt my heart beating wildly. Would he really throw me from the car? Was this why he'd lured me here?

He leaned back and draped his arm on the gondola seat. "Relax, Cecile. I'm not in a vengeful mood tonight, although what you girls put me through, no other daemon would take it, I assure you. As part of me, though, I know what you'll do before you even think of it. That's why I know that you cannot handle what we are—what *you* are. You think you can handle anything—oh, you're a *trapeze* star now, the talk of Paris," he said mockingly. "You are quite correct that your sister has killed those men. Now I know what you'll ask next."

I went to speak, but he cut me off.

"You'll want to know *why*."

It was exactly the question I was going to ask.

"Because it is the cost of the circus that you both live in. Esmé bears it, alone. Now the next thing you are going to insist…with great aplomb…is that it is unfair for her to bear such a burden. Hear me now. Are you really so naive that you think I care about fair, Cecile? Have I allowed you to so greatly misjudge me?" He leveled his eyes at me. They were cold. I saw no traces of love or even affection for me in them. Never had I been more frightened.

I knew what he was getting at. Father was the most feared of the generals and yet here he was consoling his sniveling daughter. "She hates me because of it," I said, staring off at the barren trees of the White Forest. She had gone there and endured unspeakable things because of me. Now it all made sense.

"Sadly, she will hate you more when she learns of your news." He eyes went to the tiny swell in my waist.

"How did you know?" I said, touching my stomach protectively. Beneath my fingers, I felt the warm ball below my navel, firm and round, like an orange.

"How could I not. You must know, this is not good, Cecile," he continued. "You and your sister are cambions—the offspring of a human and a daemon. You are carrying a child who is part cambion. While it can weaken with every generation, this birth—a child with the essence of a daemon—will be hard on you. You should know it's what killed your mother."

"Will I die?"

"Sadly, my dear, the Reaping is the one thing that I cannot control."

"But I have your daemon blood. Won't that help me?"

He shrugged. "You also have a fragile mortal shell, like an egg. Inside you have magic, that is true, but you are not immortal, sadly."

I considered his words. "Émile does not know about the baby."

"That is for the best."

"If he knew, he'd insist that we be together."

"I'm afraid," he said wearily, "that is not possible."

He continued gazing out at the Styx below. The river and its coal-black waters were the source of his power. This was my world. While I came and went from the circus, I was, in fact, like Doro. A creature of Hell. That I could not be with Émile was the answer that I was expecting, the one that I had known deep inside.

"It is my fault entirely that I brought this painter into the circus. I'm just sorry that you were the unfortunate pawn."

"What do you mean?" I stared off at the white sandy banks that led to the White Forest.

"I enchanted the paintings."

"I knew that."

"While I enchanted them so that anyone who gazes on the three paintings will see what I want them to see, that's not all I did."

"What did you do?" My nostrils flared and my voice rose, echoing in the cavern. He had a habit of cruel tricks. Instantly I thought of the bargain that Émile had made with him to secure the commission. Had it included Émile's soul?

"It's been dull around here this summer, so I cast a little spell." He dismissed me with his hand. "It was really nothing. I simply let Émile choose three subjects for his paintings. Each subject would fall in love with him. He painted you; you fell in love with him... Esmé, Sylvie..."

"That's cruel," I gasped. "How could you?" Again, my hand fell to my baby. The dates were important. Had my feelings for Émile been enchantments? Had anything about him been real except for the child I was now carrying? "When... when did you do this?" I was sick.

He shrugged. "When I commissioned him, of course."

I sank back into my chair, recalling the day at the market at Rue Mouffetard when Émile had bought me an apple. That was the very moment that I fell in love with him, before Father had hired him. My feelings for Émile—and his for me—had been genuine.

August 9, 1925

Doro has informed me that Esmé gave Émile a ticket to the circus. To his surprise, the tickets have allowed Émile an unprecedented third visit. I'd prepared myself to see him, but I hadn't anticipated the

scream from her dressing room. At Father's insistence, Madame Plutard told my sister about my pregnancy. The sound that came from the
room was like the wailings of a sick animal.

August 15, 1925

Émile sat in the front row at Saturday's performance, looking
miserable.

After the show, I avoided him. As I walked back to change from my
costume, I could hear Esmé's voice coming from her dressing room.
Her tone was sharp. "Get out!"

He opened the door, and I saw his face. "What has happened?"

"She is angry," he said. "She persists that she loves me. It's like a
madness. Finally, I wrote her a letter telling her that I could not be
with her and to go away. She sent me a ticket anyway, then sent the two
clowns to summon me back here. I just told her to leave me alone. She
is angry, as you can hear." He motioned to the room. "She says we will
regret what we've done."

"What *we've* done?" I cocked my head and pulled my collar tight
around my neck.

His face softened, and I knew that *she'd* told him about our baby. I
inhaled sharply. While he should have heard it from me, the fact that
my sister had felt it was her place to tell Émile my news was a betrayal.
Her door was shut tight and likely locked. I thought what I would do to
her if it weren't. "I didn't intend for you to find out this way."

"I'm not sure you *intended* to tell me at all." He winced and held his
hand.

"Are you okay?" I noticed a steady stream of blood falling to the floor from his sleeve.

"Oh, I've cut myself, that's all." He motioned to Esmé's dressing room. "There was a shard of glass near her door. I picked it up."

I led him to my dressing room, which was two doors down, so I could tend to his hand. The cut was a small gash in his palm. I cleaned the wound and wrapped it, but I feared it was far deeper in the center. "You should have a doctor look at that."

"Do not worry about me." He touched me briefly on the cheek. "I should be worrying about you."

"I'm fine." I moved my cheek away from his hand.

"If you recall, I had suspected as much when you were sick."

I gave a small snort.

"We can live in my apartment. It's not big, but it will be fine for a few years."

"I've told you." I sank into my seat. "We can't be together."

"You need to stop thinking of Esmé and begin to think of *our* child," he said. "What is your plan—to raise our child here?" He looked around the walls. "This is a place of horror. I'd been warned of the darkness here, but it seeps into your bones."

"This is my home," I said.

"But it will not be our child's home."

"Oh, Émile," I said. There has been a growing sense of dread that I have about this pregnancy. I know that I cannot live with Émile outside the circus. I don't know if that includes my child as well, but even if I could exist out there, with him, I know the artist's life is solitary. I see how Hadley and Ernest Hemingway struggle with their son, Bumby. Ernest is always writing by himself at the cafés while Hadley walks Bumby alone through the Jardin du Luxembourg, the child toddling beside her. My life at the circus has been vibrant and I've been surrounded by performers all my life. I cannot imagine another life, even if it is with Émile.

But he looked at me so expectantly, so in love. "Cecile?"

"It sounds wonderful," I lied.

August 23, 1925

It is hard to write this, but I need to capture every detail.

After my performance a week ago, I stopped at Montparnasse and was alarmed to see that Émile looked much as he did when I saw him on the street that one night. Once again he was pale, with the dark hollows under his eyes, but this time they were even more pronounced.

I insisted he join Sylvie and me for dinner. He ate very little, assuring me he was just distracted. Worried about him, I spent the night at his apartment. He woke, feverish. Fearing that he had caught something, he sent me back to the circus so he wouldn't pass it on to me and the baby; the horrors of the Spanish flu still lived large in the minds of soldiers like him. While I didn't tell him so, I was glad to be back on the other side. My leg and arm had been aching. I felt like I was coming apart; this pregnancy was already taking a toll on my body.

When I didn't hear from Émile after three days, I insisted that Sylvie accompany me to his apartment. She was hesitant at first, but she reluctantly agreed to go. That Esmé is now shattered over him has caused Sylvie to hate him even more.

The taxi left us off about two blocks from his apartment. The summer air was stifling. At cafés, women fanned themselves and angled for chairs in the shade, the sound of jazz flowing out onto the streets. "You do not like him."

Her hands plunged deep into her dress. "I don't know how you could possibly like him, let alone love him. He slept with Esmé."

"He didn't sleep with her." This was what Émile told me, and I believed him.

She snorted and spun in front of me in the street. "Do you really think Esmé would be this angry and possessive of him if she hadn't slept with him?" Sighing in disgust, she walked the block in silence.

The truth of this statement made me defensive. "You haven't been shy about conveying your opinion of him."

We turned toward the side street near Émile's apartment. She stopped and faced me again. "What do you want from me?"

"You are my friend. I don't want anything from you."

"Are you blind?" She shook her head and I saw tears in her eyes. She grabbed at her chin-length curls before taking my face in her hands and kissing me hard on the lips. When she pulled away, she had tears flowing down her face. "I am in *love* with you, Cecile. Do you not see that? He is wrong for you."

I was so taken aback by her words—and her kiss—that I felt faint. "Since *when* have you been in love with me, Sylvie?"

She dismissed me with a wave of her hand and began to walk ahead. "It has been for several months now. I was as surprised by it as you. I've been sick just watching you fawn all over him these last few months, especially after what he did to you."

"Several months?" I stopped dead. "Since the painting?"

She considered this and shrugged, her blond curls bouncing as she moved. "I guess so."

"Think." I pointed my finger at her. "When?"

She looked down at the ground. "I suppose it was then. I remember noticing things about you—things that I had seen for years, but they became pronounced. Every time you walked in the room to check on the painting, I found myself holding my breath. At first, I thought it was crazy; we've been friends since we were girls. But as you helped him sketch my face on the canvas…" She paused and looked out at the street. "I don't know; something in me stirred."

I'd known that Sylvie had a brief dalliance with a socialite she'd met at the Ritz. We'd stopped going there when the woman's husband relocated to Paris, although the woman had very much wanted to continue to see Sylvie. At that moment, I became aware of everything. The cars going down Boulevard du Montparnasse, the clink of glasses, the smell of men's sweat as they passed by too close, and Sylvie, the outline of her dress against the sun and the freckles that formed on her full checks as she stood outside. She had the most perfect heart-shaped face, like a cupid's. Then I recalled that I had signed Sylvie's painting with the EG. Father's curse had the subject falling in love with the painter. As far as the enchantment was concerned, the painting was attributed to me.

I closed my eyes. "It isn't real, Sylvie. It was a curse that Father placed on the paintings."

Her beautiful face twisted and her gray eyes went wide. "How *dare* you, Cecile," she said. "What a horrible thing to say to me. Are you the only one who can feel things?"

Instantly I regretted the callousness of my remark, but it didn't make it any less true. The enchantment that Father had cast had the subject falling in love with "the painter." He hadn't been more specific.

As we ascended the stairs, we met the landlady coming down, her face grave. "I did not know where to find you," she said. "The doctor is with him now."

I ran up the stairs to his room. It was dark and the smell—a putrid mixture of sweat and vomit—filled my nostrils. The doctor was opening the two windows, but the stifling summer air didn't help.

"He says the breeze is too cold for him." I looked over to see the outlines of Émile's body. He appeared tiny even though he was covered in thick blankets.

"What is wrong with him?"

The doctor shook his head. "Frankly, I don't know. It seems like malaria with the sweats, but it is as though he is bleeding somewhere. Yet I can't find the source of it. He is getting weaker. It could be his kidneys." The man picked up his bag. "There is nothing I can do. You should see him now. Stay with him and give him comfort, if you can."

I felt Sylvie's hand on my back. "I'm so sorry, Cecile."

I could hardly breathe. "Can you go back and tell Father?"

There was a long silence. Sylvie understood what I meant by this request. I wanted a favor from Father. "Are you sure?" Even with his children, Father didn't dole out favors freely. Something valuable would need to be claimed in return.

When I didn't answer, she turned and left the room. She shut the door quietly so as not to disturb him.

I walked toward Émile's bed. He was sleeping. As I sat down next to him, he began to heave and shake. His face was the color of stone. "I am here, my love." I stroked his cheek. It had at least a week's stubble.

He looked up at me, but I wasn't sure he recognized me—his expression remained blank. I could see him ebbing.

Father arrived within the hour. Well, *arrived* is an odd choice of words, because he didn't need to use a door. He just appeared in the room.

"He is dying." I felt his presence; I didn't even have to look up.

"It is your sister's doing." His voice was grave. "For that, I am sorry."

Sadly, I knew what his response meant. He wouldn't undo her spell.

Even when we were younger, he wouldn't reverse our magic against each other, forcing us to come to peace. "Please." I turned to face him. "This is all your fault. That curse you put on the paintings. You have Sylvie in love with me and Esmé in love with him." As the words left my mouth, I knew this was the wrong approach with Father. His face changed in front of me to his true form. Had I not been pregnant, I know I would have spent three days in the White Forest.

"I will *not* cross your sister's curse." His voice rumbled, then echoed in the quiet room like a storm.

"Can I reverse it?"

Father looked over at Émile's form in the bed. "He's too far gone and your sister is too powerful." He crossed the room and stood over Émile, studying him intently. "You want him?"

"I do." I was sobbing now.

"Will you accept him on any terms?" I knew what he was doing now, binding me to something. "I cannot give him back to you in the way you want. It is not in my power to do so."

I would take Émile on any terms. "I'll do it."

The room was silent except for the curtain rustling against the wall. When I turned to look at him, he was gone.

I sat next to Émile's bedside, expecting some improvement. By evening, he began coughing up blood, then defecating blood; blood ran from his nose, his eyes, and his penis. I mopped up sheets soaked with his blood. I took his shirts, knowing that he wouldn't be needing them, and mopped up more blood. As I wiped every inch of him, I noticed that the cut on his hand remained pristine throughout, never healing even after a week. It was then that I knew what she had done. I held his hand and stared at the cut.

When the blood stopped flowing, I felt a sense of dread. His breath began to slow, but he gasped. I didn't understand this. I had bargained with Father, but it appeared he didn't keep his promise. Before dawn, Émile died in my arms.

They took his body away and burned the sheets; the landlady didn't even wait until his body was removed before she began to strip the room in preparation for another artist who needed cheap lodging. In my haze, I'd forgotten to grab the paintings. I ran back upstairs but found them gone already. When I came back down, I found the canvases in the alley, neighbors picking through them. I spied the painting of Sylvie and grabbed it from the pile, snatching it out of another man's hand with strength that surprised him. I pored through the other paintings, looking for the ones of Esmé and me, but they were gone.

When I got back to the circus, Doro was at the entrance. "There is a new ride," said Doro's puppet. Doro the clown looked excited until he saw my face. The puppet looked up at me. "What is it, dear?"

"Émile has died."

Doro the clown took my hand. "You will want to see this ride, then." Bloodstained and weary, I was about to protest, but he took me by the hand and led me down the Grand Promenade of the arcade to a carousel. "Your father just created it this this morning around dawn," said the puppet.

I stopped dead in my tracks. "Doro, what does this carousel *do*?"

"I cannot explain it," said the puppet. "You need to ride it. It's glorious. It may be his greatest creation." He helped me onto a horse. Doro pulled the lever and the horse stepped backward. Like it was waking up, the brightly painted carousel horse began to shift in front of me and a real mane sprouted down its neck. The horse put its head down and began an odd backward trot, then finally a gallop. The lion next to me was also waking and running backward. Around the carousel all the animals—the giraffe, the elephant, and the other horses—were running in a strange backward unison.

This was madness, I thought. And then I felt sleepy. My head was heavy and I nestled into the horse's mane. He seemed to anticipate this.

The first image hit me. Émile sitting with me at Le Dôme Café. I could smell the cigarettes in the air above us. I touched his hand. This version was warm and healthy. Then the image shifted to his bed—the one he'd just died in. Only he was very much alive and on top of me. I could touch the sweat on his back as he entered me. I lingered there, sensing that this image would remain as long as I wanted it to, but then another moment revealed itself and I thought my heart would break leaving my Émile. The scene was him sketching me at the circus. The way he looked at me. Then Émile, breaking the cheese on a steaming bowl of onion soup. Me, walking at Les Halles. I could see how much he'd wanted to hold my hand, though I hadn't noticed it then. The woman in a silver gown with a tiara scurried by with a man in a black evening jacket chasing after her. I envied them their happiness and my eyes recalled the wonder at the market in the wee hours of the morning. Next I was standing in the Rue Mouffetard market, where he handed me an apple. With this scene I felt the energy of the world shift. Father was wrong. Émile could have painted me or not painted me; the outcome would have been the same. I loved Émile Giroux. The horse slowed and light began to leak through the image of him as though he were a curtain eaten by moths. And then he was gone.

When I finally looked up, satiated from Émile's images, Father sat on the control box. "Well?"

"It's not the same," I said. "It's not him."

"You said you'd take him in any form."

I slid off the horse and stepped down from the carousel, passing him as I walked down the Grand Promenade.

"You didn't ask the price," he called after me.

"It's because I didn't care," I replied.

November 30, 1925

For the last few months, as my condition has become more pronounced, I have been unable to perform. Instead I now ride the carousel. Once, I found Esmé descending from the carousel's platform. She looked forlorn and in what appeared to be a drunken stupor; then she saw me. I was livid to think that she was on the carousel lost in her own images of him. Émile and my carousel do not belong to her.

Had I not been pregnant with our child—with his child—I believe I would have killed Esmé with my bare hands and taken Father's punishment. I have never felt such anger. I hadn't spoken to her in months. As she passed me, I said, "Now neither of us has him."

"And I prefer it that way," she said, yet the pain in her face was evident. Émile was both the bond between us and the very wedge that divided us.

"Because you knew you'd lose." I had never hated her the way she'd hated me, but for once, I finally understood and matched her contempt. I didn't think that this emotion had existed in me until now. "He was never yours, Esmé."

She seemed wooden and turned rather stiffly before heading back to her room. "And he'll never be yours again, dear sister."

July 24, 1926

I haven't written much. I guess I don't care to tell my story anymore. My story—my life—has little meaning without him. Tonight is my first night back performing. I know that I don't look good, but everyone insists that I do.

The last week in February, I went into labor. I languished for two days. From the looks of Madame Plutard, who did her best for me, and even Father, I could tell this was not a good thing. I could see everyone gathered in corners and speaking in hushed tones. At this point, I didn't care if I died. In fact, I think I preferred it. The pain was unlike anything before, as though I were splitting in two. There was something about giving birth to this child. As the child grew inside me, I could feel my own essence draining. This baby is powerful, but it has weakened me. Through my haze, I asked for Sylvie. She looked fresh and crisp, in her white outfit. By contrast, I was soaked through with sweat and sitting in my own urine.

"Promise me that if I die, you will take my child away from here."

"You aren't—"

But I could read her. I saw the tightening around her eyes and I knew she was lying. I had just told the same lies to Émile months ago. I knew them well. I don't fear death. I don't know where our kind, cambions, go, but my hope is that it is near him. I'd love to see him again. "If I die and my baby lives you must promise me that you won't let *her* raise my child. Promise me, Sylvie. She will not raise *his* baby!"

"I promise."

But I lived. And so did my daughter. I named her Margot, which was Émile's mother's name. She was perfect: wiggly, pink, healthy, and screaming.

So that brings me to tonight. Sylvie has just left my dressing room, fretting again. I assured her that flying for me is like breathing, but I didn't tell her that even that has become more difficult lately since giving birth. Sometimes I have to sit on the way to the carousel. Doro has put a bench there for me. He hasn't said that it is for me, but a bench arrived at just the location where he saw me leaning against the wall.

Last week, before Sylvie left my dressing room, she turned back from the door. "I lied to you."

"About what?"

"You asked me when I fell in love with you. I told you that it was when you were sketching me, but that wasn't true. It was the first day when you crawled up the ladder to the trapeze. You kept falling and you had such determination. I hadn't seen that from you and something changed. I don't know...it doesn't matter, I guess."

But it did. Her love for me was real, yet I didn't love her in that way, and it broke my heart.

I am so weary tonight and a little distracted. It has been this way since Margot's birth, but I anticipate that old tingle that comes from flying again. My costume hangs waiting for me, draped on the covered mirror. I want to pull off the cover, but the pitiful creature whom Father has trapped in there will be peering out at me. Hesitantly, I pull back the drape. To my astonishment, I don't see one creature—but two—and they are familiar.

As I walk down into the center ring, I wonder who Father has invited tonight in the audience. He has begun sending out tickets again, thinking things will go back to the way they used to be.

But that, I fear, will never be.

25

Paris / Eighth Layer of Hell
July 3, 2005

After reading the final journals, it was taking Lara a moment to adjust to the fact that Althacazur—the daemon of *really cool shit*—was her...what? Great-great-grandfather? Oh dear. Lara felt herself sink.

Oblivious to everyone, Althacazur had his leg over the arm of the chair and was sitting like a petulant teenager, swinging his leg. "So," he began. "Let me tell you a story. Once there was this really cool gent."

"Gent?" Lara couldn't help but mock his word choice.

"Short for 'gentleman,'" said Althacazur, his eyes widening, like she was stupid.

Lara rolled her eyes. "I know that."

"Anyway," he said, annoyed at the interruption. "This gent who might have had some really great powers met this mortal actress—Juno Wagner. Such a beautiful name. Well, he fell head over heels for her—which for a major daemon is not something that happens every day."

"Father," said Cecile sharply. She was standing in the center of the ring with her hands on her hips. "Do we really have to get into all this?"

"She's family, Cecile. I promised her that she would have all the answers to her tiny, stupid, human questions if she came to Paris."

Cecile rolled her eyes.

"And so back to my story," said Althacazur, striking a different tone to please Cecile. "Where was I?"

"That I'm family," said Lara, trying to hide her distaste at the idea.

"Oh yes." He put his finger up. "Nine months later...I think you know where this story is going. My dear Juno gives birth to..." He stopped and seemed to consider something. "...a *lovely* creature."

"A creature?" Lara wasn't sure if she was supposed to be asking questions. She knew a bit of this story from reading the entry on Althacazur in The New Demonpedia.com. Juno Wagner and her child died in childbirth.

He ignored her. "Perhaps I failed to *fully* explain the rules to Juno, so enraptured with her was I. You see, my love was a human and I, a daemon. There are laws against this type of coupling. It's frankly forbidden. I mean, I didn't create the laws, but I was never much of a rule follower anyway. Well, Juno died in childbirth. All the women who bear my children die—it's too much for a human to carry a daemon's baby, no matter what Mia Farrow does on-screen. In fact, the offspring die, too. Except in this case, they didn't. Before she died, my dear Juno gave birth to an imperfectly *perfect* creature—a rare cambion. It was the perfect amalgamation of good...Juno...and evil...well...me.

"Cambions tend not to survive for a reason. Given I'm not just a daemon but a major daemon, this particular cambion didn't blend the mortal and daemon things as well as one would have hoped. It was all a bit messy. It's hard to explain to a mortal, but Esmé and Cecile were fused." Like a magician, he conjured a picture, then jumped up from his throne and presented it to Lara—a grainy, old-timey photo.

Lara studied the old photograph mounted on thick paper like

heavily sepia-toned Victorian images tended to be. In this one, an otherworldly, half-daemon child with two little heads was dressed in a single black lace gown. The girls, who appeared to be about four years old, were lovingly arranged on a chair, like dolls. Keeping with Victorian style, an oversize satin bow was perched on each of their heads, positioned carefully over tended curls—one blond set and one dark.

Whoever had commissioned this photo—likely Madame Plutard—had loved these girls and wanted them to be captured as she saw them. Studying the girls' hopeful faces, Lara saw them that way as well. "They're beautiful," said Lara. Both of their small, heart-shaped mouths were slightly slack, as though something was distracting them beyond the camera. The photo was the most heartbreaking thing Lara had ever seen—no, *felt* was a better word—because she *felt* this photo pulling her in from another time. From their faces, she could feel the suffering of these poor children. Lara counted the tiny satin slippers that dangled down from the chair—three. Closing her eyes, Lara imagined them struggling to walk. Then she knew. A protective feeling overcame her. This child *belonged* to her—was imprinted on her as the origin of her family. She looked over at Cecile, whose hands were folded in front of her and whose face showed no emotion, like she had hardened herself to the story.

"I didn't know what to do with my little creature...I wondered who would take care of it for me. I looked at my damned souls and thought, *Well, Althacazur, that's a pretty groovy idea.* So I grabbed a group of performers and assembled them with the idea that they would care for it, along with Madame Plutard, who had proven herself so loyal to Juno." He spun on his heels. "That worked until they began to grow up." He looked at his nails. "I hate things that aren't fun, Lara, really I do. So I cut them in half, creating two of them—liberating them from each other. Now, mind you, there were some issues. It wasn't clean, but inside the circus, I created a place of illusion."

Cecile looked down, like this part of the tale was painful for her to hear. Lara couldn't imagine having to endure this story.

As if on cue, he said, "Cecile, my love, perhaps you'd rather not hear this."

"No," she said firmly. "Continue. For years, I longed for these answers and you refused me."

Contrite, he motioned for Lara to join him. Cecile followed.

"Tisdale, Tisdale. It's safe now," said Althacazur as he left the center ring. "The monsters are all in their cages."

As they walked, Lara couldn't help but glance over at Cecile. She was beautiful, ethereal. "I read your diaries." Lara wasn't sure if this was a good thing or not, and she sounded like some fan or groupie.

"I know," Cecile said, smiling. "I had him send them to you. All along, I was writing them for you. I just didn't know it at the time." In person, Cecile was shorter and slighter than Lara, but their faces had a similarity—the strong jaw, the upturned nose, the green eyes.

Cecile took her hands. The woman's long silver-white hair hung in ringlets down her back. "Let me look at you."

"I look like you."

The woman put her hand to her mouth. "You do."

"Touching though this little reunion is, ladies." Althacazur was standing with Tisdale beside him, looking like Mr. Roarke and Tattoo. He motioned toward a door with a sign that read FERRIS WHEEL.

Lara stopped and turned to Cecile, remembering the entry from Cecile's diary when Althacazur had built the Ferris wheel. "I recall this ride from your diary."

Cecile looked down. "I don't care for any of Father's rides."

"Oh, come now," said Althacazur. "If you're going to pout during this tour, young lady, then you should stay back."

Cecile folded her hands and smiled, a little too warmly to be believed.

"Much better."

As Lara contemplated getting on the ride, she couldn't imagine what she was actually riding. You could call it a Ferris wheel, except it didn't go up. The ceiling was quite low, almost like a basement, and as you got on the car it traveled beneath the underworld. It was as though the world were flipped.

The little monkey pulled a lever and jumped on the cart. Althacazur looked at Lara.

"It has a delay, but I wouldn't stand there, girl. Get in. You *do* dawdle."

Lara thought that somewhere in here was a bottle labeled DRINK ME. She heard the engine lurch and jumped in the gondola. Althacazur put the safety bar over their laps, which Lara thought was as curious a move as anything she'd seen given that they were in another dimension of sorts. The car descended into what seemed to be the center of the earth. There was a river of shiny black water beneath them.

"Styx," Althacazur said, pointing. "This is a magnificent view of it, don't you think?" It meandered past a thick forest of bare white trees that looked like birches. They reminded her of the trees near Wickelow Bend. With the white soil, white trees, and black river, Lara had to admit, it was a magnificent sight.

"That's the White Forest," said Althacazur.

Cecile stared at the forest blankly, her jaw tightening.

"This place gets such a horrible reputation as a destination, but I love it...especially in *l'hiver*. You won't find me up there working in January." He pointed up. "So where was I...oh yes. It all was quite messy, and that's not even getting into the good-and-evil thing. Cecile has the uterus, but she has only one leg and one arm. And only one kidney."

Lara lurched. *She* only had one kidney. She was horrified at the

accounting that Althacazur was rattling off, but Cecile seemed oblivious to him, still staring with intensity at the White Forest.

"The other twin—Esmé—is missing her arm and is without a
uterus, but she has two legs and all of her kidneys. Physically Esmé was
the much stronger twin. But you see, cambions are only half human.
There was a bit of daemon blood flowing through my creature's veins,
so I could do some things that could never have been done to a non-
magical creature. I filled in the gaps, so to speak, with magic. Each
girl *looked*...flawless."

"You filled in the gaps?"

"I enchanted my fucking circus, so my girls looked beautiful inside
of it. They were like dolls. Outside the circus, too, if they didn't stay
out too long. Oh, my beauties were the talk of Paris. Plutard made
them costumes like little princesses, but I made a mistake." He turned
to Cecile and put his hand up. "I can admit when I'm wrong."

Cecile flashed him a rather hateful look. "You were wrong on so
many fronts, Father. It's hard to keep track."

"Well, yes, I made the mistake of putting the burden of keeping
the illusion on Esmé, but she was a brilliant illusionist. Cecile did not
fare as well when I separated them, so I decided to wipe her memories
clean so she had no recollection of being torn apart from her sister.
However, Esmé needed that knowledge to keep up the illusion."

Lara thought that sounded like an entirely unfair burden to place on
a young girl.

"What Father is hinting at but not saying," said Cecile, interrupting his monologue, "is that to keep *his* illusion that we were intact
inside this circus, Esmé was forced to commit murder as a sacrifice—
fealty—to fuel it."

"Yes, yes," he said, dismissing her. "She's so judgy now that she's
dead. Perhaps I felt guilt that Cecile here looked so much like her

mother. On her deathbed," continued Althacazur, unaware of how upset his daughter was becoming at the story, "I'd made promises to my Juno that I would care for the child. Juno was never told the entire story of the birth—that there were two. Never thinking they'd live, of course, I agreed to it, but then she died, and I was bound, you see." He looked sheepish. "It was a grave mistake as I would learn."

"You never should have split us. We were happy as we were." Cecile glared at him.

"Then that painter Émile Giroux fucked everything up," said Althacazur, ignoring her. "Although Tisdale likes to remind me that I don't know my own strength and that it *was* my fault. You see, because I'm an *artist* myself...I put a *little* spell on Giroux so that anyone he painted fell in love with him."

"What you did was unforgivable," spat Cecile, folding her arms.

Lara knew this from the journals.

"Yes, well, while I may have split you both in two physically, Giroux's knife was sharper."

"Thanks to you." Cecile sank down in her seat and rested her chin on her hand.

Lara was fascinated at this strange familial argument she was witnessing. She tried to muffle a thought she had, much like trying to stifle one of those dry coughs you get at the end of a bad cold, but the thought wouldn't stay down. *This man is a lunatic. We're placating a lunatic.*

As the thought swirled in her, she looked at Mr. Tisdale, who seemed to be able to read her mind. His eyes were now wide with alarm.

The car kept descending under a tunnel. "And as you might guess, both my girls fell in love with Giroux, so when Giroux chose Cecile over Esmé, well, she went a little crazy."

"She killed him," said Cecile.

"But not before lovely Cecile here had conceived your...well, I guess it would be your grandmother Margot. I think you saw her riding His Majesty earlier. Marvelous performer she is, much better than Sylvie ever was on a horse."

Cecile spoke through gritted teeth. "Father is wrong. I fell in love with Émile *before* he cast the spell. Only Esmé was affected by the spell. Her love for Giroux was never genuine."

Althacazur made a face that indicated he disagreed with this assessment.

Lara couldn't speak. This man—this daemon—was fucking nuts. How on earth could she make sense of this? Was this a bad trip of some sort?

"As a result, Esmé has stomped around for decades in a terrible mood over Émile Giroux. She traveled around the world for the first ten years getting into all kinds of trouble. The other daemons were furious. Then she decided to set up a residence in that horrid little town you live in. I think she enjoys killing all of the loves of Cecile's offspring as payment for Émile Giroux, who, frankly, was dull as dishwater and someone she never would have loved of her own volition."

Cecile went to protest, but he put his hand up.

"I know, I know," he said, his eyes rolling. "Greatest love, blah, blah."

Mr. Tisdale chirped.

"I know what I did to Esmé wasn't fair, but this decades-long tantrum is frankly tiring. I'm getting a lot of grief about it. Lucifer has told me that I must get her under control. So now we come to you, Ms. Barnes. You come from a long line of my descendants. You aren't entirely mortal—you're also part cambion. Perhaps you've noticed that you live in a perfect town. With no crime. Zero. Well, that's Cecile's doing. She gave Margot a spell, but I hear your mother keeps it up quite well, the way one would take care of a lawn. Audrey is a general bore, but she knew how to protect you from Esmé. Sadly, that spell doesn't work outside Kerrigan Falls, so my dear child nearly killed you the other day at the Père Lachaise."

"The woman who chased me? It *was* Esmé?"

"That was my sister who tried to kill you," said Cecile. "Audrey gave you a spell, but it didn't work or you didn't perform it correctly. I made Father intervene. Usually he won't, but for some reason he's taken with you."

"Why is she trying to kill me?" Lara shifted her gaze from Cecile to Althacazur, irritated that no one seemed to be jumping to answer what she thought was a pressing question.

Cecile looked irritated, so she began the story. "After I fell from the trapeze and died, as she promised, Sylvie took Margot and fled to America—you knew her as Cecile Cabot, your great-grandmother. My sister also ran away from the circus, but it wasn't so easy. With me dead and her gone, no enchantment was required at the circus anymore. She's a great illusionist, so she took what she learned from Father and figured that if she wanted to keep up the illusion of being young, beautiful, and immortal, she needed to keep killing. Maintaining the spell on herself has been a lot easier than on a full circus, so instead of killing each time we move, she only has to do it every thirty years, on October ninth, our birthday. On that day she finds a man and sacrifices him. Like Émile, he needs to bleed. She's a hundred years old now, but I bet she's still stunning." Cecile looked at Althacazur. "How was that?"

"Quite accurate," said Althacazur. "The bitter flourish really does add a lot."

Like a bored tour guide, Althacazur pointed at the next attraction.

"We're under the Styx right now, kind of like the Eurostar Hell Line." They came up to a white sand beach with black trees and red leaves. Lara could see animals—more accurately, animal *skeletons*—grazing on the sand.

The trees shook themselves as they went past, and leaves pelted them. Althacazur plucked the leaves from Lara's hair.

"Oh no," said Cecile, grabbing at Lara and plucking frantically.

Lara suddenly felt woozy.

"They're poisonous." Althacazur sounded annoyed. "The tree is showing off for you. Don't worry, if you stop breathing, Tisdale has the antidote in his pocket."

The monkey looked more alarmed still and patted his pocket, shaking his head.

"We need to go back now," said Cecile, leaping to her feet.

"And Todd? You told me you'd tell me what happened to him." Suddenly her mouth felt dry.

Cecile nodded and patted her hand. "She could kill any man she wanted. It doesn't matter, but killing Émile did something to her—she enjoyed it and I think it made her stronger. As I got weaker from delivering my child, she actually gained strength. In her mind, had I not been pregnant with Margot, he'd have chosen her, so she took revenge on Margot by killing Desmond Bennett. Poor Margot fell apart—she always had a wild streak, some cambions do—but the magic combined with Dez's disappearance was her undoing. Esmé killed Émile, Dez, Peter, and Todd. Every man we've loved, she's chosen for revenge."

"I blame myself. I sent Esmé to the White Forest. Sadly, she didn't come back the same," said Althacazur with true sadness in his voice. "I had thought she was just like me and could endure it, but I was wrong. For that, I have extended her liberties, but it is becoming politically difficult to continue. She must come back to the circus."

Lara wondered if anyone realized that she was fading, but they kept talking among themselves. "I don't feel well." Her head felt heavy and she had trouble getting the words out. The trio stared at her trying to understand what she was saying.

"We're almost to the top," said Althacazur.

But Lara had stopped listening to their argument, tuning it out like a radio frequency. *Todd is dead.*

She became aware of a silence. All this time, she'd realized that she'd been kidding herself that she was prepared for this news. Oh, she'd uttered grand words about wanting to know the truth, and she'd pursued the mystery of Todd's disappearance with Ben Archer like some modern-day Nancy Drew, but Lara had never, never considered what this moment would *feel* like. All hope was now lost, and the cold reality of his death hit her. Sure, she'd waited for hunters to find his body in a patch of Wickelow Forest, or at least discover fabric from his shirt or a sneaker, some evidence of doom to slow-walk her to this moment. At times, she thought she'd felt his death and steeled herself for the news that would come *one day.* And Lara found she couldn't cry. Even though she was poisoned and not concerned about herself, she refused to cry in front of these people. Audrey, Ben, Caren, yes, but these strangers...no.

"Lara." It was Cecile who spoke.

She saw a chandelier, a lovely thing really. Had she been of better mind, she would have marveled at it. Were they in a cave? She'd forgotten. Above her a chandelier twirled—or was she twirling? She'd thought she'd been on a ride, but everything in this fucked-up place was backward. Maybe Todd being dead meant he was really alive? This place was like that, turning in on itself.

For a dead woman, Cecile had a mighty grip. She held Lara up as she sank in the gondola chair.

"I'm sorry." Lara closed her eyes and swore that if Althacazur started babbling again, she'd say something that would send her to the White Forest, but she didn't care. "You said that Todd is dead?"

"He is." Cecile touched her hand. "I'm so sorry."

"You're sure." Lara focused on Cecile's eyes, locked in on them. Perhaps it was the poison, but she found she was numb all over. Her lips were dry and felt like they were swelling. She'd begun rocking.

"Sadly, yes."

"I think I'm going to be sick." Lara leaned over the gondola and threw up in the River Styx.

She was very much inside herself now, as if she were experiencing the fuzzy effects of a painkiller, while somewhere in the distance she heard Althacazur continue his monologue. "Esmé knows it's coming to an end. She knows that Lara is the most powerful creature to come down from the line. I've made you the strongest magical creature that I can for the sole purpose of stopping my daughter. That, Lara, is why she wants to kill you."

The car began to lift. Lara was still woozy and didn't understand this part of the conversation. Hell, the entire thing was confusing.

"Hold on until we get to the top. Don't die on us. It would be so anticlimactic." Althacazur cackled.

Dying. She thought she was probably close to that now, given the effect of the toxin. This would be an acceptable end to her story, she decided. As they reached the arcade lobby again, Althacazur lifted the bar and got out of the car, holding out his gloved hand for Lara, who was aided by Cecile. Tisdale scampered to turn off the machine.

Lara was still stumbling even under Cecile's grip when Tisdale came and presented her with a lollipop.

"Oh, I can't." Lara made a face. The idea of eating anything right now was impossible.

"It's the antidote," said Althacazur, taking the lollipop and handing it to her. "I warn you, though, it tastes like..."

Lara put it in her mouth and began to cough. "Shit! This tastes so foul."

"Indeed. It's actually made of petrified donkey shit from Hades, but it will save your life."

Lara lurched, fell over, and threw up again. After she'd collected herself, Tisdale motioned for her to keep sucking it.

It did have the effect of making her clearheaded again, but she needed to leave this circus and get back to Audrey and Jason...Ben. It would take time to process what she now knew about Todd, but they would help her.

Following them back into the center ring, Lara saw it was now filled with the performers, standing at attention. Althacazur walked over to Cecile and pulled her chin up. "I agree, the grave mistake that I made was separating you two in the first place. You were perfect as you were. I failed to see that. When this is all over, you two will be reunited. I promise you." Althacazur stroked her face. "I refused to intervene between you girls once, but I'm going to do so now. It needs to be by your hand, though, Cecile. I warned you once, this battle is between the two of you. I've helped you enough by bringing Lara here and making sure her magic is strong. She's the perfect weapon."

He walked around the arena, sweeping his hand like Vanna White. "So here you go. I built you a circus, Lara Barnes! Remember, when I came to visit you as a child, I told you that this circus was *your* destiny." He put his arms out. "The care of these creatures falls to you now, my dear. You see, the circus requires a human patron. You are human enough, though powerful cambion blood—mine—flows through you. This magnificent legacy needs one who cares for it and keeps its connection to the outside world, perhaps one who can convince the tickets to come back out." He shrugged. "I'd hoped that Sylvie would follow her mother and become the patron, but that was not to be. Then my hopes rested on dear Margot, then Audrey. But now with you, Lara, at the helm, I will *finally* be free of this place to go and be the daemon artist that I am intended to be."

They were all staring at her—the performers, Althacazur, Margot, Cecile, Doro, and Tisdale. Lara looked around, confused, not real-izing they were waiting for a reply. She stumbled a little, still woozy. "But I don't want a circus." What Lara needed was to think...and to mourn. This was absurd. All of it. As she spoke, though, the creatures all seemed to sink in front of her. The elephant, the winged lion, and Tisdale put their heads down. The music that was playing stopped abruptly.

Althacazur adjusted himself and Cecile started to speak, but he cut her off.

He walked toward her, Lara shrinking in his presence. Suddenly this felt like touring a time-share facility, and she now had to endure the sales pitch.

"You know what will happen to them." Althacazur's voice was calm. He pointed to the performers; gone was the jaunty ringleader. "I'll just send them all back to Hell. They've served their purpose, babysitting Cecile and Esmé." Lara saw his eyes weren't amber at all— that had been an illusion. They were black, and she saw him in his true form—with a purple robe and the head of a ram—before he switched back to the handsome man with brown ringlets and eyes the color of dead grass. She'd recalled the online encyclopedia entry on him: *Given his charm, he is often mistaken as a lighter demon, which is a grave mistake, for he is the most vain and unforgiving of all Hell's generals.*

Lara exhaled sharply and looked around the ring. The performers stared back at her like animals in a shelter.

"Ah hell, baby," said Althacazur, cackling. "They can all just burn. It doesn't matter to me. I'll close the circus and send all of you back to Lucifer—you included, Cecile." He spun toward Lara, his heels squeaking. "Then I'll let you and Esmé duke it out. You'll be dead in a day." He turned dramatically. "More fodder for Lucifer."

"Father." It was Cecile, her voice sharp. "No! You can't send them back. That would be cruel. You commuted their sentences, promising them that they could stay here for eternity. They all did as you asked." She snorted. "Now it seems that you don't want to be bothered with the burden of us all." Her face fell. "I'm sorry, Lara. I didn't realize he was bringing you here to trick you into taking over the circus."

"You helped me bring her here," said Althacazur. "Surely you knew."

"You never said." Cecile's brows furrowed.

"And you, my dear, never asked."

"Can I just speak for a moment?" Lara folded her hands in front of her, trying to compose herself. Beyond furious, she'd had it with this ridiculous world, this crazy story, and this nutty man. "I've listened to your story. I've watched the circus, which is lovely, by the way. I've gone on these fucked-up rides and eaten shit pops—a taste that I will never, ever get over. But to be clear, the *only* reason I came here is because you promised me that I'd find out what happened to my fiancé. And now I know the truth." Lara's voice broke and she paced. "He's *dead*." The word was like a razor, hard for her to utter.

Everyone watched her intently. Wiping mascara from her hands, she steeled herself and looked at Althacazur. "Now that I know what happened to him, I'd just like to go home."

Althacazur seemed oblivious and put his hands on his hips. He walked in a circle around Lara, his fury palpable. "I show you what is, perhaps, my greatest masterpiece. I offer you the universe—this fucking *perfect* circus—and you don't *want* it?" His voice mocked her and rose until the entire arena rumbled. "I've told you all your life: The boy wasn't the point. It was the circus. Always the circus. I gave you the information on the boy to lure you here to gaze upon your destiny."

Lara thought he was wrong. The mortal boy *was* the point. Todd mattered, just as Juno Wagner had mattered to him, once. Lara looked around to find them all staring at her. She'd forgotten that they all could read her mind. Aloud she said, "Shit."

Althacazur's face twisted in fury. Tisdale put his hand up to stop him from something, but he slapped the little monkey away and retreated to sink into the velvet chair. "What have I done to make this one so stupid? I tried with her, oh how I tried with this one. I made her the perfect weapon to bring my Esmé home and take over." He sat on the throne, spittle sprouting from his lips as he pointed to Lara. She feared he was going into a fit. "Why are my offspring such failures? I went to that dump of a place where this one lives and spent time with her. Poor Margot was mad." He pointed to Margot, who looked down. "Audrey's a bore. I'd so hoped that *this* would be the one worthy of the circus and able to contain Esmé." He sat sulking like a child, yet Lara could see the terror in Tisdale's face. He pointed to Lara. "You know, Esmé *should* win; she has my ambition. In thirty years, Lara, when you have a daughter, the love of her life will be Esmé's next victim. And you'll have no one but yourself to blame." He turned in his chair after giving Lara a final look of disgust. "Go back to your dreary home. Cecile, Tis...get her out of my sight, before I kill her."

"Father." Cecile crouched down beside him, her fingers resting on the arm of the chair. "You have to understand that this was terrible news to her. You mustn't be so angry at a poor human. *Please.*"

Lara could see him soften, his face relaxing. Cecile reminded him so much of Juno. Lara could see it now, the loss that registered on his face each time he looked at his daughter. This was the real source of Cecile's power with him.

"We haven't really shown her the circus. You can't blame her. She hasn't performed in it, felt it in her blood. She doesn't know what it can do."

He was leaning over on the chair, but a slow smile formed on his lips. "We really haven't shown her, have we?" He clapped his hands and jumped to his feet. "Start from the top." He softened and motioned for Lara to join him back in the center.

Lara was trying to process the evil vision of him she'd just had with the man who was now parading around like a 1970s rock star mixed with a little Lord Byron, so she approached him cautiously. "I just want to go—"

But Cecile shot her a warning look.

The orchestra began to play Grieg's "In the Hall of the Mountain King" again. Two bearded ladies rushed in with costumes and sheets. They shrouded Lara with the sheet, then quickly ripped off her dress. One of them held a costume with a sequined pink bodice, gold beading, and a matching fringe skirt. This was the leotard that Cecile had described—her signature costume. As they spun Lara, the bodice molded around her and sewed itself as the orchestra began to pluck faster at the frenzied conclusion to the song.

"Oh good. It fits." Althacazur seemed pleased.

Two men dressed in gold-and-pink-striped long leotards met her and pointed to the ladder that had appeared from the ceiling.

"You want me to crawl *up there?*"

Althacazur nodded, clapping enthusiastically. He looked down at Tisdale, who began to mirror his master's clapping. He pushed her along. "Up, up."

"But there's no net." Lara strained her neck to see how far off the ground she was expected to be, figuring forty feet at the highest point. Althacazur rolled his eyes. "Then *make* one." Lara thought he sounded like a teenage boy at the mall. He studied the signet ring on his finger, avoiding her gaze.

Lara plucked at her costume, making sure it covered everything. "I can do that?"

The daemon put his head back and closed his eyes. "Why, why, Tisdale, is this one so stupid?"

"Father!" Cecile barked.

"Yes, yes," said Althacazur, sounding slightly defeated.

Tisdale patted him on the hand, and she swore she saw the little monkey draw a line with the other hand. A net of gold appeared under the trapeze.

"Better now?" Althacazur cocked his head.

Lara sighed and climbed the fabric ladder. As she made her way up the rungs, she thought that all she wanted was to be back in Kerrigan Falls, taking time to figure out what to do next. When she got to the top and looked down, she was reminded of the scene from *Vertigo* where the camera panned in and out. This might be harder than she thought. Considering her options, she thought she'd just swing across. This was like some zipline thing she'd done in college. This was no big deal.

"We're waiting." Althacazur was sitting back on the purple throne, chomping popcorn. The scent of burnt oil and fake butter wafted up toward the ceiling. She recalled the entry in Cecile's diary about the first time she'd leapt. Not exactly knowing what to do next, she pulled down the bar from overhead and jumped from the perch. About ten seconds in, the weight of her body and gravity kicked in and she felt her arms strain. It was not unlike swinging on the monkey bars as a kid. She swung back and caught the perch awkwardly but managed to find her footing. Hoping that would be the end of it, she did a little raise with her hands like figure skaters do to illustrate a finished movement.

"That's it?" Althacazur had draped himself over the velvet throne. "Tisdale, Cecile...do something before I *kill* her."

Lara wasn't sure if he was joking or not, but she had little doubt that if he wanted to kill her, he could.

The monkey sighed and climbed the ladder easily. He grabbed the bar from her and shook it, then placed it back in her hands. The bar felt warm, like it was now enchanted. What had he just done? Magic? He chirped something, and oddly, Lara understood him.

Don't fuck this up. He chirp-pointed to the other side and spun with his finger. *We'll all pay. Get over there.*

She searched the ring but did not see Cecile. Again, Lara leapt off the perch and saw that another bar was being sent down from the other side. As if her body knew what to do, she left the first bar and somersaulted—yes, somersaulted—into the waiting hands of a man wearing a pink leotard. She swung again back toward the perch and saw that another man was now on the other side. She somersaulted back to his waiting hands. She landed back on the perch and found she was out of breath.

"Well, that didn't suck." Althacazur shrugged like some theater director or fucked-up Bob Fosse critiquing her from the front row. He twirled his finger. "Again. Niccolò, give me Villa-Lobos's Bachianas Brasileiras Number Five. And I don't care if you don't like it and it's not your composition. Play it." From the orchestra pit came the sounds of strings.

Lara leapt off the perch, preparing to simply repeat her last swing. She could see Tisdale's hands twisting and his lips moving. He was helping her, enchanting her movements. This time, it felt easier, her body lighter as she swung. She hooked up her legs on the bar, let her hands go, and shifted her gaze up for the man to catch her. Instead she found Cecile's sure hands reaching out to catch her. They swung together and Lara went to catch the opposite bar. So preoccupied was she that Cecile had caught her, that in flight on the way back, she missed the next bar. Looking down at the net, she saw to her alarm that the gold net that had once been beneath her was gone.

Gone.

Tisdale squealed.

Althacazur laughed.

Niccolò stopped the music.

A cymbal crashed.

As she fell, Lara thought that this was the stupidest death she could have predicted for herself. She thought about Gaston having to tell her mother and father that she'd fallen to her death performing for a monkey while wearing a tutu. "No," she screamed, then "fuck." She had her arms splayed and her eyes closed, bracing for impact, then nothing. Then she opened her eyes to find that she was hovering like a freeze-frame on a TV about six feet from the ground.

"Oh, thank God," said Althacazur, sitting upright in his seat. "I was getting so bored. Now we're getting somewhere."

"Shut up, Father," said Cecile, sitting on the swing above them.

Lara held herself in place, not sure what to do. Recalling Cecile's journals, Lara considered the corkscrew move. Completely confused how she could somersault from a frozen position, she rotated and found that her body held the altitude as she spun. Next, she gazed at the perch far above her, where she needed to land. In the back of her mind, she heard Althacazur tell her, *Think of spinning this flower. Don't think of the carousel.* She imagined a flower being twirled at its stem.

As she pictured it, her body began to rise and spin at the same time, mimicking the movement in her mind. Focusing on the perch, she picked up speed, like a figure skater, twisting vertically back up to the perch.

"In case you haven't realized it, you don't need a net." Althacazur was slow-clapping.

Looking over at the other side of the trapeze, Lara let the bar drop and leapt again, somersaulting cleanly through the air in a tight vertical roll, like she was drilling her way to the other side. Her body was in a tight rotation, like a football spirals in the air. She landed on the opposite platform, next to Cecile.

"Did you do that?" Lara shouted to her.

Cecile shook her head. "No. *You* did."

And Lara wanted to do it again, needed to do it again so badly that she immediately leapt off and spiraled to the other side, but then she slowed and hovered and began doing graceful spins, like water ballet in the air. A powerful feeling overtook her. Nothing in her life had ever felt as perfect as performing magic like this. Fuck a correction. Her magic didn't need to be hidden or contained. As it flowed, she felt herself becoming stronger. This power had always been inside her, but she'd never been encouraged to use it, so like an undeveloped muscle it had withered—she had withered. Until now.

Then Cecile dove off the swing like she was diving into a pool and flew like a bird down to the ground, where she landed softly.

"Now you try it," she said, calling up to Lara.

Lara hesitated, but Cecile held out her hand. "I won't let anything happen to you, but you need to learn how to do this." Cecile smiled but her voice was firm. "Come."

What the hell, thought Lara. So she dove off the platform, thinking *no* as she fell. No, she would not fall. Lara dropped more like a leaf than like the purposeful dive Cecile had demonstrated. She landed a little two-footed, but Althacazur was very happy.

Still, it was Cecile whose approval Lara wanted most. The woman walked over and embraced her. "You were wonderful. I wasn't as good my first time." Lara's legs were shaking, but she could feel the magic flowing through her like a current. She spun to face Althacazur. He had been right. *This* had been her destiny. There was a smile forming on his lips. He had lured her here with the promise of answers. Now she had them—Todd, Cecile, and what she really was.

Then, with a sweep of his hand, the performers were gone.

Althacazur sighed. "Can we discuss a little business now? I need Esmé here where she belongs. Lucifer is growing impatient."

"But I don't understand. You're the daemon of really cool shit. Why can't you bring your own daughter back into the circus? Why do you need *anyone's* help?"

"Because he can't." It was Cecile who spoke; Althacazur looked shocked. "He's never admitted it, but by seducing our mother and having us, he'd already caught the ire of the other daemons. It is forbidden, but he was the favorite, so Lucifer let it pass. But when he sent Esmé to the White Forest, it was Lucifer who found her and sent her back." She pointed her comments to Althacazur. "After she returned, your behavior toward her changed. It's my guess that you can't touch her now, can you?"

"You've gotten wise in your death, Cecile." Althacazur exhaled like he was defeated. "After what she endured in the White Forest, Lucifer won't let me touch her. He blames me, rightfully so, for banishing her in what was a rather harsh punishment, but he's putting me in an awkward position. The daemons are clamoring to destroy her because she's a cambion. They think she's cocky and too powerful. I don't want to see my daughter destroyed, but I can't help her directly."

"I don't *want* to help her," Lara snorted.

"No, you just want to live your life free of her. I want her here again, so in essence we want the same things. Even if I could lift a hand, there's pride in the daemon community. She struck Cecile first by killing Émile. It needs to be Cecile—or her proxy—that strikes back. I've helped as much as I can to build the perfect proxy. More than you know."

"It sounds a bit like the mafia," quipped Lara, wiping some dust or chalk off her hands and onto her thighs. "Well, I'm done chanting protection spells and hiding in Kerrigan Falls. If you need me to bring her here, I'll do it. I've got nothing to lose."

"That's my girl!" Althacazur clapped his hands. "Only problem is that you can't tangle with Esmé alone. Oh, granted you're a clever little thing turning the lights on and off—and that marvelous little bit of business you did with the trapeze artist at Rivoli was inspiring, not to mention what you did just now. I've built you well and I bet you're feeling *quite* powerful about now, but you're no match for a hundred-year-old child of a major daemon. So let me propose a little deal for you. Take Great-Grandmother with you, so you have a fighting chance."

At this suggestion, Lara could see Cecile shift, disturbed. Althacazur had not consulted her on this strategy. "This is not why I wanted Lara to come here."

Althacazur laughed. "So what did you think? You just tell her all about Esmé and she'd go back to her little town and vanquish your sister? Surely you see that is a fool's errand, Cecile. She can't do that. Only *you* can do that."

"But I can't leave here, Father. I'm dead."

"But she's not. And you—" He turned to Lara. "Esmé is like a cat with a toy. She knows that the daemons want her back here and that

I've been looking for someone to wrangle her. That person is you, Lara, and she knows it. Like a feral cat, she won't take the chance of getting caught. When you get back to that dreadful little place where you live, she'll kill you for sure, along with your mother and the rather handsome police detective you're so fond of."

"No." Cecile shook her head. "It's too risky."

"What does it involve?" Lara looked at Cecile. Lara's head was swimming with everything she'd learned today. She felt both broken by the news of Todd—and yet powerfully strong as magic pulsed through her veins, the cambion part of her waking up. She was open to hearing any plans.

"You must absorb me." Cecile frowned.

"And?"

"You could die once we leave here. I tried once with Doro. It went terribly wrong."

"No," said Althacazur. "It's not like with Doro. She shouldn't die. I've altered this one in anticipation of this very moment. She only has one kidney, like you, Cecile. Her body is the most like yours so she can absorb you successfully. She's the strongest of all of you. It should work."

"Glad to know I *shouldn't* die." Lara swallowed. Her body was altered for *this* moment, like a vessel. She recalled Althacazur and Margot in the field that day; Margot asking if she was "the one." He hadn't just hoped she would become the human patron. He needed a soldier, too.

"No—" said Cecile, again sharply. "Absolutely not." Cecile bit on her nail, considering something.

Althacazur turned to Lara to reason with her. "You will certainly die if she does not do it."

"I got that," said Lara. "I might be stupid, but I am present."

"I'm not so sure," Althacazur said from his velvet chair. "Any day now, Cecile."

Lara kept focused on Cecile. "I get that the big bad is coming for me. When I absorb you, will it change me?"

She nodded. "You won't have my memories, but I'll see through you and you'll feel me. You will *feel* different."

"She'll possess you, dimwit. Have you never watched a horror film?" Althacazur was picking some lint from his coat. "If you succeed—and it's a rather hefty *if*—I'll bring Cecile and Esmé back where they belong. And you will agree to serve as our human patron. I need to be free of this circus. Do you understand me?"

"I'm not killing for this circus." Lara turned and met his eyes.

Althacazur rolled his eyes. "No one is asking you to *kill* anyone. If you succeed, you'll vanquish Esmé—who should be dead anyway, so we don't need the charm anymore. Although I admit, the idea of *you* as my human patron is almost unbearable to me now. And I thought Plutard was bad."

"If you're the human patron, you won't be able to leave the circus." Cecile shook her head. "Ever. Once Madame Plutard agreed, she could never leave. She was bound to it."

Lara didn't care. Her choice was between certain death or this circus. This was the only shot she had to avenge Todd. "Can I ask you for one thing?"

"Sure." Althacazur spoke, but she'd meant the question for Cecile.

"Can I ride the carousel one last time?" Lara needed to clarify. "Before we do it."

Cecile understood Lara immediately.

"Of course."

Lara walked out of the main doors through the Grand Promenade, Tisdale following closely behind. She considered that if she succeeded, she would become the human patron of this place. It was like an otherworldly château mixed with a little Las Vegas. As she passed each room and attraction, she studied the ornate baroque walls. Outside the windows, amid the elaborate hedges, she saw clowns playing croquet and drinking tea from china cups. When they arrived at the carousel, she mounted the same horse as before and Tisdale pulled the lever. "Don't let me go poof, Tisdale."

The monkey nodded.

As the carousel went backward and the horse shook its head, Lara leaned into its mane and closed her eyes. She had one last moment alone with her own thoughts—quite possibly the last time she would be *her*.

The memories began immediately, starting with dancing with Ben at the gala. She felt his heat and the sense of safety he always brought with him as he pressed against her; then him laughing at Delilah's, his overly starched sleeves. In front of her, the image of Ben morphed—almost melted into Todd. It was here that Lara stopped and tried to slow things down. She held his face. This was a memory—a true one—but she had the ability to alter it.

Before her was the final image of him. Lara was in her car. This was the moment that had haunted her—the moment when she'd failed to catch a last look at him. What she did next, she had not done in real life: Lara turned her head back to the house to see Todd standing in his driveway. The knowledge of what would come next for both of them in the world sent her body heaving into heavy sobs. "Todd," she said, but he never heard her. Instead he turned and walked to the house, hands in his pockets. Like her, he never realized the significance of the moment. He would be dead in twelve hours.

Then as a movie cuts to the next scene, she and Todd were lying out by the river. The sun was cooking their skin, making them smell of sweat and suntan lotion. He slid over her body and kissed her. She pulled back, even though that wasn't what she'd done in the moment. Studying every line and detail of his face, she could feel tears welling up with the knowledge of what was to come for them and what would never be.

"What's wrong with you?" he said, laughing. He raked his hair and touched her chin.

"I just want to look at you," she said.

"You have a lifetime to look at me."

That he chose those words gutted her. This beautiful boy in front of her didn't get a lifetime of anything. "I'll *always* love you." She wondered if he'd be annoyed at her at this moment, like he could get when she got too sentimental, but this version of Todd didn't.

He stroked her face with the back of his hand. "I know you will."

Lara held on to him, too tightly. She knew that. In the real moment, she'd never done these things, but she felt his skin now, the warmth of it and the hair on his arms. Tears flowed down her face and she kissed him deeply. A profound feeling of sadness washed over her. The horse slowed and Todd faded in and out, like he was illuminated by a faulty lightbulb.

When the ride stopped, Lara looked up to see that both Cecile and Margot stood there waiting at the controls.

Lara could see versions of her face in both women. It was like a time-lapse projection with Margot being the bridge between Cecile's rather frost-like features and the warmer complexion that she'd inherited from Audrey.

"It's a horrible machine," said Margot, staring at the carousel. "They aren't real, you know. When I first came here, I rode it for hours to see my Dez."

Cecile touched her daughter's arm. Lara could tell how fragile

Margot was and how protective Cecile was toward her. This was her family, her legacy. And Lara considered how a painting had brought her here.

"I tried to give you clues all along," said Margot. "The record and the Ouija boards. I wanted to help."

"You sent the message in the record?" And Lara remembered the description of the woman who'd dropped off the Ouija board at Feed & Supply.

She nodded proudly. "I also sent a message to that detective of yours through the board." Margot laughed a little too loudly, her whole body rippling like it came from somewhere deep inside. "He looked terrified."

"You did?" Lara held Margot's hands. She thought of Ben Archer, so far away, yet connected to her by this mystery.

"I gave him a clue," said Margot. "To steer him on the right path."

"We've all suffered so much." Cecile's jaw clenched and she pulled Margot toward her. Then she took Lara's hand. As the three of them held on to one another, Lara could feel the powerful magic flowing through the three of them, buoying her for battle.

26

They took a cab down the Rue de Rivoli and turned up a narrow street that had a courtyard and an older building. A neon sign read:

Le Cirque de Fragonard Performance Tonight

Ben, Barrow, and Gaston found the employee entrance open, but the box office was shut tight. Inside, a tall man with suspenders leaned against the building smoking a cigarette. Barrow took the lead. "Is the manager in?"

"That depends," said the man. "What do you want him for?"

"What do you care?" Gaston seemed irritated at the man's tone.

The man shrugged, seemingly realizing he was outnumbered, and directed them back to a hallway through the open door. The three men heard sounds of horses snorting and a gait of a trot. Two men were shouting "*Allez.*"

A door was cracked open, and Barrow knocked.

"*Entrez,*" said a voice.

The three men found their way into a cramped, windowless office with circus memorabilia covering the walls.

"We are looking for the manager?"

"I am the *owner,*" corrected the man in impeccable English. He was an older man with a shock of graying hair and small reading glasses. A tiny light illuminated the office, which was filled with a smoky gray haze as the owner sat smoking a short brown cigarette.

"I am Edward Barrow of the Institut National d'Histoire de l'Art. These are my colleagues from *les États-Unis*. A few days ago, another colleague of ours was shown a painting here."

"That is impossible." The man leaned back in his chair and folded his arms.

"*Pourquoi?*"

The man shrugged. "I just returned from Rome yesterday. The circus only reopened this morning." He paused when Barrow didn't seem to believe him. "It's expensive to keep a place like this cool in the summer. No one was here."

"Are you sure?" Gaston was looking around at the paintings. "No one was cleaning?"

"Quite sure," said the man. "There is no cleaning crew here when we're not here. The place has been closed tight since April." The man ran his hand over the bookshelf beside him and held out his hand—a thick layer of dust coated his fingers. "See, no janitor."

"This painting that our colleague saw," said Gaston. "It is a painting of Cecile Cabot."

The man nodded and pointed nonchalantly to the wall. "*Oui.*"

Ben was standing nearest to the area where the man had motioned. On the wall, he noticed a small painting and leaned in to study it. The painting was surrounded by photos, many of them disturbing vintage nudes. The canvas was the same size and style as *Sylvie on the Steed*, but this one featured a silver-haired woman wearing a pink striped leotard on the second rung of a ladder. She was gazing at the painter, a small smile on her lips, her body bending as he imagined it would with the movement of a soft ladder. Ben could tell there was more detail in this painting than the one in Barrow's office. While the other had featured the relationship between the horse and the trick rider, Sylvie, this painting had only one subject: the girl.

In one swift movement, Barrow pushed Ben out of the way. "It is the second painting." The excitement in his voice was audible as he leaned down to examine it. Turning back to the man, he said, "This painting was done by Émile Giroux."

The man put his cigarette out in the full ashtray next to him. "Why should I care about who painted it?"

"Because it's a very important painting." Barrow seemed exasperated. "It's quite valuable. It should be protected and placed in a museum, not hanging on your wall, especially when you don't keep the building cool in the summer. This painting is a national treasure."

"My father was quite a collector of *cirque* memorabilia," said the man. "He found that painting in a little shop in the Latin Quarter. Someone had sold it off to pay debts along with paints and other equipment. They told him the artist had died suddenly, leaving the stuff in his small apartment. My father was only interested in that painting. It has hung on that wall *safely* for seventy years. *There it will remain*."

"Our colleague has gone missing," said Gaston.

"That is not my concern. If your colleague saw this painting a few days ago, then they broke into this building. Perhaps they have done this again and this time it did not fare so well for them. If there is nothing more, gentlemen, I have some work to attend to." He pointed to a written ledger.

Barrow took out a card from his pocket. "If you are interested in parting with this painting, the institute would be grateful."

The man did not reach out to take the card, so Barrow placed it on the desk.

Ben could tell that Barrow was eager to touch the painting again, but each of them had to settle for one last glance of Cecile Cabot as they exited the office. They were a few steps from the office when the door shut tightly behind them.

"Anyone notice anything odd about that painting?" Ben said outside on the street.

"The entire room was creepy, if that's what you mean," said Gaston.

"The woman in that photo looks exactly like Lara." Ben began to pace slowly, circling Barrow and Gaston.

"Come to think of it, the woman did look familiar, but her hair was white," said Gaston. "We're no closer to finding her than we were an hour ago. That felt like a waste of time."

"We're retracing her steps," said Barrow, who seemed lost in his thoughts since seeing the second canvas. He spun on his heels. "Did you *see* that painting? It was beautiful."

"I'm less concerned about the painting right now than I am about Lara," Ben said, annoyed.

"But who let her in?" Gaston put his hands on his hips and looked down the street as if the answer might suddenly appear before them. "As the guy so helpfully reminded us, they were closed."

"I'd say it was whoever gave her the ticket." Ben looked at Gaston gravely. "And I don't have one missing man back home, Gaston—I now have three." Ben ran his hands through his hair. "And they don't come back. My fear is Lara may not come back, either."

Gaston looked weary. "Do you think they're related?"

"I sure hope not." He shook his head. "The only one who really has ties to Lara is Todd."

"It feels a little circumstantial," said Barrow.

"Except that they disappeared into thin air." Gaston's tone was changing, softening almost like a father's. He knew Lara. This wasn't some name to him.

"Have you told Audrey?" asked Ben.

Gaston nodded. "I told her you were coming and to give you twenty-four hours. If not, she's on a plane here."

"Gaston, I hate to tell you, but my twenty-four hours is about up."

"I am aware of the hour," said Gaston quietly. On the taxi ride back to the hotel, Gaston was quiet for a long time. "If anything happens to Lara, I'll never forgive myself for dragging her here on this caper. I honestly thought she'd be fine. That it would be a nice diversion for her."

"We'll find her," said Ben. As the cab approached, Ben had an idea. "What do we know from the journal entries about the location of the circus?"

"Nothing," said Barrow.

"Not true." Gaston turned. "It usually needed a large vacant space—the space in front of Les Invalides...Bois de Boulogne."

"Exactly," said Ben. "So we're looking for a large open space within walking distance of the hotel."

"But it isn't like this circus is on the street," said Barrow. "Even if we find an open space—even if we find the correct space—it won't help us."

"But it's all we've got," said Ben. "If I can get near Lara, I'll find her."

Gaston turned to the cabdriver. They exchanged information for a few blocks. The driver took them up the Rue Favart to Place Boieldieu, where the Opéra-Comique had a large courtyard in front of the entrance.

"I don't think this is it," said Ben. "Where else?"

The cabdriver set off around the block and down the narrow streets to the Rue Vivienne. They pulled up in front of a building with pillars.

"The Palais Brongniart," said Gaston. "At night, this place is empty."

"How long would it take you to walk here from the hotel?" asked Ben.

"About ten minutes."

"And you'd give yourself five minutes to spare, right?"

"I would have," Gaston echoed as he paid the driver. The three men walked over to the café across the street and stared at the Palais Brongniart with its imposing columns. "It's a terrifying building at night. Let's get some dinner and wait for it to get dark."

Ben looked at his watch. He was still on East Coast time, but it seemed to be nearing eight o'clock. He was very hungry and tired as hell.

They asked for a table outside. As they were looking at their menus, they heard some commotion inside, near the kitchen. The waiter came by. "Apologies," he began. "We had a homeless person show up about an hour ago. They're trying to attend to her while we call the police."

Ben looked up. "*Her?*" He leapt from his seat.

"*Oui*," said the waiter, pouring water.

Gaston pointed to Ben. "*Il est gendarmerie. Peut-il aider?*"

The waiter shrugged and pointed back to the kitchen area with the empty bottle.

Ben made his way back toward the kitchen, spinning around the tightly packed café tables. Gaston was behind him, assuring him that Ben was *gendarmerie*.

"What is *gendarmerie*?" asked Ben, forming a path among the diners. "I should know."

"Police force in the smaller towns outside Paris. It fits you."

The back booth had been cleared and there was a girl lying in a ball with her back to them. The figure was a heap dressed in what appeared to be a pink swimsuit.

"It's a leotard," said Gaston. "Like they wear in the circus."

"She does not know her name," said the maître d' in English. He sighed, disgusted.

"Lara." Ben reached down to touch the woman. Her blond hair was a tangled, dirty mess. He gently turned the woman over and saw Lara's familiar features.

She gazed up at him with a blank look.

"She's burning up." Ben touched her face and then looked at Gaston. "Have them call an ambulance immediately, or we'll take her to the hospital in a cab."

Gaston nodded and took off with the maître d'.

While he waited, Ben sat on the floor so he could get a better look at Lara's face. "It's me, Lara. Ben. Do you remember me?"

Lara stared blankly, rarely blinking.

"I came as soon as I heard. You've been missing three days now. Do you know where you are? You're in Paris."

The catatonic woman in front of him was a like a shell.

A hand touched him. It was Gaston, who had now two ambulance attendants behind him. Had he really been sitting here with her for several minutes? Ben and Gaston stepped out of the way to let them attend to Lara.

"She's in shock," said Gaston, translating the conversation between the two paramedics. They administered an IV and placed her on a stretcher, pulling it up to wheel it out. The trio followed the ambulance to the Hôpital Hôtel-Dieu in a taxi.

It was as though time had stopped. In the empty waiting room next to him, a French game show blared, its laugh track grating until Ben finally went and turned it off with the remote. But the absence of the television only made him notice the hospital announcements that he couldn't understand. He'd read Lara's translations of Cecile Cabot's journals twice now and was bleary-eyed, nodding off several times, but catching himself and forcing himself to stay awake to find out what happened next. Yet nothing happened next. They just sat around in silence. He guessed this qualified as a damsel-in-distress situation. And he had to admit, flying to Paris to rescue Lara had made him feel alive again. After what seemed like hours, with the three of them sitting on plastic chairs, a doctor finally emerged. Gaston and Barrow were engaged with the man, nodding gravely. Ben cursed himself for not studying French in high school. The doctor nodded and walked off.

"That didn't sound good." Ben put his hands in his pockets and steeled himself for the worst.

"It isn't." Gaston looked defeated.

"She has a raging fever," explained Barrow. "They aren't sure if it's an infection, but right now she isn't responding to antibiotics or anything they're giving her. She's on IVs and is dehydrated terribly, plus she's in shock."

"I want to see her," said Ben.

Barrow shook his head. "They're trying to limit her guests right now. They are afraid it could be sepsis."

Gaston walked off, looking for a pay phone.

He was probably calling Audrey, Ben thought. Poor bastard. That was a call no one should have to make.

Barrow sat down on the chair. They'd taken over an entire family waiting area where the scholar pored over the composition books, particularly the passages about coming and going from the circus and Cecile not feeling well. Ben had draped himself heavily in the chair across from him.

They'd all memorized the story told within the three composition books, looking for some clue as to what might have happened to

Lara in Le Cirque Secret, not that anyone in the hospital would have believed them if the answer had been spelled out in its pages.

In fact, Ben could hardly believe it himself. While the journals were fantastic tales of another dimension, part of him still had to consider that this was entirely fiction. The Ouija board that had led him to Desmond "Dez" Bennett was something he couldn't explain away, though; nor did he have a rational answer for the ritual killings in Kerrigan Falls. At heart, Ben Archer was a rational man, so buying into this whole otherworldly answer was challenging, and without talking to Lara he couldn't make that leap. There was a distinct possibility that Lara had been kidnapped by the same person who had chased her—a human person. Only Lara could clear this up, and the only way she could do that was to wake up.

"She said it was hard on the body, traveling back and forth." Barrow pointed to the line in the notes.

Gaston was back and slid into the seat beside him. "Yeah, but while that circus operated for two years, hundreds of people traveled to and fro without harm."

"Not for three days they didn't," said Ben, interrupting the theory-building going on between the two.

"Do we think he would come if we called him?" said Barrow. He turned to the men, and it was clear from the steady gaze that met their eyes that he was serious. "When Giroux was dying, Cecile called him. We could try to call him."

"And Giroux died anyway, and all Cecile got was a fucking carousel." Gaston put his head back and studied the ceiling.

"I hate waiting." Though exhausted, Ben couldn't relax and was in and out of his chair, pacing.

"That won't help, you know," said Gaston. "Unless you want to polish the floor with your shoes."

Ben Archer felt powerless. He was a man who needed control over his environment. Now here he was, in Paris of all places, waiting for Lara to wake up and considering that, as time went on, the possibility of her recovering was becoming smaller and smaller. Over the PA system, a woman's voice called for doctors and the occasional *code bleu* in French. He hated the fact that he didn't even understand the fucking language in this country. He rubbed his neck, which was aching. His entire body felt sick, flu-like. He hadn't slept for more than forty-eight hours.

"I'm going to go to the hotel and get a shower, maybe a nap," said Gaston. The man had deep lines on his face and dark circles under his eyes. Though he consumed a steady diet of espresso and Toblerone, Gaston's clothing hung on him. "You should consider doing the same thing. You look terrible."

Ben's bag was still packed, and he hoped he still had a hotel room to check into. "I'll catch the next shift," said Ben. "You go."

After Gaston went back to the hotel, Ben settled into the chair, watching a French-language dub of *Blow-Up*. Soon he was fast asleep.

The elevator dinged and the cleaning crew moved through, mopping and scrubbing chairs, waking Ben. He checked his watch. It was six in the morning. He'd been asleep for five hours.

The sound of heels on the polished floor caused him to stir. He looked up to see Audrey Barnes passing him. Her face looked tense, almost unrecognizable, and her focus was on the hall in front of her.

It was a curious thing to see. She walked with confident intent down the empty hallway in front of her, past the nurses' station and to her daughter's exact room.

As though she'd known precisely where to find her.

27

For twenty-four hours, Lara teetered between life and death. There was no light, only the dull black behind her closed lids. The pain made everything fuzzy.

There was a voice in the distance, soft but urgent. *Lara, get up. Get up.*

But that voice didn't know about the chills. The chills were so severe that the sheets hurt anytime they shifted against her limbs. Her arms were glistening with sweat—a chilling sweat like the dew on a cold glass. She shivered and prayed to be unconscious, temporarily or permanently, it did not matter to her one way or the other.

As they'd left the circus, she'd taken Cecile's hand. That was all it required for Cecile to fully absorb into her. But then, her body had been carefully crafted to match Cecile's own.

Except Althacazur had been wrong.

When Lara had stepped back onto the Parisian street, the sun was bright and she found that instantly she felt unwell. Within seconds, a throbbing headache debilitated her, causing her to feel quite dizzy. The café across the street was busy and she made her way over there, staggering, not realizing that she was no longer dressed in her black sundress and denim jacket. Instead, she wore a sequined leotard and her shoes had disappeared. As she approached the café, the waiter shooed her away. Confused, she didn't understand what he was saying.

She was thirsty and so dizzy, but she didn't have her purse. What had happened to her purse? For a moment she panicked, wondering where her passport was until she remembered it was safely locked in the hotel safe.

She stumbled, which only made the man shoo her away harder, walking out to the sidewalk to stop her there. But Lara found her legs wouldn't move. There was also now a voice inside her. *They think you're drunk.*

"But I'm not drunk," Lara answered.

Don't talk to me, Lara. They can't see me.

"Huh?" This voice was weird. "Cecile?"

Yes. Lara, listen to me. Your body is having a reaction to me being in it. I had feared this. It will take time to adjust, if it can absorb me. If not, then we have bigger problems, but for now, you need to act normal. Do you understand?

Looking across the street, Lara could see that everyone in the restaurant had turned and was staring at her. They had spoonfuls of soup and bitefuls of duck on their utensils, mouths agape—all had stopped mid-bite and mid-conversation to take in the spectacle of her. "I understand."

Lara heard a groan followed by a sigh of frustration in her head. *Obviously, you don't.*

A man in a suit appeared and stepped in front of the waiter. "You need to leave, now."

Lara couldn't understand him, but the voice in her head did.

Do you know where you were staying before you came to the circus? I cannot help you, these streets look different to me.

"Hotel Vivienne," said Lara to the voice.

The man did not budge and pointed to the left. "Rue Vivienne. Hotel Vivienne. *Allez.*"

Lara knew what *allez* meant—"go." But she could feel her legs swaying, which made her think of the chills she was having. Violent chills.

Lara. Lara.

She wasn't sure she answered, but she could feel the impact of the sidewalk on her knees and knew they had to be bloodied.

Todd was there. Todd? He was overexposed—the too-bright sun, like the scene from the carousel that caused her to squint up at him. She was so relieved to see him. He'd help her. This version of him was glorious—square chin, brown hair that he pulled back into a low ponytail. He sat on the hood of his car, the beloved Mustang. The one he'd been separated from—the same car that had been towed through town. Now he was perched on it as though their wedding day had never happened. This was what it would have been like, Lara thought. He wore a long-sleeved black T-shirt and jeans, black high-top Chuck Taylors. He was peeling a blade of grass in two, and she realized they were parked in a field. She turned and walked up the hill, unsure of what this scene meant—trying to interpret it like a dream. "Where are you going, Lara?" he called. "Stay with me."

Lara looked down: She was in a leotard and her knees were bloody. "I can't stay with you," she said. "You're dead." Something told her this vision was a trap or a choice. This scene had never happened between them, and to accept it as real would seal her doom. She saw something peek from behind a tree motioning for her to come. It was Mr. Tisdale. *We are your destiny*, he said, without speaking words, of course. She ran toward him anyway, away from Todd, never once looking back. Then someone was slapping her lightly and turning her over. She opened her eyes.

Do we know him?

"Lara. It's Ben." Ben Archer was crouched down next to her and his wonderful face was racked with worry, but that was impossible. Ben wasn't in Paris. Oh, how she missed him. Then the chills began and everything clouded over.

Lara. Lara. Wake up.

Lara cracked open her eyes. Something was in her arm. She heard beeping. Gray walls with directions in French on how to safely lower the bed. Then nothing.

You have to stop fighting me or we'll both die.

"I'm not fighting you." She laughed at this. It was that voice again. The one that cared if they lived or died. "Poof," said Lara.

Yes, poof. And poof is bad, trust me. We'll both go poof.

A nurse came in and checked Lara's IV bag and wiped something across her forehead that beeped. The chills had subsided for a while, but now they were coming on in waves again. The woman loaded another IV bag behind the nearly empty one. A violent chill rocked Lara and then she was drowsy again.

At the darkest point, when she felt herself swinging on the trapeze, then letting go, with no visible net beneath her, Lara was reassured by the familiar touch and voice of her mother. When she opened her eyes, she found Audrey's warm hand on her face but nodded off only to wake later and find the room empty.

28

At one point, Lara's fever had spiked to 41.1 degrees Celsius. The doctors were looking for viruses, a brain bleed, sepsis, but found no cause. Nurses pushed IVs, cool baths, and dantrolene injections.

Ben was the first to spy Audrey coming out of Lara's hospital room. From the grim look on Audrey's face, he expected the worst possible news.

"Ben," she said with a wan smile. He could see she had been crying.

"Audrey." He was ready to offer to help, be useful, help make funeral arrangements. As he assembled these tasks in his mind, a hole began to form deep inside him. Lara couldn't be gone, not before they'd ever started. He wasn't prepared for this. The lack of sleep, lack of food, travel—everything from the last three days—compounded and he found himself wiping tears away.

"She'll be fine," said Audrey wearily. She took his hand and held it firmly.

For hours, they sat, side by side, in plastic chairs, silent. Then Lara's fever broke and then stayed down on its own, for the first time. It would take another eight hours for her to fully regain consciousness.

But there was something about Audrey's manner that unnerved him. He couldn't quite put his finger on it. Perhaps it was shock, but he couldn't shake the idea that Lara had only improved after her mother had arrived. Audrey had been the catalyst.

Ben filled Audrey in on the composition books when Barrow and Gaston returned to the hospital. The three took turns briefing her, correcting one another with more accurate interpretations. The best Ben and Gaston could figure was that, in 1926, the real Cecile Cabot, weakened from childbirth, fell from the trapeze and died. Just as she'd promised, Sylvie took Margot and ran, posing as Cecile Cabot for the remainder of her life.

Audrey absorbed all of this news with a stoicism that surprised Ben. They'd uncovered a hidden secret about the woman who had raised her, yet Audrey sat on the chair, expressionless. In her features he could see Lara years from now. He tried to think of Jason's and Audrey's features blending into Lara's—the fair hair, big green eyes, and upturned nose—but he didn't see any of Jason. Except for her raspy voice, Lara definitely took after her mother. Still, Ben couldn't quite put his finger on what was wrong with Audrey. Instead of being relieved that her daughter's fever had broken, he couldn't help but think that she was mourning something.

Audrey got up and walked over to the window. "I never should have let her come here."

Gaston put his hand on her shoulder. "You couldn't have stopped this. If the circus wanted her, they'd have found a way to get her. And she *would* have gone, Audrey. You know that."

Audrey nodded absently.

Ben knew what Gaston had said was true. Of course Lara would have gone.

At noon, Ben decided to go to his hotel. Before he left, he stopped by Lara's room, not asking anyone, Audrey or the nurses, if it was okay. He needed to see her. To his surprise, he found her lying there with her eyes open. A feeling of dread washed over him. The fever had been too high for too long. The doctors had warned them that there was a chance that a seizure may have caused brain damage.

"I'm not dead." It was her voice, raspier than usual, but the tone was pure Lara. "So quit looking at me like that."

It was the Lara he knew, the one from Delilah's. Ben felt he could collapse, right there in front of her, in a mixture of relief and exhaustion.

"You need to get me out of here." She focused on him. Her eyes were bright, but she looked tired, her skin translucent. He'd seen her bad before—at the beginning with Todd. The IVs had made her puffy, but he was so grateful to see that she was demanding things. "Ben? Did you hear me?"

"I'm just so happy to see you're okay—"

"You don't understand," she cut in, studying her hospital gown. "We have to get out of here. I'm not safe here."

"Let me get Audrey," said Ben, holding up a finger.

"My mother is here?"

"Lara, you've been in and out of consciousness for days. Of course she's here." For a moment, he wondered if something terrible had, indeed, addled her brain. There were flashes of rehabilitation centers and fears of a stroke, but to his amazement she was pulling at her covers with the dexterity of someone who was at least physically able.

"Ben? Is something wrong with you?"

"No." He was surprised at her clarity and focus.

"Did you hear me?" She looked around the room. "I'm assuming, given the explosion of French signs saying SALLE D'ATTENTE, that we are still in France? I'm not safe. Tell my mother we need to go home *now*."

He sat down on the chair next to her. "Can you just wait until the doctor sees you before you flee? You've been through quite an ordeal."

She snorted and looked at the wall, like she was contemplating something.

The door pushed open. "I heard noise in here," said Audrey, peeking her head in.

"Mother," said Lara. "Oh, thank God."

Audrey put her hands to her face and began to cry. "You're really okay."

"Of course I'm okay." Lara looked at both of them. "We have to get home," she repeated. "Now."

"We'll go soon," said Audrey, who perched herself on Lara's bed and smoothed her daughter's hair. "You need to rest."

"I'm in danger," said Lara.

"No," said Audrey. "You're not."

"But you don't understand," said Lara.

"I understand everything," said Audrey. "You're safe now."

Ben had a million questions to ask Lara, yet he couldn't bring himself to form a single one of them.

"You need to rest," said Audrey. "I'm here now. *Nothing* will happen to you."

"But—" Lara began.

Audrey reached out and stroked her daughter's hair. To Ben's amazement, Lara's eyes began to close and she appeared to be fighting the urge to sleep, but Audrey kept stroking her hair. "Just rest."

Before she fell off to sleep, Lara murmured, "He sent me a ticket."

"I know," said Audrey.

29

Eight hours later and with Lara's prodding, the doctors released her from the hospital, still perplexed about the cause of her fever, yet with her vital signs all healthy, and her insisting she wanted to leave, there was no real reason to keep her.

She was agitated, still wanting to go home to Kerrigan Falls. Gaston had arranged for the four of them to be on the first flight out in the morning.

Ben could see Barrow's face fall at this news. He'd hoped to talk to her about what she'd seen at the circus. At the coffee machine in the lobby of the hotel, he cornered Ben. "Has she said anything?"

"No," said Ben, as concerned about Lara's behavior as Barrow was. "She's extremely cagey right now, but she's been through a lot, so I guess that is to be expected."

While Lara rested in her room, the others gathered on the sofas around the lobby like ladies-in-waiting.

"She wants an earlier flight," said Audrey.

"We can't *get* an earlier flight." Gaston seemed frustrated.

After a few hours, Ben checked in on her in her room. He found her sitting on the edge of the bed like she was unsure what to do next. "Can we go to Montparnasse?"

"Yeah," he said, moving toward the hotel phone. "I'll just call Audrey."

"No," she said, shaking her head. "Just the two of us."

"It's almost ten o'clock. I'm not sure that's a good idea." She'd just come back from near death and here she was proposing some new scheme for them in Montparnasse.

"I'll go by myself then." She reached into her closet for a jacket.

"No, I'll go with you, but you need to make up your mind," said Ben, irritation in his voice. "You keep telling us you're not safe here, and now you want to run to Montparnasse—alone—to get into more trouble."

"I missed you, too." She smiled.

As they crossed the Seine in a taxi and cut over by Les Invalides to Montparnasse, Lara seemed distracted. Her fingers lightly touched the glass, as if the scene in front of her was fragile and impermanent. Drugstores, vendors selling televisions, restaurants with pictures of food displayed in unappetizing, plastic-looking poses—she gazed out at all of them with wonder.

"You can let us off here," she said to the taxi driver when they got to a circle. She was out the door while Ben settled with the driver and then scrambled to follow her. He found her standing in front of Le Dôme Café, looking up. "It hasn't changed."

He thought that was an odd comment for her to make, but after what she'd gone through he was just happy that she was upright and speaking mostly coherently. So he let it go, but he found that he was angry at her, too. While Barrow and Gaston were convinced she'd been abducted by an otherworldly circus, he wasn't sure he agreed. Her strange behavior, however, was only making him more suspicious.

"What do you want to do?" Ben wasn't quite sure about the purpose of this adventure, but Lara seemed mesmerized by a typical Parisian street.

"I just wanted to see the place again." Lara was turning on the street, looking around in amazement. He stopped her from rotating, because she was attracting attention. This got him wondering when she'd eaten last; maybe a meal might restore her. He'd managed to leave a note with the front desk telling Audrey where they'd gone. He figured they'd get settled in a restaurant and then he'd duck out to the bathroom and call her to reassure her mother that Lara was fine. "Why don't we eat something?"

Lara turned to him, delighted. "Oh yes, I would love that."

"Okay," said Ben, taking her hand. She curled her fingers in his as they crossed the street, finding an Italian restaurant on Boulevard Raspail that had outdoor seating. A fan sent a cool breeze past them on a rather stuffy night with the air like a bath.

"Picasso had a studio right there." Lara pointed to the right. Ben turned to see where she was pointing, thinking it was odd that Lara would know about Picasso's studio. In Montparnasse, she now seemed animated and alive, moving the saltshaker around the table, as if the act of touching things was new to her. She seemed to marvel at sports cars and clothes, craning her neck to follow a man with a mohawk and piercings as he walked by.

Ben ordered a glass of wine, refusing to let Lara have any. She frowned and took a sip of his before he'd even had a chance to taste it. He was grateful as the spicy drink hit the back of his throat. God, he'd needed a drink. Hesitating, he swirled his glass. "You want to tell me what happened?"

"You know what happened. I went to the circus." She leaned back in her seat, focusing on the traffic and not meeting his eyes. There was a childish smile on her face.

"Really?"

"What do you mean, really?"

"I thought you might have been abducted."

Lara made a face that said she disagreed. "At the gala, after I thought I'd seen Todd, there was a strange man."

"Jesus," said Ben, sitting back in his seat. "First Todd, now a strange man. That fucking gala was sure crowded."

She laughed. "It was a man I had seen before, in childhood. He told me I needed to come to Paris; he'd have answers about what happened to Todd. There was no way that I was not going after that."

"And it never occurred to you that this man might be some sick lunatic?"

"Oh, he's a sick lunatic, all right, but no," she said. "Never once, even as I sat there with Gaston and Barrow with the damned ticket in my pocket, did I consider not going." She brought her leg up on the chair, then she laughed like she often did at Delilah's—that full, throaty laugh. It was the first laugh he'd heard from her, and it made him realize how worried he'd been that she'd never return. "Tell me, would you not have gone? Even the ticket was magical. It bled when I tried to tear it."

"It's a fantastic story." He slid his wineglass away and wondered why everyone was so convinced there was something otherworldly circling around them.

She raised her eyebrow and settled back in her seat. "So, what do you think happened to me?"

"The woman who chased you might have kidnapped you and drugged you."

"Then what?" There was a change in Lara, a confidence he hadn't seen before. "She just let me go?"

He had to admit, it didn't make sense. Had someone kidnapped Lara for the painting, they'd have asked for ransom. There had been no request. He folded his arms.

There had been something that he'd been worrying about with her.

Perhaps in her grief over Todd, Lara had imagined this circus, this ticket. She might have just wandered the streets of Paris this way for days. He knew her grandmother Margot had struggled with mental illness. Was it happening to Lara, too? Was this why Audrey looked so stricken?

"I'm sure there are people who wouldn't have thought entering the Devil's Circus was a grand idea," said Lara, unaware of the narrative running through his mind, "but then I remembered that people had coveted those tickets for years in Paris. To the best of my knowledge, they all returned safely. I wanted answers, so I went. I stood outside the Palais Brongniart, and one minute there was nothing, then the next there was a circus. Not a tent, Ben. An entire *building* in another dimension. I took a Ferris wheel down past the River Styx accompanied by a monkey—who might have been a damned Benito Mussolini. The rooms were opulent. Giroux captured the way it looked. Everything has a soft focus and a sharp oversaturated color to it." She sighed. "I know it sounds crazy; I do. It's a form of Hell and yet it is the most magical, magnificent place I've ever seen."

"You were missing for more than forty-eight hours."

"Are you scolding me?" She was teasing. "I see they called the cavalry in. Tell me, does France not have police officers?"

"Apparently not ones who accept the idea of a Devil's Circus." Ben looked out in the street. "Those two were terrified." He took her hand. "I was terrified...and angry...I was very angry with them and you."

"You're still angry with me." She held his hand tightly. "It seemed like I was gone two hours at the most." She took a sip of water and gazed out at the street. "It looks so different."

"What does?"

"Montparnasse."

Ben was confused. "Different from two days ago?"

She didn't respond, tilting her body as the waiter reached over her shoulder, placing their salads with fresh burrata, tomatoes, and basil in front of them.

"So, did you get the answers you were looking for?" He stared down at his plate, trying not to let her know that the mere mention of Todd's name earlier had his heart pounding in his chest. That she'd done all of this, put herself in harm's way, all for answers—answers that he'd failed to give her. He'd *failed*, just as his father had done with Peter Beaumont.

She picked up her glass, holding it heavily in her hand like she might drop it. "He's dead."

"How do you—?"

"I'd like to just digest that information a bit if you don't mind." She gave him a sharp look that told him not to ask. She drifted away, like she was floating out to sea on a rhythmic current. "I said goodbye. There's no point in looking for him anymore. Peter Beaumont, too."

"What about Desmond Bennett?" He took a sip of wine and placed it back on the table. He hadn't told her that he had a third case.

She leaned in and met his eyes. "What do *you* know about Desmond Bennett?" Then a knowing smile on appeared on her face. "Did you get some help from a Ouija board?"

"How did you—?" said Ben. "I was at Feed and Supply when the old Ouija board spelled out DEZ. I went and pulled the files from 1944 and guess what I found."

"Desmond Bennett went missing in 1944. He was in love with my grandmother Margot. She's the one who gave you that clue. Oh and yes, she's dead and she exists in the circus." She broke off a piece of bread and dipped it in olive oil. "But you can explain everything; there's nothing magical going on at all."

"I'll admit," he said, "I've seen things recently that I can't explain." He listened to the cars accelerate down the street, heard people laughing as they walked their dogs, caught the sound of cutlery as forks and spoons hit the table, and thought about Picasso working just a few doors down. It really did feel like a magical place here in Paris. It made him realize that he and Marla should have traveled more.

"I never subscribed to the occult version of Todd's disappearance; you know that, but have you ever wondered why our town has zero crime?"

"I think you know that I wonder about it every day."

"Since Margot," said Lara, "my family has had to cast a protection spell each year—October ninth. It works except for once every thirty years, when it seems to fall apart for a night. You read the journals, right?"

"I did. My head is still spinning," said Ben. "What a tale."

"I know you're a skeptic, but everything in those journals was true. It's Esmé's doing, so now we have to find her painting. I need to see what she looks like."

"Now?"

"We're not on a flight until tomorrow at eleven. We've got twelve hours. We need to find her before she finds us."

"Lara, she's like a hundred years old," said Ben, puzzled. "Do you mean we need to find her grave?"

"No," said Lara. "She is very much alive. It was Esmé who chased me in the Père Lachaise Cemetery."

"Lara, let me repeat: She'd be a hundred years old."

"She doesn't look a hundred. She can run, too." Lara had flagged the waiter and pointed to the tiramisu. "You have a choice. Either I'm crazy and you can explain everything or I'm sane and there is some really strange shit going on. I know the truth and I want answers.

You're either going with me or not, but I don't want your help if you don't believe me. I'll get Barrow to go with me. It's up to you."

He sat back in his chair. There was a change in her since he'd last seen her on her front porch after the gala. Gone was the unsure girl who masked her grief for everyone. This Lara was confident. He'd never seen her so sure of anything, but in the year he'd known her, he'd always thought she was grounded. She deserved his trust now. Suddenly Ben became suspicious of the people around them. "Tell me everything, from the beginning."

She smiled and spun her fork, leaning back in the chair. "You'd better order some strong coffee. You're going to need it."

30

In the morning, Lara and Audrey met Ben, Barrow, and Gaston for breakfast. When she got down to the hotel lobby, they were all waiting for her eagerly.

"Bad news," said Gaston. "Our flight has been delayed. They rebooked us for tomorrow morning."

"So now we have more time to hear the story," said Barrow.

Over croissants and *pains au chocolat*, she recounted the story for them.

"We need to find Esmé's painting," said Lara, pushing her porcelain cup away.

"I've been looking for that painting for twenty years now," said Barrow, ruffled.

"And Lara has discovered two of them in a matter of weeks." Gaston sipped his espresso. "My bet is on her to find the remaining one."

Barrow conceded.

"I figure that Émile told Cecile that he threw Esmé's painting away out of shame, but I doubt that he actually destroyed it," said Lara. She could feel the ache of Cecile inside her, the burden of carrying another being. There were pangs of melancholy at hearing Giroux's name batted around among the group. Lara realized these emotions were Cecile's, yet they were now hers as well.

"I agree," said Barrow. "No artist destroys his work, especially if it is a great one. He had to know the three paintings were something special."

"Fragonard said his father found *Cecile Cabot Takes Flight* in the trash," said Gaston.

"Art was traded around in that neighborhood quite a bit, back then," said Barrow. "Giroux's apartment would be a good first place to look, but frankly, it's a long shot."

"This entire thing has been a long shot," said Ben. "Lara and I will try his old apartment building."

"I'll check the records for other art that was bought and sold around that time in Montparnasse," said Barrow, placing his sunglasses on his head as he rose from the table. It was another hot, humid day in Paris, yet Barrow's white jeans and black T-shirt looked refreshingly cool. "It might have been added to a sale if they thought there was little value to it at the time."

Lara thought her mother looked tired. "You should go back and rest. We've all been here longer and we're over the jet lag."

"I just need you to be careful," said Audrey, touching Lara's arm.

"Let's actually try to do a little sightseeing." Gaston took Audrey's hand. "Let me show you *my* hometown."

"I'll take care of her, Audrey," said Ben.

"You can join me," said Lara, placing her messenger bag across her body. "I can take care of myself."

Ben and Lara took a cab back to Émile Giroux's old apartment in Montparnasse, just blocks away from where they'd dined last night. Lara didn't need to consult a map for the street. Cecile knew the way to Rue Delambre. As they opened the foyer door, she could feel Cecile's ache inside her, especially as she gazed up at the stairs to the second floor and *his* door. *To be back in his house.*

"Are you okay?" Lara was shocked to hear herself, forgetting she wasn't alone.

"Huh?" Ben looked perplexed. "I'm fine."

"Of course you are," said Lara, composing herself. Cecile did not respond and Lara felt a tug of pity for her.

The building was not in great condition, and Lara thought that the rickety staircase had not been fixed since Giroux lived here. While the old wood was still beautiful, it was battered from neglect. The black-and-white-checkered floor was new but cheap. Everything about this apartment building felt just as transactional as it did from the days Giroux lived here.

Ben knocked on the door of the first-floor apartment.

After some time, an older woman answered the door. Her hair was a red, almost purple color, but her white roots were visible and she wore a black Adidas tracksuit.

"*Bonjour,*" said Lara. She let Cecile speak for her, in perfect French: "Are you the owner?"

"*Oui,*" said the lady. She folded her arms defensively. Her red nails were lacquered.

"Do you know who owned this house before you?" Lara looked beyond the woman into her apartment. It was cluttered, and Lara could see the walls were littered with artwork from all different periods and styles. The pastels of the Impressionists seemed to get their own wall above a pink velvet sofa.

"My father," said the woman, pulling the door shut a hair to block Lara's curiosity. "And my grandmother before him. We've owned this house for more than eighty years. What's this about?" The woman looked from Ben to Lara suspiciously.

"I'm looking for a very old painting of a circus. It would be an unusual painting of a lion tamer—a woman. The artist who painted it lived here at one time. We thought there might be a chance that the painting was left here."

"Are you saying we stole it?" The woman's voice rose as she leaned her arm on the doorjamb defiantly.

"No, nothing like that," said Lara. "The painter died. We think it might have just passed down to either the landlady at the time or one of the neighbors."

"Is it valuable?" The woman was all business.

"*Oui*," said Lara. "Quite valuable. Would you have a basement or an attic?"

"Ask her if the Germans took anything during the war," Ben mumbled, shoving his hands in his pockets and rocking from foot to foot.

The woman understood the term and shook her head. "They never bothered with us. I have not seen anything." She began to shut the door on them, but Lara was quick.

"It's very valuable," said Lara, handing her Barrow's card. "He is with the Sorbonne and can help you. We're merely trying to find it. They would pay you for it."

The woman eyed them warily and shut the door. As they made their way back out the door and onto the street, Ben put his sunglasses on. "She's lying."

"How can you tell?"

"It's my business." He stepped over to the curb and studied the house. "She thinks we're trying to steal something from her, so she's not telling us what she knows."

"It's exactly what I would think," said Lara. "If someone came to my house claiming to be looking for a painting, I'd have immediately called you."

Ben pointed to a café across the street. "If my hunch is correct, she'll make a move. Let's just hang over there out of sight and see what happens."

"Really?" Lara looked at the closed door.

"Really," said Ben.

After a few minutes, they found a table outside and ordered two café au laits and water.

Ben settled in his chair and turned it to face the house. "I think I could get used to this," he said, tapping on the table and tilting his face to the sun. He wore a crisp white shirt with rolled-up sleeves and cargo shorts. Immediately, he turned the sleeves another roll.

"It's nice to know your starched shirts made the journey," said Lara, adjusting her own sunglasses. She fixed her stare on the house and added sugar to her café au lait and stirred it with a tiny spoon. Given someone was trying to kill her, she found herself looking around for versions of the ponytailed lady. Settling into her Parisian cane chair, she thought she'd try small talk. "So is this your first time in Paris?"

"*Oui.*" He laughed, trying out his first French word. "My starched shirts and I don't travel much, maybe Jamaica and the Keys."

Across the street, the door to the apartment opened and the woman emerged from the house, shifting her weight like she had a bad knee. She now was wearing sunglasses and sneakers and it appeared she'd put on lipstick.

"I'll be damned. There she goes," said Lara. "Are we tailing her?"

"We are." He smiled.

"You go without me," she said to Ben as she flagged down the waitress.

Ben looked reluctant, but she motioned him on, so he slid out of the chair and took off after the woman. Lara could see that he only made it to the end of the block. After settling the bill, Lara joined him and they ducked behind one of the trees on the wide boulevard. The woman knocked on a door a block down from her own house.

"She didn't go far," said Lara. "Why didn't she just call?"

"Because she wants to *see* the painting." Ben held up a map and pretended to be studying it intently.

A man wearing a Brazilian soccer T-shirt answered. After a few brief words, both he and the lady shut the door and were in the house for about twenty minutes. Then the red-haired woman emerged, folding her arms in front of her and scurrying back to Émile's old house. Ben and Lara had to scramble ahead of her to avoid detection.

Ben wrote the address on a piece of paper. "We'll ask Barrow to find out who lives there. My bet is that painting is one in of those two houses. They just didn't know it was valuable."

"But how could they not know?" Lara placed her hands on her hips and paced the street before gathering her long hair up and twisting it into a hair tie. "Montparnasse was swimming with famous painters. Surely an old painting would at least get you thinking." It was a bit of a letdown to come away with nothing. She sighed, frustrated.

"You didn't really think we'd just storm in there and come out with a painting, did you, Nancy Drew?" He was amused.

"No..." But her face gave her away. "Yes," she admitted, and fanned herself from the heat with her hand.

"Leads don't work like that. You plant the seed. Trust me, we put something into motion here."

Lara smiled and looked up at him. "You're kind of brilliant for a policeman with no crime to fight."

"I know," he said with a chuckle. "Where to next?"

It wasn't Lara who answered; it was the voice in her head.

Can we go to the Rue Mouffetard?

"Maybe we can go to the Rue Mouffetard?" said Lara, echoing her head.

"The market?" Ben shrugged. "Sure."

They spent the day retracing Cecile's old steps. Lara felt like a tour guide, feeling a rush of joy as Cecile revisited every location. Lara could feel the disappointment as they visited Les Halles, the market Cecile had remembered, now gone. Despite the magical day, she kept looking over her shoulder and searching the crowd for anyone who might be Esmé.

Later the group gathered at a little restaurant, Drouant, near the Paris Opera House for a final dinner. The night was warm but a thunderstorm was threatening, so they chose a table under the beige awning and hoped for the best. Gaston ordered a bottle of Meursault and a northern Rhône Syrah to get them started.

In the span of a week, Lara had grown fond of Gaston and Barrow. She felt a profound sense of accomplishment for what they'd discovered together. Althacazur had promised her answers. He'd been true to his word, but an undeniable sadness had begun to settle in her. She'd gotten her answers. Todd was dead. After all these years, she now understood her magic, and the gravity of its origins hung heavily. She and her mother were part daemon. She would return home and either succeed in bringing Esmé back to Le Cirque Secret or die trying. In the unlikely event that she succeeded, she'd agreed, however reluctantly, to become the patron of Le Cirque Secret, likely located in the eighth level of Hell for eternity. She'd been *the one*, all right.

Looking around the table, she decided that she was going to savor everything about this evening. She'd positioned herself next to Barrow, telling him every detail of the circus. He was animated, hardly even stopping to place his order of stuffed lamb with Vadouvan herb salad.

Across the table from her sat Ben Archer. He was her biggest regret. She wanted more time with him.

Finally, Barrow held up his wineglass. "To the Ladies of the Secret Circus." Everyone clinked their glasses.

Later, Audrey fell asleep, snoring lightly. Lara lay wide awake.

"Will he change his mind?" She asked the question softly for Cecile. "Will I have to spend eternity in the circus?"

He doesn't change his mind, Lara. I'm sorry.

"Can you go to sleep or something? There is something I have to do."

Of course.

Lara crept out of the room and down the hall and found room 504. She knocked on it and Ben Archer opened it. He didn't seem surprised.

Lara held out two hotel wineglasses and a mini bottle of champagne. "This tiny bottle of champagne is fifty dollars and I'm going to drink it."

"Didn't anyone tell you not to drink the wine?"

"This is France, Ben," she said in a whisper. "You do drink the wine here."

"For someone who is in danger, you sure do run around unaccompanied a lot. Does your mother know you're here?" He opened the door wide.

"You did not just say that to me?"

He hadn't closed his drapes, and the Opéra-Comique's courtyard was lit up. Skateboarders and lovers made use of the steps near the ticket window. The view was magnificent. She heard the cork pop and the sound of bubbles meeting glass.

"I can't seem to make myself shut the drapes." He walked up and stood behind her but did not touch her.

"Did I ever tell you where my love of a man in uniform came from?"

"I didn't know you *had* a love for a man in uniform."

"Chief Brody in *Jaws*." She chuckled.

"His sleeves were not nearly as well starched as mine."

"No." She turned to face him. "They weren't."

He held out her champagne glass. "I thought you were dead. As I watched your mother walk down the hallway, crying, I had a minute where I imagined my life without you."

Lara kissed him, hard, hiding the dreadful secret that he would, indeed, be without her soon enough. She belonged to Le Cirque Secret now.

Finally she pulled away. There was something pressing that he needed to know. Both now and for the future. "In whatever state I was in, Todd came to me. He was sitting on his car and asked me to come with him. I knew it was a choice." Her eyes filled with tears. "But I told him I couldn't go with him."

With the lights of Paris shining on his face, Lara looked up. "I know now that I came back for you."

PART
3
ESMÉ'S SECRET

B ack in her old bed at the farm in Kerrigan Falls, Lara had slept soundly. The absorption of Cecile was still taxing her body. Yet the voice inside her had remained quiet ever since they'd left Paris. "Are you still there?"

Nothing.

There was a temptation to think it had all been a dream, except the desire to go to Montparnasse and the market at Rue Mouffetard that last day had not been hers. There were small signs that she wasn't alone in her body and that Cecile was observing the world, having been gone from it for over seventy-five years.

This time, there was no question that she would be staying at the farm. Since she'd gotten back last week, Audrey had been fussing over her. Her mother was out getting groceries. Lara had no doubt that she'd be picking up chocolate chips, pierogies, and turkey pastrami—all her favorite comfort foods. Caren would join them and they'd watch old Hitchcock films and eat popcorn. She could tell that Cecile's heart had quickened at seeing Audrey and Lara together. Her granddaughter and great-granddaughter—her legacy.

Like a tour guide, Lara had visited the old Kerrigan Falls Cemetery to show Cecile Margot's grave as well as the one marked CECILE CABOT that was actually Sylvie's final resting place. Lara thought Cecile would like that. "She wanted you to live on," said Lara out loud to the voice inside her. Sylvie had been the one living connection between them. They'd both known and loved her.

"What happened to her?" asked Lara finally. "I saw Margot and you at Le Cirque Secret, but not Sylvie."

Finally, the voice inside her head spoke: *Because she was human, she passed on normally. She wasn't bound to the circus like we were. We're half daemon, so we return to him. You will return to him as well, in the circus.*

"So I'll end up in Le Cirque Secret one way or another," said Lara to the voice, reassured that she wasn't alone. Having someone, even a disembodied voice in your head, sharing this secret made it bearable. "Can't you tell me what Esmé looks like?"

I can only describe her to you.

"The painting," said Lara. "You can't share your memories with me?"

No. Sadly, I cannot. But if I see her, I will tell you.

"So we just wait for her?" asked Lara. Althacazur had given them no plan; they were just blended for battle.

She'll find us, Lara. Be patient, plus enjoy the time you have here.

The next morning, the sound of her bedroom shutters snapping open woke Lara from a sound sleep. Lifting her head, she saw the morning sun filtering in on her. "Jesus," she groaned. Somewhere in the distance she heard a rooster crow and the sound of a tractor firing up. "What the hell?"

Audrey stood there, arms folded. "We're making jam today. The berries are in."

Lara covered her head with her pillow. "I'm not making jam today, Mother. I'm sleeping, then Caren is coming over."

Her mother lifted the pillow, so the sun seeped into Lara's eyes. "The huckleberries have come in this past weekend. I need help before it gets too hot." Audrey's hands clapped, and as if on cue, Lara felt a firm thump on her stomach as her Welsh terrier, Hugo, peered down at her and sniffed along her ear. Hugo shared a name with the catcher from Cecile's diary. This furry Hugo was also a great catcher…of tennis balls. While berry picking was, indeed, one of his favorite activities, apple picking in the fall delighted him even more. He mistook the apples for balls and could be found slobbering over the wooden baskets, heaping with fresh apples, one or two marred by tooth marks. Most of the top layer of apples with Hugo bites in them had to be discarded when baking pies.

"Seriously, Hugo? Why do you always take her side? It's always the tiny ones who are trouble." The terrier cocked his head and dug at her covers. "Where are the rest of them?"

"Penny and Oddjob don't care for berry picking, as you know. Hugo is going, though," added her mother, like there was ever any question about Hugo's participation. For dogs, Oddjob and Moneypenny didn't like to do much of anything except guard her. They hadn't left Lara's side since she'd gotten back from Paris, and she was surprised to find they weren't on the bed.

She put her feet on the floor and looked up to see her mother standing in the doorway, arms still folded. She snapped the duvet back and wiggled out of the tangled covers. "Are you frozen in that position, Mother?"

Audrey snorted and walked out of her room. Lara could hear her mother's shoes on the steps followed by Hugo's frantic scrambling feet behind her. Audrey called from the stairwell, "Come on."

Lara threw on pants and a gray zippered sweatshirt and pulled her hair into a ponytail, searching for her sunglasses. It was seven in the morning and it would be cold down in the groves, plus the mosquitoes could eat you alive some days. She moved like a zombie down the stairs, grabbing a cup of coffee. Then she headed out to the tractor.

Audrey had her hair in a tight ponytail and was wearing tortoise Wayfarers. She smelled of recently applied mosquito spray and suntan lotion. Starting up the dusty old John Deere, Audrey put it in gear, the old machine's cadence competing with another, newer tractor in the next field. She steered it down the windy road past the gas wells and into the wooded groves. Lara, with Hugo in her arms, was being pulled behind the tractor on a wagon with empty buckets at their feet.

It had been her grandfather Simon Webster who'd first brought Lara to the wild huckleberry groves, located in the back acres of their farm. He'd shown her the secret hiding place of the lush bushes off the mowed path. The complete opposite of what you'd expect, Simon was a masterful canner and pie maker; he taught Lara how to roll out piecrust, always making cinnamon rolls with the crust scraps. As the road wound past the wells, the house faded from sight. The tractor rumbled and thumped across a wooden bridge over a small spring as they headed into a thick forest. The sun was bright overhead, peeking down occasionally from the canopy of branches above them and shining in patches on Audrey's gold-colored hair.

The tractor slowed enough for Lara to hop out and walk ahead to investigate the ripeness of the berries. Lara and Audrey each took a giant bucket and headed out, Hugo yapping ahead of them. The sun came down in patches around her, and the stillness was welcome. Once Lara pushed through some dense thickets, the fragrant smell of the ripe dark-purple clusters baking in the sun hit her before she saw the light-green leaves of the bushes. You never knew what condition you'd find the berries in each season, and that was half the anticipation. Had Simon never shown them to her, Lara would have passed by them. Assessing the grove, Lara began plucking the berries, which fell into the basket with heavy thuds.

Audrey was humming what Lara knew to be a Hank Williams

song, "Your Cheatin' Heart"—one of her favorites. She'd move on to Patsy Cline soon enough because she couldn't yodel. Midway through the song, she stopped humming. "You took far too many chances in Paris. You know that." Audrey's voice was sharp and tight. Her berry picking came to an abrupt halt.

Lara couldn't see her mother's face. "I know."

"I was out of my mind with worry," said Audrey, her voice calm and measured. "You were gone *three* days. They said you were dehydrated and feverish when they found you lying outside a bistro." The bushes shook again as Audrey pulled them, plucking the ripe fruit from the leaves. "Are you going to tell me what happened?"

"I didn't think I was gone that long. It seemed like hours." Lara tugged at the bushes without much enthusiasm, feeling she needed another coffee. "The place was indescribable."

"Well, try."

Lara studied a leaf with a ladybug on it.

The bush rattled from Audrey picking on the other side of it. Then there was a pause. The berry bushes were still, her mother thinking.

"When I was six, I first saw him in the field. He was with a woman—your mother, Margot. They were talking about whether I was 'the one.' Sylvie told me never to tell anyone."

"You should have told me," said Audrey.

"I know I should have, but Sylvie—Cecile—whoever—specifically said to tell no one. Also, the day you showed me the spell, I should have told you that he'd been at the gala the night before."

"At the *Rivoli* gala?" Audrey shrieked, pulling the bushes back so she could see Lara's face.

"He said I needed to come to Paris. If I did, he'd give me answers about Todd."

Audrey laughed and shook her head. "Of course, he'd never do anything without something in return. I told you that I wanted no part of him. I wanted us to be normal."

"He called *you* a clever little minx."

"Did he, now?"

Lara could hear the contempt in her voice. "He honored his part of the deal," she said, plucking at clumps of ripe indigo berries, the smell of them wafting up as she pulled them from their stems. After years of doing this, she was fast. Lara tossed the berries into her bucket and pulled two lawn chairs down from the tractor and unfolded them. "It's just you and me out here, so can I ask you something?" To be safe, Lara had decided to keep the fact that Cecile was hidden inside her a secret from everyone. "Did you read Cecile's diaries?"

"I did."

"At the circus I found out that Esmé likes to kill the men we love... a sort of revenge against Cecile. She started with Émile. Then there was Desmond, Peter, and Todd." Lara bent down to pick at a blade of grass and let the last name hang in the air. She didn't want to be look-ing at her mother when she asked her what she knew she had to ask. "Do you want to tell me something about Peter Beaumont?"

Lara gazed over to find her mother staring up at the sun coming down through the trees. The cicadas—the soundtrack of a Virginia summer—were fading in and out. Audrey looked to be absorbing everything—the story, the sun—like it was precious. It was such a serene setting, the green hills lush and ripe.

"He and Jason were in the band together. They were best friends. I met Jason first, but when Peter walked in a room..." She paused, lost in thought. "I've never loved anyone like that in my life, Lara." She looked over at Lara. "Never." She took a deep breath, like she needed it to keep going. "But Peter was a wandering soul, untamed. Not unlike Todd."

Audrey stopped to let that sink in. As if a layer of an onion was peeling away, Lara was seeing a side of her mother that she'd never imagined. Her mother picked at something on her shorts. Lara was sure nothing was there, it was just giving Audrey something to do as she unpacked her history, something she'd tightly stored away from everyone.

"I knew from the beginning that he was wild. For the summer that year, it had been a bit of a triangle—Jason, Peter, and me—but I knew they were going to Los Angeles after Thanksgiving. I'd be left here." Finally, Audrey put her hands on her hips. "I've wanted to tell you this for a long time—forever—but I didn't want to ruin any part of your relationship with Jason. You clung to him so tightly. Peter is your biological father, Lara, not Jason. The day before he went missing, I had told Peter that I was pregnant. Honestly, when he disappeared, I just thought he'd bolted. Like you, I was confused. And until Todd went missing, I think some part of me always thought Peter had left to avoid the responsibility. We didn't know what to think. Jason and I were both devastated. The police were involved, of course, but they always thought he'd just up and left. His mother pushed them for years, finally getting him declared dead in the early 1980s."

"You didn't think it was like Desmond Bennett? No one did the math?"

Audrey laughed. "You have no idea what it was like back then. Simon and Cecile were so secretive about Mother. Now, knowing what you've told me, it was probably Desmond disappearing that undid Mother—along with Althacazur. I'm sure he didn't help."

"Why didn't either of you tell me that Peter was my father?"

Audrey lowered her sunglasses and met her daughter's eyes. "I never told Jason. I didn't see the point—and I still don't."

Lara inhaled sharply. Jason Barnes was not her biological father. Worse yet, he didn't even know it. There were things that Lara had clung to about her identity. That Jason Barnes was her father was one of them. She'd inherited her musical talent from him, she'd thought, but it hadn't been him at all—it had been Peter Beaumont. Then she remembered the way he'd looked at her as she'd played Peter's song. Like he'd seen a ghost.

"Are you sure?" Lara, too, sank in her lawn chair. "That he's my father?"

"Have you ever seen a photo of Peter? I mean everyone always said that he and Jason looked like brothers, but I thought that was a bit of an exaggeration. *You* look like Peter."

She'd seen the one photo. The one Jason had shown her when they'd closed on the radio station. Something had pulled her to Peter that day, but she'd thought it was just that he was the focal point of whoever had taken the photo. She'd been wrong. It had been something else, a familiarity.

Audrey stood and began tugging furiously at another patch of bushes, the berries dropping heavily into the bucket.

"It isn't my place to tell him, but *you* should," said Lara.

"I think both Jason and I had tried to move on in our own ways. I believe he knows on some level, but he loved Peter, too. One look at you and I can't imagine that he doesn't know the truth," said Audrey. "It was as though neither of us could continue without him, so you filled the void."

"Until I couldn't."

Audrey turned. "Until it was unfair to ask you to do so. The reality is that Peter would have been a terrible father. I never would have stopped him from going to Los Angeles—it was his dream, but it was never really Jason's dream. When I told him I was pregnant, he just seemed to find purpose around you. Had Peter lived, things would have turned out much different. I loved Peter, but in the end, you got the better father."

"But you settled. You said so yourself."

Audrey was silent, unmoving. "The absence of Peter nearly toppled me. I did the best that I could."

Lara looked down at her bucket. It was full. She walked over next to her mother, this mysterious creature who had always seemed so much larger than life, so put together, and began to help her mother carry buckets toward the tractor. She would drive back to the house and help her mother cook jam today. She'd pour it into little Mason jars, seal them tightly, then label and date them. Lara climbed into the driver's seat of the tractor. Everyone had their secrets and reasons for keeping them.

Forgive her, Lara. The secret inside of her was right.

When they got back to the house, Lara checked her email. There was one from Edward Binghampton Barrow with the subject line: *URGENT! Third painting found!*

Gaston et Lara:

The painting *Sylvie on the Steed* was featured in *Le Figaro* this weekend along with an article on Émile Giroux and the three paintings. We have found the third painting—the one of Esmé! With all the publicity around the paintings, we received a call from the woman at Giroux's old apartment building. She claimed to have a painting in her attic that matches the description of the missing third painting of *Esmé the Lion Tamer.* Micheau and I immediately went to see it today. I'm so excited to tell you that it is authentic. I've attached a photo!

Lara clicked on the attachment and felt her blood drain.

32

When he got back to the office, Ben found he'd missed three calls from Doyle, but there were no written messages. He hated when Doyle did that. He also had two emails from Kim Landau. He hovered over them but couldn't bring himself to open them.

There was a stack of mail that he started to work his way through, mostly junk mail; police stations got a ton of flyers. As he was tossing sale flyers into the garbage, he stared up at the board. He'd asked Doyle to take it back down to the basement, but his deputy never followed an order. Lara had said that Todd, Peter, and Dez were all dead and there was no point in looking for them anymore. He went to pull out the thumbtacks that held all the notes and photos, but he found he couldn't dismantle the board yet.

Then something caught his eye. It was the photo of Peter Beaumont that had hung up on the board for nearly a year, but today he noticed something about it. He'd been so busy thinking about the subject of the photo that he'd never thought about the photo itself. Pulling it free from its pin, he turned it over, running his finger on the edge.

He dialed Doyle's cell phone.

"Hey, boss." Ben could hear the sounds of a video game in the background. Doyle must have been home.

"What is so urgent? You called me three times. You could have just written something down."

"I thought this was something I should tell you in person."

"Then why aren't you here? In person?" Ben hated this tone in his voice, but Doyle drove him nuts.

"I've got a cold today. Anyway, you asked me to check on Desmond Bennett." A whistling noise plus Doyle's cursing indicated that he'd probably lost another troll in his video game.

"And?" Ben arranged things on his desk. Doyle must have been sitting here because everything was out of place. He imagined that Doyle tried out his chair to see how it felt every time Ben left the station.

"You'll never believe who Desmond Bennett was engaged to."

Ben waited for the answer, but he heard a crackle on the line followed by the sound of Doyle's thumb on the space bar, thumping loudly.

"So before Margot Cabot married Simon Webster, she ran off with Desmond Bennett, but she was only seventeen and Cecile wouldn't sign the parental permission form for them to marry. In fact, it was through Desmond Bennett's disappearance that Margot met Simon. He covered the story for the newspaper."

"Interesting. Anything else?"

"We had a murder while you were gone."

"What? Who?"

"I'm kidding, boss. But I had to get a bat out of someone's apartment on Jefferson Street. Hope I don't have a case of rabies," said Doyle, laughing. "I should be better tomorrow." He added, "Oh, and in fucking crazy details, this may be nothing, but Desmond Bennett was famous in his day so there was a lot of coverage on him; I left the newspaper clipping about his death on my desk."

Ben walked over and picked up the article. Desmond Bennett was as handsome as Esther Hurston had described him. He put the photo of Peter Beaumont down next to Desmond Bennett, looking for likenesses. Turning over the photo of Peter Beaumont, he flicked the paper. And he realized the answer had been right in front of him all along.

33

Checking his watch, he knew what he had to do. With his hands in his pockets, Ben walked up the hill. He spotted the still-empty spot where her car had sat all night. It was leaking oil. It was one of those days that looked like a storm—a bad one, too—was about to break open. It had been unusually humid, and so Ben found himself wishing to hear a rumble overhead that might cool things down.

He hadn't broken into a house in a long time, not since he was a kid, but he still knew how to spring a basement window free by jostling it. With a few strategic knocks, the window gave way easily, as always. Ben shimmied through the open window and landed on the dryer. He slid off the dryer and onto the basement floor.

It took a few seconds for his eyes to adjust to the darkness. He didn't want to turn on the lights, so he wandered around until he reached the area he knew to be the stairs. Ben ascended slowly, step by step. He reached the top and held his breath when it occurred to him that she might have pulled the latch to the basement door, locking him downstairs. When he turned the knob, though, the door opened freely into the kitchen. When the light shone in, he noticed several large green-and-gray bags stacked nearly three feet high on the basement floor. He left the door open and walked back down the stairs to see an additional four commercial bags of lime sitting against the basement wall.

Lime.

He walked upstairs and headed toward the hall. The long hallway led to the foyer and the staircase. To his surprise, at the foot of the stairs were three suitcases, a matching black set stacked in order from largest to smallest, the canvas giving way like they were packed full. If he hadn't been sure before, this incriminating detail was evidence enough of the fact that she was going to flee.

Yet he had to be sure. Walking back down the hall, he found the picture frame exactly where he recalled it had been. The subject was the Kerrigan River, at the bend near the old mill where it took its wildest turn, the grainy photo like a time capsule from the 1970s with its overexposed, undersaturated look. Pulling out the photo from Peter Beaumont's police file, he held the two next to each other. The tree, the hue of the photo—they were a match. These had been snapped minutes apart.

He studied the rest—black-and-whites—all in matted frames. An old photo of a demolition derby stopped him dead in his tracks. Looking closely at the photo, he could see a car with the beginning of a number painted on its door. The car design dated it back to around 1943. Next to it, he held the newspaper file picture of Desmond Bennett's car. The two scenes matched perfectly. Taken together, this arrangement was assembled like a trophy wall.

As he'd scrutinized the photos of Dez Bennett and Peter Beaumont, what had been similar had not been the men. It had been the photographer.

In 1938, Marla's grandmother Victoria Chambers had lived in this house. It had not occurred to him until now that for all Marla's love of history, he'd never once seen any pictures of her own family members. Most of the photos around the house were newer black-and-whites that Marla had taken herself, except for this cluster near the steps. But for someone who loved old photos—and someone who claimed to be so devoted to her family—there was not one single snapshot of anyone from Marla's family. In fact, Marla's mother had just died when he met her. Yet she didn't have a single photo or album of her parents. He racked his brain recalling the odd ways that Marla avoided having pictures taken of herself through the years. Wedding photos? Nope. They'd eloped. He recalled once taking a Polaroid; she turned her head and it didn't come out at all.

From Cecile Cabot's diaries, he remembered that Cecile and Esmé could not be painted or photographed. The best way not to be the subject of a photo was to be the photographer. The other night at the gala—had Marla had her photo taken? No. At the last minute, she'd pulled him into the photo, replacing her.

Laughing to himself, he realized how brilliant it had been. She was always behind the camera, never in front of it. Now he felt downright stupid. He'd been so taken with her when he'd met her. She'd been sophisticated. He'd been so desperate to hang on to her. He had asked her about her mother once, and she'd become weepy, so he never pushed it. *Why didn't I push her? Because she was a damsel in distress.*

An unfamiliar noise startled him, and his heart raced. He was about to sneak back down to the basement when he heard a latch open and then something drop. It took him a minute to realize it was the mailman. He peered out into the living room to see a neat stack of mail with a rubber band sitting on the floor in front of the door, just below the mail slot.

In the foyer, he padded past the mail pile and up the stairs. He was committed now. If Marla came home, he'd be trapped upstairs with no way out. He walked by the back bedroom—the spare where he had stayed at the end of their marriage. The room had undergone a transformation. It was as though she had erased every inch of the room that Ben had ever touched. Even the bed had been repainted white. The curtains were blue, the rug navy blue, and the room was now wallpapered in a floral pattern so busy that it would have caused him many sleepless nights.

"Jesus," he muttered out loud.

He walked down the hall and into the master bedroom, not exactly sure what he was looking for. The bed was unruly and unmade, which was also highly unusual. He sat down on the bed and touched the rumpled sheets. His hands went from the bed to the nightstand drawer. He flipped a few things over. Hair scrunchies and bookmarks. He pulled the stand away from the wall. Nothing. He lifted the mattress. Nothing again. Well, it was doubtful Marla would hide anything under the mattress, given that she wasn't an adolescent boy. He went to the tall dresser and opened each drawer, sliding his hand to the back. Lingerie, T-shirts, jeans, and scarves. Nothing. He caught his reflection in the closet mirror and couldn't bear to watch himself behaving this way. This idea was madness.

He opened the other closet door and reached back, deep into the shelves where Marla kept her shoes. Shoes, shoes, pair of boots. He made his way down through her sweaters and at the very bottom spied several pairs of her running sneakers. He had to get down on his knees and reach back behind them. His hand touched something soft. He got on the floor and pulled out an old running shoe. He tried to remember when she'd last worn this particular pair. His eye caught something in the toe of the shoe. He reached in and touched it. It wasn't an *it*, it was a *them*—a set of keys. On the chain was a Mustang logo, as well as an old Ford key and a Jeep key. He had seen its twin on Lara's key chain many times. *Todd Sutton's missing car keys.*

"Fuck." Ben sat down on the floor and threw the keys away from him as if they'd scalded him. He hadn't really thought he'd find anything here. This whole excursion had been an exercise in proving that he was wrong about her.

Ben gathered himself up, careful not to touch anything. That he was even thinking all this about her sickened him. They'd been together for ten years—ten years. True, she could be cold and prickly at times, but she was no killer—and *no way* was she was the hundred-year-old daughter of a daemon. He stopped and laughed. Despite everything that he knew from France, the idea that his Marla could be Esmé was crazy. *I have to be wrong. I need to prove I'm wrong.*

He got up and looked out the window at their small yard, which had become a palatial garden since last October. She'd thrown herself into its creation: elaborate urns and benches, exotic perennials and shrubs. Until today, he'd never noticed bags of lime in their basement. When had he been in the basement last? October or November? He hadn't noticed bags of anything. This was a curious detail, the lime.

Lost in thought, Ben wandered down the stairs and out the back door into the garden, where he grabbed a shovel. Perhaps the only outcome of all of this would be that he ended up looking very foolish, but Marla had some explaining to do anyway, didn't she? Those were Todd Sutton's keys hidden in a shoe in her closet. He scanned the garden, trying to figure out what she would have done if she'd wanted to bury someone. Spying the location where she'd put the cement bench that he knew she'd ordered last fall, he went over and shoved it away, surprised at its weight. The length was about right, and there were telltale signs of an extra layer of fresh lime mixed with the surrounding plants and soil.

He couldn't imagine how she might have dug a deep-enough hole, but then he hadn't been focused on this house and garden all those weeks after Todd Sutton's disappearance. He'd been down at Cabot Farms with Lara. He dug quickly but soon became winded. About three or four feet into the ground, Ben stepped into the hole to get a better angle. After many more shovelfuls, the blade hit something that sounded like stone but wasn't. Ben's shovel ripped free a layered piece of denim from what appeared to be a corpse. He pushed some dirt away to find a gray Chuck Taylor sneaker.

It was *the* sneaker. The one that Lara had described multiple times in police reports. He'd noticed that sneaker on every man since, looking up to see if it was attached to a man who looked like Todd Sutton.

Oh Jesus. Ben leaned against the opening he'd dug. He rubbed his jaw. *This is real.*

Struggling to process everything in front of him—the physical evidence as well as the crazy tale of the circus that he'd read—he crawled out of the hole and began to pace. Just as he was about to return to the house to call Doyle on the kitchen phone, he heard the iron gate shut.

"What are you doing here?" She was wearing a pair of jeans, a black Lacoste polo shirt, and espadrilles.

Ben followed her eyes to the pit he'd just dug in their garden. "I should ask you the same question."

Her hands were in her pockets. Her long chestnut-colored hair hung below her shoulders, and her clear blue eyes were bright. She looked exactly like the woman he'd known all these years. She peered into the hole, expressionless.

Ben pointed to the grave. "That is Todd *fucking* Sutton, Marla." He moved toward the kitchen door.

"Where are you going?" Her voice had risen a degree, but no more.

"I'm calling Doyle."

"You don't want to do that." Her movements were slow, animatronic almost. "You have to listen to me, Ben. It's very important." She took a step toward him, and he instinctively stepped back. "It was an accident. You didn't know how Todd Sutton could be. Let me explain."

He wanted to listen, really, he did.

She started to speak several times but stopped. "Let's just go inside."

"I'm fine *right* here."

She stammered her explanation. "We'd had a thing for a bit, but I'd broken things off with him. He could be violent. The afternoon of his wedding, he came by the house around one, wanting to get back together. He didn't want to marry her, you know."

"He came *here*," said Ben, pointing down to the ground. "To this house?"

Marla looked confused. "Of course...*this* house. He was trying to convince me to run away with him, but I said no. That's when things got out of hand between us. He was trying to drag me toward the car when I pushed him and he fell and hit his head. I panicked. I didn't know what to do, Ben. It was a terrible, terrible accident." She put her hands to her face. "Please, Ben. Listen to me. We can just cover his body and go on with our lives like nothing happened. Ben, look at me." Marla's blue eyes were shiny, tears brimming. "You *have* to believe me."

Her face was so beautiful and hopeful. In the years he'd known her, Ben had memorized every line, shadow, and angle of her face by heart. He'd worshipped this woman, throwing himself headfirst into their marriage. How easy it would be just to believe her and toss the dirt back over Todd Sutton, like he'd never seen a thing. But this explanation was simply bullshit.

He inhaled audibly, almost a wheeze. "I *want* to believe you, Marla, really I do, but it's just because I don't want to believe that I was married to someone who could do *that*." He wasn't dealing with a simple murder anymore. If she'd done this to Todd Sutton, then he wasn't dealing with a mortal woman. "What I'm really thinking, Marla, is that men have gone missing since 1944." He rubbed his face with his hand, sure that he'd gotten dirt all over it. "And damn if the last known location of Desmond Bennett's car was right here on this street."

"How on earth would I know about a murder in 1944?"

"Not only did you kill Todd Sutton, but you also killed Desmond Bennett and Peter Beaumont."

She laughed out loud. "Do you hear yourself, Ben? You sound crazy."

"Really? When Todd Sutton is right here in our flower bed? Peter Beaumont is probably over there in those fucking azalea bushes, isn't he? We pulled Desmond Bennett's file from the archives. Doyle just told me that Dez was last seen on this street in front of this house."

"So? I wasn't even born yet."

"We'll get to that." He held his finger up. His voice was growing louder as he was getting worked up. "I might not have noticed that little detail about Dez Bennett—it's a big street—except for the photo of Peter Beaumont. You got sloppy, Marla. There's a photo in our hallway of the Kerrigan River from around 1974. The twin of that picture is in Peter Beaumont's police file. I kept thinking there was something familiar about Peter Beaumont, but it wasn't his face that was familiar, it was the photo. For years, I'd walked past the next one you'd taken, on that very wall in our hallway."

"My mother took that photo, Ben. I have no idea when it was taken."

"And there is another one of the derby next to it. From the look of the cars, I'd say it was 1943 or 1944. What were those photos, trophies? Cut the shit, Marla." Her jaw tensed and he knew he was right. It propelled him on with the dramatics of an evangelical minister. "I thought, isn't it odd how nostalgic Marla is about her family homestead? Yet for the life of me, I've never seen one *fucking* photo of any member of her family. Not one. Then it really dawned on me. I've never seen a photo of *you*. Not even a photo from our wedding." He laughed to himself, like he'd just figured out the trickiest joke ever. "Then the entire thing clicked. It isn't money keeping you from selling our house, it's the goddamned corpses rotting in our flower beds. You didn't kill Todd Sutton by accident. Don't insult me. And I see you're leaving—fleeing, actually—aren't you? Your bags are packed." He looked down at the hole in the ground. "I can't say I blame you."

She was silent, seething, her arms folded in front of her.

"I got a call last week from Lara Barnes. She'd been chased at the Père Lachaise Cemetery. That Monday, I believe. Where were you, Marla? If I recall, there were a few papers on the front porch when I walked by. I thought that was odd, but then we aren't married any-more so I didn't think it was my business."

"Not that it is any of your business, but I was leading a group of historical society kids on a white-water rafting tour. I told you that."

"Where?"

"What?" She balked.

"Where was the tour, Marla?"

"West Virginia."

"Where? I'd like to check." He pulled out his phone. "Who can verify it, Marla? One name. Give me one name and I'll admit I'm crazy. My bet is that you were actually in Paris." Ben stood up and stepped back into the grave. With renewed energy fueled by anger and hurt, he began to dig furiously. "How did you do it? All these years? I want to see what you've done. And when I'm finished here, I'm going to start digging over there." He motioned toward a big clus-ter of bushes. "Or you could save me the trouble and just point."

Tears began to roll down Ben's cheeks with every scoop of earth. He wiped his arm on his coat as he continued digging. He shoveled until Todd's body was fully uncovered. The body was twisted unnat-urally, like he'd been tossed carelessly into the pit. Ben was thankful that he couldn't see what remained of his face due to the mass of long, tangled dark hair. The sight sickened him.

"Jesus," he said as he crawled away from the hole and vomited beside the stone walkway. He heard the sound of a power tool—perhaps an electric saw—starting up two or three houses down from theirs. A normal house with normal sounds. It was oddly comforting. And the whirring of the saw was also the last sound he heard before he felt a stab of pain in the back of his head and everything went black.

Ben woke to find his hands and feet bound by electrical tape. Marla was inching him closer to the grave, pulling his feet and torso in line with the hole to make it easier for her to roll him in. The reality hit him—she was going to bury him alive in his own backyard.

Ben began to scream. Marla put her hand over his mouth and he bit her. She pulled her hand away and then slapped him hard across the face, causing his already aching head to throb in earnest. She pulled off another piece of electrical tape and placed it over his mouth.

"You think I'm a monster." She bent down, studying her handiwork. "Well, you have no idea of monsters, Ben. I could *show* you monsters." She stood up, and he could hear her knees crack. "You asked if killing them was worth it? The answer is yes. I've lived for a hundred years. Killing is what keeps me alive. Every thirty years like clockwork, I find a willing sacrifice." She smiled. "Well, *willing* is probably not the right term. Still, I get to keep living and looking like this."

She wiped her face and then pulled Ben's legs toward the hole. He kicked at her and screamed through the tape, but the sound was so muffled with the buzzing sound that continued a few houses down, drowning out his stifled pleas.

"Esmé." The name sounded odd through the tape, but it caught her attention.

"Yes, Ben." Marla knelt beside him. She kept aligning Ben's body with the pit to dump him alongside Todd Sutton. She motioned toward the body. "It was easy to get Todd here that day. I'd been helping him find photos of a vintage truck that he was giving Lara as a wedding gift. Touching, isn't it?" She rolled her eyes. "As he was leaving, I hit him with the lion doorstop we bought at Vic's garage sale last year. You remember the one?"

What was he supposed to do? Nod that he recalled the garage sale?

"I don't have to choose one of *their* loves, it could be any man, but it makes it more poetic for me somehow. I keep seeing Cecile's face when I kill them. Her naive, stupid face. Then I place their cars at Wickelow Bend because it reminds me of the White Forest. A little offering for *him* so he knows that I haven't forgotten, either.

"The thing is that they—what I like to refer to as Father's victims— have to bleed. That's the requirement." She was on her hands and knees, getting him positioned, and she blew her hair out of her eyes. "You won't count, though; the spell doesn't work that way. I'll be on the hook for another man in another thirty years." She thought about something. "Sorry."

How had he missed this? Had he been so stubborn that he failed to see the signs? This woman he'd lived with for ten years was going to dump him in a shallow grave and then pretend to mourn his disappearance.

Marla swayed a little and she got up then sank onto the nearby iron bench, finally looking down into the hole. "You were right. I need to sell this house and get out of here, go back to Rome or Los Angeles and live again. I thought I'd try domesticity with you, but it just didn't fit." She smiled sadly, gazing at her nails as though worried she'd gotten dirt under them. She looked down at Todd's body. "I'm glad we can't see his head. I hit him on the side of his head above his ear. The doorstop kind of *stuck* in his head." She touched her hair lightly to demonstrate her aim.

"Peter was different, though. Oh, Peter Beaumont." She closed her eyes like she was savoring a memory. "He could have made me forget all about Émile if I'd stayed with him long enough. I was a friend of his mother's. He got all sentimental when Audrey told him she was pregnant and said he couldn't see me anymore. It was like Paris all over again. But I regretted killing him the most. He always took the Wickelow Bend shortcut on his way from Cabot Farms to his house, so I parked my car there by the side of the road. He never knew what hit him. And Desmond, well, he was a bit of an asshole. I fucked him right over there"—she pointed to the lattice now facing Victor Benson's home—"before gouging his eyes out. You were so funny, going on about fingerprints being wiped. They weren't wiped, Ben, I just enchanted them all. The whole thing was right under your nose, but you refused to see the magic."

She stood up and took a deep breath like she was refreshed after unburdening herself of these crimes. Then she kicked him hard in the stomach with the heel of her espadrille, which caused his body to roll. Ben fell the entire three feet into the grave, landing hard on top of what was left of Todd Sutton's uncovered body. Upon impact, the body gave, releasing putrid smells that engulfed the hole. Ben's head landed inches from Sutton's, and his nose took in the pungent decay. His eyes began to water. He squirmed and tried to sit up to get away from the smell. Marla returned to find Ben trying to stand upright in the grave. The uneven dirt made it impossible for him to gain his balance and he fell, this time directly on top of Sutton. Marla furiously shoveled dirt into the hole. "Do you want me to knock you out?" She stopped and watched him squirm. "It might be easier that way...for your sake. I don't need the blood. I don't really enjoy it, especially not with you. You're a good guy. I owe you that, at least."

"Fuck you," Ben mumbled through the tape.

"Okay then." Marla shrugged. "You can't say I wasn't merciful."

She resumed tossing dirt over Ben's feet. He sat up again and shook the dirt off. He quickly decided against getting back to his knees, which would give her another shot at the back of his head.

She walked around the hole, holding the shovel out. She positioned herself to hit him again. This time, he could tell she was going to bring the metal part down on top of his head. He moved around and lowered his head beneath the hole so she couldn't get a good angle. After a few minutes of him struggling like a worm, she hit him in the back with the shovel, hard, and he fell facedown onto Todd Sutton's faded jeans that were white from lime and felt his skin and eyes burning. He closed his eyes and prepared for the blow he knew was about to come from behind. She had a perfect shot at the back of his skull. Only then did Ben begin to laugh at the absurdity of his situation. After all these months of *looking* for Todd Sutton, he was about to die—in a hole—next to the poor missing bastard: the two of them, entwined forever in a shallow grave in his own fucking backyard.

This thought gave him one last burst of energy. He probably was going to die today, but damned if he was going to go down like this. Through the tape, he screamed, more of a rallying cry for himself. Then he rolled forward and put his legs up; they absorbed the blow of the shovel as she brought it down, sending it sailing across the stones. She scurried to retrieve it. With the shovel in her grasp, she turned back...and Ben nearly cried with a mixture of joy and dread when he spotted Lara Barnes walking through the garden gate directly behind Marla.

34

Lara stood behind Marla, unsure of what to do next. The entire scene was a mess. Ben appeared to have his mouth covered with electrical tape and had been pushed into a deep hole. Lara had a sinking feeling about what else was in that hole with him.

"Ben," she called. "Are you okay?" She could see from his expression that he was worried about her.

"Have you come to rescue him?" Marla turned, smiling. "If so, you're just in time." She held on to the shovel and cocked her head as she took in Lara. "Something has changed in you, hasn't it?" It was clear that Marla knew Cecile's essence had joined with Lara's. "What has Father gone and done now. Hello, Cecile."

"You haven't changed a bit, Esmé." Lara's tone was sharp, but the words weren't hers. Cecile had taken over. After a long sleep, Cecile had come awake. Lara could feel herself growing in strength with each passing minute, like they were fusing in strength and magic.

"Let's just say that every few years I get a little rejuvenation. How is the old bastard?"

"I'm not having a family reunion right now."

Marla shrugged. "Would you prefer I just kill him quickly?"

"No," Ben and Lara said in unison, Ben's statement coming out more of a mumble.

"How is the place? Still a prison?"

"You should see for yourself."

"Oh, I don't think so. Look, Lara, I'll make you a deal. I'm getting tired of Kerrigan Falls. It's like our circus: You don't want to stay in one place too long, people begin to notice things. I made the mistake of letting revenge go to my head; I know that now. Just turn around and go back out through that gate where you came from. I promise you won't see me again. It's a onetime deal and it's a good one. You two are kidding yourselves if you think this body-snatching routine is going to work. The two of you—even entwined—are not as powerful as I am, especially not so soon after killing." She paused, thinking about what she'd said. "Sorry, Lara."

That comment stung. Lara flinched. "Seems like you have a history of killing men who don't love you."

Marla smiled. "I'll admit, I was confounded at first that Father had chosen you. Then I got wind that he was getting a lot of pressure from the other daemons to get me back in the fold, so he needed the perfect little soldier to wrangle me like a wild horse. I've caused a bit of a scandal. The other daemons think we cambions need to stay hidden in the shadows, but that was never my way—nor Father's really, given that he created a giant, otherworldly hippodrome to put us in," said Marla. "So what's it going to be, Lara?"

"You killed Todd," said Lara. "I don't give a shit about your daddy issues. Todd, Peter, Dez, and Émile—none of those men deserved to die."

"Don't talk about Émile Giroux," said Marla. "You know nothing about him. He was *my* love. Mine. You had everything, Cecile. Do you remember us before Father split us? Have you gotten your memories back now that you're dead?"

Cecile was silent.

"Let me fill in some gaps, sister. Cambions like us didn't live. Madame Plutard was such a kind woman and she loved our mother so much. After Mother died, she agreed to give up her life and care for us as our nanny. She had a wheelchair fashioned for the both of us. Each day, she'd take us around the circus in that chair until we were ten years old. Do you remember that?"

Cecile—as Lara—shook her head.

"We'd try to take steps, but we had three legs and neither of us controlled the middle one. I figured out how to put weight on it so we could move with one of us stepping at a time with our good leg and then leveraging our middle leg like a crutch. After we'd practiced it for weeks, I made the mistake of thinking that was something great— that we could finally walk. Madame Plutard was *so* proud of us.

"Well, Father arrived at the circus. In those days, we were cared for by Doro and Hugo and all of them. Le Cirque Secret was a fun place for us, where people loved us. It was always tense when Father came back and we were paraded out to see him. We started toward him. It was supposed to be a surprise for him that we could walk. Madame Plutard had made us a satin dress—pink with a lace collar—just for the occasion. She'd taken the iron to our long ringlets and placed matching bows on our heads. Everyone was there—all the performers, Madame Plutard, Sylvie. I still recall how much joy we felt to be able to do that on our own—that one little *fucking* thing on our own.

"Well…" Marla laughed sadly, looking down at the courtyard. "In gazing up at him for approval, I forgot my step and we fell in front of everyone. You have to understand that it was difficult when we fell— we didn't exactly move together as one unit, so we struggled on the ground for what seemed like a long, long time. At first, no one moved a muscle. Then the Doros and Hugo came to help us, lifting us back on our feet while Madame Plutard ran to get our chair. I'll never forget the look on his face, Cecile. It is bored into my memory forever, and it fuels me. I'm so sorry you can't recall it, because if you did, you'd *despise him* as I do. He was repulsed by his own children," said Marla. Small sobs erupted from her, and she stopped speaking until she could regain her composure. "He told Madame Plutard that from then on we were to be wheeled to him in a chair, covered with a blanket, like *dolls in a carriage.*"

Everyone was silent. Lara found the story so horrible, so shocking that she couldn't breathe. "I'm so sorry, Esmé." Lara spoke, her voice breaking. "What he did to you was simply unspeakable. I'm so terribly, terribly sorry."

"Thank you, Lara. I appreciate that," said Marla. "Soon after the incident, he decided, against the advice of everyone, to cut us in two. It was a terrible thing to endure, Cecile. The pain was unbearable." Marla closed her eyes as her body tremored. "Even with magic, we barely survived. You were the worst. Your screams were so loud that Madame Plutard begged Father to take your pain away. So he did. The problem was that the enchantment required fealty, so one of us had to remember to keep the spell up. From then on, I had to keep the illusion of us inside Le Cirque Secret going. But even I made the grave mistake of forgetting that it was all an enchantment." Her voice trailed. "Remember when he sent me to the White Forest, Cecile? Oh, of course you do, you tattled on me like some spoiled brat. Do you know what they do to you in the White Forest? There are no illusions there. Dumped off there and separated from you, I crawled on my belly for three days across the forest floor. Defenseless, I had to fend for myself against all kinds of creatures. I ate twigs and sucked on leaves. I recall wondering what I had done to have our Father hate me *so* much.

"Finally, I got to the gate at Le Palace Noir, thinking I would be safe. I didn't know then that the other daemons look down on cambions like us, so I was tortured. I endured unspeakable things, until Lucifer found out and put a stop to it. No matter what anyone says about him, I'll always be grateful to Lucifer. He sent me back to the circus and rebuked Father horribly. Until I'd heard the gossip in the palace, I didn't know that the other daemons loathe our father."

"I never forgave myself for what happened to you." Lara could feel Cecile's sobs, causing her own heart to race.

"Well, we're even. I never forgave you, either." Marla's voice was hollow.

The story had taken its toll on everyone, yet it hadn't made Cecile more empathetic to her sister.

Lara could feel Cecile's anger, mixed with shame, heating up inside her. "It wasn't my fault, Esmé," spat Cecile. "I didn't *know*. It wasn't my fault that Father placed that unfair burden on you. You cannot blame me for something I didn't know. And you're wrong about Émile. Father enchanted the painting so you'd love him. I gave him up for you."

"You're wrong," said Marla. "He would have chosen me, if not for you being pregnant with Margot."

Marla had walked around behind Ben, and Lara instinctively knew what she was maneuvering to do. She was about to hit him over the head with the shovel. Ben knew it, too, and squirmed and twisted, but inside that hole he was a sitting duck.

"We didn't want to be separated from each other. We begged him not to do it. Madame Plutard went to the White Forest for throwing herself on us to try to stop him. Each fortnight the circus ran, I had to kill a man to keep up the illusion he wanted. I had to do whatever was required to get them near. When I first started killing, we were ten and I'd feign being hurt. I felt bad because it was always the kind ones who came over. Then as I got older it wasn't the kind ones. Yet our father didn't care about me. He didn't care about us. Once, I asked if we could send you instead. Just for one night. Do you know what he said? 'Cecile couldn't *bear* it.' All because you looked like our mother." Marla laughed.

Something occurred to Cecile. "It was you who sent the mirror to me, wasn't it? I thought it was a trick—some poor creature was trapped in there."

"That poor creature in the mirror of truth was you, my dear. That's why we couldn't be drawn. *We weren't real.* Like the way you made fun of me with my cats. That was *us*, as well. You were the one who couldn't see it. And although they thought they painted us in our illusive forms, the painters and photographers captured us as we really were. Father couldn't have them seeing those, so he'd erase the paintings and expose the film before morning. You claimed you wanted all the answers, but in the end you couldn't even gaze upon yourself. You covered the mirror." Marla searched Lara's face for a glimmer of Cecile.

"And are you happy now?" Lara had tears in her eyes. The emotion was all Cecile. "You killed Émile Giroux, Desmond Bennett, Peter Beaumont, and Todd Sutton—tormenting my family for decades. I certainly have blamed myself for being sheltered. But I am *not* the one to blame here. You are angry at Father, not me. You're a hundred years old and yet you continue on like some living waxwork seeking revenge. Or are you so warped by your hatred that you don't see that it is Father you should be angry at? Tell me, when will it be enough? Does this really make you feel better? Or do you just hate yourself so badly that you hate me, too? We may be divided, but we are still one creature. Is it yourself you truly hate?"

Marla put her hand to her face. "I'm broken, Cecile. Nothing will ever make me feel better. And I was a child. What could I have done with my anger toward our father? We were children. But I've had a fabulous life—Rome, London, Los Angeles, Buenos Aires, Sydney. I've done the best that I could. After I killed Émile, a strange thing happened to me. I got stronger, but it was like a thirst for blood that I couldn't quench. In Rome during the 1960s, I killed a man a night for thirty days. Now it's only one every thirty years."

As she listened to Marla's story—Esmé's story—Lara couldn't help but pity the poor, motherless child she recalled from the photo. Esmé had been dealt a cruel hand, all Althacazur's doing. Lara considered this to be one of the saddest stories she'd ever heard and her heart broke for that little girl.

Yet it was hard to reconcile that story with the woman standing before her. Like the many killers who were once victims themselves, at some point Esmé became the torturer. This woman had killed Lara's fiancé and her father, and despite the pity she felt for her now, Lara knew she would kill everyone here today unless she stopped her.

Just then, Lara saw Marla look beyond her. She turned to see Audrey coming through the gate.

"Mother," said Lara, alarmed. "How are you here?"

"I had a feeling," said Audrey.

Marla sighed deeply. "Not you, too. So you're all now doing his dirty work for him. I warn you all: I'm not going back there." She leaned against her shovel. "I'll admit, I'm surprised he managed to wrangle you, of all people, Audrey."

Audrey's mouth was drawn tight. "I never wanted any of this."

"Well, that makes two of us," said Marla. "Audrey, I've offered your daughter the opportunity to turn around and leave. I won't come back to Kerrigan Falls."

Audrey snorted. "No one would be foolish enough to believe you."

"Well then, since you two are still under your little protection spell, I can't touch either of you. But that doesn't apply to *him*." Marla turned to Ben and moved to swing the shovel at his head. With a flick of her hand, Lara sent the shovel flying. Marla turned to her and smiled. "It seems you *do* have some skills. He's outfitted you well."

Lara'd had no idea that she had skills other than flying. She was drawing on pure emotion.

Marla spun around toward them, wiping sweat with her arm. "Remove the protection spell and I won't kill him in front of you."

When neither Audrey nor Lara answered, Marla shrugged. "Okay then, it's your choice." She didn't even move a muscle. Ben doubled over in pain as though his insides were burning.

"Mother." Lara turned to Audrey. "Remove it."

"No." Audrey turned to Ben. "I'm sorry, but I can't risk it."

Ben nodded as he writhed in pain.

"Remove the spell, Mother." Lara's body had merged with Cecile's mind fully now, the two of them sharing power. She had never felt stronger. "Mother," commanded Lara. "Remove the *fucking* spell."

"Are you sure?"

"This ends today. One way or the other."

Audrey lowered her head and began to chant quietly.

"That's more like it," said Marla.

Marla turned toward Audrey, and Lara's mother doubled over in pain. Lara felt the fury well up inside of her. Marla then turned to Ben, who was now on his hands and knees writhing in pain.

"*No!*" Lara put her hand out, and Marla went flying backward. Lara had seen the pitchfork leaning against the wall. She began thinking about the pitchfork rotating seconds before Marla's back hit the wall, the tines turning and sliding through her body, coming out through the woman's chest. For just a moment, it looked as though the act hadn't hurt her at all, because she gazed down at the tines, as if inspecting a stain on her shirt. Then her chestnut hair fell forward and Marla slumped over like a doll.

Lara let out a breath she'd been holding.

Within moments of slumping over, Marla shook herself and stood up, the pitchfork teeth still visible through her ribs.

Lara felt the air go out of her and struggled to breathe, as if someone was gripping her throat. Someone *was* gripping her throat. Esmé was strangling her, using the same magic she'd employed. As the world began to slip out of focus, Lara could hear Audrey screaming. Then a rattle at the gate diverted Marla's attention and Lara got a moment's reprieve. She breathed, the air hitting the back of her throat, then slumped to the ground, wheezing and grabbing her neck.

"Are you okay?" Audrey was at her side.

Marla backed up as Oddjob and Moneypenny walked into the yard with a cat-like grace, sizing up their victim.

Lara was stunned by the change in their appearance. The Oorang Airedales were double their normal sizes. She had seen them stalking prey before, but nothing like this. As they paced, they continued to grow, gazing at Marla hungrily. Lara could hear their claws scraping as they moved.

"You've got hellhounds, Audrey? You have two *fucking* hellhounds?"

"I always hated magic." Audrey smiled. "But animals. That's a different story. Althacazur gave them to me as a gift when I was a child. He'd heard I wanted a pony." Audrey raised her eyebrows, suggesting it was a curious gift on his part. "These two are my pride and joy." In a flash Audrey moved and with her hand out drove Marla back over Todd Sutton's grave, radiating a power Lara wasn't aware her mother possessed. Oddjob and Moneypenny each grabbed one of Marla's arms, and Lara thought they just might rip her in two.

Lara scrambled up next to her mother and saw, for the first time, the remains of Todd Sutton in the shallow grave beneath her. He'd been buried like a pet. Anger welled up, and she turned to Marla. "Enough, Esmé. I've grown so bored by your antics. And I hate to be bored."

Marla looked at her with fury, for she knew the source of Lara's help. The words that she'd just spoken hadn't come from Lara or Cecile. Lara placed both hands on Marla's face. "I'm sorry, I take no joy in this." These were the last words from Lara before Althacazur fed her the incantation she needed.

Incante delibre
Vos femante del tontier

"My daughter. I was wrong, but now it's time you came home." Lara pressed her forehead to Marla's. As she connected with Marla, she felt Cecile pulling out of her body and fusing with her sister.

"No. No. Father. Noooooo," Marla screamed just as a lawn mower powered up across the street, drowning out her cries.

Audrey had loosened Ben's wrists, and now he was removing the electrical tape from his mouth. His face registered horror as his former wife stood there with a pitchfork through her chest. She began to deflate like a pool float at the end of summer, nearly folding over. As she did, Lara felt her strength increase and then she began to choke, doubling over gagging and coughing. Cecile had left her. The two sisters—were gone.

It is finished. Lara said the words that she knew came from Althacazur. While he had not been permitted to interfere directly, through Lara he'd placed his hand on the scales and had tipped them in their favor.

And yet, it wasn't finished, not by far.

Standing there, under the giant twisted oak tree at the top of Cabot Farms, Lara watched as Ben shoveled the final dirt over the graves, patting it down. This was a part of the farm where no one ever ventured, but to be safe, they'd purchased sod to blend in with the existing grass as much as possible.

It had taken Lara, Audrey, and Ben two weeks to move the remains of Desmond Bennett, Peter Beaumont, and Todd Sutton here for a proper burial. The three were resolute that they could never admit the true story about what had happened to these three men to anyone.

Who would believe them anyway?

While Lara had always believed in magic, everything Ben thought he knew had been challenged. While his concussion had healed and his bruises were faded, there was a light that had gone out in Ben. The logic that he believed ran the world had all been an illusion. The idea that a one-hundred-year-old daughter of a daemon had been making sacrifices of young men every thirty years would have sounded crazy—until he'd seen the things he had over the last month. And yet, he never suspected that he was *married* to her. He'd never picked up a thing, so sure was he that the world was a place of order. Of course, this manifested itself in long silences and extra Jamesons. He and Lara sat silently at the bar at Delilah's, content just to be near each other.

They'd moved Todd's body first, because he was the most recent and there were still gruesome details about him—pieces of his hair were still intact and rotting clothes still hung on his skeletal corpse. Ben and Audrey buried him without Lara. She stood at the bottom of the hill and heard the scrapes of the shovel and then a heavy thud that she knew was Todd being returned to the ground.

Next they found Desmond Bennett's body buried under a mature azalea bush, his old wallet barely holding together, but the dog tags from his stint in the army still tucked in the billfold. A week later, after digging in the night, they'd found the remains of Peter Beaumont. While Lara and Ben had offered to bury Peter, Audrey had wanted to help, so the three of them put his bones next to those of the other two men.

"Lara." It was Ben who was the first to notice something curious in one of Cabot Farms' fields.

She looked up to see the land waver and something open up. It was a familiar sight in the field and yet she had a deep dread. She'd known this time was coming, the reckoning with the devil. A trio appeared— a man flanked by two women—elaborately costumed like they were dressed to greet someone at the train. As the three came closer, Lara saw that Margot was dressed in a beautiful 1940s-style pink dress with cat's-eye sunglasses and victory rolls in her blond hair. Oddly, she held a square pink pocketbook. Cecile, with waves of platinum hair flowing down her back, was dressed as a flapper in a dress with a plunging back.

Lara was brushing dirt off her pants but stopped when she saw them. She walked toward them. "I didn't think I'd see you so soon."

"Well, we are rather attached to this lovely town," said Althacazur, dripping with sarcasm. "I see Bill is here." He nodded toward Ben.

"Ben," said Ben, correcting him from behind Lara.

"Whatever," said the daemon, who was dressed like he was headed to a steampunk convention: military brown leather trench coat, top hat, and mirrored glasses. "You did a marvelous job battling Esmé. She's back home where she belongs. I rather think she's happy to be there, although she would never admit it, of course. She sends her regards, Bill. But now it's time, my dear."

Lara could feel the tears welling up. "I'm not ready. I need more time."

Althacazur ignored her, tilting his body to get a good look at Audrey.

Confused, Lara looked around, continuing, "I did what you asked. I just need more time. Surely, I've earned it."

And yet Althacazur wasn't looking at Lara. A thin smile formed on his lips, patronizingly. "You made that *perfectly* clear." He put his hands together like the Grim Reaper, waiting patiently.

But it was Audrey who turned to her daughter, wiping tears from her cheeks with dirt-covered hands. "In Paris, when I got there. You were dying. You didn't have much time left."

Lara recalled seeing her mother in those dark hours, but then she'd seen Todd too. She knew now that she'd teetered on the edge of death, but she'd come back. Lara looked from her mother to Cecile, confused.

"Despite Father's efforts, you weren't strong enough to absorb me on your own," said Cecile gravely. "I'm so sorry, Lara. Had your mother not intervened, added her magic, you would have died."

"Intervened?" Lara shot a look at Audrey. "What do you mean?"

"I made a deal with him," said Audrey, a sad smile forming on her lips. She took the shovel and tossed it back toward the graves and shook the dirt from her pants like she needed to be tidy and presentable for what happened next.

Althacazur stood emotionless, letting the scene play out in front of him.

"No no no." A primal scream erupted from deep inside Lara, followed by a gutteral moan. She clutched Audrey. "Please, no."

"It was a necessary sacrifice," said Audrey, placing her hands on Lara to steady her. "I agreed to go with them after we defeated Esmé. It was a fair deal, Lara. *Anything* to save you."

"Oh, Mother, no." Lara doubled over and Ben scrambled to get to her, but she fell on her knees in the field. "No. No." She looked up at Althacazur. "Take me instead. I'll go now. Please."

"Oh that I could, you *delightful* girl." He leaned on his walking stick and looked down over his sunglasses. "Cecile's right, so sure was I that you were dying, I cut a different deal. I think you'd call it 'an insurance policy.' I'd thought you and Cecile would be strong enough together, but alas I needed more magic. On the bright side, it got you out of your deal, so it looks like we both got what we wanted."

Cecile shot him a look to be quiet.

Lara had bent over like she was choking. "No. Oh please no." Lara thought this was what it felt like to be gutted. She felt betrayed by Althacazur, tricked. But what had she expected?

"Ben," said Audrey, looking up at him. "I need you to promise that you'll be there for her."

He nodded.

Audrey crouched down next to Lara, who was now on her knees

near the edge of the field. She leaned to the side now, like she was unable to hold her body upright. "You and Jason can take care of everything together, Lara. All I ever wanted for you was a normal life. This was the cost, but I'm at peace with this decision."

"But I'm not," said Lara. "It's all *his* fault." She glared at Althacazur with fury.

"No," said Audrey. "He gave me a choice. I knew the rules."

Cecile stepped forward. "I'm so sorry, but Esmé and I shouldn't have been born, Lara. It was luck that we are even here. Every day of happiness that we have was more than we were designed for." Cecile put out her hand for Lara and pulled her up. The woman studied her face. "You know how much we've all suffered. The sadness, the magic, the circus—well, those things are our destiny. I'm sorry that is the legacy I have given you." Cecile brushed Lara's hair away from her face.

Lara turned to Audrey. "I'll go instead. It was me who was dying. You didn't want anything to do with this magic."

"Lara," said Audrey, more firmly now. "I cannot imagine a better fate for myself than living out my eternity riding horses in a circus— and waiting for you to join me someday."

Lara held on to her mother, both women sobbing. Finally, Cecile separated them softly. Ben lifted a shaking Lara and began walking with her up the hill. She fought him the entire way. As if they knew, Oddjob and Moneypenny both began to moan from the barn—a low, mournful sound that continued until the morning.

Before she disappeared into the night, Cecile turned back. "We will see you again, my dear. We are your destiny."

Audrey walked arm in arm with Cecile, never looking back, as if to do so would break her forever.

EPILOGUE

Kerrigan Falls, Virginia
October 10, 2006

A fter the bones were removed from his garden, after Lara's mother had gone, Ben built a stone patio, then put his house up for sale. One of the "great homes of Kerrigan Falls," declared the listing. It had an offer within a day. Marla had been living in the house since 1938, first as her grandmother Victoria, and then as her mother, Vivian. Long trips, lengthy illnesses—no one had ever questioned any oddities as Marla morphed from mother to daughter, and no one questioned them now. Lara had helped with that. While she wasn't the talented illusionist that Esmé had been, she'd made a correction so that "Marla" showed up to sign the mortgage paperwork. In fact, there had continued to be sightings of "Marla" now and then, until she finally moved back to Los Angeles permanently, to pursue her photography career.

Sadly, that wasn't the only story Ben and Lara were forced to manufacture. They'd also had to fabricate for Audrey a sudden trip to Spain about a horse. After a month, when Jason and Gaston hadn't heard from her, Ben began pressing Lara to do what they both knew was necessary. As much as Lara couldn't face it, Audrey wasn't coming back. So at Ben's prodding, they created a fake car accident, with Lara using an enchanted document as proof to both Gaston and Jason that her mother was dead.

At the memorial service for Audrey, she and Jason sat on the bench in the old Kerrigan Falls Cemetery. "You should know where he is buried, too." Then Jason took her hand and walked her around the back to Peter Norton Beaumont's grave. It was the only indication he'd ever given her that he'd known the truth all along. That—and he gave her Peter's Fender Sunburst. As they gazed down at the granite stone, Lara longed to tell him that his friend, Peter Beaumont, was interred at Cabot Farms, but she felt a need to protect him. He'd had enough.

Gaston Boucher had also become a dear friend. She could see the hope that he'd had for a different life for himself with Audrey. She and Ben stayed close to him, inviting him to dinners at Cabot Farms, an empty place at the table for Audrey.

Lara sold her own house and moved back into Cabot Farms with Ben, and they settled down into a quiet existence—if raising hell-hounds could be considered a quiet existence, although Lara found them quite lazy and content to sit by the fire.

After all that had happened, how did a person just return to a normal life? Now that she knew that daemon blood flowed through her, what could normal possible look like? So Lara found herself moving through her day like the walking dead. That first summer was the hardest. She sat out in the field waiting for *him*. Only he could fix this. Squinting in the sun, she willed him to come. Had she been nothing but a vessel for Cecile? When he failed to show, she thought she had her answer.

Yet she refused to accept things the way they were, and so she kept practicing: starting cars, locking doors, opening drawers, dimming streetlamps, cuing records, until the magic had become as reliable as breathing. While her mother had turned her back on spells, Lara found that she didn't feel the same. It was as much a part of her as her blond hair. She'd felt the magic there flowing through her veins as she leapt from the trapeze. Nothing in her life had felt that freeing. As she struggled to tell Ben, she found that words didn't describe the Grand Promenade, the carousel. True, it was Hell, but it was breathtaking and strange. And wasn't she carved from it?

Everything that Ben thought he knew had been challenged as well. They both moved around each other for a year, like soldiers who'd returned from battle. From the way he hesitated, she knew that Ben was worried about the spaces left by Todd, Marla, and Audrey, even Peter Beaumont, for she'd finally told him about Peter as well. They were two people formed by absences of others. While he never said it, she thought he worried that those who'd remained, including him, were not enough for her. At times, he wasn't wrong. She was like the mountain that had been formed by the glacier. After it tore through, valleys remained carved like scars. Yet there had been beautiful parts to the story, too. They were in this thing together now, she and Ben, their roots so deep. Early on, there were moments when she was sure the weight of everything would topple them, and yet it hadn't. He had been a gift through this all, but you didn't get one without the other. And she'd decided that she was the end of this line. There would be no children for her. While Ben had assured her he understood, she worried that it was a decision he would regret, but then again, he'd been married to a one-hundred-year-old half-daemon, so normal had changed for him as well. She recalled Cecile's words: *It was luck that we are even here. Every day of happiness that we have was more than we were designed for.*

Had Todd shown up that day two years ago, she would have been a different person. She thought back to her naive, silly self, standing before a mirror, enchanting a wedding dress. She'd been oblivious to everything—her family and its magic. Her mother had not done either of them a favor by hiding from it in a desire to make them ordinary. Audrey had clung too tightly to the idea of a mortal life, but Lara wasn't sure that she'd asked for that. She'd pursued the answers that Audrey hadn't wanted to know, but they weren't worth her mother's ultimate sacrifice. And oh, how she had missed her mother. More than Todd, the loss of her mother threatened to topple her.

Grief must have been contagious, because she received an email from Barrow that morning.

Lara:

I hope you are well, my friend. Yesterday afternoon, I visited the Musée d'Orsay. They've moved our two paintings to the second floor, overlooking the sculptures. I will always be grateful to you for displaying *Sylvie on the Steed* as part of the special exhibition and for your generous donation to the museum after the Sotheby's sale.

Sometimes during lunch, I sit with our paintings. I know that they hang on the wall due, in large part, to our conviction and the sacrifices we both made.

I confess that I am forced to recall why I was first drawn to the mystery of Jacques Mourier and Émile Giroux and this wild tale of a circus fantastique. You had asked once, and I told you, that I had been drawn to it for the scholarship. At the time, I believed that answer to be truthful. Now, in the art world, I am famous and you are rich, but I fear the cost for us was far too steep. It was the mystery that I'd loved. But the mystery—the lore—of Le Cirque Secret is gone for me now. Everything we went through has led here—to a beige wall.

How I'd hoped that people would care about these paintings! Yesterday afternoon as I ate my sandwich, bored teenagers shuffled by like ducks with earpieces, corralled by sour tour guides.

One group nodded at the duo of our paintings, then had the audacity to ask where the Monets were displayed.

The reason that I write, however, is that after my foul mood at the *musée*, yesterday I caught a cab back to the institute with the sole purpose of seeing the journals again. As I opened the vault, I found my hands shaking so hard that it took me two attempts before I could enter the correct code. It had been months since I'd seen them, so I went into the vault and pulled the box where they were stored. I'd longed to hold the composition books in my hands. The real story had been contained here—it had completed the works for me—made the paintings come alive!

Once in the vault, I flipped open the lid and breathed easy. The three composition books were still there, sitting in their plastic. It is here that I don't know how to begin. I picked them up, so desperate to touch them that I didn't use gloves. I held the first one in my hands, the cover so old it was like thin fabric. I flipped open the first page and it took me a moment to realize what I was seeing—or not seeing. I was turning page after page of dull, faded, *blank* paper.

Cecile's words are gone. The loss of them has made me wonder if they were ever there at all. I doubt myself so much now. The pages are blank and my heart is broken.

In all this time, I've begun to reflect. Much of the real story of the loss and the love between Émile and Cecile was not entirely told on the three enchanted canvases. In fact, the paintings and the journals complement each other—Émile and Cecile—their art combining to tell the most fantastical story that Paris has never known existed. The fact that the fucking circus was created so that one of the most powerful daemons in history could find a babysitter for his twin daughters is a tale so absurd that, in the end, no one would believe it.

Giroux is back in fashion these days, so I was asked to update my biography on him. At the end, I found myself struggling yet again on the Ladies of the Secret Circus chapter. The three paintings only proved that Giroux had painted a circus; they failed to validate Le Cirque Secret's existence. Nothing will ever prove that something so truly fantastic and surreal was once a part of Paris's fabric. How do you really prove magic? And in the end, do you really want to?

I confess that, for me, something was lost in the quest. Some mystery about the world has been answered, but the solution has dulled something deep in me. Solving mysteries didn't get me closer to anything. For you, I know it was the loss of your mother. I think of her so often. How she came to Paris to rescue you.

And now the journals are lost, too. I cannot help but feel it was for nothing. I miss the man I once was.

I apologize. I know that I sound dreadful. I wanted you to know. You are, perhaps, the only person who would feel their loss as profoundly as I do.

Your friend, Teddy Barrow

Tonight she was working the night shift at the station. As she sat back in the chair, she cued up "Venus in Furs" and Sam Gopal's "Escalator," then let Lou Reed's wave of discordant strings take her back to that glorious moment on the trapeze. She could feel the beaded costume and the flow of the pent-up magic running through her veins. That heady power had infected her.

Teddy Barrow was right. So much had been lost.

Yet, there had been something bothering her, nicking at her—a theory she had.

Althacazur had been the ultimate seducer. He'd lured her to the circus, and when he thought she might die after absorbing Cecile, he was so desperate for a patron that he'd traded her for her mother. But in the seduction, he'd made her stronger than any of them. Even after the deal was sealed and Esmé was returned, Lara's powers had remained. To prove her point, she stared at the clock on the wall. As she mouthed the words to Sam Gopal's "Escalator," spinning on the turntable, she noticed that it was ten minutes past midnight. She watched the second arm struggle to move, and she watched her phone hold 12:10 A.M. for more than two minutes. *I stopped fucking time.*

She typed a reply to Teddy.

Teddy.
 Come to Kerrigan Falls. I have an idea. It's crazy, but it might work.

—L

While Lara had stood in this field before trying to summon him, she might have missed the point of his instruction. He was always quick to tell her she missed the point. Perhaps he'd been right all along.

When she'd been cleaning her old room at Cabot Farms, she'd stumbled on the *Rumpelstiltskin* book; inside it was the pressed clover.

Unlike Audrey, she couldn't lock off an entire part of herself in a desire to be normal. Plus, her mother never would have left her trapped in a circus as the human patron. And so she had resolved to get her mother out. She'd arrange some deal with Althacazur to take the circus. She knew from Esmé that he wasn't popular with the other daemons. She'd use that to her advantage if she had to. As she'd plotted this, she hoped that maybe Teddy would join her, the three of them sharing the human patronage work, kind of like Hell's time share. They were powerful half creatures, she and Audrey, and didn't have to live solely in one world or another. Christ, that sounded dull. She hated dull things. In the past year, she'd painted her whole house with the wave of her hand, just like a combo of Samantha Stephens and Martha Stewart. Is this what she was going to do with her magic? What next? Tiling a wall or installing drapes when she couldn't reach them?

No, she was done with all that. It was time to embrace who she was—*the Last Lady of the Secret Circus.*

"I don't know if this is going to work, Teddy." Lara stared ahead at the field, empty as usual. She could hear his breath as he stood in lockstep beside her.

"When you were gone in Paris," said Teddy, "Ben said that all we had to do was get him near you and he'd find you."

Lara smiled. If she ended up stuck on the other side, she hoped that Ben would forgive her. He knew her well enough to have suspected that she would do exactly this—and he'd be mad at her, but he knew her better than anyone. "Well, he may have to come and find me all over again. Gaston, too."

"That's quite a love, Lara." He looked back at the farmhouse. "Are you sure?"

"It's because of that love, Teddy. I won't be half a person anymore. No one can love that for long. He deserves the best version of me. And I'm going to try to give him that."

Focusing on the clover, she held the dried sprig in her two fingers, emotion welling up inside her.

"I can't promise that we'll come back. You know that."

"I know," said Teddy, his voice low. "I've said my goodbyes."

"I also can't promise what he'll do to us when we get there. You may be selling your soul."

"I agree to the terms," said Teddy, staring out at the empty field, his chin raised. "Le Cirque Secret has called to me, Lara. Just as it called to you."

She smiled. She'd known what his answer would be. Anything for the scholarship.

"Well, you always wanted a ticket," said Lara with a chuckle. "Now we just might crash this damned circus."

Oddjob groaned. The animal looked up at her, along with his twin, Moneypenny. The hellhounds' expressive eyes bored through her. Teddy held on to their leashes tightly. Once this thing started, she hoped they'd function like magical battery packs. They were hellhounds, after all. They knew the way home—more important, they always knew the way to Audrey.

She took Barrow's hand and gripped it tightly. Spinning the clover in her other hand, she hummed "Escalator." She wasn't much for spells; she was a creature of music, and it seemed that songs could pull the other side through for her. As she twirled the flower, she thought of the carousel, of the aqua walls and dark-gold chandeliers along the Grand Promenade. How much she'd longed to see it again, to look out at the hedges and the clowns having tea. It was the most magnificent, otherworldly place she'd ever seen. The images tugged at her like a curiosity that was hardwired inside her, a haunting child's story that couldn't be forgotten. She knew that now—that she'd always be searching for it in other places. Was she homesick for it? Homesick. She thought of her mother. She was done being defined by absences. *I won't live without you any longer.* So lost in her thoughts and spinning the flower that she almost didn't hear Teddy.

"Oh my God, Lara. You should see it." His voice broke, but he held on to her hand tightly. "It's stunning. I never imagined...I never imagined it would look like *this*."

She opened her eyes to see what she already knew was there—the carousel at Le Cirque Secret. Only instead of pulling it through into her realm, she had another plan.

Lara pulled Teddy forward with her and the hounds onto the carousel's platform. As her leg brushed past the stallion, the horse flicked its tail. Beyond the platform, she spied the magnificent Grand Promenade with its gilded walls. The sun shone down through it, and she knew out each window she'd find an elaborate maze or hedge. Just then Lara thought she could see the outlines of that familiar butter-colored bob running toward them. Was that an aqua feathered headdress she was wearing? The thought of it made Lara smile.

"Oh, Teddy," she said, sighing. "You haven't seen *anything* yet."

Acknowledgments

I'm still in awe of the magic that goes into making a novel, and I'm quite fortunate to be surrounded by such a magnificent team. I want to thank my brilliant editor, Nivia Evans, for shepherding this book in the midst of a pandemic. Early on, she helped shape it and see its potential. I'm so grateful for the entire Redhook team: Ellen Wright, who is such a lifeline to us writers as these books make their way out in the world; Lisa Marie Pompilio, who has designed yet another hauntingly beautiful cover; and Bryn A. McDonald, who is the grammatic voice in my head and the author of the thoughtful comments in my margins. I always know I'm in good hands with her team's suggestions, especially Laura Jorstad's brilliant repair of my French language butchery.

The early version of this story in particular was championed by my agent, Roz Foster. I will be forever in her debt for seeing something special in my writing, and I am so fortunate to have her by my side in this fantastic journey. I'm so appreciative of the support of both the Frances Goldin Literary Agency and the extraordinary team at Sandra Dijkstra Literary Agency, including Andrea Cavallaro and Jennifer Kim.

As always, my sister, Lois Sayers, is my first and most critical voice. I trust her instincts more than my own, and her influence was especially appreciated with this book when I often felt lost. My friendship and gratitude always to Amin Ahmad for his insight and honesty. He's a developmental editing genius.

I'm also so grateful to the support from Dan Joseph, Laverne

Murach, Tim Hartman, Hilery Sirpis, Allie DeNicuolo, Anna Pettyjohn, Doug Chilcott, Karin Tanabe, Alma Katsu, Sarah Guan, and Steve Witherspoon. Much thanks to the Spark Point Studio team of Crystal Patriarche, Hanna Pollock Lindsley, and Taylor Brightwell.

If you write any type of historical novel, I think you do so partly because you enjoy immersing yourself in the research. The "lost generation" of Paris in the 1920s is a particularly rich historical period, and there are a number of source materials that helped shape this book, including: *The Circus Book, 1870s–1950s* by Linda Granfield, Dominique Jando, and Fred Dahlinger; *A Moveable Feast* by Ernest Hemingway; *When Paris Sizzled: The 1920s Paris of Hemingway, Chanel, Cocteau, Cole Porter, Josephine Baker, and Their Friends* by Mary McAuliffe; *The Golden Moments of Paris: A Guide to the Paris of the 1920s* by John Baxter; *The Found Meals of the Lost Generation: Recipes and Anecdotes from 1920s Paris* by Suzanne Rodriguez-Hunter; *Man Ray's Montparnasse* by Herbert R. Lottman; *Do Paris Like Hemingway* by Lena Strand; *Sylvia Beach and the Lost Generation: A History of Literary Paris in the Twenties and Thirties* by Noel Riley Fitch; *Man Ray: American Artist* by Neil Baldwin; *Self Portrait* by Man Ray; *Kiki's Paris: Artists and Lovers 1900–1930* by Billy Kluver and Julie Martin; and *Kiki de Montparnasse* by Catel Muller and Jose-Luis Bocquet. This book also owes so much to the HBO show *Carnivàle* (2003–2005) and the films *Trapeze* (1956) and *The Last Romantic Lover* (1978).

And finally, I want to thank Mark for believing in me, even when I often don't believe in myself. You've made me a better person, but sadly, not a better French speaker. (Le distributeur de billets est cassè!)

Meet the Author

Photo Credit: Rebecca Danzenbaker

CONSTANCE SAYERS is the author of *A Witch in Time* and a media executive who has twice been named one of the top one hundred media people by *Folio:* magazine. A finalist for Alternating Current's 2016 Luminaire Award for Best Prose, she has written short stories that appear in *Souvenir Lit* and *Amazing Graces* as well as *The Sky Is a Free Country.* Her short fiction has been nominated for the Pushcart Prize and Best of the Net.

She received an MA in English from George Mason University. She lives outside Washington, DC. Like her character in *The Ladies of the Secret Circus*, she was the host of a radio show from midnight to six for many years.

Interview

What inspired or prompted you to write *The Ladies of the Secret Circus*?

While writing my first book, *A Witch in Time*, I'd been thinking about the idea of a circus run by the devil. I pitched the story to my editor at the time as two sisters who performed in a dark circus. She really latched on to that idea of the sisters, so that became the theme.

While I do plot my novels, I honestly never fully imagine my books at the beginning, and I'm always in awe of how they grow.

Lara Barnes was a character I had from a previous book that hadn't been published, so I thought I'd begin with her as the main character because I knew her well. I was really drawn to the idea of this woman left at the altar and how that changed her. At the beginning, I had no idea how Lara would connect with Cecile and Esmé, so I began to plot that out and was happy with the synopsis, but in the writing, they all became so much more! There are just these incredible surprises that materialize in the writing process. For example, the character of Edward Binghampton Barrow was originally a minor character. As the drafts progressed, he became central to Lara's quest—almost a mirror to her. His emergence as a main character came as a complete surprise to me. There is real magic that happens between drafts if you let it. I do think that sitting down and really putting in the time allows for these bursts of creativity and connection about your story and your characters. I don't think you get the creative bursts without the hard work of sitting down every day.

What type of research did you do for this book?

I'm a huge Francophile, so prior to the pandemic, I tried to spend as much time as possible in Paris walking the very streets that Lara explores. For *The Ladies of the Secret Circus*, I had traveled Paris in the summer of 2019 and did a fair amount of research, which was great because due to COVID-19, I wasn't able to go back.

The research involved everything from the actual history of Montparnasse (Who lived there? What was the art scene like?) to costumes and food. There was an old Paris night club, Cabaret de l'Enfer, where the entrance was a devil's mouth, so I used that for the entrance to the circus.

I do write quite a lot about food, but Montparnasse in the 1920s was really a cultural center of Paris for everything—not just food but also music and art. One of the best things I found was a book called *Found Meals of the Lost Generation: Recipes and Anecdotes from 1920s Paris* by Suzanne Rodriguez-Hunter. It has recipes from Hemingway and Kiki de Montparnasse and tells what drinks they paired the food with. In my opinion, it's those little historical details that make a book shine.

***The Ladies of the Secret Circus* has many wonderful characters with some strong and widely varying personalities. Which character did you have the most fun writing?**

Althacazur. I mean, I think you can just tell I'm having fun with him. I've heard from readers that they feel guilty that they enjoy his character so much. I tried to make him terrifying yet funny and three-dimensional. He made a brief appearance in *A Witch in Time*, but he's quite the star of this book. Second would be Esmé. I mean, she needs her own book. Another favorite thing about the book is the identity of Mr. Tisdale.

How did you create such a dark, mysterious world as the Secret Circus?

I began by fleshing out the acts in the performances in Lara's modern setting, almost like I was building a show flow for an event. This process helped me establish what the circus was and wasn't. Next, I worked on Cecile's backstory, which allowed me to explore the creation of some of the rides, like the carousel (which has a very dark origin) and the Ferris wheel. With every rewrite, I tried to just keep upping the stakes and making the circus weirder and weirder through the rides or the performances. In one of the final rewrites, I got the idea of the purpose of the circus and the role of the performers in it. My goal was a completely absurd circus, but one that was haunting and touching. Seeing how the circus was created just made it so much more poignant. With every pass, I'd get a new idea and rush to put it in the manuscript. As you might be able to tell, I had a lot of fun writing that circus.

Music is also an underlying theme throughout the novel. Is music part of your creative process? Did you listen to any artists in particular while writing *The Ladies of the Secret Circus*?

In some ways, I'm more obsessed with music than with writing. My father wanted me to be an opera singer, so I took voice lessons and studied the piano for about fourteen years and entered college as a vocal performance major, but I switched to writing in my second semester and never looked back. The piano was an important part of *A Witch in Time*, so I drew on my own history there. For *The Ladies of the Secret Circus*, I used my experience as a midnight-to-six radio DJ outside of Pittsburgh. It's a lonely, spooky job, and you get really close to the music at two A.M. When I write, music is really important to me. I listen to the Apple Music Chill radio station and write to Ludovico Einaudi ("Time Lapse" and "Run" are two of my favorites) quite often because I find the music haunting and I'm trying to invoke a mood. I created a Spotify playlist for the soundtrack of each book. I also cannot end without giving a huge shout-out to Sam Gopal's *Escalator*, which really brought the ending home for me.

Reading Group Guide

1. Carnival-themed stories like HBO's *Carnivàle* or Ray Bradbury's *Something Wicked This Way Comes* often spark our imagination. As a reader, are you drawn to the Secret Circus? Would you like your own invitation to the show?

2. There are two narratives: the present day with Lara Barnes and 1920s Paris with Esmé and Cecile Cabot. How do the two narratives complement each other? Do you prefer one over the other?

3. The romance between Cecile and Émile Giroux creates consequences that impact several generations. How do you feel about the romance between Cecile and Émile? How does that compare to Lara Barnes and Todd Sutton? Or to Lara Barnes and Ben Archer?

4. Two themes explored in *The Ladies of the Secret Circus* are family secrets and the sins of the father. What do you think Althacazur is trying to do for his daughters? Do you find yourself rooting for him?

5. *The Ladies of the Secret Circus* blends several genres: historical fiction, fantasy, mystery, and horror. It starts with a missing groom and leads to a dark, sinister circus. Did you enjoy the ways the various genres were combined? Why or why not?

6. Edward Binghampton Barrow and Lara Barnes become equally obsessed with the mystery around the Ladies of the Secret Circus paintings, and both sacrifice a lot to solve it. What do you think of their obsessions? Do you believe they go too far to solve the mystery? Why or why not?

if you enjoyed
THE LADIES OF THE SECRET CIRCUS
look out for
THE GREAT WITCH OF BRITTANY
by
Louisa Morgan

Brittany, 1763

There hasn't been a witch born in the Orchière clan for generations. According to the elders, that line is dead, leaving the clan vulnerable to the whims of superstitious villagers and the prejudices of fearmongering bishops.

Ursule Orchière has been raised on stories of the great witches of the past. But the only magic she knows are the false spells her mother weaves over the gullible women who visit their fortune-telling

*caravan. Everything changes when Ursule comes of age and a
spark of power flares to life. Thrilled to be chosen, she has no
idea how magic will twist and shape her future.*

*Guided by the whispers of her ancestors and an ancient grimoire,
Ursule is destined to walk the same path as the great witches of old. But
first the Orchière magical lineage must survive. And danger hovers over
her, whether it's the bloodlust of the mob or the flames of the pyre.*

1763, outside Carnac-Ville

Thirteen-year-old Ursule Orchière knelt in the shadow of the red
caravan to watch her mother lie to people.

Agnes was very good at her job. Her dark eyes flashed convincingly,
and she spoke with just the right amount of hesitation, of warning,
and of promise.

Ursule's responsibility, one she had shouldered since she was six,
was to collect the payment after the readings her mother gave. The
pretense was that Agnes, the fortune-teller, gave no thought to money.
The truth was quite different, and Ursule had learned early that not a
penny should escape her.

The customers would arrive on foot, or in a pony cart that rumbled along the rutted road from Carnac-Ville. They wound through the field of menhirs where the clan camped, gazing wide-eyed at the circle of scarlet and blue and yellow caravans. They shrank away from the narrow-eyed, bare-chested men, gaped at the women in their gaudy scarves, and sometimes smiled at the half-dressed children running about among the stones.

Ursule met these seekers in the center of the circle, beside the remnants of that morning's cooking fire, and guided them to the red caravan where Agnes sat, shaded by a striped canopy, the Orchière crystal before her on a small table.

Often the customers glanced over their shoulders to see if anyone had followed them.

Ursule offered no reassurance. It was better if they were anxious. There was energy in their nervousness, in their fear of someone knowing they had come to have their fortunes told. Frightened customers never held back when it was time to pay.

Ursule added to her mother's drama whenever she could. She had always been plain, but her eyes were large and black and thick-lashed, and she used them to good effect, producing a flashing glance that implied danger. Sometimes she spoke in rapid Romani, and the seekers thought she was speaking in tongues. At other times, kneeling at her mother's side, she let her eyes roll back as if she were in a trance. Often she moaned, underscoring something interesting in her mother's patter.

It was an act, and Ursule was good at it, but it was the crystal that convinced the customers. It was an ancient stone, a chunk of crystal dug out of a riverbank by the *grand-mère* of Agnes's *grand-mère*. The top was smoky quartz, rubbed and polished until it was nearly spherical. Its base was uncut granite, the same rugged shape as when it emerged from the mud.

A generation had passed with none of the Orchières seeing so much as a spark in it. Agnes and her sisters swore that their grandmother could bring the crystal to life just by touching it. They widened their eyes and lowered their voices when they told the tale, claiming the crystal bloomed with light under her hands.

Ursule doubted the truth of this, and with good reason. The Orchières were notorious spinners of stories, even for their own family members. She suspected that her mother's *grand-mère* had simply been more adept than Agnes at fooling everyone.

Her mother had devised a way to make the crystal appear to glimmer as she moved her hands across its cloudy face. It required a strategically placed lamp at her feet, a twitch of her foot to move her skirt aside, a practiced motion of her hands to hide the reflection in the crystal and then, at an opportune moment, to reveal it.

Agnes excelled at reading her customers, if not at scrying in the crystal. She gave them a flood of rosy predictions, marring the optimistic future with just enough bad news to make it all seem real. The seekers handed over their money, for the most part, without demur. If they didn't, they learned how fast Ursule could run and how loudly she could shout.

Today a townswoman had come with a friend, the two of them clinging together for courage. They were dressed in traditional Brittany fashion: dark fabrics, with white scarves over their bodices and lacy aprons. They rolled their eyes this way and that, sniffing at the odors of cooked hare and boiled beans that hung over the encampment, eyeing the bright, ragged dresses of the Romani. They lifted their skirts to avoid the dirt of the camp, and shrank away if any of the grimy children came too near.

After Ursule seated the customer on a stool opposite her mother, Agnes told the woman's fortune, at great length. When the two women turned to leave, she called out to the other one. "Wait, *madame*! I have a message for you, too!"

Ursule lifted her scarf across her face to hide her smile. There would be two fees today. She was ready to add her persuasive touch to the process, but it turned out there was no need. The second woman turned back and took the stool opposite Agnes, eager to hear what her own future held. She listened openmouthed as Agnes predicted a sudden stroke of good luck that would bring money into her house. Agnes followed with a warning about being careless with the money, because someone was watching her, someone not afraid to steal. The woman nodded and cast a meaningful glance at her friend, as if she knew just who that would be.

Ursule collected the double fee and watched the two satisfied customers hurry off toward the village, arm in arm, giggling together over the success of their reading.

Her uncle Arnaud appeared at her elbow, holding out his broad dirty hand for the coins. She dropped them into his palm, and he scowled. "Where's the rest?"

Ursule blinked. "Uncle Arnaud, what do you mean? That's the payment."

"This isn't enough," he growled. "What did you do with it?"

"Me? I did nothing!"

"They cheated you, then."

She hung her head to hide the gleam of her eyes. "If they did, I didn't know it, Uncle. Perhaps I counted wrong."

"You, count wrong?"

It was a preposterous claim for her to make, of course. Everyone in the clan, no matter how odd they thought Ursule to be, acknowledged her talent for numbers. They called her clever when they wanted to flatter her, or when they needed her to translate from their patois to

French or Breton. When they were angry, they said she didn't know how to keep her place, that she should stop showing off, that she should leave business matters to the men. For those reasons and more, Ursule hugged to herself the greatest secret of her young life. Even her mother didn't know.

She could read.

The Orchière clan, like the other Romani who traveled the roads of Europe, was illiterate. It was part of their identity. Their tradition. Reading, in their way of thinking, was unnecessary. Uncle Arnaud said it was better to learn from your ancestors than from foolish words some stranger had written. Books were for churchmen or landowners, collections of words used to oppress the peasantry, and the Romani with them.

The Romani left drawings of bears or boar on trees or standing stones to mark their passing. They sang or recited their family histories. They counted on their fingers, or made slash marks in the dirt to tot up what was owed to them or what they owed. To be a reader, Ursule had always understood, was to be a rebel. To offend the traditional ways. To risk being isolated even more than she already was.

Ursule had been just three years old when she realized that the letters on shop signs or in advertising posters spoke words to her, as if the writers of those letters were whispering their meaning in her ear. Her cousins mocked her because she didn't talk until she was five years old, but that turned out to be a blessing. By the time she began, she realized that the letters that told her so much meant nothing to her mother or her aunts or uncles. She couldn't recall ever learning to read. It was simply there, the way her uncle Omas had always been able to play the harp, and Aunt Genève always knew how long to roast a hare. It was her gift, but she knew better than to reveal it.

Her clan already viewed her as a misfit, first because she had been silent for so long, and then because, when she did begin to talk, she spoke like a miniature adult. She refused to learn to sew or cook, and preferred to be alone rather than gossip with the other girls. The boys mocked her, trying to make her cry, but she refused. She was small, but her fists were hard and quick.

She was eight when she discovered there was a book in the Orchière camp. It was a single, real book, and it was in her very own caravan.

She had gone to fetch the scrying stone before a reading. When Ursule knelt down to pull it out from beneath her mother's bed, a random beam of sunlight exposed an object unfamiliar to her, a rectangular shape wrapped in burlap and tied with a strap. She believed she knew every bit and bob of their meager possessions. Surprise and curiosity drove her errand from her mind as she pulled the thing out into the light, untied the strap, and peeled back the burlap.

It was the first real book she had ever held in her hands, heavy and old and smelling of dust and ink. Ursule lifted the top cover and saw the first parchment page, the top written in French in a trembling script, with three illustrations of herbs decorating the bottom. She gingerly riffled the pages. There were dozens of them. She could hardly breathe with excitement over the treasures it must hold.

"Ursule! What are you doing?"

Ursule gave a start that made her drop the book with a thud. A little cloud of ancient dust swirled from it, tickling her nose with the promise of secrets within. "Daj, I—"

Agnes fell to her knees beside her and began hurriedly rewrapping the big book. "Never touch this!" she said. "Never ever. Promise me!"

"Why?" Ursule plucked at the burlap, but Agnes slapped her hand away. *"Daj!"* she cried. "You never told me we have a *book*!"

"And you can never tell anyone else, Ursule. It's dangerous."

With decisive motions, Agnes rewrapped the burlap and tightened the strap that held it all together. She bent to shove it as far under her cot as it would go.

"But, Daj, what is it? Where did it come from? Why do you hide it?"

Agnes settled back on her haunches, her skirts pooling about her feet. "Bring the stone, Ursule," she said tightly. "I have readings to do."

"Tell me!" Ursule demanded. She took the scrying stone into her lap and covered it with her arms. "I'm not moving until you do."

Agnes's hand rose again, but when Ursule didn't budge, she made a wry face and lowered it. "I will tell you, daughter, but only if you promise never to tell anyone."

"I promise," Ursule said. "But tell me!"

"It's called a grimoire," Agnes said. "It belonged to my *grand-mère*, and her *grand-mère* before that, and even more *grands-mères* before her."

"Why is it called a grimoire? What does that mean?"

"I don't know. My *maman* couldn't read it. She kept it hidden, and we have to do that, too."

"Why?"

"Witch hunters," Agnes said, spitting out the word as if it burned her mouth. "A grimoire is a book for witches. A book of witchcraft. If they see you looking at it, they might think you're a witch."

"I'd like to be a witch," Ursule said.

"You'd like to be burned alive?" her mother hissed. "That's what they do if they catch witches. They burn them, and stand around laughing while they scream!"

The fear in her mother's voice, even more than the ghastly images, made Ursule shudder. She never said it again. She never told anyone there was a book in her caravan. And she never looked into the grimoire— unless she was certain her mother would not find out.

Her uncle Arnaud said now, "Turn out your pockets, Ursule. Quickly!"

She did, tugging out the frayed fabric of her pockets to show they were empty. One had a huge hole in it, and she spread it open with her fingers so her uncle could see.

He glared at her for a long moment. "If you are stealing from us," he began.

Ursule promptly broke into a convincing bout of tears, and Arnaud, grunting, shoved her away from him. She stumbled back, sobbing.

"Stop that!" Arnaud snapped. When she only cried more loudly, he swore, and said, "The sooner Agnes finds you a husband, the better! You need to settle down!"

"I don't even have my monthlies yet, Uncle!" Ursule wailed.

"Well—well—hurry up with them, then!" He gave her another push, and she ran, stuffing her pockets back into her skirt.

Her mother was waiting, holding open the flimsy door of their caravan. She glared at her brother as Ursule jumped past her, up the step and inside. Agnes looped the rope lock behind her.

The lock was symbolic. Arnaud could break in easily if he wanted to, but long ago Agnes had sworn if he ever bothered her or her daughter in their own wagon she would put a curse on him. He never set foot in her caravan after that. Women had very little power, but they were known to cast terrible curses.

Ursule plunged her hand through the hole in her skirt pocket so she could fish the extra coins out of the *posoti* sewn into her drawers. She held the money out on her palm, all pretense of tears gone. "Double, Maman."

Agnes snatched up the coins and jangled them in her fist. "Well done, daughter! Well done."

"I need a new dress. This one barely reaches my calves, and the others laugh at me."

"I know they do. I'm sorry." Agnes turned to the old cracked jar she kept hidden behind a curtain and poured the coins into it. "Arnaud is right about one thing, though. You're going to need a husband soon."

"I don't want one."

"What does that have to do with it?"

"I'm only thirteen!"

"I was thirteen when I was wed to your father."

"And what a mistake that was," Ursule said. "Married to an old man. Widowed before I was born. Dirt poor your whole life."

"Well," her mother said with a shrug. "We're all dirt poor. And widowed is not so bad. I make my own choices."

"I'm going to make mine, too, and marrying some lout of a blacksmith or a basket maker is not one of them."

"Ursule," Agnes said, shaking her head but smiling at the same time. "You speak like a woman of eighty."

"Born old," Ursule said. "You've said that often enough."

"Yes. You had no childhood."

"It would be over now, in any case."

"I am sorry for that, little one."

Ursule shrugged. "It doesn't matter."

Her mother blew out a breath and began taking off the beads and scarves she wore for telling fortunes. "You'll have a new dress. We'll buy fabric when we get to Belz."

"Are we leaving Carnac-Ville already?"

"Your uncles say we must. The witch burners are about again."